CW01637035

AUTHOI

The Lady's Last Mistake is a standalone historical romance companion novel to the Bow Street Duchess Mystery series. It can be enjoyed on its own, however reading the series first is highly recommended.

The Bow Street Duchess Mystery series is complete and available on Amazon in ebook, paperback, and audiobook formats.

Bow Street Duchess readers, please note that *The Lady's Last Mistake* is a traditional Regency romance with a few scenes of intimacy.

THE LADY'S LAST MISTAKE

A BOW STREET DUCHESS ROMANCE

CARA DEVLIN

First Cup Press

ISBN paperback: 979-8987612552

CHAPTER
ONE

December 1823

Cassie sipped her second glass of champagne as she peered through the fronds of a potted palm. The ballroom had been a crush when she'd arrived, and yet somehow, he'd still spotted her. Mr. Hunt was here, somewhere, and if she valued her sanity, she needed to avoid him.

This ball was an unmitigated disaster. She had expected no less, since nothing good ever came of anything associated with Lady Minerva Dutton. The woman was brash, unyielding, and an incurable gossip, and no event she hosted ever concluded without at least one debutante erupting into tears. It was rather unfortunate then, when Cassie's good friend Marianna had accepted the hand of the dowager viscountess's youngest son.

"I told you not to marry him," Cassie said to a rather

weepy Marianna. Her dragon of a mother-in-law had just roundly criticized her, saying she looked like an overripe tomato in her gown.

Marianna sniffled. "But Gerald is sweet. He is nothing like his mother."

Her husband might not have been conniving or cruel, but he was terribly dull. Which Cassie thought might be worse.

"If you say so," she replied, her gaze still scouring the crowd.

"You're looking for Mr. Hunt, aren't you?"

"I am not looking for him, I am *watching* for him. There is a difference."

Had she known that Mr. Horace Hunt would be in attendance and would descend like a hawk upon her arrival, she would have given her regrets. She hadn't wished to attend the ball in the first place. But Marianna's increasingly desperate pleas had swayed her. The poor girl was terrified of her mother-in-law. So was Gerald, leaving them both little more than quivery lumps of nerves whenever forced to be in the dowager viscountess's company. What Cassie's presence could do to shield them was not entirely clear; Marianna had clung to her arm all evening, and Lady Dutton had still closed in for a smattering of verbal cuts. Gerald, on the other hand, was nowhere to be found.

What a hero.

"Mr. Hunt isn't so bad," Marianna said, joining Cassie in her perusal of the evening's guests through the green fronds. It seemed all of London was here. "He reminds me of a river otter."

Cassie lowered her champagne. "How is that *not so bad*?"

"River otters are adorable little creatures!"

Cassie sighed and finished the last of her champagne. Her older brother, Michael, the Duke of Fournier, had introduced her to Mr. Hunt the previous week while strolling through Hyde Park. Michael had arrived at his former Grosvenor Square home, which Cassie now occupied, and suggested a brisk walk. She'd been suspicious and had considered giving an excuse that she was on her way out. However, Michael might have asked her destination, and she wasn't prepared with a good lie.

She certainly could not tell him the truth.

So, she'd gone for the stroll, and there Mr. Hunt had been, waiting by the steely gray Serpentine. The two men had pretended surprise at running into one another, but Michael was a horrible actor, and Mr. Hunt even more atrocious. Her brother had not yet given up in his quest to find her a suitable husband, and it seemed every time she requested that he stop, he lost the ability to hear. Tonight, Mr. Hunt had swept up to her and declared his intention to have her first dance of the evening. Her swift fib that she was not dancing due to a twisted ankle had not deterred him. Instead, he'd asked for the honor of fetching her some punch. When he'd gone for the refreshments table, Cassie slipped away. She'd been avoiding him ever since.

Marianna clutched her arm. "Don't turn your head, but there is a man who keeps looking at you."

"If it is Mr. Hunt, I am climbing into this plant and living there forever. Send my belongings."

"No, no, it's not him. This man is different. He's handsome. *Quite* handsome," she said a little too breathily. "It is one of Lord Lindstrom's sons if I'm not mistaken."

Cassie's spine went rigid. "Which one?"

"I have no idea. They all look alike."

Slowly, Cassie glimpsed over her shoulder and through the palm fronds. The man Marianna had noticed stood a good head taller than the other men in the ballroom. His broad shoulders filled out the black superfine of his jacket with irritating precision when compared to the artful looseness of his cravat. Thick midnight black hair fell forward over his brow, reaching toward pale green eyes that had already spied her behind the potted palm. He formed a sly grin and tipped his drink to her in acknowledgement.

She immediately turned her back. "Blast."

"Do you know the gentleman?" Marianna asked, still staring at him in open admiration.

"Unfortunately. It is the Marquess of Lindstrom's fourth son, Lord Grant Thornton."

It had been nearly two years since she'd last seen him, and as always, there had been friction between them. They'd been at Lord and Lady Neatham's home on Berkeley Square during the birth of Hugh and Audrey's first child. Lord Thornton had been there to support his closest friend, and as Audrey's former sister-in-law, Cassie had been there too. Seeing Audrey and Hugh hold their little girl for the first time had brought tears to her eyes. However, it wasn't until she'd slipped away into the small morning room that she'd allowed the veil of joy to drop, and the sobs to take over. After a few ugly wails, drawn up as if from the pit of her soul, a throat had cleared.

"If those are tears of happiness, I do not want to imagine what your tears of sorrow must sound like."

Grant Thornton had already been seated in the morning

room when she'd entered, the tall backing of the chair obscuring him completely. Cassie had quickly dried her cheeks, wiped her nose, and chastised him for not announcing himself, as any gentleman should.

"And no lady should sound like a bleating goat when she cries," he replied. "What are these tears for anyhow? A baby has been born. It's an exultant occasion, or so I'm told."

It *was* an exultant occasion, and that was why Cassie had waited until she was alone—or at least believed herself to be —before she'd let her tears fall. She wondered whether she would ever see a newborn baby and not feel stabbing heartache first and foremost.

"My tears are none of your concern," she'd said before storming from the room. "And I do not sound like a goat!"

Now, here Lord Thornton was again. He looked much the same. Just as devilish and just as unimpressed with his surroundings. What was he doing at Lady Dutton's ball? This was a society event, and it was well known that the fourth son of the Marquess of Lindstrom, and the physician to several *ton* peers, did not go out in society. He was a flirt, a libertine, and, as Cassie had learned from personal experience, so arrogantly confident that he made her back teeth ache.

There had been a time—a very short time—when she'd harbored an attraction to him. But that had been before they'd been thrown together during a few of Audrey and Hugh's investigations. Being in close proximity to him had easily cured her of her affliction.

Cassie refrained from looking behind her again, and after several minutes in which Lord Thornton did not approach, she breathed easier.

"There you two are. I should have known I'd find you crouched behind foliage." Mrs. Jane Riverton grabbed Cassie's arm and tugged her out from behind the shrubbery. She arched a brow. "You're hiding from that man. The one that looks a bit like a beaver."

She rolled her arm free. "I'm starting to feel sorry for Mr. Hunt."

"Oh, yes, a beaver is a much better comparison than a river otter," Marianna said.

"Why are you hiding from him? He isn't so awful. You must admit, he has a better chin than Gerald."

Marianna glared at the insult to her husband. Jane had always said anything she liked without thought for whether it was nice. But ever since she'd married the wealthy and distinguished Mr. John Riverton, she'd gone from mildly pretentious to overtly superior.

"Looks aren't everything," Jane went on. "Ask Marianna, she'll tell you. Besides, I've heard Mr. Hunt is quite rich."

Marianna sharpened her glare while Cassie reached for another glass of champagne on a passing tray.

"So am I," she murmured before taking a long sip that tickled her nose.

"Not until you are married," Jane said with a roll of her eyes.

Cassie grimaced. She'd reached her majority two years ago, when she'd turned twenty-one, but her brother the duke had staunchly refused to give her the annual income it provided. Three thousand pounds per year was far too large a sum for a single woman to manage, he insisted, and it would also make her a target for any immoral, money-hungry cad looking to charm and use her. Her brother would not be swayed, and so, after many arguments and some artful calculation, Cassie had struck a compromise. She would agree to take the much smaller annual sum without complaint—*if* she could live independently from Michael and his wife, Genie.

It wasn't that she disliked them, though her brother got under her skin like no one else. But Cassie needed privacy. She needed room to breathe. Michael had agreed, albeit with extreme reluctance. She now lived alone at his former Grosvenor Square residence with a small staff, but he had continued to work tirelessly to see her married off. Case in point: Mr. Hunt.

"Darling, at three and twenty, you don't have much time left," Jane said. "The pool of peers is rapidly thinning."

"So is Mr. Hunt's hair," Cassie replied, but then felt a twinge of guilt. It wasn't his appearance she objected to. It was his sex. She wanted nothing to do with men in general, and she was quite certain they would want nothing to do with her if they knew the truth of her past. She'd trusted a man once, and he'd played her for a fool. He'd broken her in so many ways, and she'd not yet discovered how to repair all the pieces.

"I called on you yesterday," Jane said to her above the fast tempo of a pianoforte. Several couples were dancing a quadrille. "Your footman said you were out."

Cassie sipped a little more champagne than she meant to and coughed. "Yes, I was shopping." The lie was one of about five that she held in reserve for whenever an acquaintance couldn't find her at her home. *I was at the circulating library* and *I was on a stroll through the park* and *I had a megrim* were some of the others that were vague but believable, and also difficult to challenge, should one try.

Over the past year, she'd needed to come up with a host of excuses for her absences, as telling anyone the truth—that she was, in fact, running a charity home in a poor part of London for pregnant, unwed women—was out of the question. If Michael ever learned what she was doing with her paltry income, he would have an apoplexy. And he would immediately stopper the flow of her pittance. As the legal trustee of her inheritance, he would have the utmost authority to do so.

Jane leveled her with a skeptical look. "That is the third time I've called on you in as many weeks to find you not at home."

"Send a note ahead next time," Cassie said with a blasé shrug.

Avoiding explanation and elaborate apologies had worked well thus far, so she saw no reason to change her tactics now, even if it did inspire a scowl from her friend.

Cassie spent as much time at Hope House as she possibly could, but even still, it never felt like enough. Whenever she was there, a sense of purpose filled her to the brim, and whenever she left to return to her life in Mayfair, she felt a pinch of guilt. The girls and young women who found their way to Hope House would never know the safety and comfort of a large home, a full staff, or a plentiful income. They were mostly poor or working class, though a few middle-class girls had shown up inside the false front of their establishment on Crispin Street in Spitalfields. A bell above the main door was rigged to set off another bell inside the back of the house whenever someone entered, and it was

Cassie's job whenever she was there to greet whoever had wandered into the accounting offices of Mr. Hiram James & Sons. Most of the time she would find a gentleman, or some servant sent out by their employer, and she would see them out, explaining that their client list was too full to take on anyone new. But sometimes, she would find a frightened or nervous young woman who would say, "I'm here for a meeting with my friend, Miss Hope." Cassie would welcome her to come out back, where Hope House operated in earnest.

Marianna clutched Cassie's arm again, as she had when she'd seen Grant Thornton staring at her. "Oh, good heavens. He is coming over."

Her heartbeat doubled. "Who, Lord Thornton?"

"No, Mr. Hunt."

Drat! Cassie dumped the remainder of her champagne, along with the empty glass, into the potted palm. "I'll be back shortly," she said to the two women and then darted away, behind a few throngs of guests, toward the ballroom exit.

"Coward," she heard Jane say as she went. Perhaps she was. But she'd rather drown herself in a bowl of punch than endure a bland and meaningless conversation with one of Michael's potential suitors. Eventually, Mr. Hunt would take the hint and give up, just as all the others had done. There was no need to draw things out.

Cassie reached the ballroom doors and entered Lady Dutton's entrance hall. It wasn't the first time she'd been to the dowager's home, but she'd never been beyond the ground floor and main ballroom. A few ladies were coming down the stairs, no doubt returning from the withdrawing room.

There, they could have their maids refresh their hair or mend a torn stocking or use the *bourdaloue* behind a privacy screen. A glance over her shoulder showed Mr. Hunt craning his neck above the sea of guests. His eyes found her. With a jolt, she raced for the stairs.

Cassie reached the first level just as Mr. Hunt exited the ballroom. She turned left, down a darkened hall rather than the well-lit one to the right. This hall, she hoped, would lead to a servant's staircase that would take her back down to the ground floor and ultimately, to the ballroom. Once there, she could say her goodbyes to Marianna and Jane and then have a footman call for her carriage.

However, she reached the end of the darkened hall and let out a groan. No stairwell. No withdrawing room. Just several closed doors. She'd have to go back the way she came.

She turned—and went still. Mr. Hunt had reached the top of the stairs. He glanced left, then right, and hesitated on which direction to take. Panicked, Cassie grabbed the glass knob on the door closest to her and twisted. She hurried into a room and closed the door behind her. She leaned against it, her heart thrashing. She exhaled, though her anger began to simmer. How dare he follow her upstairs? Surely, he knew how improper it was. Unless...he wished to corner her. Entrap her and force a wedding. She did, after all, possess a substantial dowry. The income from it would be enough for any gentleman of the peerage to live quite well on.

She pressed her ear to the door and listened. No footsteps came. Only the clearing of a throat behind her.

"This is me announcing myself, as I have been told a gentleman should."

The deep voice raked over her back, setting her scalp to

tingling. Cassie turned, and her stomach dropped at the sight of Lord Thornton, seated in a chair. A woman stood in front of him, her foot propped on his thigh, the hem of her gown lifted to her knee.

Lord Thornton smirked. "Aren't ladies taught to knock first before barging in?"

CHAPTER TWO

Grant ran the pad of his thumb over Lady Brookfield's inner thigh and frowned. The mole she had professed concern for while they'd been in the ballroom was nothing more than a small dot on her lily-white skin. The widow barely suppressed a mewl of delight as he sat back in the chair, took in the view, and realized what she really wanted.

"There is nothing wrong with this mole, Lady Brookfield," he said as she continued to stand before him, her foot propped on his knee. The hem of her ballgown was raised above her garter.

Though nearly ten years his senior, Lady Brookfield was beautiful and shapely, and if he was at all in the mood for a rendezvous, he might have been tempted. But he was not. He didn't want to be at this ball, let alone in this bedchamber's sitting room. The only reason he'd accepted Lady Dutton's invitation was to get his father off his back. The man had been insufferable as of late, and earlier that evening, he'd made things infinitely worse. The command for Grant to find a woman to marry still echoed in his head. That he'd already been married once did not signify to the marquess. Nor did Grant's vow to never remarry.

The marquess wanted a grandson, who would keep the title in the immediate family. So far, none of Grant's three older brothers had produced anything but girls, and his younger sister, though married three years now, had not been able to conceive.

Lady Brookfield rolled her ankle, tugging his trousers and yanking his mind away from his current troubles. "Are you quite sure you shouldn't take a closer look?" she said, drawing the hem up another inch.

On some level, he'd known she'd only been trying to get him alone in a room, far away from the crush. Newly out of mourning, the rumors at the clubs were that she was making up for lost time. As Grant's reputation savored strongly of loose morality, he was an obvious choice. He didn't always care to curb the assumptions people made regarding his character, as it both nettled his tyrant of a father *and* kept young debutantes and their mothers from looking his way during the Season. Safer for everyone, all around. However, his libertine status often caused him more annoyance than it did pleasure.

He drummed his fingers on the arm of the chair. "I can see everything just fine as you are, my lady, and you are not the owner of a potentially cancerous mole."

She pouted, the little moue an implicit invitation. He swallowed a sigh. Sometimes his reputation was more trouble than it was worth.

At the sound of the sitting room door opening, Lady Brookfield's foot, awkwardly massaging his thigh, went still.

Grant looked to see who'd joined them. This was the very reason he did not *ever* dally with debutantes. Getting caught in a dark room with one of them would lead to a date at the altar, whereas getting caught with a widow would only lead to a roll of the eyes and perhaps a scowl of distaste—both of which the intruder who now pressed her ear against the door, unaware she'd entered an occupied room, would certainly do when she saw him.

Grant cleared his throat. "This is me announcing myself, as I have been told a gentleman should."

Lady Cassandra Sinclair's back went rigid. The last time he'd seen her, she'd chastised him for his failure to reveal himself inside the morning room at Hugh Marsden's home. Not that Grant had been given the chance to so much as part his lips before she'd rushed into the room and burst into wretched sobs. He'd deliberated staying silent and letting her cry. She might have left quickly after her tears dried up. But he'd been too concerned with why she was crying to trick her.

Now, she turned slowly, eyes wide, and saw him in the chair with Lady Brookfield's leg still on full display. Cassie's lips parted in shock, then slammed together again as the scowl he'd predicted emerged.

The widow lowered her hem, and to Grant's relief, withdrew her foot. She smoothed her skirt and fiddled with tendrils of curls framing her face as she cut a hasty path toward Cassie and the door.

"Wait." Cassie held out her hands. She placed her ear against the door again, and after a moment, she stepped aside. Tucking her chin, she looked at Lady Brookfield with meaning. "You haven't seen me, and I haven't seen you. Yes?"

Lady Brookfield gave a small bow of her head. "Agreed,

my lady." She then whipped out of the room. Cassie closed the door and locked it behind her.

Grant stood from the chair. "What are you doing in here?"

She hushed him and held up a palm, still listening through the wood. When her shoulders dropped, she turned to scowl at him full on. "I could ask you the same question. But I won't because it's perfectly clear what you were doing in here."

He crossed his arms and angled his head to stare down at her. She was a few inches shorter than him, and yet she persisted in acting as if she hovered high above him and everyone else.

"I was inspecting the lady for a worrisome mole, that is all," he replied. "Who are you hiding from?"

"None of your business."

"Are you in any trouble?" He considered that she might have been trying to escape an overly amorous man. He took a few steps toward the door. But stopped. What was he going to do, charge out there and confront someone who could then place him in a room, alone, with the unmarried young woman? His blood went to ice at the thought. He'd worked too hard to avoid any situation like that.

"I'll only be in trouble if I'm found in here with you," she replied, echoing his own thoughts a little too well.

He gestured toward the locked door. "Then you should leave. Immediately."

Cassie only lifted her chin and stalked toward the fireplace. A few logs had been burning when he and Lady Brookfield had come in, the room selected by some secret knowledge the lady had possessed. The thought occurred to him that she'd arranged for this room in advance. The lusty minx.

"I rather think *you* should leave, sir." Cassie speared him with a glare over her shoulder. "Unless you are waiting to inspect another woman's worrisome mole."

"Why, do you have one you'd like me to take a look at?"

Suggestive and sarcastic remarks came naturally to him, and something about Cassandra Sinclair made delivering them so much more satisfying. Especially when she blushed and scowled at the same time.

"You are a disgrace. Lady Brookfield is a *widow*," she hissed. "Have you no shame?"

"I am ashamed of many things." He made his way toward the fireplace, enjoying the little steps she took to the side, to avoid him. As if proximity would make any difference. Should anyone come breaking through that locked door, it wouldn't matter if he was on one side of the room, and she the other. She would still be compromised.

"Like how earlier, I had something in my teeth while I was speaking to Lady Dutton," he said, tapping his front incisor. "Right here. Fleck of pepper, I think it was. Utterly embarrassing."

Cassie stared flatly at him, unamused. Which only made him smile wider.

"Oh, come now, Lady Cassandra. I didn't lure Lady Brookfield into this room to have my wicked way with her. *She* lured *me*."

Cassie let out a high bark of laughter. "Oh, that is rich. You, sir, are a superficial rake."

"Believe me or don't, but I am telling the truth. Another

truth is that you are hiding in here to escape some man's attention."

She hardened again, her arms crossing at her waist. A protective motion.

"A suitor?" he guessed.

She closed her eyes. "My brother would be ecstatic if I allowed it."

Ah. The duke. "Fournier's looking to fob you off then?"

Cassie opened her eyes. The sooty gray color of them suited her black look. "No one needs to *fob me off.* I am more than capable of seeing to my own independence, thank you."

It was established knowledge that the duke's sister had avowed herself to be forever unmarried, and for a little while, it had lit up the ton like a firecracker. No one could quite understand why she was so averse to marriage, and no one had really believed she would stick to her commitment. However, over the last few Seasons it had become increasingly evident that she was not moving from her position. The talk had faded, but the disappointment had not abated. To be young, gorgeous, wealthy, and devoted to a future of spinsterhood seemed unnatural to many.

While Grant knew why he would never take vows again, Cassie's reasons mystified him. So much about her did. She was a harridan, to be sure, but not in any cold way. On the contrary, she was a flame. Erratic and opinionated, she had made it more than clear what her opinion was of him.

"Your own independence?" he repeated as he went to a table of cut crystal decanters. He poured himself a liberal amount of whisky. "You make it sound as if you don't rely on the duke's fortune."

Every additional comment from his lips seemed to ignite

more of her wrath. It was for the best. The sooner she left this room in a blaze of annoyance, the better. Locked doors only kept out those without keys.

"It is *my* fortune—"

"The income of which is allotted to you by the duke. I know how it works, Cassandra. I've an income of my own, meted out by the marquess."

Who had just threatened to sever it should Grant not find a woman by the first of the year to marry. His stomach clenched in instinctive revulsion and not a small amount of fury.

"Your situation and my own are not alike in the least, Lord Thornton." The mossy green silk of her gown shimmered in the firelight, the flames casting a warm golden glow over her skin. The bodice was free of any lace to obscure her decolletage, and Grant forced his attention to lift from the pillowy mounds, now heaving with irritation.

"You're correct, we are very different," he said. "I actually do have an independent income of my own, considering I'm a physician."

Not that his physician's income even reached to the shins of what Grant lived on from his annual inheritance.

Cassie's arms uncrossed, and she balled her hands into little fists. "Oh yes, Dr. Mole Inspector, how impressive you are."

The barb unexpectedly stung. Being the fourth son of a marquess, he'd been of little significance to his father, and thus, was allowed to enroll in medical school. The idea of spending his life as nothing more than a gentleman, plying society and politics and taking weekends in the country for shooting had been dull enough to make him panic. Medicine gave him a focus. A purpose. The marquess had, he'd later confessed, believed Grant would see sense and drop out of university. Either that or fail miserably. When he hadn't, his father had been livid. It was disgraceful to work, Lindstrom had seethed. Any profession was a stain that could not come out in the wash.

Yes, Grant's calls to peerage homes were mostly for things like gout and megrims and venereal diseases, the plagues of the rich, well-fed, and sedentary. Most of his patients were men, too, the ladies too scandalized by his reputation to permit him. But his true work, the most rewarding work, was something he couldn't speak of. The charity clinic he ran in Whitechapel under a false name had to remain a secret, and not only because the marquess would disown him. His regular patients would also disavow him. No upper-class swell would stand for sharing a doctor with poor, working class Londoners.

Likening him to nothing more than a mole inspector was facetious of Cassie, but the thorn stuck in just the same.

"I don't have to prove my profession to you," he said. "If you'll excuse me, one of us needs to leave, and it appears I am the only one possessing any good sense."

He broke away from her, only to dig in his heels at sounds of voices in the hall. They were nearing the door. And then, the doorknob jiggled.

"What's this?" came a woman's exclamation. "I didn't leave it locked."

Cassie gasped, then clapped a hand over her mouth to stifle it. Grant's stomach reached somewhere toward his knees. *Bloody hell.* The doorknob jiggled again.

"Do you have a key or don't you?" came the voice of an impatient man.

"Of course, but I am certain I didn't lock it."

Grant backed up and instinctively grabbed Cassie by the wrist.

"What do we do?" she whispered.

There was no time to contemplate and only one place to go. He pulled her toward the open doors to the bedchamber, off the sitting room. It was dark, without a single lamp lit, but they made it safely inside before the telltale click of the door's lock gave way.

"Pour me a drink, darling," the unknown woman said as Cassie wrenched her arm away. She was breathing loudly, no doubt on the verge of panic. And well she should. He was beginning to feel the touch of it himself. The man and woman, whoever they were, had likely only come here for one reason—to employ the bed that he and Cassie were currently standing next to.

Thankfully, this room had a door to the hall as well. Grant hurried to it, Cassie on his heels. But the knob was stuck.

"Unlock it," Cassie whispered.

"I would if I could," he whispered back. Damn it! What was wrong with the bloody thing? He twisted it again and again; searched for a lock but found none.

She pushed his hand out of the way. "Let me."

"Oh yes, because your touch is magic," he muttered while she fiddled with the handle. It had to be permanently locked and sealed.

A privacy screen across the room could shield them but reaching it would require them to dash in front of the open doors to the sitting room. Too risky. There was another door to their left, perhaps to a boudoir.

The knob on that door gave. "In here," he whispered to Cassie who hadn't yet given up on the sealed door.

In the sitting room, the woman giggled and moaned.

"In here, *now*," he whispered harshly.

He stepped into the darkened room and realized it wasn't a boudoir at all. It wasn't even a room. It was a shallow, slim closet. Almost as soon as he stepped in, he'd reached the end of the space. Shelving pressed into his back and shoulders as he turned to face the entrance, and when Cassie dove into the closet with him, she collided with him, treading on his toes. Grant leaned around her and shut the door as softly as he could. Cassie shifted, attempting to push away, but there was no room. Her heels banged into the door, and the noise of it blared in his ears.

He took her shoulders into his hands and held her still. "Do not move."

Christ. To be found like this, not only in a bedchamber but in a sodding closet, would spell disaster. Fournier would demand he marry his chit of a sister, and while that would certainly make Lord Lindstrom happy, Grant would be stuck. Trapped. Attached to a woman who made no effort to conceal her rancor for him.

Their uneven breathing filled the small space, and he became distinctly aware of the front of Cassie's body against his. Not only that, but when she'd slammed into him, her palms had come up between them. They were now pressed against his chest. The woman's incessant giggling from the sitting room, as her beau no doubt plied her with his hands and other unsavory appendages, corkscrewed through him.

Hell, if the pair of them came into this room and bandied about on the bed together, while he and Cassie stood like this, listening... It would be a torture unlike any he'd ever imagined.

He closed his eyes and tried to inhale and exhale evenly. With her hands bracing herself against his chest, she had to be able to feel the thrashing of his heart. It was getting hot in here. As he steadied his breaths, the scent of sun-warmed fruit brightened his senses. Apricots? Grant angled his nose toward the crown of her hair.

"What are you doing?" Cassie whispered.

"Have you always smelled of apricots?"

He'd never stood this close to her—at least not since that ungainly embrace years ago at Fournier's country home, Greenbriar. Grant had just pronounced Audrey, now the Viscountess Neatham, safely on the mend after a bullet had grazed her leg. Cassie's relief for her widowed sister-in-law had been so stark that she'd thrown herself into Grant's arms in gratitude. He still remembered the shock of her body firmly clinging to his, and even more shocking, his frozen response. He'd gone rigid—just as he had at the first brush of her body here in the closet. However now, his hands, which had been clutching her shoulders to keep her still, drifted loosely toward her elbows. While in the sitting room, he'd removed his gloves and tucked them into his jacket pocket, so his palms were now free to explore the smooth skin of her arms.

"Stop that." Cassie started to wriggle, but just then, the woman's voice grew louder as she entered the bedchamber. Grant gripped Cassie tightly again to immobilize her, but he needn't have. She'd gone to stone and no longer even breathed.

The lady hummed and giggled, most likely in thanks to copious amounts of champagne. At the familiar sound of someone relieving themselves in a bourdaloue, Grant thanked the lord he had not dragged Cassie behind the changing screen, for that was certainly where the lady had gone.

His eyes began to adjust to the pitch black of the closet, and after some rustling and more giggling, the lady returned to the sitting room.

"Release me," Cassie whispered, flapping her arms. They smacked into shelving.

"Move again and they may hear you."

"Then at least stop groping me."

"I do not grope."

"You needn't hold me this tightly."

"Woman, stop speaking. They will hear you."

"Do not call me—"

Grant lifted one hand from her arm and clapped it over her mouth. Immediately, she thrashed her head side to side to dislodge it.

"What was that?" The man's voice reached them, and Cassie ceased struggling. Her hot breath huffed against his palm. In their struggle, one of her legs had slipped between his, bringing her thigh dangerously close to his groin. Whether she planned to injure him didn't matter—he felt himself beginning to respond. He wanted to move, ease her away, but couldn't, not without making noise.

"Nothing, darling," the woman replied at last. "Let's return, I want more fizz."

Grant exhaled, and when the couple left, he leaned forward to open the closet door. He pushed Cassie's body from his, and they all but tumbled out.

"My God, woman! Did you want us to be discovered?"

She glared as she emerged from the closet. "Of course not! Why are *you* so angry? I'm the one who's just been pawed in there!"

"I do not *paw* women." His temper rose with wild recklessness. "And unless you wish to be caught in a compromising situation and forced down the aisle to a groom who looks curiously like me, you should leave. *Now.*"

"Happily," she spat, starting swiftly for the sitting room. But then she stopped, and with a viper's speed, reached out and pinched him hard on the shoulder. "That is for groping me!"

Cassie disappeared as Grant swore and rubbed his shoulder. The bloody menace!

CHAPTER THREE

The single window in Cassie's office let in the bleak gray light of an early December snow fall. The small flakes were changing over to rain, and if the temperature dropped any further, the streets would be slick by the time she left for home.

When she and her partner, Miss Elyse Khan, had purchased the lease for the three-story building on Crispin Street, it had been nothing more than a collection of shabby rooms and landings covered in peeling wallpaper, water stains, and rubbish left by the previous tenants. In some places, holes had been knocked through the walls, exposing timber beams and plaster. Fixing it up and furnishing it had taken nearly two months and had cost more than she'd budgeted for, but at last, the rooms had been ready for the young women both Cassie and Elyse knew would come.

They had met at a Lyceum lecture the previous year. Cassie's former sister-in-law, Audrey had often attended the lectures before she'd married Hugh and started their family, and she'd convinced Cassie that some were much more interesting than one might expect. The topic that afternoon had been a discourse of social reforms for the city's laboring class. Cassie had been close to nodding off in her seat when she'd felt a little nudge against her shoulder. Coming to attention, she'd turned and found a woman of about thirty seated behind her, smirking. After the lecture, Cassie thanked her for saving her from the humiliation of drooling in public.

"It was a terribly boring sermon," the woman had replied, "and his ideas for reform are flawed. He champions the banning of children under age ten from working in factories but insists an increase in wages for adult workers is too radical. Children wouldn't be in the factories at all if their parents could earn a decent wage on their own."

At her clear and confident opinion, Cassie had felt woefully lacking. In fact, she could hardly recall anything the man had said. They'd exchanged introductions, and Cassie had invited her to a nearby coffeehouse. Over the next hour, she'd learned that Elyse had been trained as a midwife by her own mother, an Englishwoman who had gone to India as a missionary. She had returned to England ten years later with Elyse, whose father had been a soldier in India. He'd contracted a fever and died, leaving Elyse and her mother on their own. Eventually, Elyse's mother proved to be a much-trusted midwife in the East End. After her death, Elyse confidently stepped into her shoes.

"Doctors are already few and far between here," she'd explained when Cassie had been stunned by how many births Elyse had presided over. "They often choose not to attend unmarried women, or women who look like me. Or anyone else with darker skin."

"Oh," Cassie replied, rather lamely.

She knew so little of the world beyond her Mayfair life. Over the next few lectures, which she and Elyse attended together, she started paying attention to a common thread in the stories of births the midwife would tell her. Many of the women were young, under the age of twenty, and nearly half of them were not married. The unmarried ones, Elyse said, usually had no support at all from their families. They were often cast out if they dared to keep their child rather than send it to an orphanage or shuffle it off to an older relative.

"Is there no safe place for them?" Cassie had asked, thinking of her own safe place when she'd found herself in the same dire circumstances: unmarried, with child, and terrified.

A middle-aged couple, Mr. and Mrs. Olsson, who had been her late brother Philip's old friends, had welcomed her into their small but caring home in Stockholm. At the time, Cassie had felt like a prisoner, separated from everyone and everything she knew, facing a moment that she dreaded with all her heart. But looking back, she realized that the Olsson's home had been a blessing.

"Not yet," Elyse had answered.

By the following week, Cassie had formed an idea. When she presented it to her new friend, Elyse had accepted on the spot.

Now, the clock on Cassie's desk ticked softly toward two in the afternoon as she read a medical treatise Elyse had given her. It went in depth on childbirth and the unnecessary use of forceps, and to be honest, much of it turned Cassie's stomach. She rubbed her eyes, the tips of her fingers chilled. Her toes were beginning to grow uncomfortably cold too. The coal delivery had been delayed several days now, and she'd forgone a fire in her own office grate in favor of making sure their current residents had plenty to keep warm. For Elyse, too. She lived at Hope House, after all, and even though the rooms were updated and comfortable, the windows still let in drafts and poor insulation kept the walls cold. All fixable, of course, but after going through their accounts, they'd agreed not until the spring. Cassie had just five hundred a year from her inheritance, and she needed to reserve what little was left of it, at least for the next five months.

The thought of money reminded her of the previous week, when Lord Thornton had so casually implied that she was nothing more than a pampered female, frittering away pin money. She gnashed her teeth. The bigheaded boor! She still simmered over his ludicrous claim that he'd been checking Lady Brookfield for a mole. Utter nonsense. The widow's hem had practically been up around her waist!

Her heart still stuttered when thinking of the several minutes she'd endured in the closet, pressed against him, as they hid from discovery. The moment she'd put her hands against Lord Thornton's chest, she'd regretted it. The hard muscle underneath his evening clothes had made her feel too hot. His scent—a rich amalgam of cinnamon and sandalwood—made her head swimmy. Cassie had been painstakingly aware of her bosom against him, and of his bare hands drifting down the backs of her arms. And then, worst of all, of the rock of his thighs as her leg stumbled between his, during their tussling. Her breathing had grown stilted when the bully had covered her mouth with his palm. And then he'd had the audacity to be furious with *her*!

A single pert knock on her office door was all the warning

Elyse gave before coming in. Cassie was too slow to wipe away her grimace.

"Are you thinking about that horrible man again?" she asked.

The office was small and cold, but it was still cozy. On numerous occasions, Cassie had considered sleeping on the couch instead of returning to her home on Grosvenor Square. However, her staff would undoubtedly report her absence to the duke. Michael was the one who employed them after all.

Cassie closed the treatise and stood, regretful that she'd told Elyse about the encounter. But she'd still been beside herself the morning after the ball, and her friend had noticed. Elyse was aware that she was a lady of the peerage and that she was keeping her work at Hope House a secret. She'd been skeptical at first, uncertain if Cassie could maintain a double life, but here they were, one year later, and the rhythm of Cassie's two lives had settled in rather well.

"Any thought of Lord Thornton is firmly in the darkest recesses of my mind," she fibbed.

"Exactly where he should be. Men like him are the very reason this house exists."

The urge to deny the accusation leaped to her tongue, but Cassie swallowed it. Why should she defend him? For all she knew, the man had sired a dozen by-blows. His reputation was cemented in the ton as a good physician but a scalawag who frequented the haunts of the demimonde rather than the typical social outlets of the peerage.

"Take Lila, for example," Elyse continued in the rising tone that usually signaled a brief ticking-off.

"What about her?" The young woman had arrived a few

weeks ago, her abdomen just barely round enough to be noticeable.

A fresh purpling bruise on the side of her mouth, and an older one yellowing the fair skin at her temple, had not shocked Cassie when she'd entered the mock office in the front of the building. Many of the women and girls who arrived sported such marks, compliments of the men they were usually taking refuge from.

"I am looking for my friend, Hope," the young woman had said, repeating the code that had been confided in her by one of the nuns or midwives in the area whom Elyse trusted implicitly.

It hadn't taken more than a single conversation with Lila for Cassie to realize she wasn't from the East End. She was educated, most likely finished at a respectable school. Her clothing didn't look to be from any of the high-end shops on Bond or Oxford Streets, but they weren't cast offs either. They'd probably been purchased readymade at a clothier.

"She was probably compromised by someone just like your blackguard."

"He's not *my* blackguard," Cassie snapped. Elyse rolled her dark brown eyes.

"You know what I mean. An upper-class rake who didn't think twice before leading a young, impressionable girl to reach just above her station," she said. "I'm almost positive she is gentry."

She and Elyse had been trying to piece together Lila's story on their own based on what little the young woman had offered. She'd only given her first name and that she was around four months gone. Nothing more.

Cassie reached for the shawl on the back of her chair and

stepped out from behind her desk. "Whoever compromised Lila, there is at least one thing that sets Lord Thornton apart from him."

"What is that?"

"He would never strike a woman." Cassie knew this with pure conviction. "He might be an egotistical idiot, but he is not a violent man."

Again, she recalled the gentle brush of his fingers down the backs of her arms while they stood in that darkened closet. The skin there tightened involuntarily at the memory. Cassie wrapped her shawl tighter around herself.

"How is Dorie faring?" she asked Elyse, eager to move away from the topic of the vexing physician.

The downward turn of her friend's mouth wasn't promising. "Her fever has worsened. She's becoming insensible. It's time we sent for a doctor."

Dorie had been with them for only a week, arriving with a head cold that had progressed into a fever.

"But I thought you said no doctor would see her," Cassie replied as she and Elyse left her office. It was tucked into the back of the house, above the kitchen. The narrow landing outside her door had a low, angled ceiling that she often accidentally smacked her head against, but once clear of it, the hallway led to two guest rooms and a central sitting room.

"Most doctors won't," Elyse said as they made their way to Dorie's room. She was from a family of Algerian immigrants, and when her father learned the man who'd gotten her with child was an Irish sailor who'd disappeared with the tide, he'd turned her out.

"However," Elyse continued, "Mabel knows of a doctor

known to treat any person who needs it, regardless of their color—or their ability to pay."

"We *will* pay him."

Elyse nodded, entirely cognizant of their dwindling funds. Mabel, however, was not. She'd joined them six months ago, when there had been five women under their roof and Elyse had needed the help of another trained midwife. Cassie could do little more than assist and run the keeping of the house. Mabel D'Costa had been Elyse's mother's friend and had helped to train Elyse too.

"He's in the East End?" Cassie asked.

Elyse frowned. "I'm not sure. Neither is Mabel. She says he runs a free clinic each weekend on Church Street in Whitechapel, and if you need him on other days, you must send word to an address on Shoreditch Road. The person there takes the information and passes it along to the doctor. We've already sent a messenger to begin the process."

"How odd. He must live outside this part of town."

They entered Dorie's room and found Mabel holding a cloth to the young woman's forehead. Mabel's silver hair was tied up into a knot and covered with a kerchief. She raised an equally silver brow. "She keeps mumbling. I can't understand a single word."

Cassie went to the water ewer. It was nearly empty. "I'll fetch more from the well."

There was one water pump out back of the house, in the alley that supplied the whole block. Cassie had never given a moment's thought to where her water came from before. That one realization had made her feel inordinately spoiled. Now she knew that if anyone wanted to drink well water, it was wisest to boil it first. Elyse even sometimes strained it through broken clumps of charcoal.

"Thank you, Miss Jane," Mabel said, calling Cassie by the name she used at Hope House. Even Elyse called her Jane, at least when others were with them.

Miss Jane Banks was a middle-class woman from Cheapside, whose father had left her with a tidy sum of family money and a wish to do good in the world. Hope House was the realization of that. At least that was the story she and Elyse had whipped up to tell anyone who asked. But the truth was, the women here usually had too many troubles of their own to pry too deeply into the lives of the few caring for them.

That being said, being open that she was the sister of a duke and a lady of the peerage would have been a folly. No one would trust her, or feel they had anything at all in common with her. Such irony. Cassie had more in common with these women than she did with most of the ladies she knew in the West End of London.

She returned from the common well and over the next hour or so, assisted Mabel as she soothed Dorie. It was Cassie's task to encourage her to sip broth, which Sister Agatha, a nun from a church in Spitalfields who came in daily to cook, had made. It was difficult work, as Dorie was nearly insensate. Mabel and Elyse had already told her that she could go for the evening, that they would handle everything when the doctor arrived. However, Cassie wanted to stay. She felt a true purpose here, even if she was just lifting a cup to Dorie's lips or changing the sheets on her bed. What would she do at home? Take supper. Have a glass of brandy.

Read. And wonder how Dorie was faring. No, she may as well just stay put.

Downstairs, the bell connected to the front office chimed.

"I hope that's the doctor," Elyse said before hurrying for the stairs.

Dorie had about a month before she was expected to deliver. After the child was born, she would decide whether to keep the baby or place it out. No matter her choice, she could stay for another month to recover. During that time, they would help Dorie plan for after she left. If she kept her baby, as a single mother, she would need an income. That was Cassie's primary duty at Hope House—to help each woman begin again. She found them lodging, employment, and continued to check in every few weeks. Only if the women wanted it, of course. Some didn't. Many turned their newborns over to the sisters at St. Paul's Church in Shadwell or St. Mary's in Bishopsgate and returned to their lives. But at least so far, all the women had abided by the foremost rule of Hope House—to only share its existence with those in need.

At the sounds of Elyse's return, and the low tenor of the doctor's voice, Cassie collected the basket holding the stripped bed linens and started for the door. The room was far too small for all of them. She would only be in the way.

"I'll bring these to the wash," she told Mabel as Elyse reentered. Cassie stood aside for the doctor to come through, and when he did, her heart stuttered to a stop.

"Mabel, Jane, this is Doctor Brown," Elyse said. His eyes went first toward the bed and his patient. Then, he turned his attention toward Cassie. Recognition flared in his peridot eyes.

Lord Grant Thornton went motionless as he stared, awestruck. She tried to breathe, tried to move, but her feet had as good as sealed to the floor. His lips parted, the space between his brows furrowing.

"Doctor Brown?"

Elyse's voice cut through the roar of panic in Cassie's ears. She'd been speaking, apparently, but neither Cassie nor Lord Thornton had been listening.

He blinked and broke his fierce stare. "Yes, forgive me. You were saying, Miss Khan?"

His eyes jumped back toward Cassie, though only for a moment, before he set down his doctor's bag.

"This is Mrs. Mabel D'Costa, another midwife here, and this is Miss Jane Banks." Elyse shot her a concerned glance. She'd noticed their mutual shock. Well, of course, she had! The whole world had come to a screeching halt. Cassie still hadn't drawn breath.

Lord Thornton acknowledged Mabel, and then turned to Cassie again. "Miss *Banks*," he said, drawing out her name.

She hitched her chin. "Doctor *Brown*."

His eyes narrowed to slits then refocused on Elyse as she explained Dorie's condition. Cassie slipped out of the room, her fingers strangling the basket handles. Her heart re-started as she set off at a charge.

Doctor Brown? What in the name of King George was he doing calling himself that? And what was he doing here, in Spitalfields? Cassie's ears continued to chime as she blindly made her way to the washroom, absentmindedly murmuring hello to Sister Agatha along the way. Once alone, she set the basket of linen down and leaned against the washroom's cold stone wall. How could this have happened?

She should have left when Mabel and Elyse suggested it. But she hadn't imagined any doctor who'd deign a charity home worthy of his time would possibly have ties to the peerage. The notion that it could be *him* had not even crossed her mind.

She needed to leave now, before he could finish with Dorie. Cassie hurried back to her office to collect her things. Her driver, Tris, had arrived in the alley behind Hope House at four o'clock, as usual, to pick her up. He was the only member of her staff who knew of her secret life across town. Although he was officially employed by the duke, Tris had vowed his silence. His sister, Anita, had been one of Hope House's first residents, and he'd said his confidence and trust was the least he could give Cassie in return.

Tris could whisk her back to Mayfair, away from this conundrum. But it would only follow her. If she didn't face Lord Thornton now, he would find some other time to corner her and demand answers. Who knew where that would be, or who else might be there? He was infuriating enough to make a show of it. So, instead of dashing off as her instinct shouted for her to do, she lingered in the hallway outside Dorie's room. The sound of his voice coming through the door was a continual stroke of alarm down her spine. Not very unlike the tremors that had come alive under her skin last week when they'd been squeezed into that wretched closet together.

Eventually, Elyse exited the room, again followed by Lord Thornton. With his bag in his hand, he looked to be leaving. He fixed his attention on Cassie, but the shock that had softened his features earlier was nowhere to be found. Wrath hardened the corners of his mouth and lit his irises like a green inferno.

"Doctor Brown, if you don't mind, I'd like a word in private," she said, and at Elyse's surprised frown, added, "It's to do with payment for your services."

"Yes, I did want to speak to you about that," he replied tightly. "Miss Khan, I'll be back tomorrow afternoon, unless you send for me earlier."

Elyse thanked him before moving toward the stairs to the next floor, the curious arch of her brow persisting. She would have questions for Cassie later, that was for certain. However, dealing with the furious lord on her heels as she led him toward her office was her primary concern.

Lord Thornton stalked into the small, cold room, and Cassie shut the door behind him.

He dropped his bag with a *thump* on the floor and threw his hat onto the sofa. He set his hands on his hips and stared down at her. "I'm beginning to think you're determined to ruin yourself, Lady Cassandra. What in hell are you doing in this place?"

Suddenly, he seemed much taller than he'd been before. Then again, the ceiling in her office was quite low. The crown of his head was nearly at the cornices.

Cassie crossed her arms, refusing to cower. "Why are you here, pretending to be someone called Doctor Brown?"

Lord Thornton shook his head. "No. You will answer my question. This is a house for ruined women. You cannot be here."

She warmed, despite the chilled temperature of the office.

"I know exactly what this place is, as Miss Khan and I are the ones who founded it."

His hands dropped from his hips and that softened, awestruck expression came back over his features. "*You* founded it?"

She held his glare. "Yes."

"Does the duke know?"

Cassie balked. "If Michael knew, he'd explode into a million pieces. He'd then cobble himself back together and murder me."

Lord Thornton cocked his head and seethed. "I share the temptation."

Cassie stepped past him, annoyed by his looming and frothing at the bit. "Hope House is important. The women who come here need help; they need care. Michael isn't cruel, but he wouldn't understand. He'd only care about protecting me."

"As he should." Lord Thornton followed her the few paces to her desk, which she placed herself behind. Putting some object between them seemed a good idea. "Cassie, if you are discovered here, you *will* be ruined. Not to mention you'll irreparably tarnish the Fournier name."

"That is why everyone here believes I am Miss Jane Banks. No one is going to discover me."

He threw out his arms. "I have!"

"Only because you are pretending to be *Doctor Brown*, the mysterious physician who pays house calls on the poor."

He hefted his chin, and the flames in his eyes banked. He'd as good as drawn shutters around himself.

"You run a free clinic in Whitechapel," she stated. "Secretly, I presume, considering not one of your upper-class patients would so much as allow you in through the front door if they knew what you were doing. Share a physician with the common poor? They wouldn't stand for it."

He shifted his jaw but said nothing as he turned to look through the window. The snow had changed to cold rain, flecking the thin, cracked glass.

"You must understand, then, why I am here," she said, somewhat more softly.

"I understand why I do what I do." He cut his eyes back to her. They sharpened. "But I cannot begin to comprehend why you would put yourself into this situation. Into this danger."

She groaned, her temper flaring. "I am not in any danger."

"You are a stone's throw from Whitechapel," he retorted, his voice rising. "You don't know the first thing about life in the stews."

"Do not patronize me, Lord Thornton." Cassie came out from behind the desk, now simmering for a fight. "We might be mutual acquaintances through Audrey and Hugh, but that doesn't give you the right to lecture me or tell me what I can and cannot do. Now, on the topic of your payment—"

"I do not accept payment," he snapped, meeting her in the center of the room, practically fulminating. "Dorie is sick with a serious fever. It's running rampant in the stews, and it is highly contagious. She must not come into contact with the other women, and only one person should provide care. *Not you.* Even if you do not listen to another word I say, at least promise me you will stay away from her."

His eyes drilled into hers, and Cassie thought she saw a glimmer of worry underneath his anger. She bit her tongue against an instant retort that she would not stay away from a single woman at Hope House in need of care. It would only rile him further, and he needed to leave. She needed him to go. His finding her here was a catastrophe, and this outburst perfectly displayed why.

"Fine," she said at last.

He stepped back, looked around for his bag, and then picked it up. Then, he fetched his hat from the shabby sofa.

"How do you get back to Grosvenor Square? Please, for God's sake, woman, tell me you don't hire a hackney cab."

She gritted her molars. "I have a driver," was all she said before going to the door and whipping it open. A clear invitation for him to leave.

He slapped his hat on and glowered. "Good evening, Miss Banks."

"Goodbye, Doctor Brown."

She slammed the door on his heels.

CHAPTER FOUR

His head had not throbbed this wretchedly in months. Not since the absinthe incident of the previous June. The green liqueur was poison to Grant, and yet he'd been persuaded to drink far too much of it one wild evening at the Fallen Arch, a club that catered to London's demimonde. June the seventh crept up on him each year. The black storm that had once accompanied the date had lessened to a dreary, cold drizzle, and Grant admitted that was probably the reason he'd blinded himself with the green fairy at the Fallen Arch.

It was only natural that the day he'd lost his wife and infant child should be shrouded in black. Eight years had passed, and with each one, the memories of Sarah continued to fade. That night at the club, he'd tried to drown his guilt, and yet he'd only succeeded in debilitating himself for the next two days.

Last night, Grant hadn't indulged in anything stronger than whisky. His head didn't ache because of that, but because he hadn't slept. All night, into the early morning hours, he'd fluctuated between tossing in bed and pacing his room, as well as the halls of his home on St. James's Square.

Miss Jane Banks. What the devil was Cassie thinking? To hide a pregnant woman from her family, or her husband, or even just the father of her unborn child was a dangerous risk. It might very well be illegal. And Cassie's safe house sheltered several of these women at a time. Miss Khan, the midwife, had briefly explained about their endeavor and purpose after allowing him out back of the accountant's office that fronted the address. Grant had come to a stop at the base of a stairwell.

"The woman is with child?" His messenger, a former patient whom he paid well to conceal the truth of his identity, had only said that a feverish woman needed seeing to, fast.

"That's correct, doctor." Miss Khan had taken the first step up, but Grant stayed planted to the floorboards.

"Is she in labor?" he'd asked, his heartbeat beginning to increase. He did not oversee deliveries. Since Sarah's death, he hadn't been able to so much as think about them without feeling the onset of shivers and sweat. For that reason alone, he'd whittled down his patients in the ton to include just men and a few older women who couldn't bear children—and who wouldn't faint over his reputation.

"Not at this time," Miss Khan had said, her keen eyes narrowing. No doubt she'd noticed his brush with panic.

Once he'd started to follow her up the steps, she'd asked for his confidence; the safety of their residents depended on his silence. Grant had given his word—and then, he'd entered the upstairs room and come face to face with Lady Cassandra Sinclair.

The onslaught of shock and stark confusion, then the slow boil of understanding had left his limbs buzzing with restlessness. It had taken all his training and focus to calm himself enough to see to the feverish woman, to put her front of mind instead of the chit he'd so recently been in a closet with at Lady Dutton's ball.

After, in the drafty back room she'd preposterously called an office, Cassie's impertinence and her refusal to grasp the reason for his anger had only further stoked his temper. And now, the bloody woman knew *his* secret. For the last five years, ever since he'd quit his daily routine of wallowing in despair, he'd run the Church Street free clinic. Every Saturday, without fail, he'd arrive with his assistant, Hannah, and from ten o'clock until five in the evening, they would be inundated with all manner of situations. From simple cuts to festering wounds; cancerous masses to ingrown hairs; severed fingers to put-out eyes; swollen abdomens to broken bones. The variety of ailments was unending, and most people in Whitechapel were content to suffer until Saturday. Emergency calls were rare, but Grant had arranged a system so that he could protect his identity. It had worked. Until now.

"Four boxes," Hannah said from where she stood at the supply cabinets in his home surgery.

Grant looked up from the medical logbook he'd been reading through. "Four boxes of what?"

"Cotton linen." Her forehead creased. "You asked me to take inventory?"

"Oh, right. Yes. I did." He barely remembered his assistant entering the room while he'd been reading through the notes he'd taken about his fever patients over the last month. "Four boxes should be plenty for now, thank you."

Hannah turned back to the cabinets. “Did the emergency call last night not go well?”

Grant closed the logbook. “How did you know I went out?”

Miss Hannah Matthews only attended emergency calls with him during daylight hours, and only when she was at Thornton House, which was usually four times every week.

“Your bag is missing a tincture of Peruvian bark,” she answered.

“Ah. Yes, of course.” Had his mind not been boiled down to suet, he would have been able to deduce her reasoning for himself. “I was summoned for a fever patient.”

In any other situation, he would have imparted much more about it to his assistant. As his late wife’s younger sister, Hannah was family. And Grant was the only family she had left. Their mother died in childbirth when Hannah was just three. Their father then left her and Sarah to be raised by their grandmother, who’d passed away shortly before Sarah became his wife. Hannah had been just eighteen when Sarah died and was suddenly entirely dependent upon her brother-in-law. Unfortunately, he’d become an utter wreck. Knowing this, his eldest brother, Lawrence, and his wife, Mary, had taken in Hannah. Over time, she began to express an interest in Grant’s work, and then, had offered to assist him when he needed another pair of hands.

Mary had been adamantly against it, saying the young lady should be getting married, not *working*—and with a physician, at that. It was beyond the pale! However, neither Hannah nor Grant had felt the need to regard Mary’s complaints, shrill as they’d been, and she’d happily stayed on the fringes of the marriage mart while assisting Grant.

Hannah was steady and serious and had a methodical sort of behavior that suited a clinic. He trusted her with all aspects of his patient logbook.

But now there was Lady Cassandra to think about. Something of which he'd already been doing too much of over the last week. He would be bathing, or reading, or eating, and on one occasion, even listening to a patient's heart rhythm through his stethoscope, when he'd realize he was not paying attention to what was going on around him. Instead, he'd be thinking about that damned closet in Lady Dutton's house. Cassie's heaving breaths, her palms against his chest. Her thigh tangling between his, her smell of apricots. He couldn't seem to stop his mind from reliving those several minutes. Or from imagining what other things could have happened, had he not fought his body's desire for her.

But it was just base lust. Had it been any woman shoved against him in that closet, he would have felt the same, he was sure of it. Probably even Lady Brookfield with her mole.

"The tincture should help," Hannah said, interrupting his increasingly cluttered thoughts. "Unless this fever is as serious as the other cases we've seen."

After their first fever patient had stumbled into the free clinic, Grant had insisted that Hannah keep her distance for a time. He was ultimately responsible for her and didn't want her to take ill. But she'd ignored his request and continued to join him.

"I fear it is."

He'd planned to wait until at least noon to return to the disguised location but now felt an increased sense of urgency. If he found Cassie in that room again, he'd wring her insolent neck.

Goodwin, his butler, appeared in the surgery entrance, and in his usual measured tone, announced a caller. "Lord James Thornton is here, my lord. I've shown him into the study."

Grant groaned and scrubbed his fingers through his hair. Two years his senior, James was closest to him in age, and by far his favorite brother. However, he never called this early in the day unless it had something to do with their father. The marquess's most recent complaints that his youngest and least preferred son was not carrying his weight when it came to providing the family title with its future heir had fallen to the back of his mind since last evening at Hope House.

"I'll return shortly," he said to Hannah, who only sealed her lips to bite back a smirk. She didn't yet know of the marquess's ultimatum, but she was perfectly aware that Grant was the black sheep of the family and was regularly hauled over the coals for his infractions.

He entered his study to find his brother seated at his desk, arms folded behind his head, and muddy riding boots up on the blotter.

"Ah, baby brother." A grin stretched James's face into the mischievous expression he wore when he knew he was being a pest.

"Get your shite-covered boots off my desk." Grant swiped them off, and James sat forward, laughing. "I take it you're here with some new decree from our loving father."

"Maybe I've just dropped in after my morning ride to say hello," he replied, standing up from the chair.

"I am not in the mood, James." Grant grabbed the decanter of single malt he kept on his desk, intending to pour himself a drink. But then slammed the stopper back in. It was too damned early, and he needed to return to Hope House.

"I can see that." James turned serious, something he could manage to do from time to time if he truly tried. "What has happened?"

Nothing having to do with Cassie Sinclair could be uttered, of course. So, Grant turned to the next most aggravating thing. "Is the marquess's order that I find a new wife and issue a son not reason enough?"

"Plenty, I suppose." James moved toward the leather Chesterfield. He fell backward onto the cushions and stretched out his legs again.

"Eight children," Grant said. "Three sired by Lawrence, three by Harold, and two by you, and none of them could be a boy? What is wrong with the lot of you?"

He would not include their younger sister in his satirized scathing. She was heartbroken that she hadn't conceived after three years of marriage, and besides, Penelope already received enough grief about it from their father.

James raised a brow, and as Grant had always been able to do, he read his brother's thoughts easily. He was thinking of the child that Grant had sired himself. The one who'd never drawn breath. Also a girl. But James knew better than to mention her.

"Perhaps we are all cursed to sire females," he said instead. He was being facetious. He adored his little girls, Letitia and Vivian.

"That is far too fatalistic an attitude for the marquess," Grant replied, eyeing the decanter once more. He turned his back to it and faced his brother. "When is the new one due to arrive again? Next month?"

It was the one last glittering hope Grant clung to: that James's wife, currently in confinement, would give birth to a boy. The boy their father had slowly become obsessed with receiving. The fact that primogeniture would safely see the Lindstrom title bestowed upon at least one of his four sons wasn't enough for the old tyrant. With no male offspring amongst those four sons, the title would eventually be shunted off to the next male heir. Some distant cousin or nephew, all of whom may as well have been common laborers for how Lord Lindstrom spoke of them.

"About a month, yes," James answered, but his tone held a warning, one he'd already illuminated before: that Grant should not hinge all his hope on the child being male. But it seemed his optimism had a mind of its own. Should Vera have a boy at the start of the new year, Grant would be off the hook.

Unfortunately, the marquess had given him only until the first of January to select a wife.

"I've come about Father's dinner tonight," James said to change the subject.

"I haven't heard about any dinner."

His brother rose to his feet, looking suddenly eager to depart. "This is you hearing. And you're to be there. No excuses. Eight o'clock."

He groaned. "I presume several unmarried ladies and their mothers will be in attendance," Grant said, pushing off from the edge of his desk as James headed for the exit.

"Our father is a hard man, I'm not ignorant to that. But you are two and thirty, brother. You should marry."

Thorns pricked the underside of his skin. "I *was* married. How is it that everyone constantly seems to forget that?"

James cocked his head. Then came forward and clasped Grant's shoulder. "No one has forgotten. We all loved Sarah. But it has been eight years." He gave a small shake of his head. "It is time to move on."

It wasn't a new sentiment. The first person to suggest it, just three months after Sarah's death, had received a broken nose and a cracked front tooth. He couldn't even recall the man's name. At that time, Grant had been visiting houses of vice nearly every night of the week to numb his incessant pain. His practice had been a shambles, his patients withdrawing to allow him time to grieve. But it was not acceptable for men to grieve for too long. He would recover, he'd been told, and find a new wife. Have more children. The comments had left him cold, and curious as to just how many men actually loved their wives.

He'd loved Sarah with blind passion. He'd worshipped her. She'd been beautiful, of course, but that hadn't been his sole reason. There had been so many little things about her, like her subdued wit, her penchant for anything pink, and her truly awful singing voice. It had been horrendously off key, and she'd known it, so she would abuse his ears with little songs whenever she felt the urge to annoy him. Not that it ever truly did. And yet, eight years on, he found he couldn't hear it anymore in his memory the way he once had.

James released his shoulder. "Besides, haven't you grown tired of superficial liaisons?"

"No." Not when they were the extent of what he was willing to risk.

Superficial rake. It was what Cassie had accused him of being when she'd walked in on Lady Brookfield showing him her mole. It was mostly accurate. He was superficial in many ways. He was a rake too, though he limited his number of bed partners to a healthy one-at-a-time—unlike many true rakes he knew.

Still, hearing Cassie accuse him of superficiality had struck with insult, while his brother's acknowledgement of it had left nary a mark.

He straightened up and cleared his throat. "I'll be at the damnable dinner, but I cannot promise I'll be on my best behavior."

He had a reputation to uphold, after all.

"You'd best try," James said on his way out. "Just pick a wife and be done with it. Father is serious about this. He holds the power to reduce your income to a pittance—"

"As I well know," he interjected, the threat like the nick of a blunted razor.

"Enough for you to get by on bread and ale alone," James went on.

"Yes, yes, do shut up and leave."

His brother winked and did just that.

Christ. Bread and ale. Had he received even a solitary display of affection from his father over the course of his life, Grant might doubt the veracity of the warning. But the marquess did not make idle threats. And should Grant's income dry up, he'd be left with nothing but his physician earnings. It wouldn't be near enough to run this household and the free clinic. One solution he'd considered had been to leave Thornton House and live in Whitechapel at the Church Street clinic. He leased the entire building, which consisted of two floors and six rooms. But he'd already shoved that option into the rubbish. He wanted to be philanthropic, not poor—which he would be, once his upper-class patients learned he was doctoring to the pestilence ridden masses.

It brought his mind back to Lady Cassandra. She knew all about Dr. Brown now. Unlike Hannah, Hugh Marsden, and the few others who knew about the clinic, like his driver Merryton and of course, Goodwin, Grant didn't fully trust that Cassie would stay mum about it. Given her short temper and her impulsivity, he felt slightly precarious about the whole thing.

"Should I ready your bag?" Hannah asked as she entered the study. "It's nearly noon, and I suspect you'll want to check in on last night's patient."

She knew him well.

"Thank you," he said as anticipation churned his stomach. As much as he hoped Cassie was not there, he couldn't deny that it would be convenient. They needed to speak. And he would not shut up until he got the answer he wanted.

CHAPTER FIVE

Lately, getting to Hope House had become more difficult, and the twinge of annoyance Cassie had started to feel for Genie, the Duchess of Fournier, had grown into a fully-fledged cramp. Considering Cassie's sister-in-law was one of the kindest, gentlest, and most likable people she had ever known, that cramp of annoyance came in tandem with one of guilt.

Genie was only trying to help Cassie discover her purpose, and by accepting invitations to teas and charity luncheons on their behalf, she believed she was giving Cassie opportunities to do just that.

"If you aren't going to marry," Genie had recently told her, "you will need to do something with your time and energy."

Cassie had bit her tongue. Telling her about Hope House was not an option. Genie was loyal to Michael and asking her to keep from him something as significant as that would have been a cruel request. Most likely, Genie would have supported the endeavor in theory. She would see the good it could do. But to be a lady of the peerage, working in the poorest parts of London, and with ruined women, was nothing short of a reputational suicide.

That was, of course, a threat that Cassie had become accustomed to. It didn't faze her as much as it might other ladies, like her friends Marianna and Jane, the latter of which had latched onto Michael's mission to convince her to marry. At least once a week, Jane would join Cassie and Genie at Violet House for tea with some new invitation to extend to Cassie, where she might meet a suitable man. The morning after Grant Thornton's discovery of her at Hope House, Cassie nearly sent her regrets to Genie for their weekly tea. But then, Jane would only come by Grosvenor Square after. So, she'd put down her head and vowed to get through the hour-long visit.

She'd slept wretchedly the previous night, beleaguered by thoughts of Lord Thornton. All night, she'd vacillated between spiraling dread that he would tell someone—probably Hugh—and crackling fury for his anger with her. The despot had no right to order her about! His command to stay away from Dorie had only made her more eager to care for the poor woman. She was ill. She needed help. What made Cassie more important than Mabel or Elyse? Why should she be shielded from potential sickness but not them?

She must have been wearing her simmering impatience on her expression, for the moment Jane sat across from her at the table in Genie's morning room, she pleated her brow.

"Why are you scowling at me?"

Cassie snapped to attention. "I'm not scowling."

Genie spread a napkin in her lap and signaled to the maid

for tea. "You most definitely are, dear. Is something on your mind?"

She took her napkin and fiddled with it. "I'm just not feeling well."

Genie and Jane both arched their brows and peered at each other knowingly. Right away, Cassie knew she'd used that excuse for the last time. Headaches and stomach malaises could only be employed sparingly.

"You're not feeling social, is what you mean to say," Jane said.

Cassie kept her lips sealed. To agree would be rude; to deny it would not be believed.

"I do have some things on my mind, as it happens," she said.

Genie brightened with interest. "Oh?"

"Last week's lecture at the Lyceum," she said, "on lepidopterology."

Jane's eyes sprang wide. "*Leprosy*?"

"No, lepidopterology. The study of butterflies."

Her friend folded her hands in her lap. "Why do butterflies have you concerned?"

Cassie had not attended the lecture as she'd told Genie the week before, when her sister-in-law had caught her preparing to leave for the day. But it was the only thing she had been able to think of just now while the two women had been staring her down. Her every thought and concern seemed to revolve around Hope House and the work there, making it difficult to find anything substantive to say during these teas and luncheons.

"Well," she said, attempting to find an answer to Jane's question. "Some are becoming extinct."

Jane narrowed her eyes in skepticism, but the maid returned with the tea service. Cassie silently thanked her for her excellent timing.

"There you are, darling!"

Michael appeared within the morning room's open door, just behind the maid. An alarmingly pleased grin stretched his mouth. Cassie frowned. She'd never seen him smile like that. Gracious, had his teeth always been that big?

"Will you join us for tea?" Genie asked.

When a gentleman entered the room after Michael, Cassie smothered a groan.

"I'm afraid not, I only wanted to stop in and introduce a friend," Michael said, his attention swerving toward Cassie. She met it with a flat stare.

Her brother ignored it and introduced Mr. Alaric Forsythe. Jane and Genie were perfectly amiable as they greeted the son of the Baron Forsythe, who was, Cassie admitted, somewhat handsome and without a single gray hair or wrinkle. Compared to a few other gentlemen Michael had gone out of his way to introduce her to, Mr. Forsythe was a gem.

"Oh, Mr. Forsythe, you must tell us all about your time to Egypt," Genie said as soon as Michael announced he was just back from a stay of six months.

Mr. Forsythe bowed and, with a bashful smile, said he would love to. "However, you might find my account tedious. I spent most of my time in Cairo studying artifacts."

"Artifacts?" Cassie asked, surprised by her own question. And at her intrigue.

He turned to her. "Yes, at an excavation site near the Nile. A tomb for an ancient pharaoh."

Michael was watching her for her reaction, and though she did suffer a moment's interest, Cassie only gave a polite nod. "I see."

"Did you find any butterfly fossils?" Jane asked. At Mr. Forsythe's quizzical look, she added, "Lady Cassandra has an interest."

"Lepidopterology? We have a common interest then. As it happens, there was a lecture on the topic just last week at the Lyceum—"

Abruptly, Cassie stood, and at the startled reaction of everyone around her, cleared her throat loudly. Anything to stop Mr. Forsythe from speaking more about a lecture she was supposed to have attended. She forced the husky sound out again, raising a hand to cover her mouth. "Sorry. Something in my throat. If you'll excuse me." She then fled through the door and into an adjacent room.

Only after hearing Michael and Mr. Forsythe depart through the front door, did Cassie return to her seat. She feigned disappointment. "Oh, did the gentlemen leave already?"

"Your throat sounds much better," Genie said with a smirk.

Cassie endured the next half hour, sneaking furtive glances toward the tall case clock. As soon as Jane departed Violet House, Cassie did as well. Although it had taken quite a bit of convincing to get Michael to agree to her living on her own, rather than under his roof on Curzon Street, it had been worth the struggle—even with the much lower annual income she'd used as a bargaining chip. If she still lived at Violet House, she would never have been able to disappear for hours on end. Someone would have always been watching.

"To the house, Tris," she said as she approached her driver, who was standing at the ready in the half-moon drive. He tipped his hat before helping her up into the carriage.

He turned out of the drive and started east. Whenever Cassie said, "the house", Tris knew that meant Hope House, while "home" was her residence at number twelve Grosvenor Square. Other than Tris, no one else knew. Not even her maid, Ruth. While it would have been more appropriate for Cassie to move about Town with her maid in tow, she didn't have the patience for such stuffy rules, and thankfully, Michael had given up on requesting she be accompanied. She also preferred to keep some distance between herself and Ruth. While her maid knew of the child Cassie had borne in secret, and she trusted Ruth to keep mum, to alert her to any more scandal would just be courting disaster.

The more people who knew, the greater the risk of being found out. Which is why Grant Thornton knowing had continued to prickle under her skin. Knowing his secret identity as Dr. Brown only gave her so much solace. The sorry fact of life was that if he were to be found out, he would suffer some minor unfortunate consequences, while she would be thoroughly ruined.

After twenty or so minutes, Tris pulled behind the Crispin Street block, into the narrow alley where he kept the carriage whenever she was there. While it was unlikely anyone from her set would be in Spitalfields to recognize it, parking along the street was an unnecessary risk.

At the back door, Cassie knocked twice, paused, then knocked three more times. The back entrance was always locked, and though she had a key, there were two chain locks that needed to be undone too. There was usually always someone in the kitchen to hear the coded knocking.

"Dorie is holding steady," Elyse said as soon as she allowed Cassie inside. Sister Agatha was at the table, chopping carrots.

"Excellent. And has Dr. Brown returned?" Cassie asked as she hung her flannel cape on the stand near the stove to keep it warm.

In the carriage, she'd shed her sumptuous velvet pelisse and fashionable hat, and replaced them with the unadorned cape and bonnet she'd purchased at a thrift shop. The exchanges couldn't cover up the fine make of her dresses, but so far neither Mabel nor Sister Agatha had said anything about them.

"Not yet," Elyse answered. Cassie's stomach dropped. She'd hoped he would have come and gone by now.

After Lord Thornton left the night before, Elyse had come to Cassie's office. She'd shut the door before saying, "You two know one another."

"He is a peer," Cassie admitted. Her friend had only nodded.

"He sounded like a toff," she replied. "I take it his name is not Brown?"

Cassie had shaken her head but had refrained from saying what it truly was. She'd already complained to Elyse about Lord Thornton and the closet fiasco. If she knew the doctor was one and the same, she might refuse to allow him back into Hope House. Dorie needed care too desperately for such stubbornness.

Thankfully, Elyse had only asked if the doctor might

inform other peers of her involvement. "No," Cassie had firmly replied. She would not allow it. Grant Thornton was *not* going to take this from her.

"Lila is restless today," Elyse said as she took a seat at the table across from Sister Agatha and picked up a half-peeled potato. "I found her in your office, looking for something to read from your shelves."

Cassie poured herself a cup of tea from the pot that was always kept hot and refreshed on the stove. "That is a first." No other woman they'd sheltered had ever taken an interest in her books. Most could not read beyond basic words, and more than a few had not even known how to write their own names. Cassie would try to teach them at least that one skill before they left Hope House, though many didn't see the value in it. Skills like sewing or embroidery would better help them provide for their families.

"I thought that girl sounded educated," Sister Agatha said, scraping the rough skin of a carrot. Her hands were deft with a peeling knife even though they were knobby with age. From the savory smells in the kitchen, she was making a roast for supper. They usually ate communally in the dining room, and Cassie enjoyed the evenings she was able to join them.

She slid into the chair next to Elyse. "I wonder what she is doing here. A girl like her should have money enough to be sent away."

"Unless her family doesn't know," Elyse replied.

"If that is the case, where do they believe she is?" Cassie frowned into her tea. "They will surely launch a search for her."

She and Elyse, and Mabel and Sister Agatha, were all aware that they could find themselves in serious trouble should a family ever accuse them of "kidnapping" their daughter, or hiding her away. It was one of the reasons they were so careful to keep Hope House hush hush. Another reason was because most of the women *were* in hiding—from unkind men. To keep them safe, not one of those men could be allowed to find them.

Elyse finished peeling the potato. "Let's not worry about that just yet. Lila hasn't said much. Maybe soon she'll be comfortable enough to let us know her situation."

The young woman had been reticent since her arrival, only providing them with the most essential details: her first name and how long she'd been with child. She'd been too frightened and untrusting to say more.

Once again, Cassie saw just how fortunate she'd been when she'd found herself in trouble. Her eldest brother, Philip, had at first insisted Cassie should be made to marry the man who'd compromised her. However, he'd been able to set his own anger aside long enough to realize it would have been a disastrous marriage. Lord Winston Renfry, the heir to the Earl of Bainbury, would have made a horrendous husband, and forcing Cassie to marry him would have been cruel. Philip had instead sent her to a trusted friend in Sweden. Her reputation had been protected, and Renfry had never learned of the child. Thankfully, she had not crossed paths with him even once since her return.

"I'm going to check on Caroline," Elyse said as she got up from her chair. Sister Agatha had gone to the sink with the peeled potatoes and carrots, so she didn't witness Elyse quickly tapping the side of Cassie's head. She startled, but then understood what her friend had wanted to tell her: She was still wearing the emerald-encrusted hair comb Ruth had speared her hair with that morning.

Before Agatha could turn around, Cassie pulled it out.

"Tell Caroline I'll stop in if she'd like to work on her sampler some more," she said as she dropped the comb into her pocket.

Caroline Rawling was a married woman with four children, and from what she'd shared, she and her husband had agreed that adding another mouth to feed would be injurious to the children they already struggled to provide for. So, she'd come to give birth in private, and then would place the baby out. To avoid judgment from neighbors and friends, she'd said she was staying with her mother in Surrey for the birth. When she arrived home without a baby, she would say it had been stillborn.

As one could expect, Caroline was often melancholy. Her decision hadn't been made lightly. Giving up a child was heart-wrenching; this Cassie knew too well. And so, she would stop in to say hello to Caroline whenever she was at Hope House, and if time allowed, they would sit and work on an embroidery hoop that Caroline had brought with her.

"Well, it's about time. The coal is here," Sister Agatha said, peering through the glass of the kitchen's single window.

"At last." Cassie got up. "My office was developing a layer of ice. I'll see the deliveryman is paid."

She reached into her pocket, which she now had Ruth sew into all her dresses. The first time she went out in the blocks around Crispin Street, a passel of hooligans had knocked into her and stolen her wrist reticule before she could even blink. They were already racing away when she realized it was missing from her arm. Ever since, she'd carried her coin purse in her pocket.

Cassie met the deliveryman as he was pouring the coal down the shute, into the cellar of the building. Enough to last them through the end of February, she imagined. She paid him the two pounds it cost, and then started back for the kitchen. A thick brume had been setting in when she'd arrived, and now, it lowered into the alley. Cassie shivered, having forgone her flannel for the short trip outside.

She would go in, say hello to Lila and Caroline, log the payment for coal in her office ledger, and leave. Before Lord Thornton could arrive and start frothing at the mouth again, anyway.

The quick scuffing of boots behind her in the alley preceded a hand latching onto her arm. A leather glove immediately muffled her yelp of surprise as it came down hard over her mouth. It was a man, and he tugged her back, against him.

"Where is she?" he hissed in her ear.

Cassie thrashed, but his formidable strength rendered the fight useless. His arms seemed to be cast of iron as he dragged her backward, her bootheels scudding over the cobbles.

"I know she is here!" he said, his voice grating and low. "Where is Isabel?"

The urge to panic and keep thrashing was instinctual, but she knew it would get her nowhere. She had to calm. Had to think. With her arms pinned at her sides, Cassie's hands flailed uselessly against her skirt. Something hard knocked into her palm. She remembered that her coin purse wasn't the only item in her pocket.

"I am going to remove my hand so you can tell me where Isabel is," the man said. "Scream and you will be sorry."

Stretching her fingers into her pocket, Cassie fished for the hair comb. The cluster of emeralds, shaped into a flower, scraped against her palm. She closed her hand around it just as the man's palm started to lift from her mouth. Cassie didn't hesitate—she captured the man's fingertip between her teeth and bit down as hard as she could against the leather. With a grunt of pain, he loosened his grip on her arms, enough for her to pull away from him. He clamped down on her wrist, but she whirled about and raked the sharp tines of her comb toward his face. And then she was falling backward, the man's hold on her completely severed as he roared and covered his face with his hands.

"Oi!" Tris's shout gave Cassie the strength to push up from the cold puddle she'd landed in. Her driver ran toward her. "Oi, stop!"

Tris raced by her, attempting to chase the man who now sprinted around the corner of the alley, out of sight. He gave up and turned back toward Cassie.

"My lady," Tris said, reaching her side. "Miss Banks, I mean, are you injured?"

"No, I don't think so," she gasped, her heart hammering erratically. She still clutched the hair comb in her shaking hand. Traces of blood glistened on the tips of the tines.

Tris took her arm and led her back to the kitchen entrance. Cassie's mind whirled as he knocked the correct code. What had just happened? The man had been looking for someone. A woman. *Isabel.*

"Miss Banks!" Sister Agatha exclaimed when she opened

the door. The warmth of the kitchen enveloped Cassie, but it seemed to only make her shivering worse.

Tris led her to the table, still gripping her elbow. "She was attacked in the alley just now."

"She was *what?*"

Cassie came to a dizzying stop at the deep voice. Grant Thornton had just entered the kitchen from the front hall, and when he saw her, his eyes blew wide. He came forward, hunting her for any injury. "Where are you hurt?"

Her legs quivered. A strange rush of numbness stole down them, making them feel as if they were disappearing. She plopped into a chair as Elyse and Lila entered the room behind Lord Thornton.

"I'm not hurt."

"Was it a pickpocket?" Lila asked.

"No, he..." Cassie took a breath, closed her eyes, and forced herself to calm. She was fine. The man was gone. She was safe.

Warm hands touched hers, and she opened her eyes to find Lord Thornton on one knee before her. He'd taken her hands in his and was now inspecting them. Her fingers, clamped into fists, were speckled with dirt from the puddle she'd fallen into. A few raw scrapes marked her knuckles.

"What did the bastard do to you?" Lord Thornton asked as he coaxed her fingers to open. The hair comb had bit into her palm, leaving imprints. He picked it up and eyed it with a propped brow. "Or should I ask, what did you do to him?"

Sister Agnes brought him a boiled cloth, and he dabbed the shallow gashes. Cassie winced at the sting.

"I can do that myself," she told him, trying to take her hand from his. He clung on.

"I will tend to them, Miss Banks," he replied, the use of her false name slightly mocking. "While I do, perhaps you can explain. If he wasn't a pickpocket, who was he and what did he want?"

"I don't know who he was. I didn't get a good look at him. He was a gentleman, though."

"What kind of gentleman would be skulking around in an alley?" Elyse asked.

"What did he look like?" Lila's question was a natural one, but the way she voiced it sounded oddly panicked.

"He was wearing a gentleman's threads," Tris confirmed. "Didn't see his face. Ran off too quickly after Miss Banks slashed at him with that comb."

A deeper scrape on her palm sent a jolt through her as Lord Thornton dabbed. She hissed, pulling her hand back. He made a *tsk tsk* sound and hushed her while regripping her wrist. She scowled at him.

"Well then, what did he want?" Lord Thornton repeated.

Where is she? Tell me where she is. The stranger had sounded desperate. Furious. Cassie's shivers had started to abate, but now, they set back in.

"He wanted to know where a woman named Isabel was."

Lila staggered backward, knocking into Elyse. She sucked in air, and horror turned her face a mask of white against her fading bruises. Lord Thornton twisted at the hip to see who'd made such a sound, at last halting his incessant dabbing.

"Lila—?" Elyse began, but the young woman turned and ran.

CHAPTER SIX

Grant followed Cassie and Miss Khan as they chased after the young woman. His muscles were strung tight, his body thrumming with pent up ire. This was exactly why Cassie should not have been in this part of London. For Christ's sake, she'd been attacked, and if her driver had not been there to intervene...

He clenched his molars as he turned into a small and modestly furnished sitting room. The young woman, probably a year or two younger than Cassie, paced the carpet, her palms covering her cheeks. He'd seen the bruises right away when he'd entered through the false front of the accountant's office and met her as she came off the stairs. She'd scrambled back up a few steps, nearly tripping before Miss Khan held out a placating hand.

"Lila, this is Doctor Brown. He's been treating another resident here. You need not be afraid of him."

If the attacker in the alley had been looking for her, he could now understand her instant fear.

"Isabel?" Cassie said, testing the name. "Is that your real name?"

Her composure had returned. In the kitchen, she'd been pale with shock, her blue eyes wild and unfocused. Grant had dropped to one knee before her without thinking, and only afterward considered his reaction might have appeared too familiar.

"Lila was my mother's name," she whispered before backing up to a chair and collapsing into it. The young woman's pupils had sharpened to pinpricks. The fear she'd shown upon Grant's arrival was nothing in comparison to what transformed her face now.

"The man in the alley," Cassie said. "You are hiding from him?"

"How did he find me?" Isabel's voice was reedy and panicked. She bent forward and leaned her forehead into her hands. Her shoulders began to shake.

Miss Khan went to her side and put an arm around her, while Cassie turned to Grant. She mouthed, *Give us a moment?* He shook his head and set his jaw. "Miss Isabel," he said as he came further into the room. He ignored the warning glares from both Cassie and Miss Khan. "Is this man the father of your child?"

"Doctor Brown." Cassie clipped his name. "At Hope House, women aren't required to answer questions they aren't comfortable with."

"The man attacked you. I want his name."

Cassie widened her eyes with another silent warning, but again, he ignored it.

Isabel looked up from her lap, her eyes red and tearful.

"I'm so sorry, I never meant for him to find me. I don't know how he did!"

"I'm not hurt," Cassie assured her. "We're only worried for your safety."

"What about your own safety?" Grant argued. "And the other women here—"

"Our concern is for *Isabel*," Cassie snapped, the color rising in her cheeks as her temper flared.

Isabel stood, pushing off the midwife's arms. "No, no, the doctor is right. I've put you in danger coming here. I should have known he'd find me."

"Who is he?" Grant asked. "Give me a name. We can go to Bow Street—"

"No!" Her shriek practically shook the walls. Isabel's chin quivered, and she broke out in fresh tears. "I'm so sorry, I'll go."

She started swiftly for the door. He stepped forward to block it. "That would not be wise. He could still be on the street, waiting."

No matter what had just happened in the alley to Cassie, he couldn't allow a vulnerable young woman to be frightened off, directly into the clutches of a violent man.

"You're safer here, with us," Miss Khan told her.

"But we can help you more if we know what we are up against," Cassie added.

Isabel sniffled. "Trust me, you'll be safer if I leave. If he tracked me down, he will be back."

Cassie sent Grant a pleading look. She was at a loss for how to stop Isabel from fleeing. The young woman was correct. The man would be back. Selfish instinct screamed for him to grab Cassie by the arm and drag her from this place to the safety of Mayfair and the world in which she belonged. But then, what would become of the others here?

He swore an oath under his breath, unable to believe what he was about to say. "I know of a safe place where Isabel can stay."

GRANT CLOSED the back door that led to the mews behind Church Street and threw the lock.

"I don't believe we were followed," he said while turning to the two women standing within the cold kitchen. Cassie and Isabel appeared tense, and for good reason. Getting from Hope House to his clinic had been a complicated operation.

Assuming the man who attacked Cassie still had eyes on the Crispin Street safe house, Grant sat in the driver's box with Tris as they departed the alley. Tris avoided the main road, instead turning off the alley and cutting through narrow passageways between street blocks. Finally, he turned onto another road and took an extended, circuitous route to the clinic. All the while, Grant kept his eyes on the conveyances behind them, making sure no single one appeared to be following.

"You're Lord Neatham's friend," Tris had said while they'd been making chaotic loops. "The physician lord."

Grant nodded. "However, here and now, I am Doctor Brown."

"Just as her ladyship is Miss Jane Banks?" At Grant's next nod, Tris had muttered, "All right, then" and continued driving. He was now staying with the carriage and horses in the mews, to make certain no one approached.

It was getting dark, and the shadows of the kitchen stretched corner to corner.

"This is your clinic?" Cassie glimpsed around the small kitchen. It wasn't much smaller than Hope House's space, but it felt vacant. Desolate.

"I only open it on Saturdays," he replied.

The rest of the week, the building lay dormant. There were three levels in the narrow residence, with room enough downstairs for the kitchen and a receiving room, which Grant had employed as his surgery. On the first floor were two bedrooms, each about the size of Cassie's little office at Hope House. A drafty attic stretched from the front of the house to the back, but Grant hadn't touched it during the five years he'd been at Church Street. He barely went upstairs at all but had at least outfitted the two bedrooms in case patients needed to stay over for observation or recovery.

He lit a lamp and gave it to Isabel, telling her to select a room and get settled in.

"I'll come with you," Cassie said, but Grant cleared his throat.

"Miss Banks, I'd like a word."

Isabel cast a wary look between them before leaving. Cassie avoided looking directly at him, and instead went to the stove and opened the grate. "I'll start a fire."

Grant frowned; it was on the tip of his tongue to ask how the devil she'd learned that skill when maids and footmen had done it for her since she'd been born. However, he bit back the comment and lit a few candles as she fed kindling and crumpled broadsheets into the cookstove. He touched a lit taper to her work and heard the rush of fire consuming the dry wood and paper. Cassie moved back, brushing some soot from the sleeve of her dress. Their eyes clashed briefly before she averted hers.

"Tell me what happened." Grant was surprised by how calm he sounded. He didn't feel it. He smoldered every time he envisioned some faceless, violent man attacking her in that alley.

"I've already told you," she replied, walking the circumference of the room, pretending to inspect the small kitchen with its few cabinets and shelves and its even fewer food stores.

"You haven't. All that has been said is that you were attacked. What does that mean? How did he..." Grant ground his jaw. "What did he do?"

She paused at the fireplace and glanced toward him. "He came up behind me. Covered my mouth, so I couldn't scream. Then he asked where she was. That is all. Honestly, I am not the one in danger, Isabel is. He was there for her."

"And yet, you were the one he put his hands on." Fire breathed to life in his chest.

She eyed him warily, as though she could see the glow of it through his shirt and waistcoat. But then gave a dramatic sigh. "I have only a few scraped knuckles, while he may have some deeper gashes to his face. I'd say he bore the brunt of the encounter, not me."

Grant had to admit, it had been swift thinking to defend herself with that hair comb.

"He's quality," Cassie said after a moment. "I could hear it in his speech, and he smelled of soap and cologne. I was too startled in the moment to think of it, but I remember now. And his gloves." She covered her lips as the man had done, as if trying to remember more clearly. It sparked another ember of fury in Grant's chest. "They were kid. Soft and expensive."

Needing to move and disburse the bottled-up ire, he went to the fireplace and crouched.

"Isabel is terrified of him," Cassie added.

"And sheltering her has made you a target." He tossed kindling into the grate. "How many other women at Hope House are you hiding from violent men? You're putting yourself in danger."

"So, I should kick them all to the street? Protect myself, not them? Are they not worth helping?"

He straightened and faced her. "I didn't say that."

"What *are* you saying?"

"That you shouldn't have been in that alley to begin with! You don't belong there!"

The words burned as he let them fly, and his gut cinched with instant regret. Especially when her eyes dulled from fire to ice.

She gave him her back. Then, after some silence, said, "Isabel cannot stay here alone."

He'd expected some other cutting retort, some argument. But instead, she'd shut him out.

A knocking on the back door—two raps, a pause, then three more—severed the tense moment.

"It's Tris," Cassie said, going to unlock it. "That's our code at Hope House."

The driver entered, his hat in his hand. "It's safe. No one's followed."

Cassie shut the door again. "Good. As I was just saying to Doctor Brown, Isabel cannot stay here alone. I would stay—"

"Your driver knows who I really am, and there isn't a chance in hell you are going to stay here."

She sliced him with a glare. "*I would stay*," the little hellion began to say again, "but if I do not come home, my staff will worry. And as they report to the duke, he may hear of it before dawn."

Grant almost wished Fournier *would* hear of it. The duke would certainly put a stop to this madness.

"I need to leave. I have a dinner I cannot miss tonight," he said, even though the last thing he wanted to do after this tangle of an afternoon was play nice for the marriageable ladies the marquess had invited.

Pick a wife, James had told him. *Be done with it.*

As he watched Cassie, nibbling her bottom lip as she tried to solve the problem of who would stay with Isabel, Grant's pulse slowed. If Fournier did hear of her connection to Hope House and her precarious work there, she'd be finished.

What would she do to prevent that from happening?

A wicked, diabolical idea began to weave its way through his mind. It was low, greasy, and unquestionably offensive. But it might just get him out of this pickle with the marquess.

Tris raised his hand, lifting his hat. "I can stay. My brother, Patrick can drive for you while I'm here, my lady. It wouldn't be a problem."

Cassie exhaled. "That's an excellent solution, Tris. Thank you."

The driver nodded. "I'll go to my brother's now. It's not far from here. I'll bring him back, and then he can drive you home tonight."

It was a muddle, but it sounded like their best option for the time being.

"I'll just go inform Isabel and make sure she's settling in." Cassie started in the direction of the front hall and stairs.

"Don't take long, my lady," Grant said, earning another tightening of her back and neck. He smiled at the reaction. "There is something more we need to discuss."

CHAPTER SEVEN

What a wreck of a day it had turned out to be.

Cassie had known some women came to Hope House to evade the men in their lives, and when Lila—or rather, Isabel—had been so guarded upon her arrival, she suspected that may be the case. However, this was the first time any man had found the safe house.

On the drive back into Mayfair, Cassie removed her flannel cape and bonnet and replaced them with her velvet pelisse and finer hat. She lifted the cushion beside her and folded the Spitalfields clothing into the hollow underneath. Tris had helped to alter the bench so she could store them there.

"That's convenient," Lord Thornton said from the opposite bench as he watched her.

"Lord Thornton—"

"You may call me Grant. We are past formalities, I think. Besides I already call you Cassie."

"That is because you're impertinent and have no respect for propriety."

He only tucked up the corner of his mouth in a smirk.

During the hour it had taken Tris to fetch his brother Patrick, she'd avoided Lord Thornton—*Grant*—and whatever it was he'd wanted to discuss by helping Isabel settle into her room. It didn't matter that Grant had offered to shelter her, or that earlier, he'd knelt before Cassie and taken her scraped hands into his with surprising tenderness. All she could hear was what he'd shouted in his clinic kitchen. That she didn't belong there. It had cut her with startling ferocity, straight down to the bone of the unspoken burden she'd carried all year, ever since she and Elyse opened the doors to their refuge: She didn't belong. This wasn't her place. She was forcing her way into a world in which she had no part.

Usually, the tasks she busied herself with drowned out these thoughts. But hearing the same accusation on Grant Thornton's tongue had exhumed them.

What a hypocrite! If she didn't belong in the East End, then neither did he.

Cassie folded her hands, ignoring the pull of her scraped knuckles.

"There is something we need to discuss," he said, the carriage lantern casting changing light over his face.

"So you've said," she sighed. "What is it?"

"My apology."

She peered at him, waiting for his well-practiced sarcastic grin. But it didn't form. He was in earnest.

"Apology for what?"

He sat somewhat slouched on the bench, against the squabs. His hat was off, his ebony hair falling across his brow.

With his long legs and broad shoulders, he looked a little like a giant on the dainty bench. The top of his head practically brushed the quilted silk of the ceiling. Cassie swallowed and shifted on her cushion when his incisive stare continued to hold hers.

"My temper, back at the clinic. I shouldn't have shouted at you."

"It was what you shouted that offended me, not your raised voice." She sat taller. "I am well aware that I'm a fish out of water in that part of London."

But she was a fish out of water here, too.

"I know the feeling," he said. "It took some time to learn how to tread there."

The carriage shook, rocking them both side to side as Cassie held his stare. "Why do you do it?"

He pulled a frown. "Run a free clinic?" At her nod, he shrugged nonchalantly. "Because it is needed. The only doctors most people there can afford are charlatans and barbers, who think they can perform surgery as proficiently as they can shave a beard or yank out a rotten tooth."

She didn't know how to respond. He'd never struck her as a serious or charitable sort. He saw her indecision.

"What, you think I have some other motive?"

"It is only that most men of the peerage don't bother to think of anyone outside their own part of society," she answered.

"Perhaps I'm not as entirely self-serving as you imagined."

"Maybe not entirely." Though he was surely no saint.

The carriage slowed as Patrick turned onto another street. Grant's knee brushed against hers, and his unyielding stare started to feel less provoking and more penetrating. As if he was trying to see something in her that had eluded him so far.

"Do you get your charitable soul from the marquess?" she asked to pierce the silence.

He seemed to recoil and then sat straighter. "About as much as you get yours from the duke."

"Michael is very charitable," she said, offended on her brother's behalf. "He and Genie support a number of foundations."

Grant hinged forward, his elbows braced on his knees. "So, he would be supportive of your safe house, *Miss Banks*?"

"You know he would not."

The galling man sat back again. "Neither would my father. He'd cut me off in a blink if he found out."

"Oh, boo-hoo," she said with a roll of her eyes.

Grant challenged her with a taunting look. "You think that isn't serious? I am the fourth son. Do you know how much fourth sons are given?"

"More than what ninety-five percent of the people in the rest of this city have a year," she replied lightly.

"You are impossible."

Cassie bit her inner cheek, pleased to be getting under his skin for once. A dose of his own medicine, so to speak. Though, it didn't dispel the vibration of friction she felt whenever she was around him, that constant urge to slap him. It also did not dispel the memory of Lady Dutton's closet. The press of his thighs against hers, the tip of his nose, brushing the crown of her head, his breaths warming her scalp when he asked if she'd always smelled of apricots.

The plague of these memories had to stop. They'd taken up residence in her mind and were driving her mad. For so long, she'd successfully pushed away all thoughts of Winston Renfry and the few times she'd allowed him liberties. However, she'd never felt the strange curling of warmth through her lower abdomen when he stood close to her, as Grant had in the closet. No, every time she thought of Renfry and what occurred between them in his bed, she could only cringe in revulsion.

She could not imagine Lord Grant Thornton had ever once made any female cringe in such a way.

They came about on Grosvenor Square and Cassie thanked the stars. It had started to feel too hot in the carriage, even with her dress still damp from her plunge into the alley puddle. It brought her mind back to Isabel and the dangerous man she was hiding from.

"I will pay you," Cassie said as they came to a full stop in front of her residence.

Grant cocked his head. "What for?"

"For the use of your clinic while Isabel is there."

He scoffed. "I don't want your money."

"Then what *do* you want? I must repay you." If anything, just to stay out of his debt. Something like that could be dangerous with a man like Grant Thornton.

He shifted on the bench. His pinched brow made him look discomfited. Was it the talk of money? It was, after all, crass to speak of such things.

"May I come in?" Grant asked.

Cassie froze. "Why?"

She'd offered to repay him... He couldn't possibly be asking for something *untoward*?

He seemed to comprehend the direction of her thoughts and groaned. "There is something more I need to discuss with you."

"Still?" Patrick opened the door, but Cassie remained seated. "Can't we leave it at your apology? I rather liked that."

"I'm sure you did. But no."

She took her new driver's extended hand. "Fine. But you will go around the back. I can't have anyone seeing you enter my house, the two of us alone."

Cassie entered through the front door while Patrick took the carriage, and Grant, to the mews. Her footman, Pierce, greeted her, and she asked for Ruth to be sent to the study. Cassie had been thrilled to take over the room when she arrived at the house; she'd always adored the small study Audrey kept at Violet House, but there was something about the dark mahogany walls, the rich, wine-red carpet, and the masculine furnishings of her brother's former study that gave her extra pleasure. To be a female in command of this space was practically heretical.

Ruth arrived there only a minute after Cassie, collecting her pelisse, hat, and gloves that Cassie had tossed onto the sofa.

"I have a visitor arriving with my new driver, Tris's brother, Patrick, in the mews," Cassie told her, glossing over the change in staff. She would deal with that later. "Can you see him in through the tradesmen's entrance without Pierce and the others learning of it?"

Ruth bobbed. "Yes, milady."

She disappeared on her task, and Cassie went to the fireplace, the flames already built up in preparation for her. Her small staff knew she preferred this room to any other and always kept it ready for her. She held out the skirt of her gown to the fire's warmth and waited impatiently.

"I don't think your maid likes me."

She turned to find Grant standing in the study behind her, the door already shut behind him.

"She is a good judge of character," Cassie replied with a goading arch of her brow. In truth, Ruth likely believed her mistress was about to embark on a tryst with Lord Thornton and disapproved. The notion sent a charged frisson through her belly. She folded her arms around her waist. "What did you so urgently need to discuss?"

Grant moved through the study, toward the fireplace. "At dinner tonight, my father will have invited at least two eligible young ladies to fawn over me."

"Lucky you," she replied. "What does that have to do with anything?"

"He has instructed me to select a lady by the first of the year. And marry her."

A quick, hot spike lanced her abdomen. She scowled at the reaction. "So?"

Grant came to her side at the hearth. "You want to repay me for helping Isabel? There is something you can do for me."

The rest of the study began to darken at the edges as the physician's green eyes seemed to reach for her. Cassie stepped back, as wary of him as she was entranced. But then he spoke and severed the thrall.

"Court me."

The two words were lost beneath the chiming in her ears.

They stole the oxygen from her lungs and set her pulse pounding.

"You cannot be serious," Cassie said, breathless.

"I know it is a rare occurrence, but yes, I am," Grant replied.

"You..." She stopped to even out her breathing. "You wish to *court me*?"

He lifted both his palms, a signal to slow down. "Just pretend to for a short while. A fortnight. Two at the most."

She snapped back, appalled. And oddly insulted. "You want to *pretend* to court me?"

The handsome, fair-faced Lord Renfry bloomed in her memory with such vivid detail that she hitched her breath again. He'd pretended. He'd led her to believe what he felt was real and lasting. Alongside his charming smile, and the way he'd looked at her with what she'd thought was open admiration, was the memory of the pearl ring he'd shown her the first afternoon they had been alone together, at his house in Knightsbridge. She had managed to slip away from her chaperone, Miss Stinton, and they'd entered his residence through the back door. Much the same as Grant had just done.

"This will grace your finger in public as soon as the duke gives his permission," Renfry had said, holding up the three pearls, twisted together in a swirled setting of gold. Cassie had been so happy, so full of excitement. He'd placed it onto her finger, then tugged her to him. His kisses had turned fevered, his hands brazen. She'd known what it was he wanted to do. And because he'd chosen her, she had allowed him to lead her to his bedchamber, that ring still gracing her finger.

She regretted that day more than any other in the whole of her life so far. Even more than she did the one that came nine months later, when her heart tore in two. It never would have happened had she not trusted Renfry and taken him at his word.

"Get out," Cassie said to Grant as she shoved down the memory.

"If you would listen—"

"No! How dare you ask me to pretend at something like that?" She crossed the room, to the one piece of furniture she'd replaced in the study when she moved in. The desk her brother had kept had been too large and formidable. This one was slim and elegant, though she kept a decanter of brandy on it just as Michael had. She took out the stopper with a shaking hand and splashed some into a snifter.

"If you would hear me out, I think we could both benefit from this courtship," Grant said as he followed her across the study. The shivers and nausea that usually accompanied any errant thoughts of Lord Renfry settled as she held the snifter to her lips. She didn't sip, only inhaled the sweet and woody fumes.

"You have one minute to explain yourself."

Grant clasped his hands behind his back and swallowed a bemused grin. Why did he always look at her like she'd said something slightly funny?

"In short, the marquess wants a grandson to carry on the Lindstrom title. He is determined that it stay within his direct line, but as my brothers have issued nothing but girls thus far, he has now hinged his hopes on me. To his discontent, I refuse to re-marry."

Cassie lowered her brandy. It was no secret that Grant

was a widower. But she knew nothing of his previous marriage and had never sought out the information. Years ago, after they first met, when she'd thought of him far too often, she'd thought that the less she knew of him, the less she could be tempted to care. And the less envious she could be of his dead wife, as ridiculous as that now seemed to her.

"The marquess has threatened to cut you off," she guessed, recalling what he'd said in the carriage earlier.

He twitched his cheek. "He has."

"You work for a living, don't you? Maybe you don't need your income from him."

"Being a physician isn't as lucrative as one might think. Especially when you work for free half of the time."

Cassie sighed and sipped her brandy. "I don't see how a fake courtship will help you. Why don't you just marry someone?"

The muscles along his jaw rippled. "It isn't as simple as that."

"Isn't it?" she challenged, still unclear on what it was he wanted from her. A pretend courtship could not go on indefinitely. "Men do it all the time."

Cold silence rushed in on the wake of her flippant comment. All warmth and civility leached from Grant's expression, and when he took a single, long stride toward her, she felt like a small animal that had suddenly become prey.

"Once you marry for love, it's a little difficult to lower your standards." Grant sealed his lips, his square jaw clenching again. He let out an exhalation and turned away from her, fingers combing through his hair.

Stunned, Cassie's fingers squeezed her glass. He'd

married for love. A streak of something unpleasant twisted through her. She chose to ignore it.

"Her name was Sarah?"

Audrey had mentioned her name once.

Grant nodded. "Yes."

She would not ask how she died. That, too, was no secret. As was the stillborn child he'd buried alongside his wife.

"You've not explained how pretending to court would benefit either of us," she reminded him, lest he start to think she was softening toward him.

"Within a month, my brother's wife will bear a child. If it is a boy, the marquess will be appeased. I'm confident he will retract his latest edict."

"And until then, you will pretend to set your cap toward me?"

The haunted look in his eyes while speaking of his late wife dissipated, and the glib, devil-may-care one returned. "And you will revel in my attention, giving my father every reason to believe I've made my selection."

Cassie began to shake her head, but he cut her off before she could speak. "Trust me, I don't want to marry any more than you do. There will be no contracts, no banns posted, no official anything. But it will get my father off my back for these next few fortnights, and I imagine it will also give you a respite from the duke's attempts to fob you off on some unsuspecting buffoon."

Cassie balked. "You are forgetting that you, sir, are a rake. A rogue. A man of ill-repute. Not to mention that you *work*. The duke will not be happy in the least to believe I have accepted your suit!"

A slick grin twisted his lips.

"Which do you think he will be angrier about? His sister, falling for a cad, or his sister, operating an East End safe house filled with ruined women?"

Cassie slammed her snifter onto the desk so hard she heard the glass crack. "Are you threatening to expose Hope House if I don't agree to this scheme of yours?"

Grant shrugged insouciantly. "We both have secrets we don't want getting out. We both have endeavors we wish to protect."

She could not believe this man! How could she have ever thought him at all charming? "Your father would merely cut you off. You would be the furthest thing from destitute. While my entire reputation would be ruined! One of us has significantly more to lose than the other."

Grant hitched his chin and took a deep breath, his sooty eyes narrowing on her. For the barest moment, she believed he would retract his disgusting ultimatum. That he still possessed a single shred of dignity. But he only exhaled and waved a hand through the air. "Then I suggest you take me up on my offer."

The rapid boiling of her blood overtook her so swiftly, Cassie wasn't even fully aware of her hand reaching for her brandy. But then, it was hurtling through the air, toward Grant Thornton's head. He barely sidestepped it, gawking at her as the snifter crashed to the floor behind him.

"Christ, woman! You could have put out my eye!"

Her chest heaved as she suppressed the urge to scream. "You ought to leave before the whole the decanter comes at your head!"

He held out his arms, as if to say, *As you wish*. He strode from the study without another word. But he wasn't a man to give in easily. This wasn't over. Not by a long shot.

CHAPTER
EIGHT

The kitchen at the Church Street clinic was starting to look lived in. Grant had come by to check in on Isabel and Tris each day for the last two days, the first time in late morning, the second day, in the late afternoon. Each time, Cassie had not been there. Instead, he'd found Tris and Isabel in the kitchen together, attempting to cook.

"She can hardly boil water." The driver's good-natured complaint elicited a mock gasp of insult from the young woman.

"How am I to know? I've never needed to learn!" she'd said with a laugh.

That one exchange had left Grant in no doubt—Isabel was quality. Which meant the man she was running from was quality too. Thankfully, she appeared less fearful with Tris. The two were getting on well.

It was improper for a young lady of her class to be living in a house, alone with a man. A man of a servant's status at that. However, whatever qualms Grant had about the arrangement were alleviated by the incontestable fact that the young lady was with child, unmarried, and thus, already thoroughly ruined.

"Miss Banks has already been by, along with Miss Khan," Tris told him on the third day. Grant had gone to the clinic under the pretenses of restocking a supply shelf, when in truth, he'd hoped to find Cassie there. It had been two full days since she'd pitched a glass of brandy at his head. Two days since he'd abandoned all honor and given her a wretched choice: agree to his plan or suffer the consequences.

Telling Fournier about Hope House would cement Cassie's hatred for Grant, and he didn't want that. What he wanted was a temporary reprieve from the godawful matchmaking his father had commenced.

The dinner Grant had forced himself to attend after leaving Cassie's home had been tortuous. Two simpering young ladies of modest means, and even more modest appearances, along with their overeager mothers and disinterested fathers had been placed near him at the marquess's dinner table. Thankfully, the ladies had barely said a word to Grant, preferring instead to flay each other with resentful glares. The two mothers played at the competition as well, lauding their daughters with increasingly ludicrous claims of beauty and talent. All the while, Grant sipped copious amounts of wine—and thought of Cassie in her study.

Her arm had trembled when pouring herself the brandy that would eventually come sailing at his head. Had it been pure anger that made her shake? Her sharpened pupils and quick breaths had resembled panic more than fury. Until, of course, he'd made his ultimatum. *Then* it had been open and unquenchable rage. With her temper pinking her cheeks, her berry red lips parted with the urge to scream, Grant had felt the virago's desire to do him bodily harm. To come at him, fists flailing, legs kicking, teeth snapping. And strangely enough, he'd wanted her to try.

Seated at the marquess's dinner table, pointedly ignoring the company, he'd felt the stirring of his blood. The thickening of breath in his lungs. Had she launched herself at him, rather than the glass of brandy, he was quite sure he'd have enjoyed the resulting tussle.

It was that imaginary wrangling that had kept his blood high, and his mind locked on Cassie Sinclair, the last two days as he went from Church Street to Hope House and back again, failing to cross paths with her at any point.

Thinking she might be hiding from him inside her little office, he'd sneaked to it after leaving Dorie. He'd peeked behind her desk to be sure she wasn't crouching—something he could picture her doing—and had seen a ledger, open on the desk. He had no excuse other than bald curiosity for picking it up and running through the columns. Cassie, it appeared, oversaw Hope House's financials, and what he'd seen wasn't good. They were operating on next to nothing. He'd put the ledger back as he'd found it and mused over what more he might be able to offer her in exchange for agreeing to a false courtship. But she had too much damn pride to take his money, even if she was in desperate need of it.

The stubborn woman would come to her senses. The courtship would be merely a temporary ruse to alleviate the pressure from the marquess, but also from the duke. Yes, she had a point—Fournier might not favor the suit of a man with a reputation like Grant's. But he was also in no position to disallow the match, not with Cassie having surpassed her majority. She *was* still young, barely twenty-three. Hell, when he'd been her age, he had not yet even met Sarah. In comparison, at thirty-two, he felt like an old man. As if he'd been run through the mill a time or two, emerging calloused and weary.

Or perhaps that was just due to the last two nights of miserable sleep.

He left Church Street after making sure Tris and Isabel had enough food to sustain them, and to warn them that come Saturday morning, the free clinic would be open for business. During that time, it would be best if they remained in the upstairs rooms. The fever Dorie had started to recover from was still running through the East End and there was sure to be some patients coming in with symptoms.

When his carriage was about to turn toward St. James's Square, Grant's impatience with Cassie's silence abruptly ended. Her residence wasn't very far from his own. He slammed a fist against the wall.

"Grosvenor Square, Merryton," he called to his driver. "Number twelve."

Calling on Cassie in the early evening and in full view of passersby on one of London's most fashionable squares would set tongues wagging—and in the direction Grant wanted.

He descended from the carriage, and to his luck, Lord and Lady Stanwick were strolling toward him on the pavements. He bowed and greeted them before approaching the front door to number twelve. Glimpsing over his shoulder, he saw the lady facing forward again. He grinned, knowing she'd seen his intended destination.

The front door opened, revealing a footman.

"Lord Grant Thornton to see Lady Cassandra," he said.

"Her ladyship is out, my lord. Would you care to leave your card?"

Out?

"Out where?"

At the impertinent question, the footman pressed down a brow in disapproval. Grant flashed what he hoped looked like a reticent smile. "I only ask because I have an important message for her, from the Viscountess Neatham. It is urgent," he added. "*Very* urgent. I've been tasked with finding Lady Cassandra. Right now."

With every ridiculous additional plea, the skepticism drifted from the footman's pressed brow. He clearly knew the viscountess and Cassie were close. Hugh and Audrey, however, had been in Surrey as of late, and Grant hadn't heard a peep from them in weeks.

"Her ladyship has recently left for the King's Theatre, my lord."

Grant thanked him and returned to his carriage, his mind cranking through possibilities. Cassie may have used the opera as an excuse and was instead on her way to Crispin Street. Or she might actually be attending the performance tonight. *The Duenna*, if he wasn't mistaken. The marquess kept a box there, and at dinner the other evening, had attempted to draw Grant into inviting one of the debs to attend with him. Ballocks to that. However, now the theatre practically glowed like a beacon.

"Home, Merryton," he said to his driver before jumping into the carriage.

If he was attending the opera, he needed to make himself presentable.

HE ARRIVED a half hour into the first act, but to his credit, he wasn't the only one. Operagoers were mingling in the foyer and in the corridors outside the house floor as Grant found his way to his father's rented box. For many, the performance was a backdrop for the true entertainment of the night—social gossip. The lighting in the house was not even fully dimmed when the orchestra in the pit began to play and the actors took to the stage. How then would the attendees be able to see who was with whom? The whispered hum of voices underneath the music always grated on Grant's nerves. People would continue to talk, uncaring of the performance unfolding on the stage. It was one of the reasons he didn't often utilize his father's box. The other reason greeted him the moment he opened the arched door and stepped inside.

The Marquess of Lindstrom twisted to see who had just joined him, a grimace fixed to the hard lines of his face.

"I see you came alone," he said, relaxing into his seat again. There were six in total in the box, which was raised three tiers above the house.

Grant removed his hat. "I thought we could have some quality father-son time."

The marquess grunted, refusing to respond to the obvious sarcasm. "Miss Green's two older sisters have born six males between them," he said. "If you are wise, you will press your suit."

"Which one was Miss Green? The one with the overly large teeth or the one whose right shoulder was higher than the left?"

Grant took the cushioned seat next to his father. He couldn't help himself; provoking him was as natural as breathing. After spending most of his youth trying, and failing, to earn even just a sliver of the marquess's regard, Grant had given up. And then he'd discovered the one thing he could never fail at with his father: needling him.

"You aren't taking my directive seriously," the marquess said. "The lady's appearance does not signify. The Lindstrom title has been in our direct lineage for five generations, and I will not see it diverted, even when I am in the grave."

Grant exhaled, having grown accustomed to this little speech. He also knew how to cut it off at its knees.

"Which one is your tart?" he asked his father, gesturing loosely toward the stage. Lindstrom was about as fond of the theatre as Grant. The only reason for him to be here, alone, would be to take in the performance of his current mistress. Actresses were his preference, though at times, he strayed to widows and even the occasional courtesan. Twenty years the marchioness had been dead, taken by influenza, but the marquess had never remarried. He hadn't needed to, what with four sons. With spare heirs aplenty, the title had been secure. Until now.

"Do not be crass," the marquess grumbled. "Why are you here?"

"I love shrill voices."

Grant leaned forward and swept a look toward the Duke of Fournier's usual rented box along the fourth tier. Four people occupied it, but only one captured his full attention.

Cassie's hair had been braided into a golden crown winking with diamond pins. Her silver gown glittered with crystals too. She stared straight ahead, toward the stage, her gloved hand resting on the railing. She looked to be utterly entranced by the performance—and completely oblivious to the man seated beside her, utterly entranced by *her*.

Who the bloody hell was she with?

Behind them sat the duke and duchess, and the choice of seating could not have been any more transparent. Cassie and the mysterious gentleman were on full view for all to see and report upon.

"*Christ in hell*," Grant muttered. He sat back and pulled at the tall stock and cravat his valet, Clayton, had fashioned in the only way Grant allowed: irresponsibly loose.

"Did you hear me, boy?" The marquess was a gnat in his ear. He'd been saying something about Miss Green's several nephews while Grant had stared at the man seated with Cassie.

"Who is that man in Fournier's box?" Grant asked.

His father had an eye for beautiful women and found Cassie easily enough.

"Alaric Forsythe. Heir of the Baron Forsythe. Why?" Lindstrom huffed a mocking laugh. "Have you diddled with his intended?"

A hot blaze ran up Grant's back, under his tailored coat. The muscles in his legs tightened, ready to spring him to his feet. "*Intended*?"

"I heard it at Brooks's. He plans to make an offer. The duke is more than amenable. A good thing too. I'm told the chit needs to be taken in hand."

Heat continued to build under Grant's jacket as he stared

across the house. She damn well did need to be taken in hand. Not one mention of this Forsythe fellow had crossed her lips. Had he been the one she'd been running from the other week at Lady Dutton's ball? If so, why would she agree to attend the opera with him now?

Grant held his glare on Cassie. He willed her to feel the burn of his attention, to break her concentration from the stage and seek out the source of the eyes searing holes into the side of her devious face. He'd stood in her study a few nights ago and proposed a courtship. A fake one, yes, but the little pest could have at least done him the honor of mentioning that she was already courting someone.

He did not relent, even when his father snapped at him to stop staring like a madman. Finally, awareness distracted her gaze from the stage. Cassie turned her head to search the crowds seated below. She held still, then at last lifted her eyes. As if pulled by some magnetic force, they collided with his. Surprise rippled over her countenance, and her lips parted. She retracted her hand from the railing, as if Grant had reached across the void between them and touched it.

Forsythe, ignorant to her astonishment, said something, and she used the excuse to nip her eyes away from Grant. She tried to ignore him for another full minute but gave in and sneaked a peek in his direction. He had not so much as blinked.

She bridled, her lips forming a tight seam. Pleasure at vexing her sealed him to his seat, and he settled in for the remainder of the first act. He didn't pay an ounce of attention to the operatic performance, and he noticed Cassie's fixed concentration faltered too. The few times she peered toward the Lindstrom box, it was to find Grant still watching her, which only made her narrow her eyes on him further. Then there was the baron's son, Mr. Forsythe, and the bothersome way he kept leaning toward her ear. He was smitten with her, no doubt. The fool.

The curtain closed on the first act, and Grant shot to his feet, determined to hunt Cassie down in the corridors.

"Miss Green," the marquess said.

Grant stopped and stared at his father. "What?"

"You will call on Miss Green." He showed the bottom row of his teeth, the way he did whenever he had reached the limitations of his temper.

There was nothing to do but smile tightly, so Grant did and, without agreeing, left the box. Arguing with his father wasn't more important than tracking down Cassie and pressing her for answers. The crowds were thick in the narrow, carpeted halls circling the house, and it was slow going as he slipped between men and women, making apologies when he brushed against them. Cassie would not stay in Fournier's box for the intermission. Forsythe, the lovesick idiot, would want to fetch her punch or the like, and she would not wish to remain where Grant would know where to find her.

So, he made for the base of the stairs that came down from the fourth-tier boxes. He arrived just in time to see her emerge into the crowd, her swanlike neck craning in search of him. As soon as her eyes clapped onto him, she spun and disappeared into another throng of black evening suits.

The hunt had never interested him. Yapping hounds and boasting men, salivating to run down a fox or buck, had always struck Grant as base and bloodthirsty. And yet, Cassie's attempt to flee ignited a bloodlust he'd not felt before. He followed her as a hound did the scent of its prey. Upon catching her, he would need to show some civilized behavior, but civility was all but absent within him as his eyes locked on the back of her golden crown of hair. It pulled him through the crowd, into the refreshments room, where she was at last cornered.

She knew it, too. As Forsythe predictably left her side for the teeming punch table, she folded her hands in front of her and met Grant with an icy stare.

"I'm relieved you don't yet have a glass in that hand of yours," he said once she was within earshot.

"What do you want?" she rejoined, her chin high as she pretended to observe the crowd.

"An answer," he replied. "I've given you three days to think over my proposal—"

"It isn't a proposal, it is coercion."

"And I would like to know what I will be doing tomorrow," he continued as if she hadn't spoken. "Will I be penning a note to the duke, or will I be paying you a call and inviting you for a drive on Rotten Row?"

Cassie stifled her fury, though poorly; a passing lady took a long, concerned look in her direction before whispering to the man at her side.

"You, my lord, have had these last three days to see the sense in your obscene proposition and every opportunity to retract it."

"I'm not retracting anything." He snagged a glass of champagne from a passing server's tray. "And I rather think you don't want me to."

Curiosity tempered her glare. "How do you mean?"

Grant raised his eyes toward the refreshments table and

the baron's son waiting patiently to edge his way in. "What are you doing here with that oaf?"

"He isn't an oaf," she said in swift defense. "He is a historian and an archaeologist. Mr. Forsythe is extremely interesting."

"Yes, which is why you haven't paid him a moment's attention all evening." She'd been too occupied looking at Grant. Something he found himself surprisingly triumphant about.

"Only because you've been watching me like...like *that*."

He laughed. "Like what?"

"Like you wanted to leap into my theatre box and..." She stopped herself.

Grant turned toward her, intrigued now. Especially when her cheeks began to turn pink. "And?"

Cassie faltered, and he presumed she would back down. He should have known better.

She turned to face him as he had her, to meet his challenge, her blue irises stormy. "And sink your teeth into me."

The hum of the room's noise muffled. The pulse in his throat slowed. It then gave a throb to catch up, and unintentionally, he let out a chuff of air. Well. He hadn't expected *that*. The image her words brought forth made his tongue thick, his brain, fuzzy. He was unprepared for the heat coiling through his groin too.

A light of victory began to cut through Cassie's turbulent eyes. He shook off the stupor and smirked. "I'm saving that for Rotten Row tomorrow afternoon."

She stepped closer. Or perhaps he'd been the one to do so. Her scent of sun-drenched apricots filled his nose.

"Tomorrow is Saturday. You would abandon your precious clinic to engage in this farce of yours?"

"Not at all. I have help at the clinic and am perfectly able to leave early to escort you, *darling*."

She fumed. "I will refuse you on the spot."

"Don't mistake my pleasant countenance for bluffing, Lady Cassandra. I *will* go to your brother."

"Are you such a villain that you would expose a charity home serving women in need?"

"No, my lady. I am only villain enough to expose *you*."

It was unctuous and repellant. And yet her simmering response to his overblown threats brought him a terrible pleasure. It was sinfully wrong of him, he knew. He wasn't a villain. At least, he didn't think of himself as one. If push came to shove, he would be hard pressed to follow through with telling the duke. However, for the moment, it was far too entertaining, too wickedly enjoyable, watching Cassie squirm.

"Ah, Lord Thornton, if I am correct?"

Cassie severed her scalding glare and whipped around to greet the newly returned Mr. Forsythe. Grant flashed his teeth. It made him think of Cassie's comment about sinking them into her. *Hellfire*.

"Mr. Forsythe. A pleasure."

The man seemed pleased by Grant's familiarity, yet he wasn't sure how the baron's son had known him. Perhaps his reputation truly did precede him.

He handed Cassie an overly full glass of punch. She took it, careful not to spill it and stain her gloves. Grant smothered a laugh.

"Are you enjoying the performance?" Mr. Forsythe asked.

Up close, Grant could see he wasn't unpleasant to look at. He would be considered handsome among the female set, in a boyish, open, and amiable way. But Cassie could not possibly be serious about this man. The duke had to have set this evening up.

With his gaze still latched onto the lady, Grant sipped his champagne and replied, "Immensely."

After an awkward moment of quiet between the three of them, a man came toward Forsythe, drawing his attention. Grant leaned toward Cassie, and his lips brushed the shell of her ear. "I will call on you tomorrow at three o'clock."

He lingered an extra heartbeat near her ear, inhaling the scent of warm fruit, before stepping away. His head did not clear as quickly as he'd hoped. That was when he knew this would be a dangerous game.

CHAPTER NINE

Cassie was beginning to think all men, no matter their rank or relation to her, were manipulative deceivers.

The previous week, Michael had pleaded with her to attend an upcoming performance at the opera with him and Genie, and to placate him, she'd agreed. But as soon as her brother had collected her in his carriage and set out for the theatre, he'd announced that they would be joined by Mr. Alaric Forsythe.

She'd been so preoccupied the last few days with thoughts of Grant and his heartless threat that everything else had fallen aside—including Michael's clear intent to pair her with Mr. Forsythe. It was the last thing she'd wanted to deal with after such a disappointing day. She'd gone to Marylebone to check in on a past resident of Hope House, Miss Emily Stafford. The young woman had turned her infant over for placement, and Cassie had helped her to find employment, to get back on her feet. But the drapers where Miss Stafford had successfully applied had informed Cassie that she was no longer employed there. She also was not at the lodging house Cassie had found for her. No one knew where she had gone, and now, Cassie could only hope that she was well.

It wasn't until she'd arrived back at Grosvenor Square feeling defeated, and Ruth had hurried her along to her bedchamber to dress, that she recalled her commitment to the opera. Being pleasant with Mr. Forsythe had been a chore she hadn't wanted. And then, when Grant Thornton cornered her, he'd drained her patience entirely.

The man deserved the glass of brandy thrown at his head the other evening. He was the lowest, vilest, most unscrupulous blackguard to propose what he had. To possess a reputation as a rake was one thing, but to compel her to help him put off his father's demands of marriage by engaging in a fake courtship was despicable. And to use the secret of Hope House as leverage was even more contemptible.

Would he truly tell Michael? She didn't know Grant well enough to be sure. He tended to treat everything like a merry joke, but he'd appeared utterly sincere in her study while laying out his proposal—or rather, his self-serving demands.

Avoiding him for the last few days had been successful, but exhausting. She'd constantly been on the lookout for him, wondering whether he would turn up at the safe house or on her front step. So, when Mr. Forsythe had turned out to be amiable company, she'd started to relax. Unlike some of the other suitors Michael had singled out for her, he was interesting—just as she'd told Grant in the refreshments room. The horrible man hadn't believed her, of course. However, Mr. Forsythe had regaled her with a few fascinating stories of his time in Egypt and the architectural explorations in which he'd taken part. He hadn't dominated the conversation with tales about himself, either; he'd asked her questions about her interests, and what places she'd enjoyed while traveling the Continent.

A few times during the beginning of the first act at the King's Theatre, she'd sneaked glances at Mr. Forsythe and imagined kissing him. Would she like it? She thought she might but couldn't be sure. She'd thought of the missing Miss Stafford then, and the things the young woman had once told her about the father of her baby. Or rather, the things she'd felt whenever the man so much as looked at her. *I couldn't help myself*, she'd admitted. *It had been like a demon possessed me. Nothing else mattered but him. Not even air.* Cassie had peered at Mr. Forsythe, curious if she could feel such a thing with him.

He wasn't very tall. Not like Grant, whose cravat knot was at her eye level. He wasn't as broad shouldered as the physician, either. Nor did he look like the sort of man who boxed regularly to keep his arms and chest muscular. Her palms had itched at the memory of feeling Grant's chest through his waistcoat inside Lady Dutton's guest chamber's closet.

Then again, Mr. Forsythe did not make her want to scream in frustration. He didn't make her feel hot or restless or accosted. He didn't look at her as if all manner of dark thoughts were swirling through his mind.

At the theatre, when Grant had stared daggers at her, she nearly felt branded. As if he was furious to have caught her with another man. It was utter tripe! She had not yet agreed to his scheme.

But if she didn't...would Grant see his threat through?

That was the question nagging her as she made her way to the free clinic the afternoon following the opera. It was just past one o'clock when she left for Whitechapel. He'd said he would call on her, but she wasn't prepared to have Grant Thornton showing up on her doorstep for all of society to observe. So, she'd decided she would go to him. She might even be able to talk him out of a stroll in Hyde Park.

Bitterness filled her as she descended from her carriage into the mews behind the clinic. Nothing Grant could say or do now would improve her opinion of him. Being at his mercy wasn't fair. Why shouldn't he be at hers? He had a secret too, one that would damage his reputation heartily. But men always recovered from scandals. They always had access to more money. Women, not so much.

As she approached the back entrance to the clinic, a single door set above three warped wooden board steps, a man with a bandaged ear emerged from within. He looked her over, then cut away, fast. Cassie stepped inside, aware she did not look at all suited for such a place. She had found Isabel and Tris together in the kitchen a few times now, their growing interest evident. Cassie's reluctance to leave them alone, to spend the nights under the same roof, had left her in a quandary. But perhaps it wasn't any of Cassie's business. Isabel was with child and needed protection; Tris was a good young man. Cassie trusted him, and apparently, so did Isabel.

Now, as she entered the kitchen, another young woman stood at the stove, holding a pair of steel tongs. She dipped a glass tube into boiling water.

"Doctor Brown is closing the clinic earlier than usual today. Unless it is an emergency—" She looked over her shoulder as she spoke and went quiet. Her keen brown eyes took in Cassie's appearance in a single sweep. "You're not here for the clinic."

"No. Though I am here to see the doctor."

The young woman wore a dark blue gown with a white pinafore, and her brown curls were piled up under a mob cap. She was pretty in a plain and straightforward way. No emotion showed on her face, except for an arch of a brow, which could have meant anything. Surprise. Condescension. Amusement.

"You must be Lady Cassandra Sinclair." She pulled the steaming glass tube from the water and laid it down on a towel. "Or would you rather me address you as Miss Banks?"

Her pulse skipped. "He told you?"

"Your secrets are safe with Miss Matthews," Grant said as he appeared in the kitchen entrance.

He'd forgone a jacket and was in his waistcoat and shirtsleeves, the cuffs rolled to his elbows. He hitched his hands on his hips, drawing her mutinous attention to the defined muscles of his forearms.

"That was not for you to decide, doctor."

He grinned at her response, as if it gratified him.

"Wasn't I supposed to call on you at three o'clock?" He took out his fob watch. "It is barely two. Why, Lady Cassandra, your eagerness gives me hope."

She glared at him as he went toward the stove where Miss Matthews was drying the glass tubing and attempting to mask her amused grin.

"Mr. Osterfield was the last patient for the day," he said. "I can take care of cleaning up the rest. Merryton should arrive any moment. He will take you home." He laid his hand on the young woman's shoulder and leaned toward her ear, to whisper something inaudible. She pulled back, laughed, and then jabbed him in the chest with her elbow. Grant rubbed the spot, pretending it hurt.

A sour sensation erupted in Cassie's stomach, all sharp corners and claws. She instantly suppressed it. Or tried to. There was absolutely no chance she was envious of this young woman for having a private, playful moment with Grant Thornton. Cassie averted her eyes when he turned back to her, all lightheartedness gone from his expression.

"Follow me, my lady," he said, and then led the way from the kitchen. Cassie knew the building; she'd been here a few times. Thankfully, when he was not present.

"How is Isabel?" she asked. It would be good to check in on her. But Grant pushed open the front sitting room door and stepped aside, an arm outstretched for her to enter.

"The last I checked she was reading Shakespeare to your driver. He was listening to her every word, rapt. Though I'm not entirely certain that is due to the bard's talent for prose."

Cassie entered the sitting room, which had been transformed into a surgery with a desk, chairs, a padded table for patients, glass-fronted cabinets, and a hulking contraption standing over the patient table. With its many chiseled lenses, it resembled a lighthouse lantern.

"Gracious, what is this thing?" she asked, going to it. The hollow interior was filled with several candles.

Grant followed her. "I had it made. The candlelight from within hits the lenses and reflects more brightly than regular lanterns. It works wonders when I'm trying to see into a wound, or in Mr. Osterfield's case, an ear canal."

She recalled that the man leaving through the back door had a bandaged ear. "What was wrong with his ear?"

Grant peered at her a prolonged moment before answering. "A sliver of wood. He sustained the injury when someone hit him in the head with a piece of a broken table during a tavern brawl. It was causing a fair amount of pain."

"You removed it?"

"He didn't come to me for me to leave it in."

Cassie ignored his sarcasm as she wandered around the tall lantern, a finger trailing along the smooth lenses. "Does Miss Matthews assist you?"

"You're asking me questions to avoid the conversation we need to have."

She gaped, taken aback at the accusation. "I am not." She'd merely been curious about the woman in the kitchen.

Grant rolled down the cuff of one sleeve. The motion was slow and oddly intimate.

"Hannah assists me here and at my home surgery, at Thornton House."

"So, she knows the truth? That you're a peer?"

At his nod, she felt those claws under her skin sharpen. Why did this trouble her? It shouldn't. She refused to let it. So what if a pretty young woman assisted Grant here and at his home? So what if he trusted her with what he'd claimed to be his most crucial secret? And now, with Cassie's.

"That bothers you," he observed.

She had been quiet too long. Lost in her own muddled head. "You should not have told her about Miss Banks without my permission."

He finished with one sleeve and then began to roll down the other. "She is as trustworthy as Tris is. Hannah is my late wife's sister. They were close. When she expressed an interest in assisting me, I indulged her, even though my brothers and father staunchly objected."

The claws retracted a little. Annoyed with her reaction over Miss Matthews, Cassie walked toward the other side of the office, if only to put distance between them.

"Why have you come?" he asked. She decided to be honest.

"To avoid having you blacken my doorstep."

"You are delaying the inevitable."

Lead slid into her stomach. She was, though she hated to admit it. Grant Thornton was not trustworthy or honorable enough for her to believe he would not see his threat through to the very end.

But even though she would play his game, she would not make things simple for him. "What of Mr. Forsythe?"

He didn't quite flinch, but she noticed the flexing of his jaw. "What of him?"

"I've grown rather fond of him," she replied.

Grant snorted. "You have not."

"Do not presume to tell me who I am and am not fond of."

As if baited by the challenge, he came toward her. Each stride radiated malevolence. "While we are courting, you will not see Mr. Forsythe, or any other man. Is that clear?"

The demand made sense, as continuing to see other men would indicate that she had not settled on a beau, and their courtship would not be taken seriously by the marquess. But it also smacked of possessive envy. It set her back on her heels.

But then, Cassie formed a saccharine grin. "Tell me, Lord Thornton, what is your plan if this nephew you're bargaining on enters the world as a niece?"

There was, after all, a fifty-fifty chance of it.

Grant reached his desk and, crossing his arms, leaned a hip against the edge. "I will worry about that when the time arrives. However, you have my word that either way, I will release you from our courtship. You may end things then as you see fit."

"I would trust the word of a gentleman, but you, sir, are not that."

A devilish grin pinned the center of his cheeks, drawing her eyes to twin dimples. It was not adorable in the least.

"Come now, Lady Cassandra, I am a gentleman at least forty percent of the time."

She pretended not to hear him. "The duke will not allow a drawn-out courtship. He will corner you before long and demand you offer."

Grant chuckled. "I rather think he will corner me and demand I sod off. But I wager we have a fortnight before that happens."

"*We* have nothing," she retorted swiftly. But then, more calmly, she returned to negotiations. "I am the one who will cry off. And it will be because you have done something wretched and unforgivable."

He assented with a nod. "That will be more than believable."

"I will allow no liberties," she added, her voice quavering while naming the condition.

Grant pushed off the desk and came near. Close enough for her to trace his scent of cinnamon and sandalwood. "I would give you my word that I will *take* no liberties, but there is that other sixty percent of the time that needs to be accounted for."

He wanted to get a rise out of her. Lead her into saying something he could use in some sarcastic remark. She wouldn't give it.

"You have something to lose too, Lord Thornton. Do not forget that." His clinic was important to him. Just as important as Hope House, she imagined.

"We both do," he conceded. "So let us agree. These next few fortnights don't have to be painful or unpleasant."

She hated that he'd led her into this scheme by force. He was dangling her freedom over her head, using it to coerce her. And then acting as if they were on equal footing. She gritted her teeth so violently, they ached.

"Fine."

He waited for her to say more, to form a new condition perhaps. When she didn't, he nodded succinctly and stepped away from her. "There is a ball Monday night. Lord and Lady Tennenbright's. I assume you've an invitation?"

She had received it last week and promptly set it aside. Lady Dutton's ball had been the first she'd attended in some time, and that had been a glorified failure.

"I do."

"Excellent. Attend. We will dance three times, and I'll keep you away from all the other men. That should signal to everyone that I have an interest in you."

The transactional performance left her cold. And furious.

"Is that all?" she asked, nipping her words.

Mischief brightened his eyes as he took his jacket from the back of his desk chair where he'd left it and inserted his arms. "It would help if you didn't look at me as you are right now, as though I resemble a slimy snail."

As soon as he said it, she felt the grimace tensing her facial muscles. She loosened them as well as she could.

"Just try to pretend to enjoy my company," he said.

"Very well. But no quadrilles." She held up a hand. "I hate the quadrille."

Cassie leaped as frantic pounding came at the front door.

"What in God's name..." Grant muttered, then headed for the front hall. Cassie followed, and the loud banging came again. Grant opened the door and a man rushed inside, a young boy in his arms.

"Mr. Mansouri, what's happened?" Grant asked, clearly familiar with him.

"It is Amir," the man said, taking the boy directly into the front room. Cassie jumped out of the way to let him pass. "He fell off a hitching post and caught his leg on a hook."

He settled the young boy on the examination table, his pant leg soaked in blood. Grant removed the jacket he'd just put on and, once again, began to roll his cuffs.

"Miss Banks," he said. She tore her eyes away from the boy's bloody leg. "Fetch Miss Matthews."

She nodded and hurried down the short hall. But the kitchen was empty.

"I think she must have left," she told Grant once she'd hurried back to the front room. The boy, about nine or ten, whimpered as Grant used a pair of shears to cut away his torn trouser.

"I did tell her to go for the evening," he said, his voice calm and measured. "Well then, Miss Banks, I'll need you to assist in her place."

"Me?" She felt glued to the spot as she looked on, the

bloody gash along Amir's calf already sending her stomach into a swirl.

Grant threw the shorn trouser leg to the floor and peered at her, slightly bemused. Then, he spoke to the boy. "Amir, this is Miss Jane Banks. She is going to be helping me."

The boy turned his dark brown eyes onto her. They were filled with doubt. When he bit his bottom lip against a whimper of pain, Cassie realized she was being silly. Of course she would help. The boy was injured, and his father was frantic with worry.

"Should I fetch some hot water?" she asked, shedding her pelisse and gloves.

"And a syringe and tincture of iodine," Grant replied, preoccupied as he inspected the gash. "You'll find them in the second cabinet, third shelf."

Cassie started moving, even though she was full of the same doubt that had been in Amir's expression. She searched for a bowl in the kitchen to fill with steaming water that remained on the stove. It sloshed over the brim and wet the floor as she returned to the office, where Grant had lit the large lantern. It sparkled light throughout the room.

"Place the bowl here, Miss Banks," he said, gesturing toward a small stand next to the examination table. She did, and then went to the cabinets for the syringe and tincture. She found them, along with a stack of clean linens.

Grant took the syringe and drew up water from the bowl.

"I have a riddle for you, Amir," he said. "What is something that belongs to you but is mostly used by others?"

The boy frowned, wincing as Grant used the syringe to

flush the gash of dirt and debris. "I don't know, Doctor Brown."

"Here's a hint. I just used it. So did your father when he brought you into my office."

Cassie bit back a grin as Grant flushed the wound a second, then a third time. All the while, Amir pinched his brow in thought. Then, he showed a toothy grin.

"My name!"

"Nicely done," Grant said while dribbling the purplish liquid he'd called iodine over the gash. "Miss Banks, hold this to the wound, please."

He placed a linen over the boy's leg and beckoned her forward. Cassie reached her hand out, hesitantly. Grant gently took it and, pulling her closer, placed her palm onto the linen. "That's right. Light pressure, like that. Good, all right, here's another for you, Amir."

As he went to his cabinets and collected some more items, he recited another riddle. "What is light as a feather, and yet the strongest person in the world cannot hold it for five minutes?"

Mr. Mansouri crushed his cap and looked on as Grant returned with black suturing floss and a curved needle.

"That don't make no sense," Amir said, then guessed, "Air?"

"Very close," Grant said, lifting Cassie's hand. "Thank you, Miss Banks," he murmured, his eyes meeting hers for a moment.

How could he be so calm? He was entirely relaxed, moving about with confidence and dexterity.

"Here is a hint: if you fall into the Thames, you best do this quick."

Amir smacked his head with his palm. "Hold my breath! That's the answer. Breath."

Grant praised him again, and then turned serious. "All right, Amir. I've got to place some sutures to close this wound. Are you ready? I promise to be as fast as possible."

The boy squeezed his eyes shut and nodded.

"How about a contest between yourself and Miss Banks?" Grant proposed as he placed the first stitch. "Shall we see who can answer this next riddle first?"

Cassie shook her head. "I am terrible at riddles."

"Amir is very good," Grant replied, "so my money is on him. Here it is: Give me a drink, and I die. Feed me, and I grow bigger. What am I?"

He worked swiftly, his hands moving with ease and grace. Amir kept his eyes pinched shut, his nose crinkled.

"A drink of what?" the boy asked.

"Water."

Cassie knew the competition was supposed to be between herself and Amir, but her mind couldn't focus on the riddle. Instead, she watched Grant with burgeoning wonder. He was distracting the boy from the pain of the sutures with these riddles, putting him at ease. It was unexpectedly considerate.

"Do you need a hint?" Grant asked, the wound nearly closed.

"No," Amir insisted. "Does Miss Banks?"

Grant laughed and shot her a quick glimpse. "Does she?"

She held up her palms. "I confess, I'm at a loss."

"I know it!" Amir said before Grant could give a hint. "Fire! Water kills it, but feeding it makes it bigger."

Cassie goggled at the boy, sincerely impressed, as Grant

cheered him. He then snipped the ends of the floss and then went to his cabinets again. He returned with a small glass jar and a roll of cotton linen.

"Miss Banks is going to wrap your leg after I apply some ointment," he said, handing her the roll before she could make any objection. He applied liberal daubs to the puckered red wound, and Cassie then began wrapping Amir's skinny calf and shin, careful not to pull too tightly. It was awkward going, and she was certain she wasn't nearly as efficient or skilled as Miss Matthews would have been, but when she tied off the wrapping, Grant nodded in approval.

"Well done. What do you think, Amir? Is Miss Banks's work satisfactory?"

The boy turned his leg gingerly. "She's good at knots. But rubbish at riddles."

Mr. Mansouri hushed the boy as Grant cracked a laugh. Cassie parted her lips in mock offense.

"Thank you, Doctor Brown. And Miss Banks," the father said. "Next week, I'll bring you something fresh from my cart, reeled in that day."

Grant helped Amir down, and as he walked Mr. Mansouri and his son into the front hall, gave instructions on keeping the wound clean, changing the bandage every day, and sending for him should the wound swell and weep anything other than clear or yellow pus. He was to return next Saturday so Grant could look at the sutures. Cassie's stomach cinched again, her head swimming a little as she grimaced.

"How do you do it?" she asked as Grant re-entered the office alone.

He went to the bowl of water and washed his hands. "Medical school helped."

"No, I mean how do you stay so calm? So composed?" She held up her own hands; they trembled, and she'd only placed the bandage on Amir's leg!

Grant noticed, and after drying his hands, went to a cabinet. He opened it and pulled out a blanket. "You should have seen me the first time I placed sutures at university. My hands shook like mad. The sutures turned out a mess, too. The patient probably still curses my name."

He brought her the blanket and draped it around her shoulders.

"I'm not cold," she protested.

"The shivering isn't from cold, it's from a rush of nerves. A bodily reaction to sudden stress." Grant didn't step away. He kept his hands on her shoulders. "Bringing up your body temperature will help reduce the shivers." He rubbed her upper arms, as if to help build friction and heat. It was oddly comforting.

"You did well," he told her.

"I barely did anything of note. Which makes my stress shivers entirely ridiculous."

"You could have refused to help me. Could have left. But you stayed." He cocked his head, forcing her to meet his gaze.

He stood close enough for her to see an amber band around each pupil, the striations radiating through his green irises.

"You were good with him. Amir," she said.

"So were you." His hands rasped up and down her arms, through the blanket.

As promised, she began to warm, and the shivers started

to ease. But something else grew in its wake. An uncoiling in her stomach.

"Where did you learn all those riddles?" she asked.

"My tutor, growing up. He liked to torture me with them."

She could hear his distraction as he gave his answer, so different than how he'd been while attending Amir. His mind was somewhere else entirely.

She held her breath as one of his hands swept up her arm again, and this time, came off her shoulder. The coarse pads of his fingers touched her cheek and stroked back, toward her ear. Instinctively, she turned her cheek into his warm palm. Cassie exhaled, her half-lidded gaze centered on Grant's cravat. The looseness of the neckcloth exposed some of his throat and, thanks to the still lit lantern, bright light reflected off his skin.

"Are you feeling better?" he asked in a restrained whisper.

His other hand drifted down her arm and continued, past the edge of the blanket and onto her gown. His fingers curved over her hip, igniting an electric current where he touched.

"Yes," she breathed in answer. "Much better."

His palm pressed against her, settling firmly onto her hip. As his thumb lifted from her cheek and rubbed along her bottom lip, Cassie closed her eyes. An involuntary sigh rose up her throat. A surge of desire muffled her hearing and beat through her body. The blanket had turned her skin into a furnace.

The scuffing of boots coming down the stairs shattered the trancelike state.

Cassie gasped and jerked away from him so forcefully she

backed into the examination table, rattling it. Grant's heated gaze cooled as he spun away from her and went toward his desk a mere moment before Tris entered the office.

Tris narrowed his eyes, but acted like nothing was amiss. "My lady, Isabel was wondering if that was your voice she heard."

Cassie tossed off the blanket, suddenly cold again, and charged toward her pelisse and gloves, where she'd left them on the chair.

"I'll come up and say hello before I have Patrick drive me home." She didn't look at Grant as she started toward the sitting room exit.

"Do not forget the Tennenbright's ball," Grant said, his voice overly incisive and commanding.

It was all the reminder she needed for good sense to slap back into her. She could not afford to soften toward him, not even in the slightest. She'd lost her wits once with a rogue and look where that had gotten her.

She wouldn't make the same mistake again.

CHAPTER
TEN

A hand clapped down onto Grant's shoulder and shoved him. He'd been taking a sip of wine, and now, a splash crested the rim of the glass and wet his upper lip. It nearly dribbled down his chin, onto his snowy cravat.

"Christ," he hissed when he saw the man who'd come to his side.

"Having a difficult time drinking, Thornton? Perhaps you should've remained in the nursery." Hugh Marsden, the Viscount Neatham, chuckled as Grant brought out a kerchief to wipe his mouth.

"What in hell are you doing here?" he asked, cursing his friend's wretched timing.

He shot a look out into the crowd, just as he'd been doing since he arrived a half hour ago. Lady Tennenbright's gala was packed to the crown moulding with members of the ton, but so far, the person for whom he had attended had yet to arrive.

"Your tender greeting warms my heart," Hugh replied.

"You're supposed to be at Cranleigh."

Not here, in London, where he would bear witness to the arrangement Grant had all but strongarmed Cassie into.

Hugh looked out into the crowd with a pinch of distaste. He wasn't fond of such events. Raised as the illegitimate ward of the late Viscount Neatham, Hugh had lived most of his life on the fringes of society, cast out as a good-for-nothing blackguard. He'd been an officer at Bow Street when he'd met Audrey Sinclair, then the Duchess of Fournier, who at the time had been married to the previous duke. Right from the start, Grant had seen his friend's interest in the duchess, even though it had taken Hugh some more time before he'd admitted it to himself. But though Audrey and the duke had married out of friendship, and the duke's romantic interest lay with men, she'd still been the wife of a peer—and thoroughly off-limits. The duke's untimely death had given Hugh and Audrey the opportunity to be together, and now, they were living in happily wedded bliss with their young daughter, Catherine.

"Audrey and I have returned to Town for Christmas, and her sister, Lady Montague, wished for her to attend tonight," he explained. Then, he glanced toward Grant suspiciously. "But what of you? Did you take a wrong turn somewhere and arrive at a society ball by mistake?"

Grant sipped his wine again. Hugh knew his habits and his preference for events hosted by demimonde rather than ton.

"I thought a change to the routine would be beneficial," he answered.

"Beneficial for whom?"

Grant lowered his glass. Being vague with a former Bow

Street officer as sharp as Hugh Marsden was destined to fail. His friend was going to learn of it anyhow. Best be out with it.

He parted his lips but faltered on the first syllable. And then, he ceased speaking all together. Across the room, a throng of guests parted, and Cassie appeared.

Her chin was high, her eyes searching the ballroom floor. For him, he imagined. Hours after Cassie had left the Church Street clinic, his palm had continued to feel the soft, firm curve of her hip that he'd gripped through her gown. He'd lost his bloody mind, touching her like that. And yet, he'd been a man possessed. Had Tris not come clomping down the stairs to interrupt the heated moment, Grant would have taken Cassie's lips in a kiss. He might have done worse. And from the little moan she'd emitted when he'd pulled his thumb across her perfectly lush bottom lip, she would have allowed worse. The sound still echoed in his ears.

She hadn't come to the ball alone. Fournier and the duchess stood nearby, as did Cassie's other brother, Tobias. The midnight blue, satin gown she wore accentuated her figure with precision, drawing Grant's attention to her modest, yet delectable bosom.

No. *No, no, no,* he had to get his head on straight.

He'd tried the last two nights to do just that. After leaving the clinic, he'd gone to the Fallen Arch in search of Miss Martha Devereaux, whom he had an off and on again, no-feelings-attached arrangement. She was a bit scandalous and tended to fall for married men. However, she also had a weakness for widowers. She'd not been at the club the first night, and though there had been plenty of other women there to take his mind from Cassie, the first such woman to sit in his lap had laughed too shrilly for him to endure her attentions for more than one minute. He'd left, cured of the painful attraction that had nearly blinded him at the clinic when he'd been so close to Cassie.

The second night, he'd forgone the club altogether and sent a note to Martha directly. However, after she arrived, something happened that had never happened before—her usual charms failed to entice.

"I'm not feeling myself, I'm afraid," he'd told her. She'd peered at him with concern, even offering to nurse him back to health—sans clothing. But in the end, he'd made his excuses, and she'd left after a drink.

What in hell was wrong with him?

"Are you going to answer me?" Hugh asked.

Grant couldn't even recall the question. He passed his empty wine glass to Hugh. "Excuse me," he said, and started across the ballroom floor.

Cassie spotted him several strides in, the flare of her eyes doing something unwholesome to him. She appeared nervous as he came through the crowds, directly toward her. He shouldn't have liked the influence he had over her, the upper hand he'd secured in this game. But he needed to maintain it. And that meant not giving in to the physical desire he felt for her.

Grant came to a stop in front of her and bowed his head. "Lady Cassandra."

Fournier came forward. "Ah, Thornton. Good evening."

He greeted the duke with another bow. "Your Grace." In any other circumstances, such formality wouldn't be necessary; he and Fournier were well acquainted already. But considering what he was about to do, the show of respect was vital.

Grant turned back to Cassie. "May I have the next dance, Lady Cassandra?"

Pink seared the apples of her cheeks. From the corner of his eye, he witnessed the duchess, Genie, lifting a gloved palm to her chest, as if in surprise. Fournier cleared his throat, and Tobias's forehead crinkled in surprise. None of them spoke. Not even Cassie.

Grant waited, holding her ever widening gaze. He had no plan for what he'd do should she not respond. To give him the cut so publicly would surely be satisfying for her, especially if she'd gone home Saturday in a high dudgeon. She'd had plenty of time to stew about his *taking liberties*, as she'd clearly stated were off the table. Was this her revenge?

Just when he thought he might have to employ some sarcastic quip to salvage his pride, Cassie murmured, "Yes."

His breath went out at the single word, which was fortuitously punctuated by the first strains of a waltz. Grant held out his hand, and Cassie fed her fingers into it. They joined a few other couples already in the center of the dancefloor, his palm settling on her upper back. His other hand gripped hers as they extended their arms.

"You enjoyed making me sweat back there," he murmured as they commenced.

She moved skillfully, her hand resting lightly on his shoulder. Her eyes would not meet his. "I wager no woman has ever made you sweat, Lord Thornton. You always get exactly what you want, don't you?"

All right then. She was angry. Rightfully so, he supposed.

"No one gets everything they want, my lady," he replied

as their legs moved in time, taking them in an expanding twirl around the ballroom. "For instance, I did not want Hugh and Audrey to return to London just now. Low and behold, they are here."

She flicked a devilish look up at him. "Worried the viscount will think you a scoundrel?"

"He already knows I am. That's not what worries me."

"Then what does?"

"He knows me better than anyone. He'll figure out what we're doing, fast."

"Do not imply that I am your willing cohort." She skewered him with a glare. Then quickly softened it, likely recalling they were supposed to be taking their first dance together as a newly smitten couple.

Grant's eyes scraped the periphery of the ballroom floor and landed on Hugh Marsden. His friend stood with his viscountess at his side, the pair of them watching Grant and Cassie with matching concern.

"I cannot lie well to Hugh," he admitted through gritted teeth, wanting to keep his lips from forming words. Here, lip-reading was as much a skill as embroidery or playing the pianoforte.

"So long as you can successfully deceive the marquess, that is all that matters, isn't it?" she replied.

The word *deceive* struck him low in the gut. However, he would allow it to stand. Yes, he would deceive his father and without an ounce of remorse.

"You keep pretending this won't be beneficial for you as well," he replied. "Two more waltzes tonight, and Fournier may well dance a jig all the way home."

Under his hand upon her back, he felt the spasm of a

laugh, quickly swallowed. The twinge of victory at having made her laugh was short lived.

"You do not know my brother," she said. "As I've already said, he thinks you are a degenerate. He won't approve of any courtship, especially one that lasts for more than two weeks. Your plan is faulty, sir."

They spun, and the close hold required for the waltz brought the front of Cassie's body into contact with his. He moved his palm inward on her back. Hell, he wished he wore no gloves so his fingertips could touch her bare, soft skin. Cassie's fingers tensed on his shoulder.

"Yesterday…at my office," he began, intending to apologize.

"Please, don't speak of it."

He peered down at her, but she was staring at his cravat. "Why not?"

"It was a mistake."

It was the same thing he had told himself time and again since it happened. And yet now his response was: "It didn't feel like a mistake."

Her attention lifted from the neckcloth knot, and he had a mere second to appear confident in his assertion rather than panicked. *Why had he said that?*

"It was, I assure you. And no, this isn't beneficial for me. Whispers will begin that we are attached—"

"That is the plan," he said, spinning her toward a less populated portion of the dancefloor.

"No, that is *your* plan, and you've twisted my arm into helping you. Hope House is my purpose, it's my life, and I won't allow you and your loose tongue to ruin it."

"Cassie, you're losing your temper," he warned, catching a glimpse of the duke's hard stare from the other side of the dance floor. Grant peeled her a few inches away from his chest.

"What do you care, so long as you get your courtship? Yes, I am going along with it, but I know exactly what sort of man you are."

He slowed them now that they'd reached the outer edge of dancing couples. "What sort is that, exactly? And softly, if you please, I've no wish to read our conversation in *All the Chatter* tomorrow."

Nonetheless, the popular gossip rag would surely feature their intense waltz. They continued to hold each other in the waltz pose, taking languid turns around a small section of ballroom floor. "The kind of man who is ruled by whim and desire and privilege," she answered.

He came to a stop and led her from the floor, toward a potted palm and two wallflowers sipping punch alone in their chairs. They had but a moment before someone descended upon them. "What is this all about? You're furious with me right now, and not just because of this scheme."

"Of course it is."

"Then where was this fury of yours yesterday in my office when you wanted me to kiss you?"

She sucked in a breath. "I did not."

"Do not lie. You wanted it as much as I did."

Cassie's teeth bit her bottom lip, directing his attention there. And then, they were no longer alone.

"Lady Cassandra." A male voice pierced the hot bubble that had formed around them. Grant dragged in a breath and turned to see Mr. Forsythe. God save him, Grant wanted to knock out the grinning fool's front teeth.

Cassie, too, inhaled sharply, and pasted on a bright smile for the baron's heir. "Good evening, Mr. Forsythe. What a pleasure that you're here."

The warm and enthusiastic greeting was a blade between Grant's ribs.

"May I have the next dance, my lady?" Forsythe asked with an overindulgent bow in which his forehead practically bounced off the floor.

Cassie twisted the blade between Grant's ribs as she held her hand out. "That would be lovely."

Without a word, Grant jerked his head in a terse bow as she left, admitting defeat. For the moment. The woman knew how to get under his skin and work him to a simmer. But he was not deterred. He would have his next two dances and secure the wagging of tongues across London by morning, even if he had to murder Forsythe and then stuff his body in the cloakroom to get him out of the way.

"What is it you think you are doing?"

Grant didn't flinch this time as Hugh joined him. The viscount's voice was low and serious.

"I merely asked the lady to dance," Grant answered as he watched Cassie and Mr. Forsythe join the next set, which was, to Grant's pleasure, a quadrille. Something she'd confessed to hating.

"You cannot dally with Cassandra, you idiot," Hugh bit off.

Audrey kept a troubled eye on their conversation from where she and her sister, Lady Montague, stood with their hostess, Lady Tennenbright.

"I have no plans to." He couldn't dupe Cassie when she was informed of everything.

Hugh signaled a passing server and took a glass of wine. "I've been in Surrey too long. What is going on between the two of you?"

"I can't share all my sordid secrets with you," Grant said blithely, though it would not pass muster. Not with Hugh. He was entirely aware that he was on a collision course with his friend's true anger.

"You are my closest friend, Thornton," Hugh began. "But if you hurt Cassie, I will knock your teeth out."

Grant split his attention from Cassie's vexed expression as she spun in and out of line for the quadrille, changing partners here and there. He met Hugh's unyielding stare. He was as serious as anything.

"You're awfully protective."

"Audrey adores her. She's a sister to her." Hugh took a breath, then a sip of wine. "And she's been hurt before."

Grant came alert, interest zinging along the back of his neck, up his scalp. "When? By whom?"

Hugh's humorless expression changed to one of smug mischief. "I can't share all my sordid secrets with you."

He wasn't amused. "What happened?"

"Not for me to say. Just mind yourself." He started away, toward his wife. Then stopped and added, "If you aren't serious about her, do not cross the line. I don't want to have to be your second when Fournier calls you out."

CHAPTER ELEVEN

Thick curtains draped the windows in the sitting room at Hope House, blocking any natural sunlight. To protect the women from outsiders peering in, Elyse and Cassie had hung them in all the windows facing the street. It made visibility a challenge sometimes, especially when Sister Nan arrived from the church in Shadwell each week to give lessons in anything from lace-making to darning to how to properly care for infants. Some of the women, like Caroline Rawling who already had children, didn't need many lessons, but it did help her to stay busy. Others learned a great deal.

Cassie's contribution was tutoring in letters and numbers. Most of the women didn't know how to read, or did not read well, so if someone expressed an interest, Cassie helped. She'd brought some of the primers that had been boxed away in Violet House's attics from when she was younger but had been careful to go through each to be sure there were no scribbles of names or anything that could reveal her identity. It was a precarious situation; if anyone in society learned of her work, she'd be ridiculed and ruined. If the women here found out she was a lady, they wouldn't trust her or feel comfortable around her. It was just the way of things. Elyse had advised her on that in the beginning, as gently as possible. She'd been right. Cassie's privilege far outweighed that of these women, and they would feel it keenly. Hope House needed to be a place of refuge that they could trust. A place where they could be on equal footing.

Two afternoons following the Tennenbright ball, it felt more like a refuge than ever for Cassie. She'd arrived earlier than usual for the second morning in a row, in time to greet Elyse as she was returning from a birth in Stepney. It had been an all-night affair, and when Elyse came into the kitchen with dark circles under her eyes and a grimace, Cassie had quickly brought her a cup of tea.

"Was it a bad outcome?" she'd chanced asking after her friend had sipped the strong brew. At her solemn nod, Cassie reached for her arm.

"I'm sorry." There was nothing else to be said that would make a difference. "I'll go stoke the stove in your room while you have your tea. You need some rest."

It was a small gesture of care, and though it didn't feel like enough, it was all Cassie could do.

When noon arrived, ushered in by Sister Nan's pert knock upon the back door, she had successfully avoided thinking of the ball, Lord Thornton, and their near kiss in his clinic by going through ledgers and compiling a list for the market stalls to give to Sister Agatha. The moment her mind veered toward a memory of Grant's hand on her hip, or his thumb tugging her bottom lip as he stared covetously at it, or the unwelcome thunder bolt though her body when he'd stalked across the ballroom to ask her to dance, Cassie simply found something else to do. So, Sister Nan's arrival was most welcome.

The older nun sat at the head of the sitting room with her knitting needles, showing Dorie and another young woman, Miranda, how to place the fragile stitches of fine cotton silk she'd brought for tatting lessons. Making lace could be a profitable endeavor for them after they returned home, or started fresh, away from their families. Caroline and Cassie sat a corner table, the primer open and a sheet of writing paper next to it.

"That's excellent," Cassie said as the older woman completed copying one of the sentences in the primer. "Really, you've a smooth hand for penmanship."

Caroline sat back to view her work. Then placed a hand on the shelf of her round stomach. She winced.

"Is something happening?" Cassie asked. But she shook her head.

"No, just regular quickening."

Cassie recalled the sensation with startling ease. What had been the light fluttering of butterfly wings in the beginning, turned into restless and sometimes painful nudging of elbows, feet, and knees as space became limited. Every movement had been a reassurance that all was well, and yet also a reminder that it was all Cassie would be given of her child. Those jabs had been a wonder to place her hand over and feel. The yearning to hold her child, to see its face, had been perilously strong, too. But always, always accompanied by the knowledge that she would give her child away to someone else.

Cassie placed her hand on Caroline's arm. She, too, faced

the same moment. It came closer with every passing day. Caroline sniffed and patted Cassie's hand.

"It's all right there, luv," she said. "Sister Nan says she's found a nice couple who can't have none for themselves. They've got a house in Islington. Even has a small yard for the tot."

Thinking of what was best for the child was the only way she would get through. Cassie knew that firsthand.

Sister Nan stood from her chair then, leaving Dorie and Miranda to practice their stitches. Dorie was still weak from her bout of illness, but at least today, she'd left her room.

"Did the woman I sent 'round ever make her way here?" Nan asked as she took the other chair at the table.

"When was this?" Cassie inquired.

"Tuesday last week."

Cassie shook her head. "No one new since Dorie." Isabel, Miranda, and Caroline had all been there for longer.

The nun frowned and rubbed her chin. "I was afraid of that. The lady was strange. She wasn't showing just yet, but she also didn't look young enough for it. Mind you, it wouldn't be the first time a woman past her prime found herself increasing quite by accident."

"What else about her was strange?"

"There was something about her manner. Can't describe it. After I told her how to find Hope House, I followed her. Saw her meet a man down the street. He'd been waiting for her, it looked like. They spoke, then they went their separate ways."

The small hairs along Cassie's arms lifted. Next to her, Caroline made a soft murmur of concern.

"Do you think the woman could have been lying?" Caroline asked. "Trying to find the location of the clinic for this man?"

It had been Wednesday, the day after Sister Nan's account, when the man in the alleyway had come upon Cassie, demanding to be taken to Isabel.

"I fear you're correct," Cassie said with an ill sweep of foreboding. "Sister Nan, I know you aim to keep every young woman's confidence but were you the one to send Isa—" She caught herself, recalling Isabel had come here as Lila. "Lila. Did you send Lila here? Three weeks ago?"

Isabel had been so guarded she hadn't mentioned who had sent her to Hope House.

At Sister Nan's nod, Cassie's stomach sank. "She was such a quiet thing. Frightened, I think." She looked around the room. "Where is Lila this week?"

Cassie should have thought to ask Nan sooner. She sat forward, fully alert. "Did she say anything about herself? Anything about her family? Or the father?"

"Bits and pieces. Sad tale. No family. Just an aunt after her parents perished in a fire a handful of years back. She was reared well, that one. I'd wager gentry at the least." Sister Nan nodded as if impressed. "As for the father of the babe, she stayed mum about him. Caught herself once when she started to say his name though."

"Can you recall what she started to say?"

"Young," Nan answered without hesitation. "Mr. Young."

Cassie sat back in her chair. Mr. Young. And maybe an upper-class gentleman. Or even a peer.

"There have to be scores of Youngs in London," Caroline said.

"Where is Lila?" the sister asked again.

When Cassie informed her of what had occurred, and that her name was in truth Isabel, her lips went slack.

"This is all my doing," she said. "I shouldn't've said a word to that woman. I knew she was shifty!"

"It isn't your doing at all," Cassie assured her. "From what Isabel said, this Mr. Young is a dangerous man. Can you describe him at all?"

Sister Nan closed her eyes and thought deeply. "Cut a fine figure. Top hat. Black greatcoat. A moustache. Brown hair, maybe. He looked like a toff."

It wasn't much to go on, but Cassie thanked her. It was at least more than they'd known earlier. And now, it made sense how Mr. Young had come to find Hope House. It felt much like a weasel having been caught circling the hen house.

"Is the girl safe?" Sister Nan asked.

"Yes," Cassie answered, though she stopped short of saying where she'd been taken. The fewer people who knew, the safer Isabel would be.

Shortly before one o'clock, she took her leave from Crispin Street. She was expected by Jane Riverton and Marianna Dutton for a shopping stroll along Bond Street, something she had no interest in but also could not avoid. The last two days, a small mountain of notes and calling cards had piled onto a tray in the foyer. Callers, including the incurably inquisitive Lady Dutton, had come by, and many more had sent invitations to tea while Cassie had hid in her room. All because of her three dances with Lord Grant Thornton at the Tennenbright ball. Jane's invitation was the only one she'd responded to. She would have rather avoided all social interaction, but it would be noted upon, and the last thing she wanted was more interest directed her way.

Cassie arrived on the busy stretch of Bond Street near Lindquist's as Jane had instructed, the command as terse in her note as it would have been in person. The fashionable dressmaker was Jane's favorite, and she was likely ordering a whole new collection for the spring. Cassie would order something too, have it put on the duke's account, and then perhaps after a visit to another shop, she could make her excuses and leave.

Patrick handed her down from the carriage. She had expertly changed from her flannel cape and plain bonnet back into her finer velvet pelisse, hat, and gloves along the way from Spitalfields. But she'd begun to wonder... For how long could she keep up this pretense? For how long could she live, split between two worlds? Grant had been doing it for five years, and by the looks of things, successfully. But he was a man. Men were not scrutinized nearly as closely as women were. Men were expected *not* to be at home, but to be out and busy doing important things.

Bond Street was one such place they might go. Tobacconists, tailors, and haberdashers were strung all along the popular street, as were clubs for fencing and boxing and other, more licentious sports. So, when a familiar masculine figure in a top hat and caped greatcoat caught her attention across the street, she should not have stopped in her tracks the way she did. Curse her wretched luck!

Grant didn't see her as he walked with hasty purpose. She hoped he'd turn into a shop before he could. Cassie held still on the pavement, not wanting to move in case it caught his eye. Ridiculous, considering the whole street bustled noisily. Perhaps it was her sudden stillness that did her in.

As if feeling her gaze on him from across the busy street, Grant glanced up. His eyes locked onto hers. He lifted his chin and slowed his swift pace. The mischievous smirk he wore so often and so well slid into place. Taking the brim of his hat, Grant tugged it gently, acknowledging her.

"Lady Cassandra." Marianna's high-pitched voice blared in her ear, and Cassie nearly jumped out of her skin. Marianna and Jane had come to stand right next to her, their hands tucked into fur mufflers and their attentions drifting across the street, toward the physician.

"We've an appointment, Cassie, do come," Jane said tightly, and then turned to go inside.

Cassie followed as a few carriages rolled by in succession, blocking her view of Grant. Once in the shop, they were settled in a private corner for their appointment, thankfully away from the front windows. After tea service was delivered, Jane folded her hands in her lap.

"Details. We want all of them. Now."

Cassie stirred a cube of sugar into her assam. "There isn't much to say."

"Hogwash," Jane tutted, eliciting a shocked gasp from Marianna. "I read the column about Lady Tennenbright's ball in *All the Chatter* along with everyone else in Town. Are you claiming you did not dance three sets with Lord Thornton?"

The gossip rag had not lied. She'd danced twice more with Grant at the ball, just as he'd wanted. And just as he'd vowed to do, he'd kept Mr. Forsythe at bay—along with every other man in attendance. As predicted, gossip had quickly taken root about their noticeable attachment. The column in *All the Chatter* had even mentioned the possessiveness Grant displayed. It should have irritated her. It should have made her feel anything other than slightly gratified, or marginally delighted. But gratified and delighted she was, and all because of that blasted moment in his Church Street office.

No, she could not dwell on it. Not again.

"People are jumping to conclusions much too quickly," Cassie said, still uneasy with the idea of the courtship going public. It made her oddly hot and her pulse exasperatingly fluttery. "Lord Thornton asked me to dance. That is all."

Marianna grinned with a deviousness she rarely displayed. "*Three times*. And you accepted *three times*. You know what that means."

Cassie lifted her cup and saucer, a quiver in her wrists. "I do."

"But the man is a notorious seducer," Jane whispered forcefully. "And he works. My goodness, a physician for a duke's sister? I never thought I would say it, but I'd rather you not marry at all than marry a man of his character."

Cassie gripped the fine china of her teacup's bowed handle tight enough to snap it. "You speak as if I am already betrothed. I am not." She gathered a breath, fighting the urge to say more. To defend Grant's character.

"It is clearly what he intends," Jane replied.

Marianna leaned forward, her manner giddier and more curious than Jane's display of admonishment. "He *was* staring at you quite decisively the night of Lady Dutton's ball."

Jane scoffed. "I'm sure he stares at every woman in such a depraved way. Take just now for example. To look at you the way he did across a public street!"

Fearing for the teacup's handle, Cassie set her cup and saucer down with a clatter. His eyes had seared her on Bond Street, but the look had been rigidly proper in comparison to what happened in his Church Street office. There, he'd eclipsed the bounds of propriety. But...what of her? More than once, Cassie had wondered what she would have done to stop him, had Tris not come downstairs. Anything at all? Or would she have allowed Grant to kiss her?

The modiste approached their alcove, and after exchanging a few pleasantries, Jane instructed her as to what gowns she was looking to have made, in what fabrics and colors, and what designs. She left little room for the modiste to make any suggestions. Wisely, Mrs. Lindquist nodded and stepped away to collect samples.

"I urge you, Cassie, out of care for you and your reputation, you must distance yourself from the physician," Jane said once they were alone again. "I know he is the Viscount Neatham's close friend, and that must raise Lord Thornton in your esteem, however..." She paused to grimace. "Mr. Riverton has it on very good authority that Lord Thornton's mistress is a scandalous woman by the name of Miss Martha Devereaux. Mr. Riverton says she frequents one of the clubs right here on Bond Street. The kind that does not hang out a sign so as not to offend passing ladies. Goodness, that might have been where Lord Thornton was coming from just now! Cassie, you are being taken in by his charms."

She squirmed in her chair. Grant's *mistress*? He'd made

no mention of a mistress. Then again, why would he? The image of him meeting with this Martha Devereaux, a faceless woman in Cassie's imagination, sent a bolt of something bitter through her. It felt maddeningly like jealousy.

"I will not be 'taken in' by any man, I assure you."

But she had been, once; by Renfry. And then, at Grant's clinic, she'd let down her guard long enough for him to grope her hip, to nearly kiss her.

At the Tennenbright ball, she'd been on edge, and Grant had sensed it keenly enough to ask why she was angry. The obvious answer had been his scheme. But he'd known it wasn't that, and now, she admitted he was correct. She'd nearly let him take liberties. Had wanted him to. Even knowing what sort of rake he was, how their courtship was all a farce...she'd still done exactly as Jane had accused: fallen for his charms, if only momentarily.

Cassie had been furious with *herself*, not Grant. No, he was only being the depraved scoundrel that he proudly was.

A scowl was still fixed on Cassie's lips when one of Mrs. Lindquist's assistants came to their seating area, followed by who else, but the subject of their current conversation. She suppressed a groan as Grant doffed his hat. But that roguish smirk couldn't be so easily discarded. He directed it toward Cassie, Marianna, and Jane with equal intensity.

"Good afternoon, ladies," he said with a regal bow. Then, his attention fully on Cassie, "Lady Cassandra."

She bit her tongue. There could be no mistaking his intention. He wanted an introduction to her friends. Not to mention, to be seen inside a dressmaker's shop with Cassie would surely inspire more gossip about their attachment.

"Lord Thornton," she said, gritting her teeth. "May I introduce Mrs. Marianna Dutton and Mrs. Jane Riverton."

He bowed again, this time even more regally, if possible.

"I did not know you patronized Lindquist's, my lord," Jane said coldly.

As it was a dressmaker's shop, there was no earthly reason any unmarried man should be present.

"I cannot say any of the fabrics on hand would suit me, Mrs. Riverton. I merely wanted the pleasure of saying hello to Lady Cassandra and making your acquaintance."

His smooth charm would not work on Jane, but Marianna seemed to be melting beneath it, evidenced by the flush along her neck. Cassie refrained from rolling her eyes.

"What brings you to Bond Street, Lord Thornton?" she asked sharply. Jane's suggestion that he'd been visiting a club where his mistress frequented had swiftly rooted in her mind. That he might have just come from her... Cassie suddenly could not sit another moment. Just as Grant began to speak, she stood abruptly from her chair. Once standing, she had no excuse for it. Grant, Jane, and Marianna all stared at her quizzically.

"Are you unwell, my lady?" Mrs. Lindquist inquired as she returned with two assistants, each young woman holding bolts of fabric in the purples, greens, and blues Jane had requested. "You look piqued."

"Yes, I'm afraid I'm not feeling well," she said. The lie swiftly became truth when she met the gaze of one of the modiste's assistants.

Cold dread cascaded into her belly as recognition shone in Miss Emily Stafford's eyes. *Oh no.*

"Miss Banks?" Emily said softly. Then, realizing she'd spoken aloud, she took a small curtsey. Cassie's body went numb, her tongue heavy as lead.

"Miss Banks?" Jane echoed. "Why do you address her ladyship in this manner?"

"My apologies, my lady," Mrs. Lindquist said, shooting her assistant a look of reproach. "Miss Stafford is new here."

Embarrassment flooded Emily's expression, and guilt stabbed under Cassie's ribs. This wasn't her fault at all. She'd had no idea *this* was where Emily had gone from her old position at the drapers in Marylebone.

"Her ladyship?" Emily murmured as confusion joined her embarrassment.

"You have mistaken Lady Cassandra Sinclair for this *Miss Banks*," the modiste said, flustered and vexed by the gaffe.

Emily's shock drew her pale brows together. She didn't look to believe it, and for all the world, appeared ready to dispute it.

"Whoever this Miss Banks is," Grant took a stride forward to put himself between Cassie and the assistant, "she must greatly resemble Lady Cassandra, and for that Miss Banks should count herself as fortunate."

It was guileless and overly complimentary, but when her panicked stare lifted to him, she saw a shrewdness in his eyes.

"Mrs. Lindquist, if Lady Cassandra requires anything today, I insist you place it on my account."

Total silence followed Grant's statement. Heat suffused Cassie's body as what he'd just said and done wove its way through her already stuttering mind.

"That is...that is unnecessary, my lord, I shall have it

placed on the duke's account," she replied, her hoarse voice betraying her astonishment.

Taking her limp hand and bending over it, Grant put his lips to her knuckles. "I insist."

Marianna and Jane stared, openmouthed at the display, Jane with abject disapproval and Marianna with thrill. He could not pay for her clothing! It was indecent. It was what husbands did for their wives, or betrothed men did for their intended brides. Worse still, it was what men did for their mistresses.

As Grant took another bow and bid them a good afternoon, he cut Cassie a knowing arch of his brow. He was aware of what he'd just done. And as his eyes slid past Miss Emily Strafford—the disruption over calling her Miss Banks now completely overshadowed—she comprehended *why* he'd done it. To help her. And yet, in doing so, he'd also solidified the rumors of their attachment.

Cassie suffered through the first round of fabrics that Mrs. Lindquist showed to Jane, all the ladies pretending nothing untoward had just occurred. When the modiste left to fetch another few bolts in a different color palette, Cassie stood and apologized, saying that she was expected at Violet House. The lie wasn't contested, and she took her leave.

When she arrived home, she unpinned her hat roughly and impatiently shrugged out of her pelisse.

"A servant from Thornton House delivered this not long ago, my lady." Pierce, her footman, said as he presented a letter that topped yet another small mountain of notes and calling cards.

Cassie took it and detached the dark blue wax wafer,

pressed with a T. Inside, a brief message had been scrawled in the center of the paper.

I will pick you up at 8 o'clock tonight. - G

CASSIE LOWERED the paper with a fluttering of her pulse. What on earth was the interminable nuisance planning now?

CHAPTER TWELVE

As they entered the gallery inside Madame Archambeau's Kensington estate, Grant reluctantly treasured the sensation of Cassie's hand tightening around his arm.

"I don't recognize anyone," she said softly as they strolled across the black and white marble tiles.

"That is because we have stepped outside the bounds of polite society," he told her, keeping his voice low as well.

"And straight into the realm of depravity," Cassie rejoined.

Grant laughed. She had no idea what true depravity the demimonde had to offer. "This is as tame as a church sermon, Lady Cassandra." He leaned closer to her ear. "Did you truly believe I would take you to some illicit club?"

She stiffened at his side, her hand releasing the pressure she'd kept on his arm since walking toward the estate's front entrance. He regretted teasing her. She was in no mood for it. He'd sensed it when he'd arrived at number twelve Grosvenor Square at eight o'clock just as his message had informed her.

The footman who opened the door had bowed and said that her ladyship was not in. Grant had come prepared. "Please tell her ladyship that if that is the case, I have a dinner with the Duke of Fournier to attend."

He'd waited in the foyer while the footman delivered his response, and to his delight, Cassie had come to the top of the stairs, backlit by wall sconces. She was beautiful when she was furious.

"I could have a dinner with the marquess, if that is the game we are going to play," she'd said.

She'd been dressed and ready, as if she'd known she wouldn't be able to get out of their evening together. Or perhaps, hadn't been willing to try very hard.

"I don't think you would enjoy that very much," he'd replied. It was the truth, too. His father was an arse.

"About as much as I enjoyed the stunt you pulled at Lindquist's, I imagine," she'd shot back as she'd come down the stairs.

"It got their minds off Miss Banks, now didn't it?"

Cassie had not spoken again, ending all conversation until they'd been on the carriage ride to Kensington.

"I don't understand why we have to be at odds," Grant had finally said.

"Stop threatening to tell my brother about my work and perhaps we won't be."

"It isn't safe, Cassie. Look at what happened with Isabel's beau."

"Do not patronize me," she'd snapped. "Hope House is just as important as your clinic. And the father of Isabel's child is a shining example as to why."

Grant hadn't been able to argue with that. Once the heat of her temper had subsided, she'd drummed her fingers upon her thigh, draped in the burnt umber silk of her gown, embroidered with black thread and onyx crystals. Wearing it, she'd looked like a flame. Inviting, yet dangerous.

"Do you know a gentleman by the name of Mr. Young?" she'd asked.

He'd run the name through his mind, attempting to find a memory of it. But shook his head. "It isn't familiar. Why?"

She'd explained about the nun from St. Paul's unknowingly giving away the location of the safe house to a woman connected to who they now presumed was the man from the alley, Mr. Young.

"We should ask Isabel about him. Maybe she feels safe enough to tell us more," Cassie had suggested.

He'd not missed the way she'd included him in her plans.

"It would have been nice to know in advance where you were taking me tonight," Cassie now said, dragging Grant back to where they were, inside Madame Archambeau's vast manor. A short distance from Kensington Square, the home was fashionable and a bit wild. The city itself was a few miles east, and out here, it did feel more like countryside, with the spires of Town on the horizon.

"I thought I would surprise you," he told her as they joined a circle of guests surrounding a statue. It looked to be carved from pink marble. It, and a number of other statues, had been placed on plinths inside the large gallery. Madame Archambeau was a great patron of the art.

"I don't like surprises," Cassie replied as two guests in front of them stepped aside, allowing them to move closer.

But then, she tugged on his arm to keep him from taking another step.

"Grant!" A blush tinged her cheeks. Following the direction of her shocked stare, he looked to the statue. And immediately understood her reaction.

The pink marble had been chiseled into a detailed carving of a man and woman. The woman was on her knees, her arms stretching up to clutch the man who stood behind her, bracing her between his legs. One of the man's hands reached into her unbound hair, the other, cupped her breast. Their mutual expressions of rapture were well detailed.

"What kind of art is this?" she whispered, trying to tame her reaction when a few others glanced her way.

Grant drew her from the statue. "The kind that would never be admitted into the Royal Academy."

She stole another look as he directed them toward a servant holding a tray of champagne. The servant wore all white livery, a white curled wig, and his skin had been dusted with white powder. Grant took two glasses from the unblinking man, who had been made to look like a statue himself and pressed one into Cassie's hand.

"Madame Archambeau and her companion, Miss Stone, enjoy supporting anything polite society shuns," he explained. "Which is the reason I've brought us here tonight."

She sipped the champagne, her eyes peering around the gallery as though expecting to see more erotic sculptures. It was a good possibility she would.

"To show me indecent sculpture?"

He chuckled darkly, enjoying her scandalized reaction. "No, to introduce you to a potential benefactress."

Champagne went down her throat too quickly, and she spluttered. Her blue irises, ringed with steel gray, met his, looking just as shocked as when she'd seen the statue. "For Hope House?"

He gave a nod. "And for my clinic."

Cassie pondered that for a few moments as she cleared her throat.

"This is your next plan for if you do not receive a nephew," she said astutely.

"An alternate solution, yes."

Earlier that morning, James had called on Thornton House, and Grant had been reminded that he needed such a plan.

"The duke's sister? Really?" his brother said as he'd strode into Grant's study. "I heard Forsythe was pressing his suit."

The idea of the handsome young heir pressing anything toward Cassie had made Grant scowl. "Haven't heard of him," he'd said.

"He has Fournier's blessing."

"But he does not have Lady Cassandra's," Grant replied lightly.

That Forsythe might still be lurking about once Grant was no longer in need of a fake courtship, and that Cassie might actually declare him acceptable, unexpectedly grated.

"Father is having a dinner at Lindstrom House next Monday," James said.

Another dinner? Christ. Grant considered his next move. "Tell him to uninvite the debutantes, especially if one is Miss Green. I would like to introduce him to Lady Cassandra."

James's skeptical look had been sharp enough to draw

blood. "If you have some gambit in mind, I advise you to think twice. The duke will not take kindly to his sister being used as a pawn."

Grant ignored the warning. "Is your wife in labor yet?"

James had seen through that question too. "Don't hinge all your hope on my child being a boy. You'll only be disappointed."

Grant knew it wasn't wise to bargain everything on that child. But last Saturday, Mr. Mansouri's visit with Amir had only demonstrated just how essential the clinic was. Without proper cleaning and sutures and bandaging, Amir's wound would have become infected. In the end, he could have lost his leg. Or his life.

Cassie set her unfinished glass of champagne on a tray held by another statue servant, this one liveried in all red, with a tomato-colored wig and matching red powder on his face.

"Hope House doesn't need a benefactress," she said without meeting his gaze. "I have enough to keep it afloat."

Grant didn't know how much her per annum was from the duke, but the state of her ledgers had not shown thriving numbers.

"You are nearly insolvent, Cassie," he said. At her contemptuous glare, he admitted to his snooping in her office.

"You wretched, devious, interfering man!" she exploded, drawing some interested looks from around them. Thankfully, these were the kind of people who did not mind shows of impropriety. They generally looked forward to them.

"Do you have any other colorful adjectives to sling at me, or can I introduce you to Madame Archambeau?"

He understood her upset; he'd been snooping, and it had been completely out of line. Cassie had every right to upbraid him for it, however, just then he caught sight of the benefactress standing near another sculpture. Her usual white hair, powdered light blue, was piled atop her head in a regal Marie Antoinette fashion, and her gown was an array of all the different colors of the liveried servants scattered around the gallery. She was an eccentric, and proudly so. She was also unfailingly supportive of anything society frowned upon.

Cassie crossed her arms in a huff. She wouldn't look at him. "You had no right looking into my finances. My annuity is sufficient. I shall see a replenishment soon."

It would be paid out to her by Fournier near her birthday, most likely. A bank note that she would then turn in for ready cash.

"You're cutting it fine," he commented. "I sorely hope you weren't considering approaching a moneylender to tide you over."

She all but gnashed her teeth at him. "I am not that foolish, Lord Thornton."

The use of his title exposed her frustration. He exhaled and vowed not to rile her further.

"Just let me introduce you to Madame Archambeau." He held out his arm, and she shifted her jaw before assenting with a stiff nod.

Had the older woman been interested in men, he might have planned to charm her into funding the free clinic. But as it was common knowledge that her chosen companion was Miss Stone, who was never far from her side, Grant couldn't employ that tactic to his advantage. No, if she was going to lend her assistance, he would have to appeal to her based on the value of the charity alone.

At their approach, Madame Archambeau's mouth twitched into a curious grin.

"My, my, Lord Thornton. It has been ages since I've seen you at one of my exhibitions," she said, casting aside the conversation she'd been having with another guest.

"Madame," Grant said, sketching a bow. Then also bowed to her companion, who wore a far more understated gown. "Miss Stone, it's a pleasure."

She was the unmarried daughter of a gentry landholder, about ten years Madame Archambeau's junior, and almost completely devoid of facial expressions. How someone so serious and bland could have captured the affection of one of the demimonde's most eccentric personalities was a mystery. On the surface, they appeared to be complete opposites.

"And who is this magnificent creature on your arm, Thornton?" Madame Archambeau inquired, turning her interest toward Cassie.

He was nearly certain the woman already knew but made the proper introduction just the same.

"Ah, yes, Lady Cassandra of the three waltzes," she said with a fanciful wave of her gloved fingers. She turned toward Miss Stone. "It seems our wayward physician has stumbled out of the dark wood and found his way onto a well-trodden road at last."

Cassie's arm stiffened around his. Being likened to a "well-trodden road" could certainly come across as an insult, though he was rather hoping Madame Archambeau was referring to the road many take toward marriage.

"What fortunate artist has convinced you to display their

sculptures tonight?" Grant asked to redirect the conversation.

"Miss Constance Plumly. Isn't her work divine? I can introduce you if you like."

While he'd enjoyed seeing Cassie blush at the erotic sculpture, the art had not been his reason for attending tonight.

"Is it all..." Cassie began to say as she peered toward the closest statue. That one, carved of alabaster, resembled a lily, however the closer Grant looked, the more it appeared to be a representation of the female genitalia.

"All what, my lady?" Madame Archambeau said with a knowing smirk. "Indecent?"

Cassie chose another word. "Forthright."

Miss Stone's dour expression cracked with a small twitch of her mouth. "Bravo," she commented. "There is nothing indecent about the female form or the pleasure it can both give and receive. Only society and religious establishments try to convince us there is."

It was the most Grant had heard Miss Stone say at one time. Even her companion looked slightly taken aback.

"And yes, Miss Plumly's sculptures all follow the same theme," Miss Stone went on, answering Cassie's question.

Madame Archambeau shifted her inquisitive eye toward Cassie once again, as if wanting a second inspection of the person who had inspired Miss Stone to speak so passionately.

"Of course, magnifying such artistic talent is incredibly important," Grant said, striking while the iron was hot, "however, have you ever given any thought to throwing support behind charities that benefit those who are willfully overlooked by high society? Say..." He paused as if trying to think of a charity. "Vulnerable, unmarried lower-class women who are with child?"

He didn't have to look at Cassie to imagine her clenched jaw and rolling eyes. Admittedly, it had been a clunky delivery, but it got the job done. Madame Archambeau snapped her fingers and a servant dressed head to toe in banana yellow brought her a new glass of champagne.

"You have a charity in mind, I presume," she said.

"I do. Have you heard of Hope House?"

Cassie took a deep breath; he felt her ribs expand against his arm.

"I have not," Madame Archambeau answered. "Tell us about it."

Through his jacket, Grant felt Cassie's fingers pinch him. "Yes, that sounds fascinating, Lord Thornton. Do tell us more."

She couldn't do the honors herself. To be knowledgeable about it would only indicate that she was involved. And while the two women bucked convention at every opportunity, they were also shameless gossips.

So, Grant laid out the premise of Hope House as he knew it: a safe house for unmarried women, either wanting to have their baby in private and arranging for parish nuns to place the babes with good families, or escaping from those who would harm them and their unborn child. Cassie pinched him again, indicating he'd left something out. He had no idea what, however.

"I imagine such a place would serve women coming from many different situations," she said for him a moment later. "Those who are frightened or ashamed or feel they've nowhere to turn."

"How very true, Lady Cassandra," Miss Stone said, her grave expression now one of concern.

"Where is this Hope House?" Madame Archambeau asked.

"Its location is private," Grant answered. "Apparently, it is found via a sort of whisper network."

Sparks of interest flared in both women's eyes. The two exchanged a look and a nod. "Bring the organizer to us," Madame Archambeau said. Then with an inquisitive glance, said, "How very fortunate for them that you've learned of their endeavor."

He could have easily taken advantage of the moment to say he'd learned of Hope House through his free clinic, which also needed assistance. But their minds were trained on the safe house's mission; to falter at this moment could dilute their interest.

"I help where I can," he replied vaguely.

Madame Archambeau sipped her drink and gestured toward the rest of the gallery. "Do enjoy the rest of the art, Lady Cassandra."

"In a most *forthright* way," Miss Stone added with a playful smirk. The two women linked arms and moved along, ready to mingle with others.

Cassie turned her face toward his once they were alone again, wonderment dilating her pupils.

"Does that mean they want to help?" she whispered.

"I'd say so," he answered, grinning at her expression of breathless delight. Cassie nearly sagged against his arm as they walked aimlessly across the gallery floor.

"This is so wonderful. Oh, Grant, I never thought... I'll send Elyse! She can tell them everything, answer every question." She hopped twice, giddily. "When will you take her? Should you go tomorrow? Maybe that's too soon. But what if they forget about our conversation?"

"They won't forget," he assured her, pleased by her reaction.

Cassie's bright and bubbly reaction was a salve against the lost opportunity to make his own pitch. But there would be another time. He'd see to it then.

"We don't have to stay for the rest of the party," he told her as they entered a thicker crowd in the center of the gallery. "Unless you have a secret yearning to see—"

The suggestive comment, which would have likely earned him a jab in the ribs, was cut off as another guest slammed into him. Grant was solid and tall enough to not be spun around by the force of it, but it did send a splash of champagne over the lip of his glass. It also shoved Cassie aside, for which he turned to spear the clumsy offender with a glare of annoyance. He was met with a red-cheeked man who stood as tall as Grant, his cravat loose, his eyes unfocused from too much liquor.

"Ho, there, friend, sorry about that. Thornton, is that you?" the man said, clapping Grant on the shoulder. It was then that Grant recognized him. He looked a bit sloppy and soft around the paunch and jowls. But he was nearly certain this was Lord Renfry, the heir to the Bainbury earldom. The sleazy cad had seduced his own stepmothers, both of whom had died. Both murdered, in fact. The investigation had been one Hugh and Audrey had solved a handful of years ago, and Renfry's reputation had spiraled into the gutter since then.

At Grant's side, Cassie's arm transformed into inflexible granite. So, she knew of the degenerate, did she?

"Think nothing of it," he said, and then started away. Cassie's feet, however, stuck to the floor. Renfry clapped his hand onto Grant's forearm, this time to stop him.

He looked pointedly at the drunkard's hand, then to Renfry's face with the intent to sear him with reproach. But he was not paying attention to Grant. Renfry's eyes were hinged on Cassie.

"Lady Cassandra?" A mischievous grin pulled his wet lips into a leer. "It's been quite some time. You look well. Extremely well."

Grant had the urge to punch that leer clean off his mouth, but when he looked to Cassie, he forgot the urge. She'd lost all the pink coloring that had flooded her cheeks after leaving Madame Archambeau and Miss Stone. Her lips were slack, her pupils pinpricks as she stared up at Renfry. Her nostrils thinned as she took small, panicked breaths.

"My lady?" Grant whispered, alarm slowing his pulse.

Renfry chuffed a laugh, and instantly, Cassie averted her eyes. She turned her whole face away and loosened her grip on Grant's arm, as if she was about to flee. He tightened his hold.

"We were just leaving, Renfry," he said with more force and vitriol that necessary.

"Of course you were. Enjoy your evening, Thornton." The man snorted again before moving off, but Grant and Cassie were already walking away, her gait stiff and awkward at his side. She clutched his arm.

"I'm not feeling well," she said, breathless. "I'd like you to bring me home now."

He murmured yes, of course he would, while his mind spun in circles. It had not been difficult to interpret Renfry's tone when he'd wished him a good evening. The man believed Grant would be winning Cassie's favors. Why the hell would he suggest it? He clenched his jaw as they collected her pelisse and his coat and summoned the carriage.

He lost his patience as they waited outside on the crushed gravel drive, Cassie's quick breaths fogging the crisp night air.

"When did you make Renfry's acquaintance?"

She was no longer on his arm. Instead, she'd wrapped them around herself, her eyes on the drive, as if staring could make their carriage appear faster. She didn't answer.

"Cassie," he prodded.

"Some time ago."

"How did you meet him?"

"I don't recall."

Her brief answers worked underneath his skin. He kept his mouth shut as his carriage and driver came forward. Once they were enclosed inside and Merryton was turning them back down the drive, Grant spoke.

"I've never seen you this rattled."

"I'm not rattled. I told you—I'm not feeling well."

Her voice was high and panicked. She wouldn't look at him.

"What happened with Renfry?"

Cassie squeezed her eyes shut. "Please stop asking questions. *Please.*"

He rolled his shoulders, restless. Agitated. The way Renfry had looked at her, as if remembering something satisfying, pricked like a briar. Something had taken place between them. As they crossed out of Kensington and onto the well-lit King's Road, to travel through Hyde Park, he recalled what Hugh had said to him at the Tennenbright ball.

He'd had cautioned Grant against hurting Cassie; that she had already been hurt before.

He curled his hands into fists where they rested on his thighs. It had been *Renfry*.

"What happened between the two of you?"

Unshed tears glistened in her eyes when she opened them again, the interior carriage lantern illuminating her beseeching expression. "It is none of your concern. We are not truly courting, so I don't have to tell you anything."

The tears slipped, cutting down her cheeks. Angrily, she swiped them away.

Grant's whole body strung tight with the urge to pummel something. To leap from the carriage and go back to Archambeau Manor and hunt down the dissolute cretin.

"Did he harm you?" Vehemence pulled his voice low.

"Leave it alone. Grant, please," she pleaded again.

"I won't. Talk to me, Cassie. I know what Renfry is like. Did he..."

"Stop!" The word broke on a sob. She dropped her chin and covered her face with her hands. "I can't. Please, just *stop*."

Incandescent fury swarmed. It had been a long time since he'd felt this kind of rage. Unhinged. Directionless.

Grant dragged in a breath but said nothing more. If she wanted him to stop speaking, then he would stop. For now. But he would have answers. If Renfry had harmed her... The black thought drove him mad. Why hadn't Hugh *said* anything? How could he have allowed the man to remain breathing?

The rest of the ride back to Grosvenor Square was silent. Cassie refused to look at him, and when Merryton pulled up to the residence and opened the door, she all but leaped out.

As soon as Cassie had been safely received through the front entrance by her footman, Grant knocked the carriage wall. “To the boxing club, Merryton.”

He wasn’t ready to go home, and he had the powerful desire to hit something.

CHAPTER
THIRTEEN

Ruth said nothing as she set the breakfast tray on the foot of Cassie's bed. She didn't need to speak a word for her concern to come across plain as day. The lady's maid could control her tongue, but she'd never mastered controlling her expressions. The furrowing of her brow and the nibbling on her bottom lip gave her worry away.

"I'm not unwell, Ruth," Cassie assured her as she pushed herself up from where she'd been lying stretched on her side, staring out the window into the milky mid-morning sunshine. She sat against the bolster pillows and accepted the cup of tea her maid offered.

"Forgive me, milady, it's just that you're usually up long before now."

"I suppose I needed a morning to laze about," she said, hoping it would placate her.

Lazing about wasn't something Cassie did well. She liked to be busy, not bored. But that morning, she'd found all motivation sapped right out of her as soon as she opened her eyes. It was as though the muscles in her legs and arms simply didn't want to work. Sleep beckoned her, causing her to wake then fall asleep again, however light the slumber was. It was how it had been all night. After returning from the art showing, she'd gone to her room and held herself together while Ruth undressed her. Once the maid had finally taken her leave for the night, she'd crumpled. Literally.

The soft, thick pile of the carpet had padded the strike of her knees as she'd folded, sobs and tremors wracking her body for what felt like hours. Eventually, she'd crawled into bed and, exhausted from crying and from the overwhelm of seeing Lord Renfry again for the first time in years, fallen into a black, fathomless sleep.

But when morning arrived, the truth was waiting for her. It was why she'd stayed abed so long. She'd wanted to avoid it.

Cassie sipped her tea without tasting it. "I'm not hungry, Ruth. If you'll draw me a bath, I'll get ready."

There was no point avoiding anything now. Her unexpectedly wonderful meeting with Madame Archambeau and Miss Stone, all thanks to Grant, had been tainted by the appearance of Renfry and her disappointing inability to control her reaction to him. She thought she'd overcome everything that had happened. Countless times, she'd imagined what it would be like to meet with him again. The cold, stony glare she would level him with, how she would exude detachment and serenity, as if she thought nothing of him. Her poise and disinterest would assure Renfry that he was nothing to her.

Instead, she'd frozen. Her pulse had throbbed in her neck, her breaths becoming stilted and panicked. In that moment, with Renfry looking at her like she was something amusing, making her feel small and filthy, she'd been transported back years in time, to the very moment she'd read the wedding banns in the society pages for Lord Winston Renfry and Miss Evelyn Rothchild, the exorbitantly wealthy daughter of a shipping merchant. This, weeks after he'd promised to visit her brother Philip at Fournier Downs in Hertfordshire to ask for Cassie's hand in marriage. Weeks after he'd bedded her while whispering vows of love. And three days after she'd realized she was carrying his child.

All that pain, disappointment, and fury had surged up again last night and threatened to drown her. To make things cataclysmically worse, it had all happened in front of Grant Thornton.

She hadn't been able to look at him, too afraid he'd see the truth in her eyes. But of course, he needn't have made eye contact with her to know something had occurred between her and Renfry. His stifled anger, his hot confusion, had filled the carriage on the way back to Grosvenor Square. At least Grant had done her the honor of respecting her plea to stop asking questions.

It would not last.

She set her tea down and stood from bed. Her legs still felt heavy as she went toward the window. Looking out over the square, she could only think about what a tenuous life she led. Within a glass room, it seemed, where one crack in the thin wall could send the whole thing into shambles. First, her secrets about Hope House, and now, about Renfry and the baby. Good God, what would Grant think of her if he knew everything? As soon as she thought the question, she shook it off. Why should that matter? He might not be as depraved at Renfry, but he was still using her for his own gain. Would he truly go to Michael and reveal everything he knew about Hope House if she no longer played along with his scheme? Cassie didn't want to believe it. But she'd been wrong before. She'd made an awful misjudgment of character with Renfry. What a fool she'd been!

She would not make that same mistake with Grant Thornton.

Cassie bathed and dressed, and then jotted a letter to Emily Strafford, apologizing for what occurred the previous day. She thought to send it to the shop directly but after wondering if Mrs. Lindquist might open it, crumpled the letter and rewrote it. She wrote as Miss Banks instead, who had just heard from Lady Cassandra of the mix-up. She expressed hope that she was getting on well in her new position. There was no way to know if Emily would be able to infer the truth from the cryptic letter, and after sending it off, Cassie rubbed her eyes. Once again, she questioned how much longer until her life in Spitalfields erupted into her life in Mayfair.

Concerned though she was, she still set out for Crispin Street. Elyse was in, and when she saw Cassie, she drew her aside, into the privacy of her small bedchamber.

"I heard about Sister Nan's visit, and what she revealed about Mr. Young."

Instantly, Cassie flushed with guilt. She hadn't given anything to do with Mr. Young or Isabel a lick of thought yet that morning. She'd been too self-absorbed with everything having to do with Grant, Renfry, and Emily Stafford.

"I'm worried," Elyse went on, and indeed, the press of her brow emphasized it.

"As am I." Cassie felt the same jittery alarm as she had the afternoon before, when Sister Nan had explained how the man had tracked Isabel down. "If he knows our location, what is to stop him from breaking in? We have a few locks. No guard."

"Or he could make it public," Elyse added. She began to pace the braided rug, her fingers rubbing her temples. Cassie wished she knew the answer. Wished she could do something to put Elyse at ease. She'd given herself to this place. Her time, her energy, her skill. She was here day and night, while Cassie was able to come and go as she pleased.

She sat on the edge of Elyse's bed. "It's been over a week since he approached me in the alley—"

"He *attacked* you, Cassie, he didn't approach you."

"Yes, all right, attacked," she conceded, though she didn't like to make it sensational. Playing the matter down helped her to deny how dangerous the situation really had been. "My point is, it's been days. If he hasn't tried again, he might not be coming back. Perhaps he began to doubt Sister Nan's information. Or the woman who obtained it."

Elyse stopped pacing and then perched on the bed beside her. "I hope you're right. I would hate to have to shut this place down."

Cassie knocked into her shoulder. "What's this? Shut down? That wouldn't happen. We'd simply find a new location." She turned to face her friend. "I know I don't do much around here—"

"Stop it, that's not true."

"—but I can at least manage to keep a roof over everyone's heads."

Elyse smiled but looked doubtful. "I've seen our ledgers, Cass."

So had Grant, she thought, again prickling with annoyance. But that put her in mind of Madame Archambeau. With an excited hop that jounced them on the bed, Cassie told Elyse about her meeting with the benefactress the evening before. Elyse leaped to her feet when she heard about the invitation to call on them.

"You want me to go?" she exclaimed.

"It should be you," Cassie replied. "You're the one who runs Hope House."

Elyse eyed her curiously. "We run it together. Why are you discounting yourself?"

Cassie stood up and smoothed the skirt of her gown. "I'm not. I'm just being realistic. I can't apply for their aid—they know me as Lady Cassandra. I can't show any knowledge of Hope House without risking them saying something to the wrong person."

Elyse crossed her arms, nodding. "All right. I'll go. But goodness, what will I say?"

"We'll think of something," Cassie said, "though right now, we should visit Isabel."

As it wasn't a Saturday, Grant wouldn't be there. Hopefully. They left Hope House in Mabel and Sister Agatha's capable hands and took Cassie's carriage to Church Street.

On the way, Elyse inquired more about the benefactress, including how Cassie had even come to be introduced to her.

"There is something I should tell you about Doctor Brown," Cassie said. "His real name is Lord Grant Thornton."

Elyse jerked back, her eyes popping wide. "The rake you were stuck in a closet with?"

"Yes."

"Why did you not tell me before?"

"I don't know really. I suppose I didn't want you to despise him."

"Whyever not?"

What to say? That any time someone said something disparaging about Grant, she wanted to defend him? Even though she was constantly complaining about him herself. It made no sense.

"Well, for one, he's the reason we have the interest of Madame Archambeau," she said.

Elyse perked up. "Is he?" She frowned. "Well, that is kind of him. I suppose he received an invitation as well, to discuss his free clinic?"

Until then, Cassie hadn't thought of it. But Grant hadn't uttered a word about his clinic.

She shook her head, and Elyse sighed. "What is his game then?"

The midwife had never been very open about her private life, but Cassie could tell she had reservations about men and their intentions. But then, she huffed a laugh.

"A lord with a charity clinic and a *nom de guerre*." She arched a brow at Cassie. "How much you two have in common."

She nudged Elyse, refusing to rise to the bait. But her friend had a point. The clinic was of paramount importance to him, just as Hope House was to her. And it wasn't the clinic itself he cared about; the people it served were important to him. He'd shown that clearly with Mr. Mansouri and his son, Amir.

Cassie was thinking of the riddles he'd put to Amir, to distract the boy from the pain of his injury, when they arrived at Church Street. Patrick let them off down the street, out of caution, since they couldn't be sure if Mr. Young had still been watching the Crispin Street building. She and Elyse walked to the corner of the block, then went around and onto the mews lane. When Elyse knocked twice, then three times more, they heard footsteps approach. Tris appeared and ushered them inside before he shut and locked the door again.

"You're in time for stew," Isabel said gaily as she stood at the stove, stirring a steaming pot. Her flushed cheeks appeared fuller, and her eyes fairly sparkled when Tris joined her.

He had doffed his hat, allowing his black curls to spring unrestrained. "It's the rabbit stew my mum used to make," he said, leaning over the pot. "Though I think this smells even better than I recall."

"I thought you said I couldn't even boil water," Isabel replied.

He shrugged bashfully. "I suppose you've learned a thing or two since then."

The two of them looked at each other for a moment longer than strictly necessary, and Cassie exchanged a glance with Elyse. They both suppressed their grins. It appeared Tris was completely smitten with Isabel, and she with him. And here they'd been, alone together all week, allowed the freedom to converse and get to know each other. Cassie didn't want to think anything untoward had occurred between them. However, she easily recalled the moment in Grant's office, when the intensity of his closeness nearly stole away her good sense. Imagining a whole week alone with Grant in this house, with no one to interrupt them, made her belly flutter.

"The stew smells delicious," Elyse confirmed. "How are you feeling?"

Isabel let out a small laugh. "Mostly just tired."

Tris took the spoon from her hand. "Sit, and I'll stir."

She sighed as she sank into a chair, a look of appreciation cast toward Tris's back.

"Isabel," Cassie said after a few quiet moments. "I regret having to bring it up, but we spoke with Sister Nan yesterday. From St. Paul's in Shadwell."

The young woman frowned and nodded. "She told me of Hope House."

"Yes, and she thinks she knows how the father of your child came to find you there." Cassie briefly explained about the woman pretending to be with child and the man Sister Nan saw her meeting with immediately after.

Isabel paled, the healthy flush of her cheeks draining. "It must have been my aunt."

At the stove, Tris put down the wooden spoon. "How did that horrible woman know to go to Sister Nan?"

Elyse sighed. "The more women we help, the more risk we face. One whisper is barely audible. One hundred whispers together become a roar."

"Elyse is correct," Cassie said, knowing that something would have to change if they were to continue offering a safe haven. She then peered at her driver. "Tris, you know about Isabel's aunt?"

"I've told him everything," she said. Then blushing, "I should have told you too."

"You only have to share what you want at Hope House," Elyse assured her.

She looked to Tris, who nodded. Then, Isabel explained. "My aunt was the only family I had left after my parents died, so I had to go live with her, even though my mother had deliberately cut her out of our lives. Lydia...well, she..."

Tris settled his hand on her shoulder, encouragingly.

"She supplies men with companions. High quality ladies," she continued.

Cassie tried not to let her shock show. How awful it must have been for Isabel, to be made to live with such a woman. No wonder her sister had cut her out.

"One of her clients saw me one day. He was charming, bashful almost. Or so I thought, at first."

Cassie nodded. "Mr. Young?"

Isabel sat up straighter, surprised that his name was known. But then, she corrected Cassie. "Mr. Young*dale*. My aunt warned him that I was not an option, but he would not accept it. His offers for me became exorbitant. And at last, my aunt was too tempted."

Cassie gasped in revulsion. "She *sold* you to him?"

Isabel nodded. "In a fashion, yes. With the stipulation that he marry me. He was obsessed, though I cannot account for why. He didn't know me at all."

She was pretty and young, but perhaps it had been the quest for her, or for her innocence, that had held him in her thrall, not actual affection.

"The witch didn't even ask Isabel before agreeing," Tris

put in, his hand still on her shoulder. Isabel covered it with her own.

"Lydia said I was her burden to do with as she wished."

It was barbaric and cruel. How someone could be so twisted as to do such a thing to a family member left Cassie grasping.

"Who is this Mr. Youngdale?" Elyse asked. "Is he gentry? A peer?"

Isabel took a bracing breath. "He is the third son of a baronet and quite wealthy. At first, he didn't seem so awful, and I did want to be free of my aunt, so I didn't put up a fuss. But..." She shook her head forcefully. "He is no gentleman."

Cassie peered at Isabel's left hand. She wore no wedding band. "*Did* you marry?"

"No. He found excuses to delay the wedding, as well as to pay Lydia. But that did not stop him from..." Her chin quivered. "From treating me as if we *had* married."

The poor woman. She'd been manipulated and used, and she'd likely felt as though she had no one to turn to for help.

"He was already married once before," Tris said. Then gave her shoulder a gentle squeeze. "Tell them, Isabel."

She nodded. "She died. He said she fell down the stairs and broke her neck, but he's said other things to me, warning me that if I disobey him or make him angry, I might just find myself at the bottom of some stairs too. I think... I think he pushed her."

From his anger in the alley, Cassie didn't doubt Mr. Youngdale was a violent man. But if his wife died in such a manner, it had to have been investigated. Cassie thought of

Hugh and Audrey, and wondered if they might be able to find out more.

"I hid the fact that I was with child for as long as I could, but then, he noticed my growing middle. After accusing me of being unfaithful, he said he was going to marry me at last and keep the child." Isabel frowned. "But he made it sound like he wasn't going to keep *me*. I got scared. So, I ran. I'd been moving around for a week when I heard of Hope House and..." She shrugged. "And here I am. I won't marry him. And I won't allow him anywhere near my child."

Cassie reached across the table and clasped her forearm. "You won't have to. We'll protect you."

They would find a way.

"We'll make sure you're safe," Elyse agreed.

"And we can arrange for you to leave London before your baby is born," Cassie adds, thinking of Fournier Downs or Greenbriar. She had resources, and she wanted to share them with Isabel more than anything.

Isabel's eyes shone with tears. Tris stood beside her, and Cassie knew he would not yield. He cared for Isabel, even if the affection was new and formed under difficult circumstances.

As she and Elyse took their leave, a weight settled onto Cassie's shoulders. This was becoming more complicated. And dangerous. Mr. Youngdale was wealthy, and he likely had many connections to people with power.

Well, so did Cassie. Yet only one such connection knew of her ties to Hope House and her involvement with Isabel. She had no choice—she had to ask Grant for his help. As much as she dreaded seeing him again, Isabel's safety was more important than her own damn pride.

CHAPTER
FOURTEEN

The note Cassie sent ahead to Thornton House, informing Grant that she would be visiting him that night, had been somewhat cryptic—*T.H., rear entrance, 11 o'clock*—but she hoped the meaning would be clear to him.

She also hoped it would prevent him from having his mistress present when she arrived.

Her stomach flipped at the thought of the woman's name: Miss Martha Devereaux. Why had Jane felt the need to tell her about her?

As Patrick pulled his carriage down the mews lane behind Thornton House, she swallowed the urge to call for her driver to turn around. If not for Isabel's dire situation, she would not have come at all. Visiting an unmarried man's home this time of night, alone, in such a manner was precarious. If anyone were to learn of it, their false, short-term courtship would not be able to end as planned. Not without disastrous consequences for her.

Cassie squared her shoulders and, grateful for the pitiful lamplight in the mews, slipped up to Grant's tradesmen's entrance. After a single knock, the door opened, and she was looking up into the physician's face. A single candle illuminated his expression of censure.

"You are asking for trouble by coming here, Cassie." He took her arm and pulled her inside swiftly before shutting and locking the door. They stood in a small vestibule off the kitchen.

"I assumed your servants would be abed by this hour," she said, inhaling the air between them, trying to trace any lingering scent of perfume. The more she thought about his keeping a mistress while they were pretending to court, the more it began to rankle.

"They are," he said. The single taper in its holder was the only light in the kitchen beyond the vestibule. "But you may have been seen, or your carriage could be spotted in the mews."

"I'm having Patrick drive around. He's going to keep checking the lane, and I said we'd place a candle on the step outside when he's to come back."

The plan did little to assuage Grant's discontent. But he turned and began to lead her through the kitchen without a word. His anger over her presence was slightly insulting. The risk of being found with her here was no less severe than when they'd been huddled together in Lady Dutton's closet. His aversion to having to marry her was likely causing his sour attitude.

"Have I interrupted your evening?" she snapped as she followed him through a door and a short set of stairs, into a corridor.

She'd been in his home once before, shortly after Hugh and Audrey had uncovered a debased secret society near Vauxhall where a few women had been killed. Grant had been with them, and he'd been beaten badly, a few of his fingers broken. He'd endured torture rather than give up the location of his friend. Cassie had seen then his loyalty, and it had impressed her. She and Audrey had come to visit him, to be sure he was recovering. But in true Grant fashion, he'd brushed off the injuries with humor.

Though now, he didn't show a single drop of humor.

He pushed through a pair of doors, and Cassie followed him into a room similar to his Church Street surgery.

"Yes, in fact, you have," he answered.

He stalked through his home surgery and rolled open another pair of doors, these leading to a study. Annoyance rippled off him in waves as he went directly to a decanter on his desk and poured.

Coming here had been a mistake. With a sinking stomach, Cassie stood in between the surgery and the study. Firelight lit the masculine space. She could easily imagine him entertaining a woman on the wide leather Chesterfield before the fire. With that image in mind, the study seemed more like a den of sin.

"Your mistress had to leave early, I take it?"

He stilled the decanter.

"If I am not permitted to see other suitors, then I think it only fair you should not see Miss Devereaux."

Grant looked over his shoulder at her. He made no reply and went back to pouring. He filled a second glass, presumably for her.

"You won't deny she is your mistress?" Cassie pressed.

"I won't." Grant came back toward her and extended the drink. "How do you know of her?"

She stared at the glass but didn't take it. Couldn't look at him as a whistling sound filled her ears. "Jane. She said you frequent a sporting club on Bond Street where... Is that where you were coming from the other afternoon when I saw you?"

He lowered the drink. "I box at Gentleman Jack's, which is also on Bond Street, and had just left there when I saw you." Before she could start to feel miniscule for having asked such a question, he added, "But Mrs. Riverton is not wrong. The club is called the Fallen Arch. I have met Miss Devereaux there in the past."

Her fingernails bit into her palms as she clenched them.

"However," he went on. "I have not partaken in Miss Devereaux's special *attentions* since our deal was struck. Nor any other woman's if that is what has you all twisted up in knots."

Her fingers relaxed, her nails likely having left indentations. "I'm not twisted up." She grabbed the drink from his hand, perturbed with herself. And a little injured. He didn't want her here. He was downright angered by it.

"Give me your candle. I'll place it outside for Patrick." She held out her other hand, waiting for it.

"You are not leaving," he said. "Not until you tell me what was so bloody important that you'd risk coming here."

"You came to *my* study through *my* tradesmen's entrance," she reminded him.

"That was different."

"How so?"

Grant sipped his drink, his eyes not leaving hers. "You

had the safety of your staff on hand. A lady's maid who knew I was there and who stood just outside the door. There is no one here now to protect you from me."

A quiver of apprehension went through her. "Do I require protection from you?"

The question sounded far more suggestive than she'd intended. Grant didn't answer right away. Instead, he took the time to sip his drink again. The corner of his mouth twitched, and the dimple in his cheek showed itself.

"Maybe," he said, but his grin assured her he wasn't serious. "Sit, Cassie. Tell me why you've come."

She broke free from his penetrating gaze and went to the leather Chesterfield, adjacent to the hearth. A fire leaped in the grate, lighting the cut crystal glass in her hand as her fingers traced the chiseled edges. "Elyse and I went to the clinic and spoke to Isabel." She perched on the sofa. "The man's name is Mr. Young*dale*, not Young. She told us what happened and... Grant, it's just awful."

Cassie described what had been revealed about her aunt Lydia and Mr. Youngdale and also about the suspicious death of his first wife.

"She doesn't believe it was an accident," she explained. "He's threatened her, and she's frightened that he means to keep the baby once its born but dispose of her."

Grant scowled into the fire. "Youngdale," he murmured. Then, he set his glass on the hearth mantel and went to his desk. He pulled open a drawer and extracted a thick text.

"What is that?" Cassie asked.

"My copy of Debrett's. It should have something on the Youngdale baronetcy."

He brought the guide to the Chesterfield and took the

cushion beside hers. As he opened the book and began to flip through, she considered that this was not at all the image of Grant entertaining a woman on said sofa that she'd had just moments ago. Some of the tension left her back. Cassie couldn't account for it. She shouldn't be at ease, not while she sat here, alone in his home with him at so late an hour. But his concern for Isabel was evident as he turned pages. He would help the young woman. So many others would never have lifted a finger to give aid, but he would. Even if he was upset with Cassie for being there.

"Why do you keep a guide to the peerage in your desk drawer?" she asked.

"I like to know a little about my patients before I attend them," he replied while turning pages. "Plus, I'm incurably nosey. Ah. Here we are." He stopped flipping and put a finger to the page. "Mister Gregory Youngdale. Third son of Sir David Youngdale, deceased and succeeded by his eldest son. Child number three, Gregory, is nearly forty years of age, according to the birth date listed for him. This is the 1818 edition, so a few years old now, but it looks like the wife, Mrs. Alicia Youngdale was still alive when this guide was published. Married in 1815." He closed the book and tossed it aside. "There's nothing more than that. Officially, Youngdale is not a peer, so he wouldn't be part of any upper-class society, at least none that I know of."

"The demimonde then?" Cassie suggested.

Grant leaned against the Chesterfield's back cushion, his arms folding over his chest. He wasn't wearing a jacket, or a cravat. Just his shirtsleeves and waistcoat, the latter of which he'd likely only kept on because he knew to expect her.

Otherwise, by this time of night he'd have been in a state of dishabille. The image that flared in her mind wasn't ladylike. It was slightly alarming, in fact, especially when her attention drifted toward his unbuttoned collar, open to reveal the smooth skin of his throat. Thankfully, Grant didn't see her perusal. He was staring straight ahead, brows pressed low.

"Perhaps. I'll ask a few friends if they've heard anything about him." He shifted his gaze to her. "A part of me is relieved he's not as connected as a peer, but that also means his actions can go overlooked more easily than someone of more significance."

It was a good point. Anything could happen behind a closed door when no one cared enough to look.

"We must help her," Cassie said.

Grant sighed heavily. "I'm not sure what more we can do. Isabel can't be forced to marry him, but once the baby is born, if he *is* the father, he'll have a right to his child."

A surge of sudden, unchecked anger made her ill. "Why should he? After what he's done, he shouldn't have any right at all. He is violent. He killed his first wife!"

Grant held up a hand. "We don't know that for certain, and there is likely no proof."

"Isabel doesn't need proof to be afraid, or to know what kind of man he is. She has the right to protect herself and her child!" Cassie couldn't sit another moment. She got to her feet, the motion splashing the drink, still untouched in her glass, over the rim.

"I agree," Grant said calmly, his eyes following her as she set the glass on the flat arm of the sofa. Her wrist trembled. "However, there is little the law can do for her, and many would say she'd be better off married than unmarried when the baby is born."

"She should not be made to marry him!" Cassie said, her anger unspooling. "It isn't her fault that she doesn't have the sort of family who loved her or cared for her enough to keep her away from him, to understand that she didn't deserve to be punished with an unwanted marriage." She clasped her hands together, her fingers twisting as once again, she saw his face—*Renfry's* face—looking down at her at Archambeau Manor, all but leering as his mind took him back to the few times he'd successfully lured her into his bed. How *stupid* she'd been. How naive and desperate and silly. Her eyes stung as she stared into the fire.

"It isn't her fault her aunt didn't love her enough to send her away for her confinement before anyone could notice her increasing. To formulate an excuse that the whole family upheld to protect her. And then to bring her home afterward and continue to pretend..."

Her voice caught, and she couldn't go on. She shouldn't have said so much. Her whole body flushed as she realized what she'd done—and that it might not have been a mistake. The smallest part of her, a part she'd avoided listening to, had wanted to confess. Wanted to know how Grant would react. If he chastised her, despised her, she could hate him again.

The flames in the hearth entranced her as she waited with her back to him. Grant didn't speak as she heard him rise from the sofa. He continued to stay silent as he approached. Without looking, she knew he stood behind her. The warmth of his body pressed against her back. His hands touched down on her arms, bracing them, and her nerves lit with a galvanizing stir.

"Look at me, Cassie," he whispered. "Please."

She sniffled and blinked back the stinging tears. "I don't want to."

His palms tightened around her arms, and he closed more space between them. He angled his head toward her ear. "Why don't you want to look at me?"

Because she knew she wasn't going to see disdain or disappointment. She wasn't going to see censure or repulsion. And then she wasn't going to be able to hate him.

Slowly, she allowed him to turn her. And even more slowly, Cassie lifted her eyes from the sliver of skin at his unbuttoned collar. His green eyes, usually clear and pale, were now dusky. There was a tenderness in them that she hadn't expected. And yet, glaring fury too.

"You are no longer talking about Isabel," he said softly.

She gave her head a small shake. The muscles of his jaw jumped, and Grant tucked his chin, unblinking. "It happened to you."

She closed her eyes, feeling as though she was about to step over the edge of a precipice, not knowing what lay below, or how far the drop would be. A tear slipped free and wet her cheek. It was too late to reverse course now. He knew. Even if she said nothing, he would know. Cassie gave another jerky nod. Just one. Grant's grip on one of her arms released so that he could bring his thumb to her cheek.

"You're still not looking at me," he said as he cleared the dampness from her skin.

She gathered all her mettle, all the strength she'd convinced herself she possessed these last many years and split her wet lashes apart. Grant nodded, still holding her in a direct stare.

"It was Renfry?"

God, why was she doing this? Why did she *want* to tell him?

Her lips quavered uncontrollably. "Yes," she managed to whisper, the single word a hiccup.

Grant's hands fell away from her. His chest heaved as he took deep breaths, his expression suddenly devoid of any tenderness. Instead, it tightened with barely contained wrath. He strode several steps away, rubbing the back of his neck. Cassie rocked back onto her heels, her pulse beginning to throb in her ears.

"I shouldn't have told you," she said, the words tinny from panic. How could she have been so bloody daft? "We worked so hard to keep it secret, and I've never told anyone else, I don't know why I..."

Grant spun back around and closed the space between them, taking her arms again. "The truth is safe with me. Breathe, Cassie. Just breathe."

She inhaled a shallow breath, then another. It took a third for the chiming in her ears to subside. All the while, Grant's palm stroked her arm, elbow to shoulder and back down again.

"You said 'we'," he said after a moment. "Who knows? Not Renfry?"

"No, God no." A shiver worked down her spine, though it might have been from the soothing scrub of Grant's hand. The slow, intimate caresses had tempered her panic.

"Hugh and Audrey?" he guessed.

Cassie nodded. "And Michael and Genie."

Grant's hand stilled. "That is surprising."

"Michael loves me, even if he is inflexible and conventional to a fault. He would never have forced me to marry the man who lied to me. Who used me and...and threw me over."

Again, Grant stepped away, his aggravation visible in the flexing of his hands, into fists and out again. Cassie brought her arms around herself, her hands replacing where his had been soothing her. It didn't work half as well.

He raked a few dark strands of hair from his forehead, appearing overwhelmed. So was she. Never in a thousand years would she have thought the first person she'd tell, outside her protective family circle, would be Grant Thornton.

He seemed to hesitate. But then met her eyes. "The child?"

The child. Those two words blasted apart the glass casing she'd erected around her heart. There had been cracks in it, of course, fissures and fault lines. But Grant's simple inquiry ruptured them all. Cassie barely made it to the Chesterfield before her legs disappeared beneath her. She leaned forward, burying her face in her hands as the memories of that wretched day swarmed. The horrible pain, the relief of it ending, and then more stabbing pain in her chest when she'd seen her. She could still hear her daughter's shuddering wails as she was cleaned and bundled by the midwife, and then laid into Cassie's arms for the first, and what would be last, time.

The sofa cushion beside her dipped with Grant's weight. He didn't touch her, but his presence was enough.

"You needn't tell me anything," he said softly. "However, nothing you do tell me is going to change how I already see you."

Cassie moved her palms to uncover her eyes but continued to cup her wet cheeks as she peered at him. "How is that?"

Right then, she felt like a disaster. Weak and vulnerable. She didn't want anyone to see her this way.

Grant leaned forward, bracing his elbows on his thighs just as Cassie was doing. His hands clasped together, and he knit his brow in thought. "Brave," he said. Then, "Caring to a fault. You're strong and stubborn and a warrior for others."

She shook her head, even as his compliments made her feel the slightest bit radiant. "I'm not strong. I'm broken, and I feel like I'm breaking apart more and more every day." A sob caught in her throat, squeezing off that last word.

He nodded and rubbed his palms together, but he remained quiet. He didn't push her to say more, or console her with well-meaning words. He simply sat next to her, waiting for her to either say more, or not. The purposeful silence said it was to be her choice.

"I don't want to talk about Renfry," she finally said. "He doesn't matter. He is nothing."

And that was the truth. He'd injured her, to be sure, but it had been the product of that injury—*the child*—that had scarred her, not his ill treatment.

"I will never say his name again if that is what you want," Grant said.

It was perhaps even more generous than the words he'd just used to describe her. She sat up a bit straighter and rested her hands in her lap.

"Philip sent me to Stockholm, to be in the care of friends there. The Olssons. They were kind, and they found a family for the baby. I tried to prepare myself, but when she was born..." She shook her head, more tears welling. "I knew I could not keep her, but giving her away, coming home without her... I left a piece of my soul behind." Her throat closed off again, feeling as though it was being crushed.

Grant reached for her hands, which were twisting the fabric of her gown over her knees. He laid his palm over them, his large hand easily encompassing her own. His skin was coarse and warm, and the touch instantly calmed the tremors shuttling up and down her spine. Cassie looked at him, and to her surprise, his eyes were glistening. They were full of pain and sympathy, and she felt suddenly wretched for not considering that he knew a similar pain.

"When I wrapped my daughter in her burial shroud, I felt a part of me die too," he said, his voice a rasp. "It's why I cannot attend births anymore. I'm too afraid."

He shifted his position on the sofa to face her. "And yet, here you are, helping women going through something you've endured. Every time you walk through the doors of Hope House, you face your pain. You're not weak, Cassie. You are stunning."

He lifted his hand and with the ridge of his knuckles, brushed her cheek. She turned into the touch unthinkingly, only wanting to feel the comfort of it. Just as she had the evening in his clinic. And like then, the reckless desire for Grant to kiss her erased every other thought in her mind. His lips were so close, the fullness of his lower lip mesmerizing. She couldn't draw her eyes away from his mouth, or her imagination from how it might feel to kiss his lips. The senseless, imprudent yearning for him to fit them against hers overrode all reason.

But unlike Cassie, it seemed he wasn't without reason.

Grant dropped his hand from her cheek and launched to his feet, breaking the spell. He cleared his throat roughly and pulled on the points of his waistcoat before fidgeting some more by smoothing the deep green fabric with his palms.

Cassie's legs quaked as she, too, got to her feet. Her mind reeled and her cheeks flushed. "I should go."

"Yes, it's late," he replied swiftly. Grant stooped to pick up the copy of Debrett's that he'd tossed onto the floor. "We'll speak to Hugh tomorrow. He might know something regarding Mr. Youngdale."

As he led her from the study, back through the surgery and into the corridors toward the kitchen, he stayed a few steps ahead. Telling him the truth had been bewilderingly easy, and his response, even more puzzling. He'd been supportive and kind. And yet, he'd pulled away before he could kiss her.

Gracious, she was such a fool. Why would he wish to kiss her now that she'd admitted to having a child out of wedlock? To being ruined? It was the very reason why she'd never allowed herself to become close to any man. Intimacy would be impossible. Her brother wanted her to marry, but the moment any husband saw her bare stomach, he would know the truth. The baby had left marks on her skin. Unassailable evidence. She would be betrayed on her wedding night, and the man would know himself to be betrayed too. While Grant may have been sympathetic, it had likely altered whatever attraction he might have felt for her. Even if it was a frivolous and fleeting attraction.

They entered the mews lane outback just as Patrick was driving past the entrance to it. He turned and drew up to them. Grant opened the door for her.

"Cassie," he said as he helped her onto the step. She forced herself to look at him. In the dark, at least he couldn't see her blushing. "Thank you for trusting me."

She nodded, but as he shut her into the carriage and told Patrick to carry on, she feared it had changed everything. And she wished she'd kept her damn mouth shut.

CHAPTER
FIFTEEN

At just two years old, Miss Catherine Neatham outshone all the finely turned-out ladies inside Hyde Park, firmly placing herself as the center of all envy and attention. She gripped the sides of her father's face as she rode his shoulders, calling out a giggly "Hello!" to everyone walking by on the Serpentine path. Almost everyone said hello in return before nodding or bowing their heads toward the Viscount and Viscountess Neatham.

"You look deranged, you know," Grant said as he walked alongside his friend. "Like you've allowed Basil to purchase you a chubby little adornment for your hat. Or perhaps for your collar."

"Basil would never select anything that produces this much spit," Hugh replied. His valet was notoriously fussy about the viscount's clothing.

"She's going to topple off if you don't hold her legs," Sir admonished as he strode along Hugh's other side.

The young man was exceedingly protective of Cat, and Grant presumed it was because he saw her as an additional baby sister. He already had three of his own, the young girls all living with their mother in the country, on Hugh's estate.

"I am holding her ankles," Hugh replied. "She isn't toppling anywhere."

Sir made a doubtful snorting sound.

"Are those the gentlemanly noises they're teaching you to make at Charterhouse these days?" Hugh asked, smirking over at the young man.

Sir, whose name was in truth Davy Givens, had started working for Hugh as his errand boy of sorts when Hugh had still been with Bow Street. He'd been a scrappy, smelly street urchin back then. Now, at about age fifteen, he was nearly as tall as Hugh, filling out with some muscle, and dressing like any one of the young gentlemen in Town. He attended a boarding school for boys in Surrey but was on a short break for the holidays and had come to London with Hugh, Audrey, and Cat.

Sir had come a long way in just a handful of years, and all because Hugh had taken him in as a ward. However, Grant suspected Sir was much more to Hugh than that. He was like a son, and Sir saw Hugh as a father.

"Leave Sir alone," Audrey called from where she walked a few strides ahead. "He only has Cat's best interests in mind."

Walking next to the viscountess, Cassie kept her attention trained on the pewter water in the Serpentine. She'd sent a note earlier in the day to say she would meet him at Hyde Park at the fashionable hour, and that she would bring Audrey and Hugh. She'd held to her plan and had been with the viscount and viscountess, as well as Sir and Cat, at the entrance to the park. However, she hadn't met Grant's eyes more than a few times.

It was for the best, even if her avoidance of him since starting on their stroll was sinking his stomach with every additional step. The previous day, he'd been irate when her note had arrived at Thornton House, warning him of her near to midnight visit. And not just because if she were to be seen visiting his home at that hour, their false courtship would have no choice but to become one in truth. He'd been irritated because picturing her in his home late at night, with his bedchamber so easily accessible, had also aroused him. His attraction to Cassie had become a powerful problem. But it wasn't something he could act on, especially now.

After Cassie's confession last night about Renfry and the baby, Grant did not know what to think or feel. His heart had ached when she'd wept, trying so valiantly to keep her composure. That's what she had been doing for years now: pretending. Being strong. Pushing away the pain. Closing herself off.

He'd been an arse all these years, thinking her a cold fish, calling her Lady Freeze. After what she'd had to endure, she'd turned cold for a reason: to protect herself.

But last night, she hadn't been cold at all. She'd let down her rigid guard and exposed herself to a man who'd given her no reason to trust him. A man who was coercing her into a charade that would benefit him. A man who was using her. Not in the same way as Renfry, of course, but still using her.

On the sofa, Cassie's eyes, her lashes sparkling with tears, had beckoned him to kiss her. He'd wanted nothing more than to give her what she wanted. What *he* wanted. God, how he wanted to know those lips against his. The glide of her tongue, the touch of her hands. The yielding press of her body. He wanted it with a keen pain that wasn't at all familiar to him.

And yet, he'd have been no better than Renfry if he'd taken advantage of her in that vulnerable moment. His rejection had stung; he'd seen it in her expression, and he'd lain abed until dawn with a tight ball of regret rooting in his stomach.

A dog being led on its leash crossed the path ahead of them, and Cat's little hand slapped the side of Hugh's face in excitement.

"Down, down!" she exclaimed, kicking her legs and nearly clipping Hugh's nose. He promptly did his daughter's bidding, lifting her from his shoulders and setting her feet onto the gravel.

It wasn't at all common for peers to carry their children around Hyde Park on their shoulders. However, Viscount Neatham had never intended to be a common peer.

"See, I told you, she doesn't like heights," Sir said, reaching for Cat's hand.

"She likes heights just fine. She saw a dog and wanted to pet it," Hugh insisted as Sir led the toddler toward the animal.

"You may as well give up," Grant told him. "You've been overthrown by your protégé."

Audrey paused long enough for Hugh to fall into step beside her. She latched onto his arm and leaned her head against his shoulder. The loving display was also something that wasn't prevalent in Hyde Park, where those of the ton walked primly and properly, with the expectation that every eye was watching and judging. Audrey and Hugh did not care what others thought.

Cassie, however, didn't move to join them. Instead, she followed Sir and Cat as the little girl made a dash for the white fluffball of a dog. She appeared to be anything but a woman strolling happily with her suitor. It was a fine afternoon, and the park was full of people who would gladly exchange the news of having seen Lady Cassandra and Lord Thornton together. They would also speculate as to why the lady appeared forlorn.

"Grant," Audrey began now that Cassie was out of hearing distance. He knew what was coming and braced himself. "I hope you know what you're doing. The rumors I'm hearing..."

"You shouldn't listen to rumors, my lady," he said with a playful grin.

She arched a brow. "Is there any truth to them?"

"That depends on what you're hearing," he replied.

"Thornton." Hugh held out an arm to stop him from taking another step. It was smoothly done, in a way that would not draw any attention. And yet, Grant knew he was serious. "I've heard rumors too. About Lindstrom and his demand that you marry again."

Hell. His second eldest brother, Harold, had always possessed loose lips. Especially when he was in his cups. He should have known the knowledge would make its way out into the gentlemen's clubs, then swiftly around London.

"I can handle the marquess," Grant said.

Hugh stared at him with plain doubt. "I don't know what you're playing at with Cassie, but my warning to you stands."

Grant bristled. "Why do you assume I am playing at something?"

"Because I know you." Hugh's each word was sharp and dangerously quiet. "The marquess has made a demand, and you will not have liked that. If you are using Cassie in some harebrained way—"

Audrey laid a hand on her husband's arm as his voice began to rise.

"If you do know me, as you so claim, then do not insult me by presuming I have set out to harm Lady Cassandra." Grant stepped closer to Hugh, unexpectedly furious. "I am *not* like Renfry."

Audrey parted her lips in surprise, and Hugh hitched his chin. He inspected Grant another long moment. "She told you?"

Grant could say nothing before Cat screeched, diverting her parents' attention. The little girl clasped her hands together as if she'd been nipped by the little dog.

"She's fine," Sir called to assure them. "Just a mean mongrel."

The servant that had been walking the animal gawked at Sir and then strode away. Sir then picked up Cat and brought her closer to the water, to distract her. Cassie didn't follow this time. Finally, she met Grant's eyes, and seeming to take a bracing breath, came back toward them. She kept herself a good arm's length from his side.

"Sir is good with her." It was one of the first things she'd said since beginning their stroll, but it lacked the brightness of her usual tone.

"He is a natural," Audrey agreed, looking at Grant one last time before welcoming Cassie with a grin.

"How are Sir's mother and sisters?" Cassie asked. At the

water's edge, Sir had crouched and was letting Cat sit on his leg.

"Doing well in Surrey," Hugh answered. Then sighed. "I hate to say it, but Harlan Givens's death was the opportunity they all needed."

Sir's father had been a brute, abusive, and neglectful, and his whole family had been under his thumb. Hugh had given Sir a refuge, but there wasn't much he could do for Mrs. Givens and her other daughters. Not until Mr. Givens had been killed a few years ago.

Cassie licked her lips, and with a meaningful glance toward Grant, asked, "There must be something that can be done if a man is known to abuse his wife."

They'd invited Hugh and Audrey on this stroll for a reason—to ask about Mr. Youngdale. How they would explain their interest in him would be challenging, as would be explaining how Cassie knew Isabel. He and Cassie had not had the chance to confer and agree on an approach.

"Unfortunately, there isn't much Bow Street can do in those situations," Hugh replied. "Unless the lady's family calls him out or takes vengeance into their own hands."

Audrey's mouth thinned in distaste. "A woman is the property of her husband, and he can rule her as he sees fit. It is shameful. There should be laws against it."

"I agree entirely," Hugh said.

"But what if the lady in question is not married to the abuser?" Cassie asked. "What if she is simply carrying his child?"

The question startled the viscount and viscountess into momentary silence.

"That is rather specific," Hugh said. "What is this about?"

With a look toward Grant, Cassie nibbled her lower lip. She was stuck on how to explain her interest.

Thinking only to alleviate some of the pressure, Grant said, "I have a patient at my Church Street clinic. She is in this situation."

Cassie exhaled with some relief. It only lasted until they saw Hugh glowering at them. "How does Cassie know of this woman?" Then, with alarm, "Have you taken her to your clinic?"

"That isn't the important point," she quickly said. "This young woman is hiding from a dangerous man, a Mr. Youngdale. He's the third son of a baronet, and we wondered if you knew anything about him."

Audrey asked, "Where is she hiding?" at the same time that Hugh asked, "What have you two gotten yourselves into?"

Cassie's rosy cheeks marked her as flustered, but even with Hugh's pointed questions, Grant could only think that they looked lovely.

"She is staying at my clinic," Grant supplied. "Youngdale. Do you know him?"

The viscount shook his head. "The name isn't familiar. You say they are not married?"

Cassie nodded. "She escaped before he could force her. Her aunt sides with him, so she has no one to protect her."

Hugh and Audrey exchanged a look, then cast it toward them. Their thoughts were of Renfry no doubt, and the fact that Cassie had shared her deepest secret with Grant. It smarted that his closest friend didn't trust him not to hurt

Cassie. Perhaps Grant had been blind to just how dissolute his reputation had grown to be.

"The best thing to do, perhaps the only thing, would be to get her away from him," Hugh said.

"There is a place I've heard of," Audrey whispered. "Greer mentioned it once. A house of hope, she called it, but apparently one must find a nun in a parish to receive its secret location. It all sounds mystifying, but I could try to find out more."

Cassie's eyes rounded and her jaw went slack. Grant's own went a bit loose as well. Cassie turned her shocked stare toward him, and for the first time since meeting with Madame Archambeau—it felt like years ago—she grinned.

"What is it?" Audrey asked, peering between them.

Cassie wiped the smile away. "That is quite all right, Audrey, you needn't learn more. She is safe at Grant's clinic for now."

"She won't be if this Youngdale fellow finds her there," Hugh said. "There are laws against assaulting a woman who is not your wife, as paradoxical as that may seem. So, as long as she doesn't marry him, Youngdale can be brought up on charges if he harms her. If she does become his wife..." He shrugged as if to say, *it's over*.

Sir and Cat returned from the edge of the Serpentine then, the little girl's shoes and hem soaked.

"She saw minnows," Sir explained bashfully.

"It is December. There are no minnows in the water," Hugh replied as Audrey picked Cat up.

"We best get you home, little troublemaker," she said, touching the tip of her nose to the little girl's.

Their party turned back toward Rotten Row, where their

conveyances and drivers waited. Distracted by their fussy daughter, Hugh and Audrey weren't listening when Grant chanced addressing Cassie.

"May I drive you home? There are some things we should discuss."

"I expect we'll take a turn through the park first, so all and sundry can see us *courting*." She was angry. About last night? Because he had not kissed her as she'd so evidently wanted? Or perhaps it was because she regretted letting down her guard.

"Perhaps we should sit on the same bench," he replied, thoroughly annoyed by her sudden change in attitude now that Audrey and Hugh were not listening. "I will whisper something in your ear, and you will laugh as though I am the cleverest man of the century."

"If I stoop to that, everyone will surely know the whole thing is a farce," she replied, picking up her speed.

He matched it easily with longer strides. "I did not force you to tell me anything last night, Cassie. If you are having regrets, don't take it out on me."

She came to a lurching stop and glared up at him. "I do regret it. I regret giving you one more thing to hold over my head. To coerce me with—"

Instant offense lit through him. Unthinkingly, he took her wrist. "I would *never* hold that over your head. Ever."

Her hard, skeptical glare diminished, but Cassie still appeared timid. She did not know if she could trust him. Just as Hugh hadn't known if he could trust his intentions with Cassie. With Hugh, Grant had felt slighted. But with Cassie, he had the intense urge to prove what he said was true. He wanted her to trust him.

And yet how could she when he'd given her no reason to?

"Thornton." Hugh's bark came from a distance. Releasing Cassie's arm and breaking their drawn-out stare, Grant sought out his friend. He stood on Rotten Row with their driver, Carrigan, Grant's driver, Merryton, and Cassie's driver, Patrick. And standing next to Patrick was another man—her original driver, Tris.

Cassie gasped and started toward them. Fresh bruises riddled Tris's face, and his right eye and bottom lip had swollen to a grotesque size.

"What in hell happened to you?" Grant asked as he and Cassie reached them. It was a scene, one that did not often occur on the most fashionable stretch of road in London.

"Where is Isabel?" Cassie inquired.

Tris shook his head, his swollen face even more distorted as emotion gripped him. "They took her. Came crashing through the back door at the clinic and set upon me, four to one." He whipped off his cap and crushed it in his hands. "When I came to, she was gone."

Dread pooled in Grant's stomach. "Youngdale. He found her."

Sir came over from where he'd been standing with Carrigan. "Youngdale?"

"Do you know the name?" Grant asked.

Sir nodded. "Some lower toff? A baronet or some such?"

Grant focused on the young man. "That's him. How do you know of him?"

"He's a high roller at Duke's."

Hugh fixed him with a glare. "What are you doing at a boxing club?"

Sir patted his cheek. "Not ruining this handsome mug. Just betting a little. Got mates there."

Before Hugh could reprimand him for frequenting a boxing club and gambling, Grant held up his hand. "Is he there often?"

Sir shrugged and nodded. "Whenever there's a fight. Sits with some other toffs like he owns the place."

"When is the next fight?" Cassie asked, her eagerness worrisome.

"There's one tonight," Sir answered. She brightened, and Grant could easily guess what she was thinking.

"You are *not* going to Duke's."

She set her jaw and whipped toward him. "No, I'm not. Not alone at least. You can take me."

Grant fixed a sarcastic grin into place. "I'm not offering."

Cassie fumed and parted her lips to give a retort, but Hugh cleared his throat. "Cassie, on this, I must agree with Thornton. Duke's is in a rough part of Limehouse. It's not suitable for you—or fifteen-year-old boys," he added, tossing a harsh look at Sir. The boy rolled his eyes. "I'll come around later, Thornton. We'll discuss a plan."

After a bow toward Cassie, he gathered Audrey and Sir to leave. Audrey sent her an apologetic glance before getting into the carriage. Once Carrigan began to drive away, Cassie broke from Grant's side and started for her own conveyance.

"Wait," he said, catching her arm. "We need to talk."

"I've nothing to say."

"Cassie. *Stop.*" The command was a bark, and much too loudly done. Heads turned in their direction. Cassie did stop her retreat but looked as if she'd have liked to rip out his tongue.

"Take my arm," he said more softly. Pink flushed her cheeks.

"No."

The stubborn, mule-headed woman!

"Fine. If you won't trust me, then at least trust Hugh. Duke's is no place for you."

"Just as Crispin Street is no place for me?" He recalled what he'd said before—that she didn't belong there. It had hurt her.

"I am only thinking of your safety," he said, his temper rising.

"I do not need you for that."

His jaw locked with the sudden urge to take her over his knee. The image both stoked his temper and stirred his loins wide awake.

"I think our stroll has reached its end," Cassie said, still holding his hard stare. "Unless you still wish to take that exhibitive ride in your carriage?"

He flashed his teeth, the grin more of a snarl. He snatched her hand before she could pull it away. Grant raised it to his lips and took a protracted amount of time—several moments at the least—to drop kisses along her gloved knuckles. Long enough for some passersby to see the display. "No need, Lady Cassandra. I've rather lost my interest in it. I'll take Tris with me to tend to his injuries. Good afternoon."

Grant lowered her hand, released it, and walked away from her, toward his carriage.

The bloody woman was going to drive him straight into Bedlam.

CHAPTER
SIXTEEN

"I'm not sure about this, milady." By the light of the carriage's interior lantern, Cassie's lady's maid appeared wan. Even more so than she'd been when Cassie first informed her of the plan for the evening. Ruth squirmed. "Limehouse isn't the finest part of Town, and we've only Patrick in the box for protection."

"We aren't going to need protection," Cassie said. She was beginning to regret bringing Ruth. It had been an attempt to show some propriety, but her maid's complaints were growing tiresome.

Cassie drew in a breath to calm herself. Her frayed nerves weren't entirely Ruth's fault. No, her true annoyance was with Grant. And Hugh if she was being honest. The two of them had shut her out, deciding what wasn't appropriate for her, when Isabel was her responsibility. Not theirs.

Once Grant had left with Tris in his carriage, her face still hot from his ardent show of kissing her hand, Cassie had fled back to Grosvenor Square, where she'd told Patrick to plan for an outing to Limehouse that night. He had not been pleased. Her assurance that they would simply wait outside the club and see what they could see had not been enough to put him at ease. Since she could not enter the club alone, watching from the carriage window would have to suffice. Staying in at home and twiddling her thumbs while Isabel was out there, in danger, was not an option.

Duke's was located in a repurposed warehouse near the river, and several minutes after Patrick had parked the carriage on the street outside, Cassie's spirits lifted. Men in fashionable suits and top hats were entering the club, and women were in the mix as well. By all appearances, the attendees were not lower class. While a few women were unaccompanied, most were on the arms of men.

Cassie slid forward on her seat. "I say we go in."

Ruth balked. "No, milady, we couldn't. It wouldn't be safe—*ah!*" The maid screamed as a hand pounded on the carriage door, and Cassie practically jumped out of her skin.

"Cassie, is that you in there?"

Her heart re-started when she recognized the voice. "Tobias?"

She reached for the door handle, and Ruth screamed again. Cassie gritted her molars. "It is just my brother," she told the maid, who didn't look at all relieved.

"I thought I recognized this carriage. What in Hades are you doing here?" Tobias asked the moment Cassie flung open the door and saw her brother on the pavements. She extended her hand, and he saw her down.

"I'm attending the match, of course," she said, immediately taking his arm. "With my favorite brother."

He was more agreeable than Michael, and quite the young blade with his walking stick, skewed top hat, and loose cravat. However, he was no pushover. Tobias peered at her skeptically.

"You had no idea I would be here," he said.

"Perhaps I did. Maybe I am having you followed," she replied lightly. "Patrick, stay here with Ruth."

Her driver bowed his head. "My lady. Lord Tobias."

"Are you boxing tonight?" she asked him as she tried to begin walking toward the warehouse.

Tobias kept his feet planted. "I don't box. I bet. And no, you may not come in with me."

"There are women going inside, Toby. Plenty of them."

And an increasingly large part of her wanted to be one of them. If Mr. Youngdale was at the boxing match, he might have Isabel with him. If not, it might be possible to follow him afterward. He could very well lead them straight to her.

"These matches are no holds barred," Tobias said. "They're quite gruesome at times, and besides, Michael would serve my head on a platter if he found out I'd taken you to one."

"He won't find out through me," she replied. "Though, he might find out how you're spending your allowance if you do not escort me inside."

Gracious, now she sounded like Grant Thornton.

Her brother scowled. "Fine. But you will stay right next to me the entire time. Is that clear?"

She promised she would, and at last, they started for the warehouse. Whatever goods the structure had stored in its previous life had been lost beneath its new incarnation. A vast space with high ceilings and worn wooden floors housed four sets of staged seating, all surrounding a raised boxing rink. Lights blazed from lanterns hanging from ceiling beams, and the noise as she and Tobias entered arm in arm stunned her. Men spoke loudly and in teeming throngs. Those they threaded through seemed to be placing bets and discussing the odds of the night's match. The chaos of the floor brought a smile to Tobias's lips, and he raised an arm as he caught sight of someone. He pulled her along while Cassie scanned the lively crowds for the two men who would not be at all pleased to see her there. *If* they had come, that was.

"Forsythe, you've met my sister, Lady Cassandra," Tobias said, and suddenly, she was staring into the face of Mr. Alaric Forsythe. He quickly removed his hat and bowed.

"This is a surprise, my lady. I had no idea you attended boxing matches."

She gaped, belatedly remembering that he'd sent flowers to her after the opera. And also after Lady Tennenbright's ball.

"Cassie doesn't attend boxing matches," Tobias provided when she continued to stare. "I don't know why she's here, but trust me Forsythe, whatever the reason, you likely don't want to be part of it."

She longed to tweak her younger brother's ear but contained herself. Mr. Forsythe ignored Tobias's advice and animatedly invited them to sit with him. Tobias pounded him on the back, calling him a good chap, and Mr. Forsythe led them toward the far side of the boxing ring.

"I hope you don't mind the front row," Mr. Forsythe said as they filed onto the benches.

"I'm not sure what I prefer," Cassie said honestly. "This is my first match."

He blinked, his curiosity plain. "What has brought you out?"

She had no ready excuse, and with the crush of viewers near them in the stands, Cassie felt slightly panicked. It was hot and close, smelling of salty brine from the Thames, smoke, and sweat, and her heartbeat was beginning to pick up speed. The noise was overwhelming, and though she darted looks all around, she couldn't see any sign of Isabel. Or of Grant and Hugh.

"Lady Cassandra?"

She faced Mr. Forsythe. "I'm sorry, this is all rather—"

A high roar erupted in the room, and people all around them shot to their feet. Mr. Forsythe took her elbow, and they stood as well. Two large, muscled men wearing breeches and nothing else climbed into the boxing ring. All around her, men and women cheered and clapped, and then just as abruptly, everyone retook their seats. Cassie was slow to do the same, her ears ringing, her mind still spinning. A few seconds behind the others, Cassie had started to sit, but then froze. Across the ring, in the opposite stands, one man remained standing. He linked eyes with Cassie, his own blazing with pure wrath.

She'd found Grant. Or rather, he'd found her.

Tobias tugged her arm and brought her back onto the bench with a thump. Across the way, Grant smoothly lowered himself into his seat. Hugh and Sir were with him. The viscount shook his head after seeing her and leaned over to whisper something in Grant's ear. However, the physician didn't shift his glare from her. As the two men began to circle one another in the ring and throw jabs with their fists, Grant's attention slid to the man on Cassie's left.

"I think I have discovered why you're here, Lady Cassandra," Mr. Forsythe said, leaning toward her ear as people all around them cheered on the fighters. He had to practically shout to be heard above the din, and it made her eardrum ache.

She peered at him, confused as to how he could possibly know. But then, when he directed his attention across the ring, into the stands where Grant was seated, she understood his meaning. Embarrassment stained her cheeks.

"Oh, no! Really, that's not why," she said, but Mr. Forsythe only laughed.

"I do not read the gossip columns, but even I am aware that the gentleman has set his cap at you. And if the way he is looking at you is any indication at all, he is not pleased to see you here at another man's side."

While Sir and Hugh were looking off toward another section of staging, Grant continued to blister her with a glare. But she wasn't here with Mr. Forsythe! They'd simply bumped into one another. No, what Grant was angry about was her being here at all after he'd told her she couldn't come. Well, that wasn't up to him, was it?

"His interest is evident," Mr. Forsythe continued to say as the two men in the ring circled one another. "And dare I say, yours as well?"

She felt a twinge of shock, then an equal one of guilt. "Mr. Forsythe, I don't think you under—"

He held up a hand again and smiled. "No, no. No need, my lady. You should know that I've made arrangements to return to Egypt next month. Not because of a broken heart," he added with a laugh. "But because it is where I belong, at least for right now."

The announcement left Cassie speechless. She began to feel silly as she gaped at him.

"Oh. Well, then... I am happy for you." She genuinely was. Relieved, too. Cassie did feel terribly that he had fallen for the ruse she and Grant were perpetuating, but she could only hope that he was in earnest, and his heart was not injured.

"I only pray the gentleman endeavors to deserve such a treasure," he added, with a final nod of his head. As if to say, *and that is that.*

Blushing fiercely at Mr. Forsythe's presumptions, Cassie turned away. She could not look at Grant, however, and followed the direction of Hugh and Sir's attention instead. In the staging adjacent to hers, every row was filled. In the gaps where there were no seats, men and women stood, and several men continued to collect bets being wagered on the opponents.

Her eyes tripped to a stop on a man in a top hat. There was nothing remarkable about him, and without doubt, she would not have given him even a second glance—if not for the healing scratches on his right cheek. Cassie held her breath as the cheers and jeers of the crowds around her faded behind a ringing in her ears. Four long lines stretched from under the man's eye to the corner of his mouth, the gashes red and scabbing over.

In the alley behind Hope House, she had defended herself by raking her hair comb along her attacker's face. Blood had been left behind on the sharp tines, proving she'd cut him.

This was Mr. Youngdale.

His full attention was on the fight unfolding in the ring. He sat stiff and unemotional, unlike the others around him, who were shifting in their seats, standing or clapping or shouting when one boxer landed a punch and sent the other staggering. The more she watched him, the more Mr. Youngdale's cold inspection of the fight began to chill her.

And then, the disturbing spell was broken.

The boxers in the ring barreled into one another, flying up against the ropes directly in front of Cassie, Tobias, and Mr. Forsythe. One man slammed his bare fist into the other's face, and in a blink, a spatter of blood arced through the air. Wetness splattered against Cassie's face, shocking her. She raised her hands to her cheek. Her fingers came away with blood on them.

Laughter for her predicament erupted in the rows around her, and when she looked toward Mr. Youngdale again, his hard stare had fastened upon her. For a moment, she thought he did not recognize her. But then, he raised his gloved hand to his cheek and touched the healing gashes. His lips twisted into a mean grimace.

"Here, take this, Lady Cassandra." Mr. Forsythe pressed a handkerchief into her hand. She peeled her eyes from Mr. Youngdale and attempted to wipe away the gore. The last thing she wanted to do was look across at Grant, so she didn't.

In the ring, one of the opponents received a blow to the jaw and slumped to the stained canvas floor, unconscious. The warehouse erupted into cheers and moans. Tobias, however, was still howling with laughter at her expense.

"You should have seen your expression." He acted it out in absurd exaggeration, and Cassie kicked him in the shin.

"Ow!" He rubbed his leg as everyone around them began to stand.

The entire fight hadn't lasted more than ten minutes. She looked to the stands where Mr. Youngdale had been, but with everyone standing and moving, couldn't see him.

"Try this." Tobias whisked the handkerchief from her fingers and uncapped his flask. He poured some spirits onto the cloth and began to dab roughly at her skin.

She snatched the cloth away. "I can do it myself, you buffoon."

Tobias threw up his hands and turned to speak to some other acquaintances. After wiping at her cheeks, Mr. Forsythe's wince hinted that she had not been totally successful. He gestured for her to give him the handkerchief, and when she did, he applied it to her nose, then forehead.

"Awful luck," he said. "I'm afraid you've some in your hair, too."

Cassie felt silly having her face cleaned by him. Not to mention, his ministrations were blocking her view of the stands where Mr. Youngdale had been. She pulled back from Mr. Forsythe. "Really, it is fine. I'll be—"

Her voice cut off as a scorching presence seared her. Like the pressure of a hot wind, she did not have to see Grant to know he was there. Cassie rose to her feet and, steeling her spine, faced his wrath full on. He towered in front of their row, his eyes like two emeralds on fire.

"May I have a word, Lady Cassandra?" It was less of a request and more of a terse command. He held out his hand.

Cassie eyed it, dreading his certain scolding while at the

same time, eager to put her hand in his. It made no sense. She blamed the chaotic surroundings and the shock of blood spatter that had lashed her across the face.

After thanking Mr. Forsythe, whom Grant had pointedly refused to acknowledge, Cassie slipped her fingers into Grant's waiting palm. He locked her hand in his and began to walk, saying nothing as he hauled her toward the exit.

She dug in her heels. "Stop! Mr. Youngdale is here."

"I know."

"We have to follow him." She again struggled against his route toward the warehouse exit. She tried to look over her shoulder, but the crowds were milling, and Grant was still dragging her forward.

"Hugh and Sir have gone after him. I would be with them, too, if not for your foolish antics."

Cassie ripped her hand from his. "You do not need to concern yourself with me. We are both here for the same reason. Let us find him."

"I don't need to concern myself? Have you lost your senses?" Grant held himself rigid, and close, looming over her. "Not only is this place utterly inappropriate for a woman of your standing, but Youngdale *saw* you. He recognized you. Did you not think of that before coming here with Tobias—and with *Forsythe*?" He spit the name.

"I did not arrive with either of them. I met them by chance." Though she knew that wasn't the larger problem. If Mr. Youngdale learned who she was and could place her at Hope House...he could expose her.

"I didn't think of Mr. Youngdale seeing me," she admitted softly. And how it pained her, too.

"No, all you heard was someone telling you that you couldn't do something, and like a child, you did it anyway."

The chiding burned, and Cassie glared, her contrition consumed by a rush of indignation. "Very well, your opinion is noted. Now, I have no need for your protection, Lord Thornton, so you are free to join Hugh and Sir."

She started toward the exit but did not make it two strides before Grant overtook her. He slid in front of her, so close her feet practically tripped over his.

"They are gone, and I am taking you back to Grosvenor Square."

"No, thank you," she bit off, teeth gnashing. "I have my own carriage."

He hooked her arm as she tried to pass him again.

"Unhand me," she commanded. Grant cocked his head, the intensity of his stare enough to thicken the breath in her throat.

"Woman, this is the second time today that I've wanted to bend you over my knee and paddle your hide."

The growled words burrowed under her skin—and ignited. The rest of the club vanished as Grant's eyes dropped to her lips. His vexation with her brimmed to overflowing, and an increasingly reckless part of her delighted in it. That heedless little demon inside her relished that she could push him to the brink of losing control. It wanted to keep pushing until he snapped. What might that look like? What would he do? The attention he was giving her mouth gave her a suspicion.

"Ah, Lord Thornton, I see you've apprehended my harridan of a sister," Tobias said as he joined them. Purposefully, Cassie was sure of it. Grant wasn't exactly masking his anger, and as petulant as Tobias could be, he wouldn't stand back while someone manhandled his sister.

Grant released Cassie's elbow and stepped away. "Lord Tobias, can I ask you to walk your sister to her carriage. She was leaving."

The utter gall! "Do not order me about. I'm not yours to command."

"The match is over anyhow, Cassie," Tobias said, without giving Grant a chance to reply. He hooked her arm and tipped the brim of his hat to Grant, bidding him a good evening.

Her brother pulled her along, and when they'd taken several strides, he leaned closer. "What have you done, dear sister?"

She balked at him. "*Me?*"

"Thornton looked like he wanted to rip off your head."

Or take her over his knee. Outside, Cassie welcomed the cool air and dragged in several gulps. "I didn't do anything. He is simply unpleasant and bad-tempered."

Tobias frowned down at her. "And yet rumors swirl that he is going to propose."

Cassie blushed. "Nothing will come of that."

Grant did not intend to propose, only court her. And none of it was real anyhow.

They turned toward her carriage. "Good," he replied.

Cassie slowed her gait. "Why would you say that?"

Her brother laughed lightly. "The man's reputation is less than pristine. Michael respects that he's friends with Viscount Neatham but as a match for you? Absolutely not."

Patrick leaped from the box and opened the carriage door for her, but as Tobias released her arm, Cassie swayed. It wasn't as if she was going to marry Grant but hearing that Michael would disapprove of the physician rankled.

"Is it because he works?" Cassie asked before Patrick could shut the door.

Her brother shrugged. "That. And the fact that he has several mistresses."

Disbelief poured through her. "*Several?*"

Tobias shrugged again. "From what I hear."

He tipped his hat, and Patrick shut the door. Surely, Tobias had to be exaggerating. Or the rumors he'd heard were false.

"Milady, is that...*blood* on your face?" Ruth's warbling voice drew Cassie out of her whirling thoughts. "And in your *hair*?"

As Patrick drove them back toward home, Ruth fretted over the dashes of blood that had also landed upon the collar of her pelisse. The whole thing would be lost now, stained irreparably. Cassie half listened to her maid's vexing, and when at last they arrived home, impatiently waited for her driver to come hand her down.

Just then, a coach, made visible by its exterior lanterns, appeared in the streetside window. Had it gone by swiftly, Cassie wouldn't have noticed it. But the coach slowed to a crawl as it passed them, practically stopping entirely as their windows aligned. It was far too dark to see inside the coach, but a strange prickling lifted her skin. She felt eyes on her.

Patrick opened the door, and Cassie quickly took his hand to descend. By the time she was on the pavements, the coach had picked up speed again and was continuing away.

"That coach," Cassie said to him. "Was it following us?"

"Now that you mention it, milady, I did notice it behind

us since Limehouse," Patrick said. They watched it go around the oval-shaped square, then out of sight.

"Is everything all right, milady?" Ruth asked.

"Yes," Cassie lied. Her maid would have dissolved into panic if she told her the truth: that she was quite certain they'd been followed since leaving Duke's. And that she was almost positive Mr. Youngdale had been in that coach.

Now, he knew where she lived.

CHAPTER SEVENTEEN

Nothing had gone according to plan at Duke's, and though Grant had at first laid all the blame at Cassie's feet, it didn't take him long to realize *he* had been the larger problem. Not her.

The moment he'd seen her walking through the roiling crowds at the boxing club, he'd been both incensed and vindicated—he'd known she would come. He'd been looking for her as soon as he'd stepped inside the warehouse. Telling her to stay away, that it was no place for a lady, might have worked for any other typical woman of quality, but for Cassandra Sinclair, it had been woefully inadequate. It been all but an invitation.

As Sir had searched the crowd for the high roller he regularly saw at boxing matches, Grant's mind had been on Cassie and whether she would come alone or with another—and who that *other* might be. Hugh had sensed his distraction and attempted to recapture it by knocking his elbow into his ribs.

"Are you listening? Youngdale is here." Hugh discreetly

looked toward a grouping of men on another section of staging around the raised ring. Sir began to describe which one he was, but it wasn't necessary. The healing gashes along one man's cheek were all the proof Grant needed.

"We'll follow him after the match," Grant said, and he'd had every intention to do just that.

But then, a vision in dark rose pink had stolen his entire focus. Across the ring, Cassie had approached the staging opposite his with her younger brother and the nettlesome Mr. Forsythe.

She didn't see Grant right away as she took her seat, conversing mainly with Forsythe while Tobias stole sips from his pocket flask. That she would arrange to attend the boxing match with another man, one who was *truly* pressing his suit, pushed a thorn right into his side. It continued to grow and twist as the match began, his temper stoking only higher when Cassie at last saw him. He'd remained standing so that she would. The pleasure he'd taken in seeing her rattled, in watching her squirm, had been alarming, even to him. It had been disturbingly arousing to see the effect on her. And when Youngdale had taken notice of Cassie after the strike in the ring sent blood spattering onto her face, Grant hadn't been able to stay in his seat another moment.

He hadn't been there in the alley to protect her when she'd been attacked, and with Youngdale's eyes on Cassie again, Grant's sole desire had been to shield her. He'd been no better than a caveman dragging her away from Forsythe and Tobias, and the fight she'd put up had been just enough for him nearly lose his wits.

"I'll pour you another if you insist but trust me—it

won't help erase whatever is eating at you," Hugh said from where he stood at his desk.

Grant had gone to Hugh's Berkeley Square home after leaving Cassie with Tobias in Limehouse. The viscount and Sir had shown up shortly afterward, though their expressions had said everything: they had not succeeded in following Youngdale.

"The blighter vanished like smoke," Sir had said.

All was not lost.

The previous day, while Grant had been cleaning up Tris's battered face, the driver had shared more about Isabel's aunt. He had a name and address, thanks to Isabel placing her trust in him, and Tris shared it in the hope that the aunt might know something. Grant and Hugh would visit the aunt, and perhaps she would know where to find Youngdale. Failing that, they would visit Youngdale's brother, the baronet. His residence had been listed in Debrett's, and if they could come up with a believable story, the baronet might reveal where his brother resided.

Hugh poured the third finger of whisky despite his warning and handed it to Grant. The two of them were alone, Sir having gone off to his room.

"Something tells me you're not pacing my study near to midnight because you are concerned for this missing woman."

"Of course I am concerned." He wasn't cruel or unfeeling.

However, his friend was correct. Isabel's unknown whereabouts wasn't why he'd downed his first and second fingers of whisky so quickly. With every next sip, he hoped the spirits would douse the coals in his gut.

Why couldn't he stop thinking about the reckless woman? He hadn't been this out of sorts for years. Not since the last time Cassie had twisted him up with a distorted tangle of irritation, amusement, and longing. That had been in Dover, when Audrey had been accused of murder, and Grant had followed Hugh to the seaside town to help in any way he possibly could. That Cassie had been detained alongside Audrey had, of course, been a concern too.

He lowered his glass of whisky.

Reflecting on that case, Grant allowed that he'd thought of Cassie more than a few times as he'd taken the Dover Road from London on horseback in freezing temperatures. He'd arrived no better than a block of ice. And Cassie's icy reception of him had put him in an irritable fit of pique. From then on, he'd been certain to cut with sarcasm and wound with acerbic wit. It had kept her loathing him. It had kept her at a good distance. Far enough away so that he couldn't begin to so much as like her.

Any proximity would be dangerous. *She* was dangerous, as was the way his body responded to her. No other woman —more experienced, worldly, or confident—did this to him. Made him feel mixed-up and in such disarray.

"All right, you're concerned," Hugh assented. "But you have another concern, and she consumed your entire focus tonight."

Grant swirled the whisky in his glass. His friend was correct. She *had* consumed his focus. He'd nearly lost control.

"Our conversation earlier in the park was cut short. What do you know about Renfry?" Hugh asked after another moment had passed. "Everything?"

"Everything." He put the glass to his lips, but then lowered it. "Including about Sweden."

Mentioning a baby explicitly would be too free. There was always the chance a footman or maid could be listening at the door.

The viscount's inspection narrowed. "She trusts you."

Grant heard another question underneath the statement: *Why?* He didn't have the answer to that. Cassie shouldn't have trusted him, not after the stunt he'd pulled with the false courtship. And yet, she'd willingly told him about Renfry and the baby. Albeit, the way she'd been acting since, she regretted doing so.

"Speak plainly, Marsden," Grant said irritably. "Say what you want to say."

"If you are aware of what happened with Renfry, then you will understand our concern for her."

"That I will misuse her the way he did?" Grant set down his whisky, no longer inclined to linger.

Hugh shook his head, but he still looked conflicted. "No, I know you will not. But you've made it clear in the past that marriage is not something you will revisit. Why are you spending time with her if you don't intend for anything serious, and what does it have to do with the marquess's demand that you marry?"

Grant had considered telling Hugh about his father's threat to cut him off. As he knew about the clinic, he would understand why Grant needed that money, and he would have most likely offered to fund it himself. But he could not have accepted his friend's charity. Grant's pride was too damn fierce for it. Applying to a benefactress like Madame

Archambeau, with whom he did not have any ties, was much more palatable.

The knocker on the front door slammed down three times, saving him from answering Hugh's question. In the quiet of the house, it was as loud as a pistol shot. Hugh went to the entrance hall, to see who could be calling at such an hour. Grant followed, and they arrived in time to see Basil, Hugh's valet, approaching the door.

"Where is that lazy footman?" Basil asked, exasperated. "I am a valet; I am not supposed to be opening doors."

He wore his nightrobe and a cap, and if Grant had to wager, he'd been on his way to the kitchens for a midnight sweet.

"The *viscount* is more than capable of opening said door if the *valet* thinks it is too beneath him," Hugh grumbled.

"If it is beneath me—and it is—then it is miles beneath yourself. A viscount should never open his own front door." Basil rushed to beat Hugh to it, muttering under his breath. He and his longtime valet often traded barbs. In fact, it seemed to be their preferred method of communication. However, Hugh would never have dismissed Basil; the valet's fussy loftiness could not mask his true affection for the viscount, and as Basil was with him long before he became a peer, Hugh trusted him implicitly.

Basil whisked the door open, and standing on the front step, wearing a dark velvet cloak, was a woman. The hood was pulled up around her so thoroughly, it nearly engulfed her face.

"May I help you, my lady?" Basil intoned, his request drenched with annoyance.

She pushed back her hood, and Grant swore under his breath.

"Cassie?" Hugh crossed the entrance hall as Basil stepped aside, allowing her to enter. As soon as she did, she set eyes on Grant and came to a halt.

"I didn't know you would be here," she said.

He hardened himself to her obvious disappointment and said nothing.

"What are you doing out at this hour?" Hugh asked. "Has something happened?"

She hesitated as she looked at Grant, but then commenced removing her cloak. Basil collected it and her gloves, and then with a raised brow—likely of censure—moved off. Cassie started for Hugh's study with all the familiarity of a frequent guest. "I was followed home from Duke's."

Grant went rigid. "Followed by whom?"

Hugh shut them into the study after asking Basil to summon the viscountess.

Cassie went directly toward the fire. She was still wearing the dress from the boxing match, but her face had been cleaned of any blood, and her hair had been loosened and plaited into a single thick braid. It rested over her shoulder. "I have no proof, but I believe it was Mr. Youngdale."

Grant stalked to the window and peered outside into the square but saw no conveyances outside the viscount's home. Not even Cassie's.

"Tell me you did not walk here," he said, letting the curtain drop. Her home was less than a five-minute stroll from Hugh's, the two squares adjacent to one another. But it was late, and if she'd been followed, whoever it had been might still have been hanging about.

"If it would make you less upset, then no, I didn't walk." She paused. "But you should know that is a lie."

Grant flexed his hands into fists. What had she been thinking, going out alone?

"Why would he follow you?" Hugh asked before Grant could react. The viscount's ability to remain focused on the immediate problem only highlighted Grant's own much narrower focus. It converged entirely on the woman holding her hands to the flames.

"That is my question too," she replied. "If Mr. Youngdale has Isabel, why would he care to follow me?"

"You've likely left his face scarred," Grant reminded her. "He could be interested in revenge."

"Whatever the reason, he now knows where you live," Hugh said with a heavy sigh. He tossed back the rest of his drink.

Cassie wrapped her arms around herself with an appropriate amount of apprehension. "That is why I came here. I instructed my footmen to lock the doors and windows and not allow anyone inside for the time being, but I didn't want to stay there tonight."

"Fournier will hear of it soon," Grant said.

Cassie grimaced. "I am aware of that, thank you."

"If you'd simply stayed away from Duke's, like I asked, this wouldn't have happened." The moment he said the words, he regretted them.

Her fingers tightened where they clutched her arms. "You have already made yourself perfectly clear on that point,

Lord Thornton. Would you please stop harping before I am driven to slit my wrists?"

"I'll stop when I believe a modicum of good sense has leaked its way into your reckless mind."

Her eyes flashed. "Do not boss me about! You have no right."

"Even if it is for your own good? Your own safety?"

"I will decide what is and isn't safe, *for myself*!"

"You've done a hell of a job of that so far!"

Their shouts ebbed, and at a soft clearing of a throat, Grant belatedly remembered they weren't alone. At the study doors. Audrey stood with Hugh, and they looked on with interest.

Cassie turned away and attempted to compose herself.

"Cassie will be staying with us tonight," Hugh murmured to Audrey, who looked intrigued but refrained from questions.

"Of course. I will tell Mrs. Carrigan to prepare your guest room," the viscountess said, then, with a hand to her husband's arm, added, "There is a matter I'd like to discuss, if you have a moment?"

Hugh showed reluctance to leave the study, but with a sharp look from his wife, conceded. It was evident Audrey only wanted to draw him away to give Grant and Cassie a moment alone.

Once they were, and the flames crackling in the hearth were the only sounds in the room, his storming temper calmed. He'd probably looked and sounded deranged just now. Running a hand through his hair, he blew out a gust of air.

"I'm sorry," he said, breaking the silence. "I shouldn't have shouted at you."

She eyed him warily, as though questioning if the apology was genuine. Grant went to Hugh's desk and poured her a finger of whisky. The other night at Thornton House, she'd seemed more settled when she held something in her hands.

He brought it to her, and she accepted, her fingers closing around the cut crystal. He'd never truly observed her hands before. They were small, her fingers slim and dainty. For a heartbeat, he recalled the press of them against his chest in Lady Dutton's closet. He dashed the image away.

"I don't usually raise my voice," he said. It was true. He found a silver-tongued remark, or some well-timed sarcasm could be just as effective. More so, even. But with Cassie... his temper had never fluctuated so rapidly or easily.

"Neither do I," she said, absentmindedly sliding a fingertip over the rim of the glass. "Well, that's not necessarily true, I do shout. Though usually just at Michael."

Grant wasn't entirely certain he liked being lumped in with her brother.

But at least for the moment they'd found a tenuous peace.

"Youngdale attacked you in that alley, and now he may have followed you home." When Cassie began to rise to her own defense again, he held up a hand. "I don't want any harm to come to you, that is why I get angry. When I think of any man hurting you, causing you any pain, I want to crush him in my bare hands." At the awed parting of her lips, he caught himself. "Forgive me for being a boorish male."

She deflated, the argument she'd been about to

commence fizzling. Instead, she took a deep sip of her whisky and shrugged.

"If you can apologize, I suppose I can make the effort as well." She gathered a breath. "I wasn't needed at Duke's. My presence there made no difference and likely made things worse. I'm sorry." She spoke hurriedly, and then took another sip of her drink. To chase away the discomfort of the apology, he imagined. Grant tried to suppress a smile, but she still saw it.

"Are you laughing at me?"

"Not at all, but did that apology draw blood? It looked painful."

Cassie affected insult but let out a light laugh. Some of the tension left his shoulders.

"I like the sound of that."

She continued to smile. "Of what?"

"Your laughter. I haven't heard it in a while."

He remembered one time in particular when he'd raced her to the top of the Grand Shaft in Dover; she'd tripped on a step, and when he'd caught her, she'd giggled. It had been utterly girlish and so unlike her that he'd worn a wide grin the rest of the way to the top. They'd arrived gasping for air and in between gasps, argued over who had won. It seemed ages ago now. Another lifetime.

And yet, even then, she'd been keeping her secret about Renfry and the baby. Cassie was a *mother*. One who had been forced to make a heartbreaking sacrifice. Her pain had to be fathomless. He wished he could fix it. Take it away or make it better somehow.

Grant realized she was no longer smiling. Neither was he.

They stood in close conference in front of the fire, the flames lighting half of her in a golden dance.

"There aren't many reasons to laugh lately," Cassie said.

He was suddenly desperate to make her smile again. To make her laugh. The corners of her eyes bowed upward whenever she did, and the bridge of her nose crinkled adorably.

"I want to change that," he said, before he could think.

She cocked her head. "Why?"

His immediate answer was simple: Because he wanted her to be happy. But there was much more to it. Why did he care about her happiness? Why did the things she thought and felt seem to rule him as of late?

And why did his attention keep diverting to her mouth?

On impulse, he reached for her. His hand brushed tentatively against the deep rose silk. To touch her was the only thought firing into his brain. Once his fingertips made contact, Cassie's lips, which he'd been so studiously watching, parted. Grant filled his palm with silk as he pressed his hand against her hip, the same way he had at the clinic. Her top teeth bit the soft mound of her bottom lip, and her whisky glass, loose in her grip, tipped. He caught the glass, supporting her fingers around it.

"Grant," she whispered.

He gently prized the glass from her and placed it on the mantel, his full attention never leaving her eyes. Her breaths shortened, and her pulse visibly beat against the curve of her throat. He placed his fingertips against her warm skin there and felt the quickened throb.

"Cassie." He heard his voice, but it was trancelike. Far away and muffled. He hardly recognized it.

She didn't respond, but kept her face lifted to his. As her eyes dipped toward his mouth, he read the unmistakable invitation. Stronger and surer than the one in her eyes the other night in his study. He'd resisted then. He should now, too, but as the tip of his nose came against hers, and her warm breaths gusted against his mouth, the last scrap of Grant's resistance foundered. His lips grazed hers.

He'd intended for a gentle, appraising kiss, to give her the chance to pull back or push him away. But at the first caress of her velvet lips, all gentlemanly intentions dissolved. He fused his mouth to hers, and the fingers gathering the silk at her hip dug in and hitched her closer. Grant reveled in the feel of her body pressed against his, and in her soft, decadent whimper when he impatiently nudged her lips apart. In a strike of victory, Cassie's indecision evaporated. Her tongue met his, and the world around them fragmented and fell away. There was only Cassie and her mouth and her sumptuous figure, sealing itself to him. The smoked spice of whisky on her tongue curled through him as he consumed her kisses, one after another, each rising in fevered need. He filled his palms with as much of her body as he could, spending an ungodly amount of attention to the lush swells of her backside.

Breathless and mindless, he barely stopped himself from sweeping her feet from the floor and cradling her into his arms. This wasn't his house. He couldn't toss her over his shoulder and climb to his room where he'd lay her down on his bed, peel the silk from her body and sink into her. He groaned at the sinful image. Cassie, feeling the vibration of it, gasped into his mouth. Her palms, braced against his shoulders, slid down his chest. Then lower, against his stomach. Any more of this and he wouldn't be able to stop.

With more fortitude than he'd ever shown in his life, Grant clamped his hands down over hers and broke away from her mouth. Her swollen, pink lips competed with the invading reality that this was Hugh's study, and that he or Audrey or one of their nosy servants could come barging in at any moment. She breathed heavily, her eyes two smoldering coals as she came down from the same frenzy.

"Cassie," he said again, his own breaths ragged.

He wasn't given a chance to say anything more. Sprightly footfalls in the entrance hall beyond the closed study doors drove them to release each other. Grant raked a hand through his hair and scrubbed at his mouth as Cassie whirled toward the fireplace to straighten her gown and hair. He was smoothing the lapel of his jacket when Hugh entered, followed closely by his housekeeper, Mrs. Carrigan.

"Cassie, your room is ready. Thornton, Norris can drive you back to your home—"

"I will walk," Grant interrupted him, desperate for the cold air to douse the fire consuming his good sense.

"You're sure?" Hugh asked.

"It's less than a mile, I'll be fine," he said, far too abruptly to be anything other than suspicious. He turned his back on Hugh's narrowing stare and met Cassie's red-cheeked and red-lipped face. Hugh would certainly recognize the complexion of a recently plundered mouth. *Christ.* Grant bowed. "Good night, Lady Cassandra."

"Lord Thornton," she said, still rather breathless.

He left without a glance toward his friend, though he felt

Hugh's eyes on him. As he collected his coat and hat, and then emerged into the brisk December night air, he could still taste Cassie on his tongue. Could still feel her warm body against his. Bloody hell. Grant walked faster, the notion that everything was about to go to shit snapping at his heels.

CHAPTER EIGHTEEN

Thick green carpet absorbed the steady sound of Cassie's pacing. The blush of dawn painted the bare tree limbs in the park at Berkeley Square a pinkish orange, and on every turn at the window, she paused to observe the coming daylight.

She'd gone to bed several hours ago but had barely slept. After Grant left the study, Hugh had been gentlemanly enough not to mention what he and Mrs. Carrigan had so obviously interrupted. Cassie's lips had felt distended, and her flush had been so thorough, her palm had been like ice when she'd pressed it to her hot cheek. Wholly out of sorts, she'd bid the viscount a distracted goodnight and followed the housekeeper to an upstairs room.

A maid waiting for her there had efficiently removed her gown and dressed her in a borrowed nightrail; one of Audrey's, to be sure. When Cassie had finally been alone, she'd perched at the edge of the tester bed and put her trembling fingers to her lips.

She'd still been able to feel Grant's mouth, his bruising kisses, and the ardent, nearly desperate kneading of his hands. Her skin prickled where he'd touched, and where he hadn't, there was a hollow ache. A few times now, Cassie had wanted him to kiss her, and when he hadn't, she'd imagined what it might have been like. However, none of her imaginings measured up to the reality. In the study, when he'd crushed her to him, he'd seared her with a fire inside him, one he'd barely been holding in check.

It hadn't been anything close to what she'd felt with Renfry. With him, her mind had been spinning during his kisses, thoughts and doubts and questions all swarming. But under Grant's mouth, only one word had filled her head: *more*.

At Hope House, some of the women had spoken plainly about the pleasures of coupling. There seemed to be a consensus among them that they were often made weak by it. Cassie hadn't understood, not truly, considering her wholly unpleasant first—and only—experience. But now, after Grant's kiss, when her sole desire had been for his hands to touch more of her, his mouth to stay on hers... How different might the act of lovemaking be with someone as skilled as Grant?

She stopped at the window overlooking the square and gripped the embrasure. Her pulse picked up speed and a fine sweat bloomed on her neck and back. Thank providence things ended the way they had. She couldn't afford to be made weak-minded. With Renfry, she'd allowed passion to dictate her actions—though not her own passion. Her concern had been for Renfry's pleasure. *His* passion. Pleasing *him*. She'd been so consumed with giving Renfry what he desired and thus ensuring her place as his wife, that nothing else had mattered.

But with Grant's devouring kisses and impatient hands practically incinerating her, pleasure was all that had mattered. Cassie released the embrasure and touched her lips again. If Grant's kisses alone could affect her so thoroughly, she wondered what spending the night in his arms would do to her.

She whisked her hand from her mouth and curled it into a ball. *Stop*. What was she thinking? In a fortnight or two, Grant Thornton would have no more use for her. They were only spending time together because of the ruse, and because he'd coerced her to do so! And yet, she'd still become a willing lump of desire in his arms. Where was her bloody backbone?

Grant Thornton was a Lothario, and everyone knew it. *Of course* she had become a thoughtless puddle of need—he was well practiced in making women turn into them.

Their argument last night had merely stoked their tempers and with their blood high, things had gotten out of hand. It didn't mean anything. It certainly didn't to Grant.

Gripped by sudden restlessness, Cassie rung for a maid. Though it was still early, the staff would be awake and preparing for the day. She needed to dress and go home. Grosvenor Square was so close, she could see the rooftops of its houses from the guest room window. Mr. Youngdale might have followed her home, but by the light of day, she didn't feel nearly as afraid as she had after seeing that coach slowly roll past her own. She was safe, while Isabel wasn't. There was work to do if they were going to find her.

The maid came to help her back into her gown, already

having freshened it, and she was bringing up Cassie's hair when Audrey knocked upon the guest room door.

"Tell me you're not leaving already. I thought we'd take breakfast together."

Cassie sat still as the maid pinned her hair and avoided making direct eye contact in the mirror with her former sister-in-law. Surely, Hugh had told her what he suspected happened in the study.

"I'm not very hungry, and I should return to let my staff know I am safe. Thank you for allowing me to stay the night."

Audrey came to stand near the maid. Several beats of silence passed. Finally, Cassie gave in. She looked into the mirror, and the viscountess's brow arched with mischief.

"That will be all, Ann, thank you," she said, dismissing the servant after the last pin was placed.

Cassie sighed as the maid left. "Hugh told you."

Audrey moved to a set of chairs near the fireplace. She appeared more tired than usual as she sat, and Cassie suddenly felt guilty for having imposed on them last night.

"He suspected that Grant may have..." She waved a hand. Cassie spun around in her chair to face her.

"He kissed me." The confession sent a surge of unexpected trembling down her arms and up her back. Thinking about it was one thing; speaking of it was another entirely.

In her chair, Audrey sat up a bit taller. "You gave him permission to do so?"

Briefly, Cassie recalled parting her lips and welcoming the thrust of his tongue. She'd moaned against his mouth, and while she'd at first been humiliated at making the involuntary sound, it had only seemed to make Grant clutch her more possessively.

She nodded. "I did."

The viscountess blinked a few times and seemed at a loss for words. Though only for a moment. True to her style, Audrey got right to the point. "So then these courtship rumors are true?"

A spate of panic cinched Cassie's throat. As close as she was with Audrey, she couldn't tell her about Grant's scheme to put off his father's demands, or his threat to expose her involvement with Hope House if she did not go along with it. Not only would it reveal Cassie's secret life, but it would cast Grant in an awful light. And well it should! Gracious, had she lost all her wits? The man was a reprobate for intimidating her into this entire fiasco. If he'd simply turned a blind eye to what he'd found at Hope House when he'd come to treat Dorie, none of this would have happened. Instead, he'd found a way to manipulate the situation to his benefit. Good lord, *why* had she allowed him to kiss her?

And despite everything, why did she so desperately want him to do it again?

Cassie shifted in her seat, then stood up. "I don't know."

It was a pathetic answer, and Audrey's stern look said as much.

"Do you have feelings for him?" she asked. "Real feelings, I mean."

Cassie frowned. "As opposed to false feelings?"

Did Audrey suspect something about the courtship ruse?

The viscountess stood, and though she was no taller than Cassie, she possessed a forbidding conviction. "No, as opposed to girlish infatuation. Years ago, before Hugh and I married, I suspected that you might have an interest in Grant."

"I thought him handsome, yes," Cassie said. "But all he had to do was speak a few times and I found I loathed him more."

He'd been arrogant and sarcastic. Just being near him had set her nerves tingling with irritation. It wasn't much different these days, only her tingling nerves now stemmed from something else altogether.

Audrey gave her an indulgent smile. "Yes, loathing was what it appeared to be. You certainly pushed him away with an abrasiveness you didn't implement with anyone else."

"What are you saying?"

"You put up walls around yourself whenever he was near," she answered readily.

Cassie shrugged. "He was infuriating."

"I understand completely," Audrey said with a laugh. "Hugh drove me mad when I first met him. Everything he did and said would anger me. There was a reason why, but it was one I didn't want to understand, so I chose not to."

When Audrey met Hugh, she'd been married to Cassie's oldest brother, Philip, the Duke of Fournier. While away in France, he'd drowned, and after a year of mourning, Audrey had accepted Hugh's offer of marriage. Of course, Cassie knew that her former sister-in-law's feelings for the Bow Street officer had developed long before her mourning ended. In fact, she'd suspected they had begun even before Philip's death.

The viscountess's expression turned solemn, and she looked to her hands, folded in front of her. "I was quick to anger because I wanted to protect myself from what I was feeling for Hugh. I wanted to keep him at a distance, and antagonism is an excellent way to do that."

Cassie nodded. What Audrey said made sense, and she had to admit that whenever she and Grant argued, it gave her a reason to walk away. It was the moments when she could find no fault in him, like at Church Street after his thoughtful handling of Amir, and last night, when he'd apologized and then made her laugh, that she felt in danger of liking him too much. Because if she admitted to liking him a little, what was to stop her from liking him more than that?

"I told him everything," she said. "About Renfry. About the baby."

And he had not pushed her away. He'd shown compassion, not judgment.

Audrey nodded. "Because you trust him."

But how could she? It was utterly foolish. She'd been a fool before with Renfry, and she'd paid an awful price for it.

Cassie shook her head. "It doesn't matter. I've proven to be a terrible judge of character before. Now, I really must go."

She started for the door, eager to be gone. Audrey's long exhalation was audible, but she didn't say anything more as she followed Cassie and summoned a carriage to bring her back the short distance to Grosvenor Square. The viscountess held up a hand at her assertion that she could reach home on foot faster than it would take for a carriage to be prepared for her. She gave in and had tea with Audrey while waiting for Carrigan to come around the front of the residence. No more talk of Grant ensued, thank goodness, though she could see that Audrey was still thoughtful about him.

Once at home, Cassie informed her small staff that they

were to continue being cautious, but that there was likely no immediate danger. After bathing, her sleepless night sneaked up on her and she couldn't keep her eyes open. She slept until noon. Almost as soon as she opened her eyes, foggy from sleep, the question of why Mr. Youngdale would have followed her carriage was waiting for her. Proper sleep seemed to have returned her priorities.

Grant suggested he might want revenge for scarring his face, but she wasn't convinced. If he had Isabel back in his clutches, what was he doing out at Duke's? Why had he spent time following Cassie, when he could have been with Isabel, forcing her to marry him?

Around two o'clock, she summoned Patrick. She'd sent a message to Elyse the evening before, informing her of Isabel's disappearance from Church Street, but now wanted to be at Hope House, if only to distract herself. Ever since Grant had come to the safe house as Dr. Brown and discovered her there, she'd started to feel the divide between her two lives more keenly. Not to mention everything involving Grant and his scheme had occupied more of her time and energy. She needed to get back to what she'd been doing before and reorganize her priorities.

"Milady," the footman, Pierce, said as she entered the foyer to make her way out front. He presented a bouquet of hot house flowers, a small card inserted between the green stems and foliage. With some reluctance, she took the card and read it:

Dinner Monday night at Lindstrom House. I'll fetch you at six.

A barb of dread partnered with a tremor of anticipation. She could not think of anything she would like to do less than attend a dinner with Grant's father. And yet at the same time, the thought of seeing Grant again stirred the phantom pressure of his lips against hers, the greedy clutch of his arms, and the hard muscle of his abdomen when her hands had slipped to his waist.

She gritted her teeth and pocketed the note. If she'd thought for one moment that the physician would wake up with a change of heart about his scheme, she'd been proven wrong. The courtship was still to play out.

CHAPTER NINETEEN

By the time Monday night arrived, frustration had settled like a stone in Grant's chest. Dinner with his father had loomed like a ominous black cloud for the last two days, and it had cast its shadow over everything, it seemed.

Saturday at the clinic, plenty of patients had come in for one thing or another, but he had not seen Amir or his father. The boy's sutures needed checking; without proper care and attention, they would fester. Surely, Mr. Mansouri would have sent for him had Amir turned feverish, or the wound red and infected. Still, he and Hannah waited an extra half hour past their regular closing time to give them a chance to show. They hadn't.

Then, arriving home, a message from Hugh had been waiting. Mrs. Lydia Montrose had denied any knowledge of where her niece could be. In the aunt's opinion, the ungrateful girl had captured a wealthy man's heart and had squandered it by running away. The only helpful thing she provided was Youngdale's address, but when Hugh had called on him, the staff said their master was out and that Miss Isabel had not been seen as of late. With no solid legal reason to force entry, all Hugh could then do was place someone as a look out. Unsurprisingly, Sir had volunteered. But there was still no sign of Youngdale. Sunday night, Grant returned to Duke's for a match, but he had not been among the spectators either. It was as if he'd disappeared. Or was lying low.

And, of course, there was Cassie.

As Merryton pulled along the curb outside twelve Grosvenor Square, Grant regretted every single decision he'd made for the last fortnight. But none so much as the one he'd made Friday night in Hugh's study. Though, kissing Cassie hadn't been as much a decision as it had been a compulsion.

Grant had cursed under his breath the entire walk back to Thornton House. Storming inside, he'd barked at his butler to lock up for the night, taken the stairs to his room like a tempest, and slammed the bedroom door in his valet's face. But one look at the bed in which he'd so recently imagined laying Cassie down on, stripping her gown from her body, and making love to her, and he'd ached with the solitary need for release.

He wasn't often in a foul temper, and so the servants were sure to talk, but he did not care. He'd lost control in Hugh's study. Hell, if he'd been assured of their privacy, he would have laid Cassie onto the carpet in front of the fireplace and taken her there and then.

Had that happened, when the sun rose, he would have had no choice but to go to Fournier and offer for Cassie's hand. *In truth.*

That was something he could not do. That he would not do.

Cassie's footman allowed him in, and Grant held himself rigidly while he waited. He'd forced all his frustration from the last few days to stay lodged where it had accumulated, right in the center of his chest. He would make no more mistakes.

He was staring holes in the parquet flooring when a throat cleared softly. Cassie had come to stand in front of him. He straightened but didn't look her directly in the eye as he murmured a good evening. She held still and quiet as her maid helped her into her pelisse, thankfully covering up the emerald satin gown she wore; a hasty assessment had shown it displayed a healthy amount of decolletage. Grant refused to let his eyes linger.

Without more conversation, they got underway, the two of them alone, enclosed in the interior of his carriage. He breathed evenly and kept his attention on the window. Flakes of wet snow collected on the glass. The silence intensified with every passing minute. His fingers drummed on the black superfine encasing his thighs. He needed to say something.

Grant turned away from the window, and she was waiting for him. Their eyes connected, and he could not look away. Not without appearing cowardly.

"Mr. Youngdale hasn't been located."

Cassie lifted her chin, and he saw her disappointment. She wanted to speak about the kiss. He could not think of anything he would like to discuss less.

"Hugh suggested he could be keeping Isabel in an undisclosed location. Or perhaps the aunt was lying, and she is helping Youngdale after all."

He kept his words flat. Emotionless.

Cassie took a bracing breath. "Shouldn't we speak of what happened the other night?"

His eyes clashed with hers again. He then squared his shoulders. "No. It was a mistake. Let's leave it at that."

Cassie stared at him as if a realization was dawning, one that now slid through her like oil. She made no reply, and Grant again looked out the window. "The marquess is going to test the veracity of this courtship. Are you prepared to keep up your end of the bargain?"

"*My end*? You rule over all of this charade, Lord Thornton. Not me."

He looked at her again, the void between them yawning wide and hollow. *Good*. It was what he needed.

"Can you make the marquess believe you are interested in my suit or can you not?" he asked.

Cassie breathed thinly, her temper beginning to visibly flare. And why shouldn't it? He was being unforgivably callous.

"I will make him believe it." She ground out each word. At the chilled glare that followed, Grant had the notion that she was devising something in that crafty mind of hers.

Neither of them spoke another word as the carriage bore them across the Thames, toward Lindstrom House in Kennington. For as long as Grant could remember, he'd considered the place a prison. Though it faced the distinctive and landscaped Oval, it was the wild lawns out back of Lindstrom House where Grant had preferred to spend his time when he'd been younger. There were some outbuildings where he'd taken shelter if the weather was cold or rainy, and he'd kept them stuffed with supplies—hampers of food, pilfered bottles of his father's good whisky, books, and blankets to keep warm.

Almost always, one of his brothers would find him and drag him back to the house, where he'd receive a lecture from the marquess regarding his irresponsible behavior and commands to strive to be more like Lawrence or Harold, or at the very least, like James.

As the carriage stopped, Grant realized he was about to lead Cassie into a house that had, from the beginning, seemed to swallow him whole whenever he entered it. Not once had he possessed even a shred of true confidence within these walls, and if he was going to pull off these next few hours with any semblance of success, he would need all the confidence he possessed.

Grant handed Cassie down onto the pavement out front of Lindstrom House and noted that her slippers made deep impressions in the snowfall. By the time they made it to the front step, they would be soaked.

"I can carry you, if you'd prefer to keep your feet out of the snow," he said, though immediately wished he hadn't offered. He could not put his hands on any part of her body again.

"Carry me? Don't be absurd," she snapped, and then started forward without him.

Half thankful and half vexed, he followed, flecks of snow shuttling into his eyes. The front door whisked open before he could bring down the knocker, and upon entering, the voices of his brothers and their wives barreled into his ears. They were a loud lot and always had been. His father's longtime butler, Harding, greeted them with a bow.

"Welcome, my lord. My lady," he said, taking a second bow toward Cassie. The footman, a new one Grant did not know, divested her of her snowy pelisse and gloves, and then took Grant's outer trappings.

"The marquess and his guests are in the drawing room," Harding intoned.

The butler started away, expecting them to follow. With an arm gesture for Cassie to proceed, she gave Grant her back and crossed the entrance lobby. Gray was the overarching theme inside Lindstrom House. A cold pewter. Grant recalled yellows and greens when he'd been young and his mother had been alive, but after her death, the marquess had tried to eradicate all traces of her. Any memory of her would be salt in an open wound. When Sarah had died, it was the closest Grant had ever been to understanding his father.

A moment before Harding announced them, Grant braced himself. Then slipped his arm under Cassie's, hooking it. The touch sent a bolt through him, and surprise was still bright on her face too when they entered the room together.

His father stood, along with Lawrence, Harold, James, and Penelope's husband, Alfred.

"Lady Cassandra, may I present my father, the Marquess of Lindstrom; his heir, Lawrence, the Earl of Cranfield and his wife Lady Cranfield; Lord Harold Thornton and his wife, Lady Priscilla; Lord James Thornton; and Mr. Alfred Farrington and his wife, my sister, Mrs. Penelope Farrington."

Had he been in any typical humor, having spat out that

mouthful of introductions, Grant would have made some quip about his family having more members than the Houses of Parliament. But he couldn't find it within him. A heaviness had settled in his chest and stamped out any humor at all.

His siblings and their spouses, and his father too, greeted Cassie in turn, who continued to clutch Grant's arm. He was almost positive she was tightening her grip due to nervousness. Even still, he was entirely too aware of her arm against his.

"We wondered if the snow had hampered your carriage," Harold said.

Grant frowned. "It's nothing. A dusting at most."

"It's going to increase," Harold, ever the fusspot, argued. "I think we'd be better off leaving for Town sooner rather than later."

The marquess scoffed. "Stop stewing over the weather and act like a man, for God's sake."

Harold's wife, Priscilla speared her father-in-law with a look of animosity. It had never been much of a secret that she did not care for the marquess or his unrestricted ridicule. Just as it had never been much of a secret that the marquess did not care for Priscilla. Or *Prissy* as he tended to call her, both behind her back and to her face.

"Now, Lady Cassandra, what will you have? Peters, bring the lady a glass of wine."

The footman stationed near the table of decanters leaped to his task.

"Perhaps you could allow the lady to choose her own drink," Grant said, his jaw tight.

His father waved away the suggestion even as Cassie's

hand on his forearm flexed. Then, as if realizing that she still clung to him, she released him and stepped away.

"Ladies prefer wine, son. Or sherry. What of that, my lady, would you prefer sherry? Peters! Sherry."

The footman had already poured the wine but now lowered the carafe and reached for the sherry.

"I'll have a whisky," Cassie said. The room silenced.

Instantly, Grant recalled the intoxicating taste of whisky on her tongue as it curled around his Friday night. He swallowed a groan.

The marquess did not say a word as Peters splashed a finger of the good single malt into a glass. Penelope and her husband Alfred exchanged an amused look as Cassie took the whisky. In contradiction, Lawrence and his wife, Mary, could not mask their matching sneers. It was a rare thing for Lawrence or Mary to differ in opinion from the marquess, and right then Lindstrom was arching a brow in distaste.

"It isn't often a lady in Lindstrom House partakes in *uisge beatha*," James said, shifting his entertained grin toward Grant. Thought she was in confinement, James's wife Vera was the luckiest of them all for getting to sit out this dinner party.

Grant was scowling at his brother when he felt Cassie's hand glide against his. Startled, he stared at their joined hands, their fingers lacing together. He looked up and saw the glint of mischief shining in her eyes.

"I find that I prefer to toast good news with the water of life, Lord James," she said with a fetching grin as she affected an adoring gaze on Grant.

"And what good news do you bring, my lady?" the marquess asked.

A prickle of premonition arrived too late. Grant could not open his mouth and deflect her answer fast enough.

"I have accepted your son's offer of marriage, Lord Lindstrom," Cassie said as she stared into Grant's eyes, watching for his reaction.

He stopped breathing, but sound tolled through his ears —the rush of blood and shock and not a small amount of panic. *Offer of marriage?* The infuriating little hoyden! She'd promised to convince the marquess of her interest in his suit, and *this* is what she had settled on?

As he met her acerbic smile with a menacing grin of his own, voices began to feed back into his eardrums. His brothers' stiff congratulations and Penelope's genuine exclamation of surprise were pops of sound that grated on him. But his father's voice was the loudest. Even though Cassie had just shoved Grant one step closer to giving the old man what he wanted, he didn't offer well wishes but more criticism.

"Glad to see you've finally drummed up some sense, boy. That perpetual keening over a woman, dead nigh on a decade, was becoming rather tiresome."

The scornful remark was nothing new for Grant and so it did not lash at him as it had the first several times the marquess voiced it. However, Cassie's triumphant gleam snapped off, and she jerked a look of horror toward the marquess.

"How could you say something so cruel?"

The pleased grins all around turned to stone and cracked. The pressure of Cassie's fingers increased around his as she glared at his father. Grant gently squeezed her hand.

"Don't pay him any mind. He says what he thinks without concern for how it might sound," he told her. She blinked, the color rising in her cheeks. It wasn't embarrassment. No, he knew this particular shade of pink. It lit her face whenever she was provoked, and Cassie was truly appalled at Lord Lindstrom.

"You clearly do not know your future husband as well as the rest of us, Lady Cassandra. He's a stubborn, melancholy profligate that I expect you to take in hand."

She rocked back onto her heels, stunned anew. Grant should have warned her what his father was like. The threat to cut him off financially had not been a manipulative tool. It had been sincere as a bullet to the heart. Now at least she would believe him.

Coming through the drawing room doors, Harding announced dinner. Everyone leaped to flee the unexpected tension. Penelope came toward them, interest bowing her lips.

"Lady Cassandra, why don't you walk with me?"

Cassie's fingers loosened from Grant's and fell away. He shouldn't have felt the loss of them as keenly as he did, especially given the stunt she'd just pulled. It had been hasty and ill-judged, and she was going to regret it once her temper receded.

He followed Cassie and Penelope to the dining room, where the seating was arranged to make sure no one sat directly next to their spouse. Cassie was placed to the marquess's right, and to her right was James. Grant took a chair across the table, diagonal to her. While the wine was poured and the soup course delivered, her mouth remained a grim slash, her eyes furtively taking stock of Lord Lindstrom. For once, she was directing her discontent toward another man, and Grant found he was rather enjoying the show.

"Lady Cassandra, has my brother ever told you the story of his first patient?" James asked after the serving of the roast and a rather dull monologue from Lawrence about a finance bill moving through the House.

Cassie lowered her glass of wine and tossed a droll glance toward Grant. "He has not."

"It's nearly as tedious as that finance bill," Grant said with a shake of his head. This story never failed to amuse James, and every time he told the sodding thing, he injected more fanciful imaginings.

"The bill is an integral piece of legislation, Grant, though I don't expect you to know or care," Lawrence muttered.

"Monsieur Quack," James began, affecting a French accent and ignoring their oldest brother.

Cassie arched a brow. "Who?"

"Grant's first patient. Our pet duck."

"*James—*" Grant sighed, but his brother held up a hand.

"He loved that duck."

"I bloody hated the creature," he said. But James continued as if he'd said nothing.

"And when Monsieur Quack received grave wounds while fending off an attack by a vicious dog—"

"It was a broken wing from our aunt's decrepit poodle."

"—he spent all night tending to it, doing everything he could to save the poor thing."

Grant tossed back the rest of his wine. "I set the wing. It took ten minutes."

"It was then that we all knew he would be a marvelous physician," James concluded. Then with a wink toward Cassie, whose lips were pinned together against an amused grin, "Or perhaps just strangely attentive toward waterfowl."

Groans from around the table followed the well-worn finish to James's story. However, Cassie released a genuine laugh. The sound charged through Grant like a wallop of victory.

The marquess cleared his throat and put an end to the fragile good humor. "Here is another story, Lady Cassandra. When my youngest son expressed an interest in medicine, I told him to do as he pleased. You see, I didn't believe he had it in him to see through university let alone lower himself to actually work as a doctor."

Cassie's smile slipped, as did everyone else's.

"Imagine my surprise and horror when he hung out his shingle," Lindstrom went on, fingers tapping the table—a signal of his mounting displeasure.

Cassie cut her gaze toward Grant, but he didn't wish to meet it. No doubt it would be full of pity and disbelief at the marquess's derisive remarks. Instead, he kept his attention on his father, whose forehead creased with an expectant look.

"It is high time you put all that nonsense behind you, son. A new marriage is a fresh start, and I doubt His Grace will approve of his sister marrying a man who takes his profession more seriously than he does his title."

His father's disapproval had become so engrained in him that it often felt like an extra layer of skin. Not only did Lord Lindstrom despise the fact that his son worked, but he was also embarrassed by it. While the boy in him longed for his father's approval, the man in him did not require it. Both parts of him took an indecent amount of pleasure in the marquess's humiliation.

However, as he had not sufficiently warned Cassie of his

father's shortcomings, she once again balked at the old man. "Give up his profession?"

"Yes, quite right," he said.

"Or at least give up Miss Matthews," Mary said. "It is untoward for the young woman to be working alongside you, Grant, and well you know it."

"The girl is ruined. No one will have her now," the marquess went on, cutting his hand through the air dismissively. "But Lady Cassandra, surely, you do not desire to be the wife of a doctor. And well you shouldn't!"

Cassie didn't desire to be his wife at all, Grant thought, but she had just turned their courtship into a betrothal out of some fit of pique. Here was one such consequence—being subjected to his father's edicts.

He was oddly curious as to how she would handle it.

"Being a physician is entirely respectable." She brought her hands to the table, laying them flat on the lace cloth. "As is being the wife of one."

Grant hitched his chin, unable to peel his eyes from her. By her solemn expression, Cassie was entirely serious. The marquess, though, bayed laughter.

"I thought I told you that you would have to take him in hand, my lady," he said, busily cutting the meat on his plate instead of looking at her. "You must stand up to him or his selfishness will taint your position in society far faster than you might imagine."

Cassie leaned forward, her hands pressing against the table. "I think everyone here would be better served if someone were to stand up to *you*."

Someone at the table dropped a utensil onto their plate. All other noise ceased. The marquess set his fork and knife down. Slowly, he looked at Cassie as if he'd never seen her before.

Grant tensed, ready to intercede.

"That is an interesting observation, Lady Cassandra. Do explain your point." His father's solicitous tone was anything but genuine.

"I can see now why Grant has said so little about you," she started, undaunted. "Your willingness to disparage him so vocally to me upon our first meeting can be nothing compared to how callous you are toward him in private."

The marquess scoffed. "I have nothing to hide."

"Perhaps you *should* hide better your dislike for your son. It is entirely unbecoming, not to mention unfounded. He has helped countless people as a physician, and rather than be embarrassed by it, you should be proud."

Cassie pushed to her feet and with mounting wonder and admiration, Grant marveled at the picture she made as she glared down at his father, who looked as if he'd gotten a piece of gristle stuck in his throat.

The marquess touched his napkin to his mouth then tossed it onto his plate. He pushed back his chair and stood to meet Cassie's challenge. "Why you saucy little chit—"

Grant's fist came down onto the table like a pistol shot, rattling china and crystal all around. He was on his feet before his father could utter another sound.

"You will address her as Lady Cassandra, or you will not address her at all."

The marquess curled his lip, and Grant's reflexive ambition to always push his father one more inch took over. He met Cassie's wide eyes and added with a smirk, "Besides, I am the only man in this room permitted to call her a saucy little anything."

She struggled not to grin, but when James leaned back in his chair and chuckled, she gave in. Cassie covered her mouth and retook her seat. Down the table, Penelope cleared her throat and in a low, theatrical voice, said, *"I am the only man permitted to call her a saucy little anything."*

Priscilla snorted a laugh while taking a sip of her wine, which only caused James to laugh louder. The alarmed mood around the table shifted back toward normalcy, the tension breaking and vanishing in a wink. This was how it always was with this family, and as Lawrence admonished Penelope to show more reserve, and Harold asked Alfred, seated next to Priscilla, to pat his wife's back before she choked, even the marquess could not stop himself from rolling his eyes in capitulation.

Grant's attention sealed on the woman across from him as he retook his seat. Cassie's laughter joined that of his siblings, and as he had the previous night, he relished the sound of it. That she'd so swiftly stood up to his tyrant of a father should not have surprised him. But that she would defend him at all, after everything he'd done, left him curiously humbled. He didn't deserve it. Perhaps in this instance, his father had been correct after all.

The rest of the dinner unfolded without any more cross words or arguments, unless a debate about whist being the superior card game to *vingt-et-un* counted as cross words. The marquess had wisely forgone speaking to Cassie, allowing James to rule most of her attention, though several times Grant caught her furtive looks across the table.

The marquess had stood to announce brandy in the

billiards room and sherry for ladies in the drawing room when Harding joined them.

"My lord, I've reports that the roads to Town have become all but impassable. Several of the drivers are saying the snow has turned to ice. Perhaps it would be prudent to prepare guest rooms?"

As if magnetically, Grant's eyes went to Cassie just as hers landed on him. Words weren't necessary to know what was going through her mind. To be stuck here, in this house, under one roof for the night was more than just not ideal. It was dangerous. He swallowed hard, past a pulse of panic in his throat.

"Bring my driver. I will speak to him myself." Grant started for the door. Merryton would simply have to try to take them back across the river and toward home.

"Don't be a fool," Harold called. "You'll only be stranded in your carriage all night should you go off the road."

Grant slowed his stride. As overly nervous as his brother usually was, he had a good point. He could not risk an accident that would put Cassie in danger. Not even if the image of Cassie, sprawled in a bed in a guest room down the hall from him, gave him the first twinges of arousal.

"Prepare the rooms, Harding," Lindstrom snapped.

"I've been telling you for years to lease a house closer to Town for the winter months," Lawrence complained loudly to their father as everyone shuffled off toward their respective after-dinner rooms.

With a last wary glance toward Grant, Cassie linked arms with Penelope and followed them.

Hellfire. This was going to be a disaster.

CHAPTER
TWENTY

The guest room at Lindstrom House was ten paces across, from door to window, and eight paces long, from fireplace to the head of the tester bed. An hour after Cassie had been installed in the room, she had measured the width and length several times over with her restless walking. A maid had helped her undress and had given her a shift and dressing gown, the second night in which she'd needed to borrow such items.

Outside, the winds had increased to a howl. Icy snow pelted the glass windows. A fire in the small hearth was giving out some heat, but Cassie was producing enough for herself as she moved from one corner of the room to the other. The encounter with Lord Lindstrom had left her twitchy and impatient, her nerves frayed. But if she was being honest, the dinner had become an irreparable mess the moment she'd raised her glass of whisky and announced their betrothal.

Her sole aim had been to lash out at Grant for his wretched behavior in the carriage, to force him to sweat a little. His father wanted a wedding and moving from a mere courtship to a formal betrothal would certainly put the scare into him. She would cry off, of course, but the move had been shortsighted, made in the rush of anger. And perhaps also in the offense she'd felt at his coldness toward her. He'd hardly even looked at her on the way to dinner, his dismissiveness pointed and intentional.

How dare he treat her that way after such an inflamed encounter...one that would have been enough to ruin any unmarried woman. But she was already ruined, wasn't she? Grant knew it, too. Perhaps that was what had made him think she would not mind his advances in Hugh's study.

In the carriage, Cassie had nearly demanded that he take her back to Grosvenor Square. But if he could so swiftly turn on her, how much more swiftly would he follow through with his threat to tell Michael about Hope House? No, she could not trust him. So, she'd busied herself conjuring ways in which to convince Grant's father of the veracity of their courtship, as Grant wanted—and to make the scoundrel suffer for it.

However, even though she would cry off before any gossip could spread, as she must, Michael would likely still hear of it. And then there would be hell to pay.

She'd been rash and reckless, and to make everything worse, the effect she'd wanted had not come to pass. Instead of fulminating anger, Grant had been oddly subdued. Once seated around the table, and Lord Lindstrom began to impart his coarse and revolting opinions about his fourth son, Cassie began to understand his quiet restraint.

She couldn't comprehend the marquess's treatment of his son. It wasn't merely that he disliked that he was a physician and worked for a living; he seemed to view Grant as a complete failure. An embarrassment. And worst of all, Grant had taken his verbal mauling on the chin, without so much as a complaint. He'd sat back and waited for it to be over. Not one of his brothers or his sister had tried to stand up for him either, which had only spurred Cassie on to do so.

The instinct to tell the marquess that he was wrong, that Grant wasn't a selfish profligate, had filled her so swiftly that she'd been near to bursting with it. But...*wasn't* he exactly that? Running a charity clinic did not in and of itself make him a good man, especially when he would lower himself to coercion for his own benefit. And to kiss her the way he had...and then turn cold as iron, as though it had not affected him at all. Had *that* been his true character showing? Could Grant simply kiss women in such a fashion and then treat them as if it was nothing?

Cassie stopped at the fire, the tiled floor around the hearth warming her bare feet. She stared at the flames, shaking her head. If not for her conversation with Audrey earlier that morning, about people using anger and antagonism to protect themselves from true feelings, she might have believed Grant to be the emotionless and cold man he'd been in the carriage earlier. But Audrey's observation had wiggled into Cassie's mind all day. She didn't believe Grant had been unaffected by their kiss. She couldn't, not when she remembered so vividly the way he'd nearly lost control. It had not been just a kiss; it had been as though he was trying to possess her. As though he'd been trying to absorb her.

She put a flat hand to her stomach, to the spiraled tension that kept fluttering between her hips whenever she thought of it. It could have been the darkened corners of the room, or the ripping snowstorm outside, or the fact that they were stranded away from Town for the night, but try as she did, Cassie could not put the image of bidding Grant a good night earlier from her mind.

They'd climbed the stairs together, behind a maid with a lantern. At the landing, Cassie turned right, following a maid toward the guest room. After a few steps, sensing Grant was no longer with her, she turned. He'd gone left at the landing and was standing at the open door to another room down the hall. For several protracted moments, he'd watched her. Then, he'd gone in and closed the door.

She now knew where his room was. Had that been his intention? Had he wanted her to see where to find him that night? The idea of going to his room made her dizzy and hot, and yet, so did just standing here thinking of him undressed. In bed. Knowing that he was sleeping just down the hall would make her own slumber impossible.

Was he thinking of her in the same way?

Cassie wanted to throttle herself. All this time, she'd accused Grant of being a libidinous ingrate, and yet, look at her now. She was nearly panting with thoughts of him in his shirtsleeves—or less. *Get ahold of yourself, Cassie!* No self-respecting woman should suffer breathlessness from mere *thoughts*. However, as much as she chastised herself for it, she could not lie to herself any longer. Grant infuriated her. He was unscrupulous and impulsive and held some questionable principles.

Yet, she could not bring herself to care about those things now that she knew what it felt like to have his mouth against hers. His hands on her body. Now that she knew what the corded muscles of his abdomen felt like beneath her own hands, her mind had come alive with progressively more unvirtuous imaginings.

Heaven help her, she wanted to feel it all again. All of it and more.

Cassie eyed the door to her room. An unrelenting whisper of a notion had plagued her since Grant had gone into his room. Had it been invitation in his eyes, or a warning to stay away? To go to him would be unconscionable. It would be reckless and hypocritical of her. This was a staged courtship, and one she had battled against. Now, it was a false betrothal that would end the next day. Soon, they would no longer see much of one another.

The drop of her stomach propelled her feet from the tiled hearth and toward the door. Commands to stop, turn back, be sensible, streamed through her mind as she peered into the hallway. It was dark, the candles having all been doused, but the leaded windows at the turn in the stairwell cast some bluish light on the landing. As softly as she could, Cassie latched her door and padded along the carpet toward it. If she were to be found right now, she could always whip up some excuse as to why she had left her room. But if she were found standing outside Grant's door, or worse, knocking upon it, there could be no acceptable justification. That was why, as she came to the door he'd gone through earlier, Cassie forwent bringing her knuckles down on the wood. Instead, she put her hand to the knob and gave it a twist. Unlocked. Her heart strummed in the base of her throat as she pushed the door open a few inches, slipped inside, and closed it behind her.

Grant sat on the edge of his bed, his back to her. The fire in the hearth was the only source of light in the room.

Without taking a breath, she stood immobile. For the briefest moment, in a surge of doubt, Cassie wondered if she could slip back out again without him noticing. But his back stiffened. He cocked an ear toward her, and his eyes swiftly followed. Grant sprang from the bed and faced her, unable to mask his astonishment.

"What are you doing in here?" he asked before coming around the large bed, toward her. "Are you insane?"

She stepped away from the door. "I might be."

He'd undressed for bed, tossing off his jacket and waistcoat, and his cravat and stock. He was now in his shirtsleeves, untucked from his trousers. At his open collar, a triangle of his throat and chest drew her attention. He was barefoot, too, completing his look of dishabille.

Grant took in the sight of her in her dressing gown and his mouth tightened. So did his jaw. "Announcing our nonexistent betrothal to my family was one thing, but this... Cassie, you need to go."

She'd expected him to say as much. "I know it was rash, and I'm sorry, but I wanted to make you angry."

"You never fail to succeed in that." He huffed and shook of his head. "Why did you want to make me angry?" He hitched his hands on his hips, looking discomfited. "Because I kissed you?"

"No. Because of how you treated me afterward."

His brow pinched, and he lowered his hands. "How I treated you?"

"On the way here, you were cold and dismissive." She shrugged. "You acted as if...as if you wished you hadn't."

"That *is* my wish, and it should be yours as well." Cassie jerked back at his harsh rejoinder. "I lost control for just one moment, and now the only thing in my mind is the memory of what you taste like. Damn it, I can't look at a glass of whisky without thinking about your tongue."

The air thickened in her throat. She shouldn't have doubted her instinct. He *had* been affected. Grant turned away and released her from his stare. She took a half breath, but it wasn't enough. She was still lightheaded.

"You regret the kiss because you...*liked* it?"

He looked askance at her. The firelight cut through the thin linen weave of his shirt, revealing the silhouette of his chest and stomach. "You thought I didn't?"

"I didn't know what to think when you began acting like a stranger."

"To keep you at arm's length." He let out a gruff laugh and gestured to the room. "Apparently, it didn't work. Cassie, if you're found here, you won't be able to cry off. You need to go. Now."

She knew he was right. But his confession had emboldened her. It had made her certain about what she wanted, especially before this charade of a courtship was over.

"I will," she said with a shaky breath. "After you make love to me."

She held still, air trapped in her lungs as delayed comprehension dawned on Grant's face. His lips parted, and a furious, mystified stare drilled into her, sealing her feet to the carpet. "You don't know what you're saying."

"I do. I'm not a simpleton, Grant. I'm also not a virgin."

He clenched his jaw and emitted a soft growl, stepping back and to the side as if her comment had been the glance of a fist. "I do not want to think of you with him."

The strain of jealousy gave her wings, but she pretended otherwise. "My point is, I cannot be ruined twice."

Grant scrubbed a hand over his chin, then hitched it on his hip. He breathed hard. "Why are you doing this?"

"The other night, the way you kissed me..." She hesitated. But so far, she'd been utterly honest with him. She'd made herself vulnerable. It frightened her as much as it exhilarated her. "It did something to me, in a way nothing else ever has."

Though he'd turned to granite, his chest rose and fell with rapid breaths. "It was just a kiss."

He was still trying to keep her at arm's length. She could see through it this time.

"I know you felt it too." She then reconsidered. "Maybe with all your mistresses, you've felt it before, but I haven't. And I want to."

He cocked his head. "*All* my mistresses?"

"I hear you have several, not just Miss Devereaux."

"Is that right?"

"Yes, and what is one more, for just one night?"

Grant shook his head and raked his fingers through his hair as he strode away from her. "Do not push me, Cassie. I might be a gentleman, but I am no saint." He faced her, looking undone. "Are you trying to drive me mad? Is this revenge for bullying you into a courtship?"

"No!" That hadn't even gone through her mind. Though perhaps it should have. "I want—" She cut herself off, suddenly unsure. She'd hoped that once in his room, once she'd presented herself, he would accept her without challenge. But challenge was all he'd been doing.

"Tell me," he said softly, his green eyes now glimmering jet. "Tell me what you want."

Cassie's voice shook with nervousness, but she forced out the words. "I want to know what it feels like to be with a man and feel pleasure rather than...indifference."

Grant's breathing visibly escalated, his chest swelling with every breath. He bowed his head, but his eyes stayed on her.

"If I take you to my bed, I'll need to marry you, and that is something I cannot do."

She twisted her fingers into the sides of her robe as irrational envy spiraled through her stomach. "Because of your late wife."

"I barely survived," he whispered. "I refuse to go through something like that again."

Why hadn't she seen it before? The anguish from losing his wife had burrowed into him so deeply that it was now a part of him. It had found a home within him, and it had settled with permanency. In that moment, Cassie wished she could magically steal away all his pain. Free him of the burden.

"I would never force you to marry me."

Rather than setting his mind at ease, it only seemed to offend him. "I am not Renfry," he growled. "I will not use you and set you aside."

"What if I ask you to?" Incomprehension swept his face, but she only felt a new stroke of clarity. "Renfry lied. I gave myself to him because he told me he would make me his wife. With you...you're not making a false promise to lure me in. I *choose* to give myself to you simply because *I* want it."

Grant scrubbed his palm over his mouth again. And with

his unbroken reluctance, pangs of shame began to heat her cheeks. Here she stood, practically begging him to make love to her...and yet he hadn't wavered in his resistance. The great Lothario, the debauched physician lord, the man who was rumored to chase anything in a skirt...would not have her. She licked her lips, the desire to flee formidable. But her pride was too fierce to run back to her room in humiliation. No, she would go with her pride intact.

"I see," she said, her voice tight. "The risk is too great for you. I understand. Forgive me."

Cassie turned and with her back straight as an arrow, reached for the door. A hand slammed up against it, holding it shut. Grant had crossed the room and come up behind her at lightning speed.

"Please," she said, the presence of him hot against her back. "If you don't want me, let me go."

"You have no earthly idea how much I want you." Each rasping word scraped up her spine and pressed underneath her skin. Her legs went soft as the hand not bracing the door curled around her waist. He hauled her against him, and her eyes fluttered shut as the hard wall of his chest caught her, his thickly muscled thighs bracketing her legs. Cassie gasped, and the sound was joined by another: the unmistakable click of the door's lock as Grant engaged it.

Her blood bubbled as he wrapped both arms around her and sealed her to him.

"Are you sure this is what you want?" he whispered against her neck. Then, with his lips against the lobe of her ear, "Are you absolutely certain?"

She nodded, or at least tried to. Her body wasn't responding to what she wanted it to do.

"I need to hear it, Cassie." His hands curved inward around her hips, splaying wide and reaching lower.

"Yes," she sighed, the pitch broken and pleading. It would have embarrassed her to have sounded so undone—if Grant had not spun her around and smothered her half-formed answer with his mouth. He chased it with a coarse groan of his own.

She draped her arms around his shoulders and clung on as the assault of his kiss began. The last of his resistance cracked and dissolved. Grant's tongue twined around hers, the kiss claiming and desperate and she couldn't breathe. Nor did she want to if it meant parting from his mouth. Carnal sparks lit off inside her as he walked them in small steps closer to the bed, his fingers tugging roughly at the sash on her robe.

She took in a gulp of air as Grant shifted his mouth to her throat, where he pressed hot, openmouthed kisses.

"Cassie." His teeth abraded her skin, and his hands pushed the robe from her shoulders. It fell to the floor. "My God, the things I want to do to you." He filled his palms with her backside and kneaded her through the linen shift. He lifted his head to look at her. Firelight played over his face, his eyes dark with craving.

"I want those things too," she whispered.

His gaze dimmed with a glint of warning. "You might come to regret saying that."

She went still, though her heartbeat thrashed. Was he still trying to push her away? She wouldn't allow it. "I'm not afraid," she said. "Tell me. What are you going to do to me?"

With a devilish grin, Grant released her. She lurched,

despondent, as he took a step backward and put an arm's length between them.

"As you were the one to come to my room, I believe I am *yours* to command tonight. So, you tell me, my lady—what do you want me to do?"

Cassie's mouth went dry, and she was suddenly nervous again. "Isn't what I want clear?"

He shrugged, attempting for nonchalance. But his eyes were busily devouring her, the firelight likely rendering her shift near transparent, as his was.

"I'm a man who likes detailed instruction."

She faltered. It had taken more courage than she'd imagined just to come here and tell him that she wanted to feel pleasure with a man. To tell him every detail? Cassie's stomach flipped. She couldn't do it.

Grant saw her doubt and winked. "Might I make a suggestion?"

She nodded, slightly embarrassed by the eagerness of it.

"Perhaps I am wearing too many articles of clothing," he said, pulling at his shirt with his thumb and forefinger.

Oh. She licked her lips, her pulse stuttering again as she understood. "I...I want you to..." She could not believe she was going to say it. "Take off your clothes."

A slow, sinful grin bowed his lips, and with languid motions, Grant gathered his shirt with both hands. Lifting his arms, he peeled it up, over his head, and then discarded it onto the floor. Cassie's pulse quivered in her throat. Firelight gilded his taut shoulders and the chiseled lines of his chest and abdomen. Her breath ceased entirely when she realized his fingers were moving at the buttons on the fall of his trousers. He wasn't stopping. He was heeding her command.

On the next unsteady throb of her heart, his trousers and smalls were on the carpet, his feet stepping free of them.

There was no longer a single drop of air in the room. Heat stole over her as her eyes roved over the gloriously muscled figure standing proudly erect before her. He was beautiful, his brawn a revelation, and instinctively, she reached for him. Her fingers touched down on his chest, and instantly, he covered her hand with his, flattening her palm to his skin. She felt the powerful thudding of his heart.

"Next," he said, his voice a rasp.

It took her distracted and sluggish mind a moment to understand his meaning. He wanted his next command. There was only one thing she craved, and that was to feel his bare figure against her own.

"Remove my shift?" she asked.

Grant did not move slowly this time. He bundled the shapeless linen in his hands and hauled it over her head and off the tips of her fingers. The material disappeared behind her, and his eyes wolfed in the sight of her. Cassie felt a change in him as the intensity of his stare narrowed.

"Fuck, you're perfect," he groaned, the coarse word signaling his disintegrating control. His flexed his hands, but he didn't reach for her. Instead, he lifted his searing gaze to hers and growled, "*Next.*"

In that moment, she knew she could say anything, demand anything, and he would give it to her.

"Take me to your bed," she whispered. "Make me yours."

CHAPTER
TWENTY-ONE

Make me yours.

Never in his life had Grant been given a command he'd so desperately and instantly wanted to fulfil. He closed the gap between them and, with a ruthless tug, crushed Cassie to him. He let out an involuntary groan at the decadent caress of her warm, naked skin against his, and at the softness of her lips as they tried to match his battering kisses. With an easy lift, her feet left the floor, and Grant did the very thing he'd been envisioning since kissing her the other night: he draped her onto his bed and covered her body with his.

Their fused mouths were in a war, each of them in a frenzy to reach deeper, as if to claim or punish or possess. He wanted all three, and as Cassie whimpered into his mouth, he gave in to the reckless turmoil of the conflicting desires.

As soon as he'd seen her standing within his room, a part of him had known that he would not allow her to leave it. He'd tried. Tried to deny her, tried to stay furious with her for pushing him even further than she already had that evening. He'd tried to be firm and send her away. But when she'd walked for the door, attempting to maintain her pride and composure, his mind shut down. The need he'd buried for so long had taken over, obliterating the last shred of his honor. Cassie wanted him. This was *her* choice. And like hell if he wouldn't give her what she wanted.

No more games. She didn't have to tell him what she wanted him to do; he could read her desires as she writhed beneath him, her hands exploring his back, his hips and chest, and then, more boldly, his arse.

"Grant," she pleaded as he trailed hot kisses down her throat, and lower. His lips closed around the mound of her breast, and she arched her back with a soft yelp.

"Yes, say my name," he murmured as he grazed her nipple with his teeth. He wanted to wring all sorts of nonsensical sounds from her throat, but he wanted his name on her tongue the most. Cassie gave him that, gasping it, and raking her fingers through his hair as he worshipped her other breast.

As if instinctively, her hand reached toward his groin, but he caught her wrist and pinned it to the bedcover. He was rock hard with the ache of desire. It would not take more than a few strokes to finish him off. But this wasn't about him. She'd come to him with one need in mind: pleasure. Her own.

Grant eased back a little, enough to take in the divine sight of her sprawled underneath him, her lips red and puffy, her perfectly shaped breasts on full display.

"You're so beautiful. I can't stop looking at you," he said as he brushed his fingers down the valley between her breasts, to the flat of her stomach, and lower, to the apex of her thighs. She squeezed them together, and Grant stopped. He waited. And then, the muscles of her thighs began to relax.

"Are you still sure?" he asked. He would never forgive himself if she'd changed her mind but had been too reluctant to tell him.

Her eyes glittered like jewels in the firelight, dusky blue and leaden with need. "I'm sure. I want this, Grant. I want *you*."

Her declaration pummeled into him like one of the snowy gales battering the windows of his room. Rationally, he knew what she meant: she wanted him to make love to her, to pleasure her, here and now, in this bed. For this one night. Nothing beyond that. But for a few missing heart-beats, he interpreted the words differently. For a dangerous moment, he considered it as something potentially more.

Cassie writhed beneath him again, and he realized he was still gazing at her, still pinning her wrist to the bed. The tension in her thighs had melted completely, and reading the invitation, Grant drew a finger along the seam of her core. Her eyes flared, her lips parted, and he took her mouth again. His tongue plunged in deep as her hips bucked up to meet his hand.

Grant reined in his quickly collapsing control and forced himself to breathe. To move slower. She wasn't a virgin, but that didn't mean she was experienced. At the fleeting image of Cassie underneath Renfry, of the rogue spreading her open to him, taking his pleasure and treating her as nothing but a vessel in which to slake his lust, Grant's mind recoiled. She wanted more than that from him tonight, and he would not disappoint her.

As he touched her, his plunging tongue mimicked his

fingers, building heat and friction and wringing the sounds from her throat that he'd so desperately wanted to hear her make. Circling her hips, Cassie's moans vibrated through his mouth, into his chest, and when she screamed her release again and again, he swallowed the sound, rather than let it blare into the quiet of the sleeping house.

"I didn't know... I had no idea..." she murmured, panting and mindless as she came down from her delirium.

With a small huff of laughter, he settled onto the bedcover next to her. No longer strung tight as a bow, she relaxed into his arms. The sound of her contented sigh and the rosy pink of her cheeks nearly made him forget the painful state of his arousal.

Cassie pressed her mouth to his shoulder and kissed a trail up his neck, her soft lips buzzing under his skin and adding more pressure to the granite coil of his groin. Naked as they both were, she could not overlook the sight. Her eyes took in his condition, and when she met his hooded gaze again, she bit her lower lip.

"Are you going to ask?" she said.

He ran his finger down the slope of her pert nose and then across her chin. God, she was gorgeous like this, her golden hair loose around her shoulders, her lips swollen, sweat glistening in the hollow of her collarbone.

"Ask what?"

That rogue hand of hers slipped again toward his hips. He caught it, stilling it. "Next," she said.

He felt ready to explode just from that one word and the intent behind it.

"This was about your pleasure, not mine," he said, even

though he was nearly blind with the single-minded need to be inside her.

Cassie lifted her chin from his shoulder, and a curtain of her hair swung forward to cover one eye. He pushed it aside and tucked it behind her ear.

"I asked you to make love to me, Grant Thornton." She rolled her wrist free from his grip. But she only touched a finger to his upper lip. She drew it down, tugging his bottom lip. "I'm still waiting."

His pulse slammed in his neck. "You have no notion of what you do to me. Do you?"

Grant pushed her onto her back, and his mind silenced. All potential consequences muted beneath the sounds of their rough breathing as he nudged her delectable thigh aside and aligned himself with her. He clamped his mouth to hers and thrust forward, muffling her reflexive cry. With painful restraint, Grant went still, aware he might have hurt her.

"Don't stop," she breathed and clutched him closer.

He exhaled in a rush and seated himself to the hilt, reveling in the tight clasp of her, of her uneven breathing as he began to rock forward and back. She clutched the sides of his face, her nails likely leaving indentations, but he didn't care. Grant watched her, the tips of their noses brushing together and apart, as she began to gasp and drown in the pleasure that she'd come here for. That she'd shoved aside all pride, all fear, all doubt, to reach for. She was bloody magnificent.

Cassie's mewls and moans began to rise as he deepened each thrust, closing in fast on his peak. He'd known he would not last long, and as his body tightened, he stopped breathing. Though it was practically torture, he tore himself free at the last moment and dropped his forehead to Cassie's. They each struggled for air as he held her to him, their bodies slick with sweat.

"My God, Cassie—" He collapsed next to her, their legs still entwined. She wrapped her arms around his torso so tightly her heartbeat thudded against his ribs. There was an unnerving trembling in his arms and wrists as he held her to him.

Grant sealed his mouth shut without finishing the thought that had bolted into his mind. A perilous thought that frightened him with its truth. That one night with Cassandra Sinclair would never be enough.

THE CARRIAGE TURNED onto Grosvenor Square, and Cassie's stomach plummeted. "Oh no," she murmured as she stared through the window.

Grant followed her gaze, his hands still adjusting his cravat. "What is it?"

"My brother." Michael's coach was parked near the front of her residence.

Grant sat back against the burgundy quilted cushion of his carriage. "Damn."

They'd wasted no time at Lindstrom House, departing even before the early breakfast had concluded. When Cassie had stepped outside her guest room that morning, Grant had been waiting for her at the landing of the stairs. As she approached, her legs suddenly quivering like warmed honey, a wicked grin had tucked into the corner of his mouth. It brought her mind directly back to the early morning hours spent in his room, in his bed, before returning to her own room before the servants woke. As they descended the stairs together, Cassie had wondered if she should say anything about the night. Or if they should pretend nothing had happened.

Breakfast had been quick and quiet, with just the two of them, and Lawrence and Alfred at the table. Cassie had been ravenous, filling her plate generously at the sideboard. Grant smothered a grin every time she caught him looking at her from across the table, as if he knew why she had such an appetite. The snowy world outside reflected the sunlight and brightened the morning room, turning it warm and stuffy. The marquess had been joining them when Grant and Cassie stood to leave. She was grateful that he'd refused to be drawn in by his father's complaints that it was far too early to already be leaving.

"If you are worried for the lady's reputation, there is no need. You can be wed as soon as you have secured the special license," the marquess had said as the footman was bringing them their outer trappings.

Cassie considered crying off right then, making up some excuse that they had quarreled, and it was over. But both she and Grant had exchanged a tense look and with unspoken agreement, left with their lips sealed.

"Fournier's not going to be happy," he now said as his driver brought them around the square.

This she already knew; however, she'd successfully put it from her mind during the carriage ride back into Town. She'd half expected Grant to choose to sit up with his driver so that they would not be enclosed into the interior of the carriage together. But he hadn't, and they had barely left the

Oval before their wordless staring match culminated with Grant reaching for her. He'd dragged her straight off her bench and onto his lap. Mind numbing bliss muted all the reasons it was a terrible idea as he'd kissed her with the same fervor he'd shown the night before.

When evidence of his arousal pressed against her, she'd once again devolved into a burning mass of need. Grant had been suffering the same affliction, rising from it only long enough to ask her if she was, again, certain. With her ragged yes, he'd bunched her skirts, and she'd unbuttoned his fall. Their uncoordinated motions were only awkward until he'd been inside her once more, and Cassie had marveled at how perfect and right it felt. And though he'd pulled from her, to avoid spilling his seed, he'd continued to cover her lips and neck with kisses for most of the ride home.

Now, with their hair and clothing repaired, they stepped onto the pavement. The snow from last night's storm had been swept but a layer of ice crunched beneath their feet as they approached the door. Walking exacerbated the soreness of her inner thighs where she'd straddled Grant, and though it was ridiculous, she had the irrational fear her brother would know.

She braced herself as they entered the foyer and saw Michael storming down the stairs toward them.

"Where the devil have you been?" His eyes landed on Grant. "Thornton, explain yourself. Immediately."

"Michael, please, calm down," Cassie said, removing her pelisse with Ruth's help. Her maid's eyes were wide with alarm and no doubt some fear for her mistress. Grant shook his head at the footman, signaling that he would keep his greatcoat on. He would not be staying long, then.

"Last night's snowfall caught us by surprise, Your Grace," Grant said. "It prevented the entire dinner party at Lindstrom House from returning to their homes. Lady Cassandra was given a room. She is perfectly safe."

Michael's nostrils flared, and the black look he shot at Grant spoke volumes. He was suspicious enough to make Cassie's pulse skip.

"I suppose that is understandable, however I have also learned this was not your first night away from the residence." He turned his incisive glare onto her. "This is my household, my staff. They are merely at your disposal. Did you really think that I would not find out you went to Neatham's for the night? And that there was some concern about a man following you from a boxing club in Limehouse? What in God's name were you doing there, Cassandra?"

The footman and Ruth had disappeared to give them privacy, but Cassie still did not want to have this conversation in the foyer. She gestured toward the front sitting room, beckoning her brother inside. It would also give her a moment to think. Poor Patrick. Michael had to have cornered him with questions.

"It was my doing, Your Grace." Cassie turned to stare at Grant as they entered the room. With a furtive glance, he silently told her to go along with it. "I invited Lady Cassandra to Duke's for the match."

He even appeared properly chagrinned as Michael's contemptuous glare increased. "You thought a place like that was decent for my sister?"

"Michael, please stop." Cassie stepped between her brother and the man she still could not quite believe she'd made love to. Twice. If they remained in the same room for any longer, she feared Michael would pick apart the truth of it. "Lord Thornton, thank you for delivering me safely home."

It was a polite dismissal, and with a deep bow, and a glance toward the duke, Grant moved for the door.

"Thornton," Michael said, dragging Grant's heels to a stop. "The duchess is hosting a dinner at Violet House Saturday night. I expect you to be there. It appears we have important matters to discuss."

Grant bowed again and, likely with great relief, took his leave. The moment the front door shut behind him, Cassie whirled to face her brother. "I will ask you not to involve yourself in my relationship with Lord Thornton."

That word—*relationship*. She had even less of an idea what it meant now than she did before.

Michael's shoulders slackened some, his show of hostility abating now that Grant was gone. "He is not suitable for you, Cassie."

Tobias had warned her that their brother would not approve. She crossed her arms as she went to the front window overlooking the square. Grant's carriage was pulling away from the curb. Whether her brother approved or not hadn't mattered before, especially since it was a fictitious courtship. The barbs of irritation she now felt from his pronouncement were unwarranted.

"He is Lord Neatham's closest friend," she said. "And Audrey approves of him."

"While I respect the viscount and viscountess's opinions, there is no question that his reputation is tainted. Not to mention his methods are crude. Offering to put your order at that modiste's on his account! What was he playing at, treating you like one of his mistresses?"

Jane and her enormous mouth had likely divulged the incident to Genie, who in turn had told Michael.

"He is doing no such thing," Cassie replied, even as a vivid image of his naked form, gilded by firelight and moving over her, made her blush.

Michael shook his head, unconvinced. "You've been taken in by one rogue already, and I was ignorant to it. I will not turn a blind eye again."

Cassie bristled while trying to maintain her calm. Her brother had confessed before that he blamed himself for not keeping a better eye on her after she'd met Lord Renfry. What he couldn't quite understand however was that it had nothing to do with him. She'd made her own choices, poor though they'd been. And now, he was likening Grant to one of the worst blackguards in London.

"Grant is nothing like Renfry. *Nothing*," she said, her ire growing. "You shouldn't judge his character based on the rumors you hear at White's."

"Not just at White's," he argued. But she would hear no more of it.

"It's been a long night, and if you don't mind, I'd like to change my gown."

Michael exhaled, and though he appeared to want to say more, he relented. "Very well. You will come to dinner Saturday night too, of course?"

She nodded, thinking there was nothing she would like less. Except perhaps another dinner with Lord Lindstrom.

Her brother left, and small shivers set in. She wasn't cold.

Exhaustion weighed her down as she summoned Ruth and had her prepare a bath.

Michael infuriated her at times. He'd been pestering her to marry for years, and yet the man she'd finally chosen to court was not good enough? She squeezed her eyes shut. No, she had not *chosen* him. She wasn't courting him at all! Even now, after their night together and their frenzied coupling in the carriage, Grant did not plan to ask for her hand. She'd laid out their agreement firmly. Cassie had wanted to know pleasure; now, he'd given it to her. She pushed aside a strange, hollowing sensation. She'd told him she wouldn't demand anything more, and she would not go back on her word.

CHAPTER TWENTY-TWO

As the carriage pulled into the mews behind Hope House, the constriction around Grant's throat intensified. It felt as if he was inhaling and exhaling through a slim, hollow tube. Sweat gathered under his suit and at his temples.

Patrick brought the horses to a stop, and Grant descended straightaway, his doctor's bag clutched in his hand. He wasn't prepared for this in the slightest.

When Cassie's driver had shown up at Thornton House shortly past five o'clock, Grant had just returned from Jackson's on Bond Street. His home had been too quiet for the past day, ever since he'd returned from their night at Lindstrom House. He'd needed a distraction from the relentless barrage of images. Of Cassie coming apart in his arms, of her blushes during breakfast the next morning, of the exquisite pleasure of sinking into her while she straddled him in the carriage and rode him with unbridled passion.

He'd spent the rest of Monday in his home surgery, seeing a few patients whose ailments battled for his attention, though barely triumphed. He told himself to be thankful for the work. Otherwise, he might have devised a way to meet with Cassie again. Getting through the night, alone in his bed, had been a study in torture. He could have gone out, to the Fallen Arch or another club, but it would not have helped. In fact, it might have made things worse, especially if Martha was there to drape herself over him. He wanted no one and nothing but Cassie.

Tuesday, he could not stay at home while his blood continued to boil, so he'd taken himself to the boxing club to replace his unchecked desire with blunt pain. It had worked. Somewhat.

But it was the urgent message Patrick carried with him from Hope House that had successfully dashed away every lingering carnal thought, replacing them with cold trepidation.

Grant knocked twice on the back door, then thrice more after a two-second pause. The door opened an inch, and the face he had not been able to expunge from his mind stared up at him, her blue eyes pleading.

"You came," Cassie breathed out in a rush, allowing him into the kitchen. She shut and locked the door behind her.

"Did you expect me not to?"

At Cassie's flinch, he realized it had come out more harshly than necessary.

"It is only that I know you don't attend births," she replied, her strain evident in the crease between her brows. Curls of hair had come loose around her face, too.

Had anyone else called on him to attend a birth, he would have directed them to some other doctor. However, it was Cassie asking, and Patrick had said she was alone at Hope House. That had spurred him on ever faster.

"What has happened?" Grant asked. "Where is Miss Khan?"

Cassie led him from the kitchen, toward the slim corridor and stairs. He noted that the door leading to the staged accountant's office at the front of the building had a new second bolt lock. Good. They'd taken action following Mr. Youngdale's attack.

"Elyse left a few hours ago for her dinner with Madame Archambeau and Miss Stone."

"That is tonight?" The benefactresses had sent him an invitation in which to pass along to Hope House's organizer, and he had. But he'd lost track of the days since then.

"I've sent a messenger to her there, but I don't know how long it will take. And Mabel has been out for another birth. Everything was fine when they left," Cassie explained as she started up the stairs. "But then one of the residents went into labor, and it's progressing quickly. Faster than usual, and it's only me and Sister Agnes here, and I didn't know who else to turn to—"

Grant reached for her hand sliding up the railing and stilled her. She turned, eyes wide and a bit wild. "Breathe, Cassie. Everything will be fine. You're not alone now."

She exhaled, visibly attempting to calm. Then, more evenly, she told him what the problem was. "Mrs. Rawling has four children. This is her fifth. She says something is wrong."

Panic started thumping at the base of his skull, but Grant stopped it in its tracks. Cassie was already in distress; he wouldn't add to it. She'd called on him. Needed him to be strong. As did Mrs. Rawling.

"Take me to her."

Cassie led him to a small room. Well-furnished and comfortable, the room was simple but cozy. The woman on the bed, however, was in supreme discomfort. Red-cheeked and glistening with sweat, she grimaced as she held her round abdomen. Sister Agnes stood to greet him, appearing frazzled.

"I never learned a thing about birthing babies," she said. "I'm so glad you've come, Doctor Brown."

Grant shed his greatcoat and jacket and got to work. He'd attended several births before Sarah's death and like most things having to do with the practice of medicine, the knowledge came back to him without delay. A swift birth was normal for a woman who had already borne several children, and Mrs. Rawling was fully dilated and ready to push. But after an examination, Grant understood what she had meant about something being wrong.

The constriction around his throat set in again. He met the mother's imploring eyes, and then Cassie's.

"The baby is transverse. That means it's in a crosswise position. It should be facing head down by now." Mrs. Rawling closed her eyes. She knew what this meant. "Were any of your other children breech?"

She shook her head. "Oh, Mother Mary, help me."

Cassie took her hand and looked to Grant. "What can you do?"

Most babies stuck in the breech position and thus, unable to come down the birth canal did not live. Neither did their mothers. But with Cassie looking at him, expectant and hopeful that he had some answer, he would do anything not to let her down.

"It means we need to turn the baby into the correct position," he said. "I've seen it done a few times, and it can be successful." He removed his cufflinks and rolled up his sleeves. "Sister Agnes, we need more hot water. Bring several basins, bathing soap, and linens. Miss Banks, do you have any laudanum on hand?"

Cassie released the woman's hand and stood, nodding. "I think so."

"Good. I don't generally like opium, but turning the baby is going to be painful. A small dose would relax you, Mrs. Rawling, making the turning easier."

The woman nodded, eager for anything that might help. Cassie found the medicine in Miss Khan's office, and within minutes of administering no more than five drops, Grant began to press the woman's abdomen in the fashion he'd seen from a few of the more progressive male midwives at university. Applying pressure against the womb to influence the baby to turn was complicated, but if external manipulation was successful, he may not require the forceps he had placed into his bag. The device would often kill the baby while sparing the mother. It would be a last option.

Cassie gripped Mrs. Rawling's shoulders while he worked slowly between contractions. At last, he felt the resistance give as the baby slid away from his prodding hands. After an examination, he nodded. It had worked. The baby was now in the proper position. He motioned for Sister Agnes to ready the linens and dampen several cloths with soapy water. He was in the minority of physicians who advocated for cleanliness, but as so few of his patients developed infection, he would continue with the practice, even if other physicians mocked him for it.

The crown of the baby's head presented, and after only two more contractions, the infant emerged. A boy. The umbilical cord had looped and tightened around his neck, likely from the twisted position in the womb. Grant freed him, but the baby's silence and the blue cast of his skin stopped his own breathing. He wrapped the boy into a warm blanket and took him into his lap, then began to rub his little chest vigorously. For several seconds that felt like hours, Grant saw again his own daughter, serenely silent and ashen when the midwife had put her bundled figure in his arms.

"Come on, little one. Fight," he whispered as he continued rubbing.

The baby twitched. And then a wail split the quiet. A rush of color flooded the baby's skin as he howled, and Grant joined him, letting out a cry of relief. Mrs. Rawling sobbed, but when he tried to hand her the child, wrapped and warm, his fists flailing, the woman shook her head. "No, no," she gasped, turning her face away.

Puzzled, he looked to Cassie, whose expression was a crush of pain. Sister Agnes bent to take the baby from him. Just then, a rush of footfalls came up the stairwell. Miss Khan dashed into in the room, busily removing her cloak, hat, and scarf. "I got your message and came as quickly as I could," she said, out of breath. But at the sight of the infant in the nun's arms, she beamed at Grant. "Doctor Brown, we might just get accustomed to having you here."

He stood when Miss Khan prepared to take over for the delivery of the afterbirth; he was more than happy to let her. His hands shook as he washed them. Cassie gathered his things and beckoned him to follow her. He did so on legs that were soft at the knee. His blood pumped hard and erratically, though now it was with thrill rather than dread.

Cassie led him to her office and shut the door. It was still just as cold as it had been last time, the brazier again unlit. But after the heat of the birthing chamber, Grant dragged the chilled air into his lungs with pleasure. She placed his bag, greatcoat, and jacket onto the lumpy sofa, then took up a hooked blanket from the arm. She came back and, just as he had with her after she'd assisted him with Amir, draped the blanket over his shoulders.

"There," she said, rubbing his arms as he had, to assuage the trembling that had afflicted her. He pulled her to him with a sudden burst of gratitude. Cassie embraced him, resting her head on his chest. "You were magnificent, Grant."

He buried his nose and mouth into her crown of hair. The scent of warmed apricots curled through him, and after several moments, his pulse slowed. His breathing evened. But just as he began to regain his composure, he heard Cassie sniffle. Grant pulled back to peer down at her. "What is wrong?"

Any hope of the tears being happy ones dissolved when the corners of her mouth turned downward.

"Caroline—Mrs. Rawling," she said softly. "She's here because she is going to leave her baby with the nuns for placement. She can't afford another child, and so..."

Grant nodded. That was why she had not wanted to hold him. It would be too painful to then give him up.

He held Cassie closer, his lips brushing her forehead.

"I know how devastated she is," she whispered. Grant nudged her chin with his thumb, and when she looked up at him, he kissed her cheek, wet and salty from her tears. Her lashes were damp, the tip of her nose red. She appeared so vulnerable, and yet he knew she wasn't. At least not all the time.

"The world can be cruel," he said. "You're doing the best you can for Mrs. Rawling. She's grateful for that, I'm sure."

Cassie rested her head against his chest again. She didn't attempt to disentangle from his embrace. Instead, her palms rubbed his back. She turned her face into his chest, her nose scuffing side to side. He felt the press of her lips through his shirt and waistcoat. His body replied, instantly going hard.

"I'm sorry about Michael."

Grant had shaken off the duke's reaction the morning after the snowstorm. In all honesty, he could not blame Fournier. "He thinks me unsuitable."

She nodded. He rubbed circles against the small of her back.

"I am, you know."

Cassie lifted her head. "Don't say that."

"Why shouldn't I? It is true."

She frowned and started to pull away, but he wrenched her back into place. Her body came flush against his, and her eyes widened as she felt his arousal.

"You see?" He gripped her waist and lifted her to sit on the edge of her desk. The blanket around his shoulders fell off. "I am entirely unsuitable."

He kissed her, her lips salty from tears. Her thighs fell apart, and Grant stepped between them, stretching the fine wool of her skirt.

"The only thing I've been able to think about, dream about, for two days, is being inside you again," he said against her mouth. "Is that not depraved?"

Cassie hooked her hands around his neck and pulled him lower, her tongue first to delve into his mouth. After one long, scalding kiss, she replied, "Then I must be depraved too, because I want that. I want you. Grant, please."

The sound of her gasping his name awoke a sleeping dragon within him. He had the insensible desire to collect a thousand such gasps from her and hoard them like jewels. Christ, he needed her skirt up; the blood in his veins throbbed for it. But he could not entirely dismiss where they were. Or what they were doing.

"Cassie," he whispered as her thighs clenched around his, as if to draw him closer. "This is getting out of control."

She shook her head. "I don't care."

In truth, neither did he. Grant covered her mouth with his and pushed her back onto her desk, rucking up the hem of her skirt. He'd gathered it around her stockinged knees, exposing her garters, when a knock resounded on the office door. The spell gripping them shattered, and Grant stood straight, tugging Cassie off the desk, to her feet. Her skirts swayed into place as the door opened.

"Are you in here?" Miss Khan called as she popped in her head.

Cassie whirled away from the midwife and went behind her desk. Grant half-turned, entirely aware of the bulge in his trousers. "Oh good, Dr. Brown," Miss Khan said, coming inside the office. "I wanted to thank you again for your assistance. Mrs. Rawling and her baby seem to be doing just fine."

He kept his back to her as he swiftly reached for his things on the sofa. "I was happy to help." He barely looked toward Cassie, who was pretending to be busy at her desk.

Her flushed cheeks were telling, however. "But I'm afraid I'm late for another appointment. Send for me if there are any complications. Good evening to you both."

He hastily departed the room, incensed they'd been interrupted, and yet also relieved. This was madness. It had to stop. He could *not* touch her again, not even once. As he took the stairs, the squalling of an infant sounded from another room. He thought of Mrs. Rawling and the strength she'd possessed to not hold her baby. One touch, and she might not have been able to give him up.

"Christ," he muttered.

He was in trouble. Deep, deep trouble.

CHAPTER TWENTY-THREE

Elyse had been invited back to Archambeau Manor to dine again the following Saturday—this time, with any luck, uninterrupted. Madame Archambeau and Miss Stone had shown great interest in Hope House during her first short visit before she'd been summoned back to Crispin Street, and afterward, Elyse had been walking on air. Cassie wished she could feel as buoyant, but her last few encounters with Grant had kept her trapped between rapturous bliss and agitated uncertainty.

He'd been slinking into her every thought over the last few days, and when the benefactress sent Elyse a second invitation, Cassie realized something. Having now met the marquess, Cassie knew the threat of severing Grant's income was not an exaggeration in the least. However, at the art opening at Archambeau Manor, Grant hadn't so much as uttered a word about Church Street. Instead, he'd put forward Hope House. He'd put forward *Cassie*.

"I suppose we should find some way to thank Lord Thornton," Elyse had said the day after Caroline Rawling had her baby. Then, with a wry twist of her lips, she added, "Or perhaps that is what you were doing in your office when I walked in?"

The blood had rushed to the tips of Cassie's ears, and Elyse had broken out in laughter. But then, more seriously, she'd touched her arm. "Be careful. I worry about his intentions."

She hadn't known how to respond, so she'd just promised that Elyse needn't worry.

However, that seemed to be all Cassie had done for the bulk of the next few days.

LIKE ELYSE, she was to attend a dinner Saturday evening too, this one at Violet House. Afterward, Michael would drag Grant into his study, pour him a scotch, and demand he ask for Cassie's hand.

After staying the night at Lindstrom House, Michael's already thin patience had snapped. Especially when a column earlier in the week in *All the Chatter* hinted that the unexpected snow had pushed "*Lord T*" and "*Lady C*" into an inescapable position, in which the lady's honor may even hang in the balance. Cassie was certain it was the marquess's doing. He'd probably sent word to the gossip rag himself.

With the rumors at play, Grant needed to offer at the dinner Saturday night or cease courting Cassie entirely. He, of course, would not offer—gossip or no gossip. Michael would then toss him out and warn him against speaking to his sister again. The false courtship would be at an end.

Cassie should have felt relieved. She should have felt

happy. What she most certainly should not have been feeling was *bereft*.

If only she could go back to despising him. To believing he was a shallow lordling who practiced medicine but was not especially serious about it. But now... Now she knew Grant used riddles to distract his youngest patients from their pain. She knew he employed his dead wife's sister against his family's wishes. That he felt insecure about his father's love and used humor to deflect those feelings. Cassie knew that he hated to think of her with another man and that he shouted when he worried over her safety. She knew that he gave pleasure freely, demanding nothing in return. Most importantly, she now knew what it was like to be the object of his desire.

She'd seen parts of Grant that he kept hidden from everyone else. And she *liked* them. All week, she'd grappled with that realization, half wondering if she should send a note to Thornton House, telling him not to come to dinner. She didn't want him to have to face her brother.

Heaven help her, she didn't want it all to end.

It was nearing four o'clock when the correct sequence of knocks at the back door of Hope House announced Sister Nan's arrival. Cassie was glad for the timing. She needed to return to her residence to prepare for dinner. She hadn't sent the note to Grant, knowing deep down that it would only prolong the inevitable.

"How is Mrs. Rawling?" Sister Nan asked as she came inside. She set a long wicker basket on the table. Cassie eyed it, knowing what it would carry away from Hope House. It was why she'd insisted on making the trip to Spitalfields that day. She'd told Ruth that she was having tea with an acquaintance, leaving it vague, as she so often did. However, she continued to feel the thinning of the barrier between her two worlds.

"She's recovering well. No signs of any infection," Cassie reported. Sister Nan looked sideways at her. Her health wasn't what the nun had been inquiring after.

"She won't hold him," Cassie said. "Mrs. Powers is still here, so he's at least content."

Mrs. Powers was a wetnurse that Mabel and Elyse both knew from the area, and she provided her services to infants whose mothers had either died or were otherwise unable to feed them.

Sister Nan sighed and nodded. "The sooner we take him from here, the sooner Mrs. Rawling can begin to recover." She started for the corridor leading to the stairs, but then stopped. A hesitant frown creased the wrinkles on the bridge of the older woman's nose. "I wanted to say again, how sorry I am to have sent Isabel's awful man here."

All week, Cassie had been frustrated by the fact that Mr. Youngdale had not been at his residence, and that Isabel had yet to be found. Hugh had kept her informed on the lack of news, as since Tuesday night, she hadn't seen or heard from Grant. It was, of course, for the best. She still reeled from how Elyse had nearly found them on her desk. Her lack of decorum had been insupportable, her thoughtlessness disconcerting.

"You didn't send Mr. Youngdale here," she said. But the nun wouldn't have it.

"Yes, I did. Not to worry, though." She reached out to pat Cassie's arm. "The young woman is safe again."

At her coy wink, the small hairs on Cassie's arms raised. "Do you mean you know where she is?"

Sister Nan nodded. "She got away from those ruffians after they snatched her from the doc's. Said they didn't lock her into the carriage properly and went to get a pint. Bloomin' idiots."

Of course! Mr. Youngdale had followed Cassie from the boxing club in Limehouse not to terrorize her, but because he hadn't had Isabel in his possession after all. He'd thought Cassie would be able to lead him to her.

"She's been at the church?" At the sister's confirming nod, she leaned against the wall, lightheaded with wonder.

"Just for a few days. She was hiding in some abandoned house but then she started feeling ill and decided to risk coming to the church," Sister Nan said with a grimace, popping Cassie's bubble of elation.

"Fever?"

The sister nodded, and Cassie worried her bottom lip. Grant had expressed concern for a fever going around the slums.

"Mr. Youngdale isn't going to stop looking for her," she said, "and if she is ill, she should have a doctor."

Isabel could not come back here, to Hope House. Neither could she go to Church Street again. As Mr. Youngdale had followed Cassie home, she could not take her to the safety of Grosvenor Square either. Hugh had suggested getting her out of London altogether. Michael had Fournier Downs in Hertfordshire and Greenbriar in Kent, but each of those estates were fully staffed. She could never sneak in a pregnant, unmarried woman.

But she was getting ahead of herself.

Cassie checked the clock. Grant would still be at the clinic, though not for much longer.

"Sister Nan, did you bring your rig?" The older woman nodded. "Excellent. I'll come with you and the baby to the parish church."

While the nun went to collect the baby from Mrs. Powers, Cassie opened the back door and flagged down Tris. He had relieved Patrick just that morning, the bruising on his face still evident but explained away to the other servants as the result of a neighborhood brawl while he was caring for his sick mother.

"Drive to Lord Thornton's clinic," she told him, "and tell him to meet me at St. Paul's Church in Shadwell. Isabel is there, and she needs our help."

His expression brightened, but with some reserve. "Is she hurt?"

She shook her head. "Feverish. Inform Lord Thornton. And tell him she needs a new safe place, preferably out of London."

GRANT REACHED inside the lantern in the surgery and raised the wick. The resulting light over the patient bed was nowhere near enough by which to see properly. Swearing under his breath, he fiddled with a few of the reflective lenses.

"Did you move the lenses, Hannah? I've told you before, leave them where they are." He jostled one glass lens set on a pin hinge. It had most assuredly not been angled like this the last time he'd been at the clinic.

Last week. Before the snowstorm. Before spending the

night with Cassie at Lindstrom House. Before everything had started to unravel.

"I was attempting to give you more light with which to look up Mr. Brinkley's nostril," his assistant explained. It was the third time she'd done so, but it didn't erase his irritation.

Damn Mr. Brinkley and damn the rock he'd somehow gotten lodged in his nasal cavity. Grant had spent nearly an hour digging it free and the man had complained and howled the entire time.

Suddenly, the pin hinge snapped, and the squared beveled lens broke free into his hand. A groan scraped up his throat as Grant dashed it toward the floor. Hannah watched him warily, a hint of reproval on her raised brow and pursed lips.

"You've been doing that all day," she said, continuing to calmly roll a ball of cotton linen.

He stomped to where the broken lens had landed, scooped it up, and brought it to his desk. He'd repair the damn thing another time. "Doing what?"

"Grunting."

He frowned at her. "I have not."

"Yes, you have. You were even grunting while you were pulling that stone from Mr. Brinkley's nasal cavity."

He tossed up his arms. "Of course I was grunting, I couldn't get the bloody thing out!"

Hannah set down the roll of gauze. "Does this have to do with the rumors?"

Grant chucked the lens into a drawer and slammed it shut. He sent Hannah a baleful stare. "No."

The rumors she referred to were the inevitable aspersions

being cast against Cassie's character for her overnight stay at Lindstrom House. It did not matter if Mother Nature had given them no other choice, or that his entire family had also been required to stay the night. Hell, had Cassie had a bed made up in the entrance hall and been guarded all night by half a dozen footmen, there would still be whispers about Grant ruining her.

The problem was that the rumors were utterly true.

Of a fashion, at least.

"They say you must propose," Hannah said. "Or that you already have." She tried not to sound very interested, but he knew her too well.

There had been a time after he'd stopped actively mourning her older sister when she had soured toward him. The rumors of his lascivious behavior had reached her, and she'd told him it might be best if she resigned her post. They'd had a frank discussion, where he'd explained he would not be taking another wife, but he also would not be living a sad and celibate life. Grant promised not to flaunt women in front of her, and she'd given him a second chance. It had worked, and over the years, she'd loosened up considerably.

But some member of his family—most likely the marquess himself—had fed the betrothal news to the gossips, and the rumor was quickly tangling itself up with another rumor—that he'd ruined the lady.

Pangs of conscience locked up inside his chest, and he stepped away from his desk. "I have not proposed," he told Hannah. It was the truth. After a bracing breath, he exhaled, and then told Hannah everything about the courtship scheme. About the marquess's demands and ultimatums, and how he'd used Cassie to put off his father, at least for a little while.

Used Cassie. A slick twist of his gut accompanied those words as they came out of his mouth, Hannah's puckering expression increasing. When at last, he'd finished explaining, Grant held out his arms in defeat. "So, no, the rumors that we are betrothed are not true."

Hannah continued to pucker her brow. "What of the other rumor?"

That he'd ruined her. Grant rubbed his chin, discomfited. "That is a complicated answer."

"It's not. The answer is either yes or no."

He trusted Hannah, but Cassie's past with Renfry was off limits. He would not attempt to explain it away. If he needed to take responsibility for that, too, he would. "Yes."

She set her hands on her hips. "And yet you will not marry her?"

"Cassie doesn't wish to marry," he replied. "And without going into detail—"

"I thank you for that," she muttered with a nauseous grimace.

"She made it more than clear *before* the fact."

The corner of her mouth pressed downward, hinting at disbelief. But she moved on. "All right. She doesn't wish to marry you, and you don't wish to marry her. So why have you been in such a high dudgeon all week?"

It hadn't been *all* week. The exhilaration of delivering a baby had stayed with him for at least a few days. Despite his fear, he'd done something he'd firmly believed he would never be able to do again. But Cassie had needed him that night at Hope House; his fear had not. After, when she'd praised him, he'd reveled in it, while his fear had never given him anything in return but more weight on his soul.

The whispers and printed lies regarding the need for a hasty union between him and Cassie had dulled that exhilaration considerably. A decorous courtship could have gone on for some time. One dogged by rumors of iniquitous behavior, however, could not. Fournier would expect Grant to formally propose tonight, at the dinner. A dinner that he now could not attend. He also could not see Cassie again. The courtship was over.

And to top things off, the previous evening, a message from James had arrived.

"James's wife has delivered their new child," Grant said to Hannah now. "A perfectly healthy baby boy. Mother and infant are well," he added because Hannah would want to know. She liked Vera and James the most out of his family.

Her eyes popped with glee. "A boy! Well then, that is wonderful news. The marquess has his grandson. Surely this means his demands of you are unnecessary."

Grant took out his fob to check the hour. The afternoon was closing in on five o'clock, when he would shutter the clinic for the rest of the week.

"Yes. Good news. I'm sure the marquess is in raptures and has forgotten entirely that he threatened to see me destitute should I not fall in line."

The false courtship would have ended anyway, he reminded himself, with or without the chatter about Cassie's night at Lindstrom House. Everything was always supposed to go back to normal, and now it would. Tonight, Grant would go directly to Lindstrom House after closing the clinic and abolish the betrothal rumors. He'd tell his father that

Cassie had cried off when she found him kissing another woman, or some such rubbish. He would believe it, and that was all that mattered.

"Perhaps you should speak to Lady Cass—"

A few quick knocks on the clinic's front door bowled over Hannah's comment. Thank God. No, he could not speak to Lady Cassandra outside of a letter to inform her that she was released from his scheme. She would be pleased. He'd been an arse to her from the start. He'd lied through his teeth too. He'd have never told the duke a thing about Hope House, but how was Cassie to have known? He'd exploited her doubt, and for that, he would likely rot in hell.

Hannah went to open the clinic door and brought in the next patients. Grant's spirits lifted marginally to see it was Mr. Mansouri and Amir. The boy limped in, but he had a crooked grin on his face as he avidly leaped onto the table.

"We couldn't make it last week, what with a busy day at the wharves," Mr. Mansouri said, extending a newspaper-wrapped bundle to Hannah. She was accustomed to taking the offerings some of the prouder patients made in place of money and left to deliver the fresh catch to the kitchen.

"You made it this week, that's what matters," Grant said. "How is your wound healing, Amir?" It was promising, at least, that he'd not heard from Mr. Mansouri.

"My scab's tight and itchy," Amir answered. His father said, "He is hoping the sutures can be removed."

Grant rolled up the boy's trouser leg and was relieved to see the shin was wrapped in clean bandages. He'd sent plenty home with them, and it appeared they'd kept up with the changings. Unraveling the cotton linen, he prepared to see infection. But the gash was healing well, without swelling or weeping.

"You're in luck," Grant said. "The sutures can be removed, and it looks like the most you'll suffer is a wicked scar to tell tales about when you're old."

Amir's toothy grin gave him another infusion of good spirits. But not enough to lift him entirely from his high dudgeon, as Hannah had called it.

She returned to the surgery and brought forth the required tools. The boy grimaced in preparation for pain.

"It won't hurt half as much this time," Grant promised him.

"I came prepared anyhow," Amir said.

"Prepared in what way?" Grant made the first snip of the black floss.

"What can you break, even if you never pick it up or touch it?"

Ah. A riddle. Grant smiled. "That is a challenging one. Let me think..." He snipped another section of floss and pulled it from the scabbing wound. He'd heard this one before but took his time. "A promise," he answered after another moment. Amir groaned.

"All right. What about this: Why do bees have such sticky hair?"

He chuckled. "Do bees have hair?"

"Just answer it," Amir said, though his father scolded him for being rude. Grant snipped and pulled more of the stitches, unbothered by the boy's impatience. It was rather endearing.

"It must have something to do with honey," he mused aloud.

"They use honeycombs," Hannah said smugly, and Amir clapped.

"Know-it-all. I nearly had it," Grant said. "Very well, Amir, we've time for one more before you're ready to run out of here, completely healed."

He swung his legs over the edge of the patient table. "This one's hard: You keep me even after you've given me to someone else. What am I?"

Grant cocked his head and pushed back onto his heels as the answer came to him instantly. It might not have, had he not been wallowing all week. His mind had been spinning around the truth of his foul mood, refusing to stop and acknowledge it. But Amir's riddle had finally brought him to a standstill.

He should have been overjoyed to have a nephew, as he'd wanted. To be off the hook with the marquess. He should have been relieved to know things could now go back to normal.

But he wasn't any of those things.

"Well?" Amir prodded. "You don't know, do you? Giving up?"

Grant shook his head, but his throat was too thick to speak.

He didn't want it to be over. He didn't want Cassie to walk away. To leave him. Grant wanted to be with her every night and every morning. He wanted her everywhere, wherever he was. The thought of her somewhere else, *with* someone else... Bloody hell.

He was in love with the woman.

When in Christ had this happened?

"Doctor Brown?" Hannah said softly. He blinked and turned, meeting her stricken gaze. "What is wrong?"

"A heart," he said, looking to Amir. "You keep your heart even when it belongs to someone else."

Amir clapped again and whooped as he hopped down from the table. "You got that one, doctor! I'll think of more for next time."

"Amir, as much as I like riddles, let us hope there is no next time."

Mr. Mansouri shook Grant's hand, thanking him, and they left. He stayed where he was, still rocked by the revelation that had just smacked him in the back of the skull. What was he going to do?

The clamor of the front door opening and shutting, then footfalls coming toward the surgery, distracted him from the overwhelming question.

Tris barreled into the room, and Grant snapped to attention.

"Lady Cassandra has found Isabel," he panted. "She wants me to bring you. She says Isabel is sick, too."

Grant broke from his numbed hold and hurried to his desk, for his medical bag. "Where?"

"A church in Shadwell. St. Paul's."

He knew of it, and it wasn't far. "Hannah, close up the clinic and have Merryton bring you home."

"Grant—" she began, but then stifled her objection. "Just be careful."

He kissed her cheek and nodded, then followed Tris as he raced from the clinic.

CHAPTER TWENTY-FOUR

St. Paul's Church, near the river, still had the gleam of newness about it. The parish's previous church had been demolished and this new one, a commissioners' church, had only recently been erected, along with the adjacent rectory and school. Sister Nan often lamented the new design, saying the original structure had been more impressive, and besides, Parliament could have put the money that was used to build it to much better use. "*The parishioners can't eat limestone or brick, can they?*" she was fond of saying.

As Sister Nan guided the small wagon toward the church, Cassie held the basket firmly in her lap. Caroline's baby boy was wrapped snugly in flannel and wool, and as Mrs. Powers had just finished feeding him, he'd slept contentedly as they wended through the streets. Now, however, he made little sounds as he wriggled and stretched awake. His fist popped out from the wrappings, and Cassie carefully eased it back in.

He was the most adorable thing, with wisps of black hair and a pouty bottom lip that made her smile. Maybe Caroline had been wise not to hold him, so as not to grow attached. If she had no memory of what he looked like, would she be better able to heal? It was possible. But Cassie could not go so far as to wish she had done the same after her daughter had been born. She cherished the short amount of time she'd held her baby too much to wish it gone from her memory, even if it was excruciating to remember at times. The determined strength of her little girl's hand as she gripped Cassie's pointer finger, the impossibly soft skin of her wrinkled feet, and the sweet, immaculate scent of her head when she'd kissed it, murmuring a promise to never forget her, were memories that could fill her heart and keep it beating as easily as they could rip apart small pieces of her soul.

"You've done this before with your own," Sister Nan said as she turned the horse toward the rear of the churchyard.

Cassie looked up from the basket and met the nun's gentle, knowing smile. She saw no judgment, no censure. "How could you tell?"

"The look in your eyes when you watch him." She slowed the horses to a stop inside a small, enclosed gravel square between the church and rectory and pushed the hand brake into position. Then, the older woman rested a hand on Cassie's arm.

"I know the pain myself, so I can see it in others easily."

Cassie blinked, stunned. This Anglican nun couldn't possibly... But when Sister Nan nodded in confirmation, she felt ashamed for doubting her. Cassie had presumed too much.

"Does it ever get any easier?" Cassie was suddenly desperate to know.

"Yes," Sister Nan said with a thoughtful nod. But then she frowned. "And no."

Cassie knew her meaning without having to ask.

"But we do our best," she went on. "We find new things and new people to love."

At that word—love—a face sprang to mind, unbidden. His vibrant green eyes, and his dimples whenever the playful quirk of his lips converted to a wicked grin. His unruly black hair that always seemed to draw her fingers toward it. But it wasn't just Grant's handsome face that came to mind; it was how she felt when she was with him. Yes, he infuriated her. Yes, he had pressured her into a false courtship that had been a hindrance from the start. And yet, there was no use denying that even with all that, whenever he entered a room, she felt better than she had before, when he had not been there. The truth was, Cassie would rather be locked in an argument with Grant than be alone, or with anyone else. With Grant, she was accustomed to feeling her blood rise, but lately, it was with more thrill than it was with irritation. Now, after their night at Lindstrom House, the difference was even more pronounced.

How could she have been so rash? How could she have not seen that she was already in love with him, and that one night would never be enough? Without even knowing it, she'd given away her heart to yet another man who would not offer for her. And this time, she'd asked him not to.

"Come now," Sister Nan said. "I'll show you to Isabel."

Now that it was evening, lanterns and candles lit the inside of the church, but it was the large rectory and school she led them toward.

"The rector knows we take in orphans to place out," the

nun said as they entered a side door to the rectory. "But he wouldn't approve of sheltering an unmarried mother here. So, I've kept Isabel's presence to myself."

She took Cassie down a corridor, toward where Sister Nan and a few other nuns resided. She explained that the rector's rooms were on the opposite side of the building, and since he never trespassed here, so long as Isabel stayed inside and was quiet, he would not notice her.

The nun stopped at a door and knocked lightly before unlocking it. Isabel sat on the edge of a narrow bed, back straight and tensed in preparation to run. But then she saw Cassie, and her shoulders sagged. "Miss Banks, thank goodness, it is you."

It was a simple room, with a single bed, a washstand, and a dresser. A low table dressed in prayer candles and a statue of Mary in a penitent pose was the only other ornamentation. Several more candles lit the room, and the wavering light showed healing bruises under Isabel's eye and on her cheek.

Cassie handed the baby basket to Sister Nan and went to the bed, where Isabel was already laying down again. After pulling the blanket up over her, she peeled off a glove and pressed a palm to her forehead. It was scorching. She turned to the nun, recalling what Grant had said about keeping others away. "Take the baby, sister. He shouldn't be in here."

Sister Nan nodded and left, closing the door behind her.

"Your fever is high," Cassie told Isabel. "But Doctor Brown is coming. He's going to help you."

She shook her head on the pillow, her hair damp with sweat. "I have nowhere to go. Nowhere to hide. I can't do this."

Cassie went to the small table with a basin and pitcher

and poured out some water. She wet a cloth and then folded it over Isabel's forehead.

"Yes, you can. You will. I promise, Isabel, you're not alone."

In the corridor, footsteps scuffed lightly along the tiled floor. How had Grant already arrived? Cassie stood to meet him, but as the door opened, her body went rigid.

Mr. Youngdale entered, his cloak and hat as black as his menacing grin, puckering the scabbing gashes on his cheek.

"No!" Isabel yelped, jerking upright in the bed.

"Thank you for leading me to my wife." His voice, though smooth and modulated, ran with an uncurrent of hostility. So did his expression as he looked between Isabel on the bed, and then Cassie, who stood between them.

"You were still following me," she whispered, cursing herself for her stupidity. He'd left Grosvenor Square after trailing her from Duke's, and she'd presumed that had been the end of it. But it hadn't been. He'd been watching her ever since, and she'd naively led him straight to his quarry.

"I am not your wife," Isabel said through gritted teeth. She shook, her forehead glistening with sweat, and her coloring had paled. She was ill and in no state to fight.

"You will be, if only to give me my rightful property when it is born." A long blade dropped into Mr. Youngdale's palm, and he made a low, swiping gesture with it toward Cassie. "Move aside."

Her pulse throbbed as her mind jumped to Sister Nan and the baby and if they were safe. Then to Grant and Tris and when they might be here. But she couldn't depend on their arrival. She had to defend Isabel herself somehow.

"No," she replied to Mr. Youngdale. "She is not your property, and neither is her child. Leave here, now."

He wouldn't. Cassie knew that even as she said it. He stepped forward.

"You may be the sister of a duke, but when people learn you've been secretly operating a home for pregnant whores, I doubt they will be surprised that you met your end in a Whitechapel alley, which is exactly where you'll be found."

He lunged. Isabel screamed as Cassie barely escaped the slicing path of the blade. In her dive to the side, her toe snagged on the foot of the bed, and she lost her balance. Landing hard on the floor, Cassie twisted to see Mr. Youngdale latched his hand around Isabel's arm and hauled her from the bed. She fought, thrashing and screaming. Cassie needed a weapon, but the room was utterly spare—except for the prayer table near her shoulder.

She grabbed the first thing she could think of—the statue of Mary. It was surprisingly heavy, made of stone or marble, rather than hollow ceramic as she'd imagined it would be. As Mr. Youngdale struggled to drag Isabel toward the door, Cassie rolled into a kneeling position and swung the statue, bashing it into his knees. A sickening crunch preceded his animal like howl. He lashed out at her with the knife, but she'd fallen back to the floor, out of reach. Isabel shoved him and kicked, and keeping her hands on the statue, Cassie staggered to her feet, prepared to swing again, this time, for his head.

The door to the room crashed open, and then Grant was barreling inside. He slammed into Mr. Youngdale, his momentum driving them both into the washstand and knocking it over. The basin and pitcher shattered onto the floor.

"He has a knife!" Cassie screamed, terrified that he would plunge the blade into Grant as they smashed into another wall.

Cassie gathered a sobbing Isabel to her feet and urged her toward the door. But she couldn't leave Grant, who now pinned Mr. Youngdale to the wall. He thumped his arm repeatedly until the knife dropped from his grip and clattered onto the floor. Cassie kicked it further away.

"Go! Fetch a constable!" Grant shouted.

Isabel darted from the room just as Tris was rushing through the door. They caught each other's arms, but only briefly basked in seeing each other again.

"The sister is shouting for help, go!" he told her, and Isabel left with the task.

Together, Grant and Tris shoved Mr. Youngdale to his stomach and pinioned him to the floor. The man howled some more, and when Grant knelt on his legs to keep him still, he screamed.

"My knee!" he sobbed. "The bitch shattered it."

Heaving for breath, his hat lost in the scuffle, Grant peered between the discarded statue on the floor and Cassie. He grinned. "That is the sort of divine fury I wholly support."

He got up, leaving Tris to stay with Mr. Youngdale. He wouldn't be going anywhere. He lay flat and moaning, utterly whipped. Grant took Cassie by the shoulders and inspected her.

"Are you hurt?"

She shook her head, but when she started to reply that

she was fine, her voice squeezed off. Her limbs quaked as the full extent of what just happened struck her.

Grant pulled her to him, crushing her in his arms and pressing his lips against her forehead.

"You found us," she managed to say.

"We heard screams as soon as we entered the churchyard," he explained.

Cassie closed her eyes and rested her cheek against his shoulder, letting him hold her. But then, he peeled her away and tipped her chin up to meet his eyes. "There will be patrolmen coming. You need to leave. You can't be found here."

"What about you?"

"Don't worry about me. I'll take care of Isabel, and Tris will take you home."

"No, I'll go to Hope House," she said. "Meet me there afterward."

"My knee!" Youngdale grunted, struggling under Tris's weight. "Get off me. I need a doctor!"

Grant released Cassie, whose shivering had only increased at the thought of avoiding the constables. Of leaving Grant to clean up this mess.

"Sit him up, Tris," he commanded. Her driver did as requested, bringing the man into a sitting position while pinning his arms behind his back.

"A doctor you say?" Grant asked. "You're in luck."

He struck Mr. Youngdale in the face with a hard crack of his fist, knocking him flat onto the floor and out cold.

CHAPTER

TWENTY-FIVE

It was well past nine o'clock, and Cassie had still not left Crispin Street. Michael and Genie's dinner had been scheduled for seven, and by now her absence, alongside Grant's, would have surely elicited concern. Her brother would send a footman to Grosvenor Square. When Cassie was not found there, Michael would likely go to Thornton House himself. When neither of them were found, she could only imagine what her brother would suspect.

She should have left for Mayfair immediately from St. Paul's Church. Logic and reason and self-preservation all demanded it of her, and yet, she'd gone to Hope House anyway. How could she attend dinner and pretend as if a crazed man had not just attacked her with a knife? And was Grant to arrive as well, pretending as though he had not subdued the man and saved both her life and Isabel's?

So much pretending. She was tired of it all. Utterly exhausted by it.

Elyse paced the sitting room, her arms crossed. "This is exactly what Madame Archambeau was worried about."

She had returned from the benefactress's dinner just minutes ago, and Cassie had explained everything that had happened at the church rectory.

"This area is too dangerous, and our location too insecure. We're often hiding women from their men and families, just like Mr. Youngdale, and what happened with him is a prime example of how weak our whole arrangement is."

Each word was a stake through Cassie's heart.

"But that is our purpose. It's why we started this home to begin with. To give women a safe place, a private place, with no judgment."

Elyse quit pacing and, still wearing her dinner gown of golden amber silk, she came to sit next to Cassie. "If we promise safety, we must be able to deliver it. The same goes for privacy. That wretched man is going to try and defend himself by denigrating Hope House, exposing it, saying we've kidnapped women—"

"We don't know what he will say," she argued, but she feared Elyse was right. She usually was. Her wisdom outpaced Cassie's by a long stretch.

"Madame Archambeau will support us financially; she's given us her word. But we need to consider improvements. More protection."

Cassie nodded. "Stronger walls."

Elyse covered Cassie's hand, which was resting limply on her lap. "What is it you're thinking right now?"

Her throat cinched tight. "I'm not entirely sure."

"Does it have to do with Lord Thornton?" she asked with a playful waggle of her brow.

She nodded, then sighed. "Yes. A little bit."

Elyse squinted, her lips pursing into a discerning grin.

"He seems to be a good man. What with his bravery tonight and his help with Isabel. And he has kept your secret."

This seemed to impress Elyse, though Cassie was certain she would change her tune should she learn about the courtship scheme. But she said nothing. She didn't want Elyse to despise Grant, not when Cassie could no longer despise him.

So much had changed over the last few weeks. Her secret life had been running with such smooth, oiled precision until Grant had walked into the middle of it all. The wall separating her two lives was rapidly dissolving now. And with Madame Archambeau's support assured, more changes would be coming. It should have frightened her more than it currently did.

"Elyse," she began. "I'm not sure I can be Jane Banks anymore."

Her friend shifted on the sofa cushion to fully face her. "You were never going to be able to be her forever."

"I love it here. I feel purposeful, and I'm proud of what we've started. But...you don't need me. Not anymore. Not now that you'll have Madame Archambeau's money behind you." Quick as a cricket, Elyse smacked Cassie on the arm, startling her. "Ow! What was that for?"

"For being stupid. It isn't just your money that makes you useful. Your place is here, whether you're managing the costs of operations or not. And whether you're Miss Jane Banks or Lady Cassandra."

She dropped her hand from rubbing her shoulder and blinked back tears. She blamed them on exhaustion and the tumultuous events of the day.

"That's good to know, since my brother will cut off my income when he learns the truth."

Elyse's lips parted on a gust of air. "You will tell him?"

She felt a surge of trepidation—and determination. "I may wait until after the holidays so as not to ruin them for everyone, but yes. Yes, I think I must."

Elyse had been right; she was never going to be able to be Jane Banks forever. All her secrets, her little lies, and vague excuses that had at first been diverting and insubstantial, had finally started to weigh heavily. Telling herself that it was all worth it because of the good she was doing had reached its limit. She *was* doing good. But at what expense? Her lies to her family and to those who cared for her and trusted her no longer felt light and merry. They were just plain deceitful.

"So," Cassie went on, "before he can evict me from Grosvenor Square and lock me in a room a Violet House for the rest of my life, what do you say to coming to tea tomorrow? We can discuss improvements to Hope House."

Elyse was difficult to stun, but right then she looked utterly bowled over. "You're inviting me to your home? As Lady Cassandra Sinclair?"

Nerves fizzled out along her extremities, and she got to her feet, suddenly restless. But also resolved. "Yes. I should have done so long before now. I am finished with being a coward."

Elyse shook her head, surely about to tell her she wasn't that. But Cassie raised a hand to stop her. "I want to be *me*, whatever the consequences. And I would like my friend to come to tea to discuss business matters. Will you?"

Male voices coming from the kitchen accompanied the bright grin stretching over Elyse's lips. "Say one o'clock?"

Cassie nodded. "Perfect."

Elyse left to go to her room and change from her dinner gown, and Cassie made her way to the kitchen. As she suspected, Grant had arrived, and Tris, who'd been on watch at the back door, had let him in.

She pulled up short when she saw him. A purpling bruise discolored his bottom lip and there was a small bloody cut near his eye.

"It's nothing," he said in response to her flaring eyes and halting steps toward him. "I'm fine. As is Isabel. I took her to Thornton House. It's safe there, and her fever isn't the same as Dorie's. A simple head cold, I'm sure of it."

Thornton House? He'd exposed his true identity to Isabel by taking her there.

"And that devil bastard?" Tris asked, scowling. He then bobbed his head toward Cassie. "Forgive me, my lady."

"No need." She looked to Grant. "Has he been arrested?"

Hesitation dimmed his expression, and her heart sank. "Yes, but I'm not sure what will come of it. Assault charges usually result in minor punishment, and with his connections, he is sure to be released. At least a constable will keep guard over him at London Hospital where he was taken for his knee, which I think is indeed shattered," he said with a wry grin.

Injuring him wasn't enough, but it would be a fantasy to believe someone like Mr. Youngdale would meet with proper consequences for what he'd done. At least Isabel was somewhere secure for now.

"He should be locked up," Tris said. "He all but admitted to Isabel that he pushed his first wife down the stairs."

But as there had been no investigation at the time, that would not matter.

With a defeated sigh, Tris slapped his cap back on his head. "I'll go out to the horses, my lady."

He left the kitchen, and Cassie locked the door behind him. She felt Grant's eyes on her back as she went to the stove.

"Tea?" she asked. When she picked up the kettle, her hand shook. Maybe from exhaustion or frustration. Or simply because they were alone.

"No, thank you." He joined her at the stove. There was something he wanted to say. She could feel it. Though, she knew it would not be about tonight's altercation, nor about Isabel or Mr. Youngdale.

She set the kettle down and blurted out, "I'm going to tell him."

Grant frowned. "Tell who, what?"

"My brother. About Hope House and Jane Banks and that I've made my choice, and he can either support me or he can turn his back on me." She dragged in a breath, suddenly short on it.

Grant cocked his head. "That is a bold move."

It was. It also meant that it no longer mattered if he followed through with his threat.

"Cassie," he began. She could not think of another way to stall him. "I'm an uncle again. James has a son."

She stepped away from the stove, and from him. Her fingers twisted together as she floundered for what to say. There was only one acceptable thing. "That is wonderful."

"It is," he agreed.

She kept her back to him, her eyes burning all the sudden.

"The marquess will retract his ultimatum now, I imagine. You must be relieved. You've gotten what you hoped for." She didn't mean for it to sound bitter. Bitter wasn't what she was feeling at all.

"That was the hope," he said, agreeing again. It was getting on her nerves.

Cassie turned, stiffening her neck and shoulders. But she could not quite look him in the eye. "I will tell my brother that he no longer needs to discuss matters with you. And you can inform your family that I've cried off. Now that this charade is over, it would be best if we did not see each other again—"

"Cassie." He took a stride toward her. She backed up a step to compensate. Grant stopped and held still.

"As for Isabel," she said. "Can I trust that you will take care of arrangements for her?"

Though she was still unable to look him in the eye, she felt his answering glower. "Of course. But there is no reason for such finality."

"There is. You know there is." She closed her stinging eyes, resolved to not let one singular tear slip free. "I haven't been myself, and now, with Madame Archambeau's support, there is so much to do. I need to get back to what matters most, and that's Hope House. Please, Grant. Please go."

He didn't move. Not for several breaths. Not until she turned to the side and continued to refuse to look at him. From her peripheral vision, she saw him go to the door. He reached for the handle. Then paused.

"I was never going to tell your brother. I lied to you to get what I wanted. I used you. I said I was nothing like Renfry, but I am."

Cassie whirled toward him, ready to refute that, but he held up his hand.

"At least do the me honor of despising me as much as I despise myself. I deserve no less, and it will make things more bearable for us both." He opened the door. "Goodbye, Lady Cassandra."

The door closed behind him, and Cassie's legs folded. All strength depleted, she collapsed into a chair and wept.

CHAPTER TWENTY-SIX

It was Christmas Eve, and as with most December twenty-fourths, Grant spent the bulk of it dreading the marquess's annual fireside dinner. It was the one sentimental tradition his father had kept from the time Grant's mother had been alive.

Though he'd been young when she'd passed, he still recalled how the servants would decorate the drawing room, dressing the hearth and mantel with greens and ribbons and pinecones, and how instead of dining around a table in any formal way, they would eat as they would a picnic, with plates on their laps or on small folding tables. It was always a messy affair, but Grant's mother had thought it cozy and rustic and good fun. The marquess must have enjoyed it too, though he hardly ever let on that he remotely enjoyed anything at all.

However, this Christmas Eve, Lord Lindstrom was as chipper as a schoolboy, and all in thanks to the arrival of the grandson he'd been impatiently waiting for.

"All is well and good, well and good," he said from his

leather chair, for what must have been the tenth time since the evening had commenced. "I knew it would it happen, as it should. A healthy little lad, too."

Slumped into the corner of a sofa, Grant leaned his head back and groaned. The marquess pointedly ignored him, though Penelope, seated next to him, laughed softly. Her husband, Alfred, was still happily eating his rum and currant pudding, a napkin tucked into his collar. Lawrence and his wife deplored the whole tradition and had hardly touched a thing on their plates, though Harold and his wife had made more of an effort. An unfortunate streak of gravy had dribbled down his cravat and Priscilla had spent a ridiculous amount of time trying to scrub it out with her napkin. On the carpet in front of the blazing hearth, Grant's nieces played a game of jacks.

"Of course, it *is* always preferable to have a spare heir," the marquess went on.

Grant lifted his head, the roasted fowl they'd been served earlier now churning in his stomach. "You are perpetually unsatisfiable, aren't you? You've had your prized grandson for less than a week, and already, you're angling for another."

His father harrumphed. "Not from you! I should have known better than to encourage you toward marrying again."

Grant sat upright. "*Encourage*? You threatened to cut me off, bone dry, unless I found a wife by the first of the year."

"And look how well that went," the marquess said. "The duke's sister has given you the old heave-ho!"

Grant clamped his jaw shut, refusing to rise to the old man's bait. The last week had passed in a blur of action, keeping his mind off Cassie and their parting at Hope

House. He'd hired a lady's companion for Isabel and arranged for them to be taken to his hunting lodge in Essex, where she would be kept safe from Mr. Youngdale. As expected, he'd been released from custody after paying a simple fine for the charges of assault. Hugh had informed Grant that some Bow Street officers had agreed to do him a favor and look deeper into Youngdale's first wife's death, but there were no guarantees. Isabel would be safest at the lodge for now.

Cassie was relieved. He'd sent a note with the plans for Isabel, and she'd responded with a brief thank you and an announcement that her driver, Tris, had stepped down from his post. He was going to Essex, to be near Isabel. Otherwise, there had been no contact between them. Just as Cassie had requested.

Thinking of her hurt. It was a gasping, hollow ache in the center of his chest, and no amount of whisky or rounds in the boxing ring at Jack's could dull it. There was no getting around the plain truth: He'd done everything wrong.

"A damned shame, too. The lady had a backbone, at least," his father went on, snorting a laugh.

"Father do leave him be," Penelope said.

"What happened? How did you drive her away?" the old man asked, ignoring his daughter. "My guess is that Fournier wouldn't allow it."

"The duke does not tell her what to do," Grant said tightly.

She would have told Fournier by now about her secret life. He'd had to bury the urge to write and ask how the news had been received. No matter how incensed the duke was,

Cassie would not give up on Hope House. She was too damned stubborn.

"Ah, so she rejected you all on her own, did she?"

Grant gritted his back teeth. "Yes."

His father sat forward in his chair and slapped his thighs, as if he'd just heard a raucous joke. As if he was pleased rather than disappointed that a woman had rejected him. He'd been the one to demand a marriage, but the fact that Grant had failed seemed to be the outcome he'd actually desired.

Grant met Harold's bespectacled gaze, a pleat of pity cutting into his brother's forehead. Lawrence avoided Grant's eyes by checking the time on his fob. Their wives exchanged discomfited looks, too. Had James been here, rather than at his home with his wife and newborn son, he might have interjected with some well-timed quip to ease the marquess's focus from Grant. But other than Penelope's feeble attempt, no one dared stand up to their father. No except Cassie. His heart squeezed when he recalled how she'd defended him at that dinner. For once, the marquess had been roundly stymied.

"That makes you happy, does it?" Grant asked. His father's grin slipped. "That I've failed to meet your expectations and fulfil your edicts. I wonder, why did you even bother to dole out that ultimatum when really, all you wanted—all you've ever wanted—was for me to fail?"

Lord Lindstrom's mouth turned down, and his expression went to stone. Grant got to his feet. He could no longer sit and say nothing. The thought of it suddenly made him ill. He didn't want to be like Harold or Lawrence or even James or Penelope, too cowed by their father's bitterness, his sharp tongue, and his constant disappointment to dare to speak up.

But Grant was already guilty of the same cowardice, wasn't he? To evade his father's wrath and displeasure, he had manipulated Cassie, applying pressure to one of her weak points—Hope House—until she'd given in. He'd valued keeping his father happy, and keeping his father's money flowing toward him, over his own honor. He'd told himself it was nothing, a prank, that no harm would be done.

Ballocks.

"Congratulations, my lord." Grant spread out his arms. "You have what you want."

"Believe it or not, I do *not* want a failure for a son. I want you to be a gentleman for Christ's sake. Doctoring is lowly work, and no lady of the peerage will ever stoop to being a doctor's wife. Lady Cassandra has made that clear."

"Do not speak as if you know Cassie's mind. You do not." He spoke calmly, evenly, even though he did not feel an ounce of peace right then. And he wouldn't. Not until he stopped pretending.

"She approves of my work. Every facet of it." He paused. "Including the charity clinic I run in Whitechapel."

The room had already been quiet, but now, it was as if even the fire in the hearth had stopped its crackling. Slowly, the marquess rose from his chair.

"I hope this is another one of your jokes," he seethed.

"I have never been more serious in my life."

Lawrence spluttered, "Whitechapel? That place is a cesspool."

Grant held his father's lowering glare. "That's right. I tend to the masses, father. The poor, the destitute, men and women of different colors and creeds, prostitutes—" At that,

Lawrence's wife gasped. But Grant only smiled. "And a hell of a lot of criminals."

"Uncle Grant said hell, mummy," Lawrence's daughter, Emmaline said from the carpet. His nieces had abandoned their game of jacks. Grant belted out a laugh as a weight he'd not known was even there lifted from his shoulders. Miraculously, he could breathe again. How long had he been struggling for air?

"What are you thinking opening a clinic in the slums?" Lawrence asked. "Mingling with the diseased?"

"Now, let us all calm down—" Alfred began to say, but he was disregarded.

"This is unacceptable!" the marquess shouted. "I knew medical school was going to bring nothing but trouble. I should never have indulged you!"

"Did you say Lady Cassandra knew of this clinic?" Penelope asked.

"That is what he said, Pen. Do listen," Harold chided.

"Mummy, what is a prostitute?" another of Grant's nieces asked.

He threw back his head and laughed as Mary and Priscilla got up from their chairs to shepherd the little girls from the room.

"That is it! I am finished with being patient," his father said. "I am cutting you off until you close down that clinic and give up your profession. You will marry and you will be a gentleman, as I've raised you to be. And by God, you will not bring shame upon this family!"

It was the very threat Grant had been desperate to circumnavigate before. The one that had led him to manipulate Cassie. As Grant stood in the center of the room, his brothers and sister bickering between themselves and his father blasting off at the mouth about the repercussions of such selfishness, a surge of exuberance unlocked something inside him.

"Take your money," he said, tossing up his arms. "Go on, take it. Cut me off. I will no longer be beholden to you. I am finished, too, Father. I'm finished caring what you think. I am a doctor. I treat people who need help, and I don't give a damn if they live in Mayfair or Wapping or if it might damage my reputation."

He'd never felt so alive, so free as he did right then. Shocked silence descended over his family. They knew he was not in jest. He could see it on their expressions.

"I will make my own living, if I must, and if that means I am a destitute lord without two ha'pennies to rub together, then so be it. It will be worth it to not have to come crawling to you with my tail tucked between my legs. And if I marry," he went on, unable to curb his erupting confession. "If I marry, I will do so because *I* want to. Not because you want a spare grandson to ensure the title passes within your line. I will marry because I am in love, and I can't imagine my life without her. Because she is the only thing I can think about, even though she makes me want to tear my hair out, and even though she makes me feel like I'm a bottle of brut about to explode." He turned in a circle, raking his fingers along his scalp. "And she's not replacing Sarah, no, it's not that. I can't compare them. They are both incomparable. But Sarah is my past, and Cassie..." He dragged in a breath. "Is my future."

He fell quiet and waited for the guilt to weigh him down again. But it didn't. After several breathes, the idea of a future with Cassie had still not filled him with any guilt at all. Only anticipation. And then, uncertainty.

She didn't want him. She'd made it clear that she didn't wish to marry, and after the way he'd used her, how could he blame her? Cassie may have come to his bed willingly, but that had been on her terms, and for just one night. She'd gotten what she'd wanted from him, and now, she'd asked him to stay away. Was that what *she* wanted, though, or was it because of his inflexible avowal to never remarry? *Hell.* He had to find out.

"I thought Lady Cassandra turned you down," Lawrence said.

Snapped from his stupor, Grant saw his family all staring at him with bemused expressions. "She didn't turn me down," he replied. "Because I never even asked her."

"What are you talking about? The girl said you were betrothed!" his father spluttered.

He could keep spluttering for all Grant cared. "I have to go." He broke for the door. "I have somewhere more important I need to be."

CHAPTER TWENTY-SEVEN

For a week, Cassie had planned what she would say. And for a week, she'd struggled to find the right words. Whenever she thought she'd settled on the perfect way to announce to her brother what she had been doing for over a year, she would practice saying it, cringe, and start over. Until finally, she realized that there was no combination of words in the English language that could possibly make such a confession sound agreeable.

"Milady? We are here," Ruth said from the opposite bench inside Cassie's carriage. In fact, they had arrived at Violet House several minutes ago. Patrick, whom she'd hired after Tris left for Essex, had opened the door. He was still waiting for Cassie to emerge.

Her body was a pile of lead on the bench. Every time she meant to move, she found she could not. It was Christmas Eve, and inside her brother's home, a family dinner was underway. Hugh, Audrey, Sir, and little Cat would be there, as would Tobias.

When Cassie had missed the previous dinner at Violet

House on the evening Mr. Youngdale had followed her to St. Paul's Church and rectory, she had sent a note to her brother, announcing that she had ended the courtship with Grant and that she needed time and space. He'd given it to her, only asking that she come for Christmas Eve. Being with family may help her to restore herself, he'd said.

So, for the next handful of days she had lingered at home, in bed mostly, devising her confession. And thinking of Grant. Again and again, she heard the closing of the back door at Hope House as he left, and her own voice telling him to go, that it would be best if they did not see each other again. In genuine self-loathing, he'd likened himself to Renfry and asked her to do him the honor of despising him. It would make things easier, he'd said. He'd been right, it would. She'd tried, but just like her need to come clean about Hope House, she needed to face the truth that she didn't despise him. She couldn't. She couldn't even be angry with him for his pledge to never remarry out of dedication to his dead wife. How could she be when it was one of the things that she loved about him?

"My lady?" Patrick said. He still had his hand extended.

Cassie forced herself to sit forward and take his hand. The action physically drained her. Her pulse grew thready as she walked to the front door, the footman already there, waiting for her. He took her pelisse, hat, and gloves, and Cassie followed the lively voices toward the drawing room. Her somber march into the room was met with wide smiles and welcomes, and Genie and Audrey both stood to come greet her.

They'd heard of the courtship's end, of course. All of

London had. She'd avoided reading the gossip columns but when asked, Ruth confirmed it had been reported upon.

"They're speculating you cried off when you caught him with his mistress," Ruth had told her. Cassie's insides had felt as if they were imploding, crushing her from within. He would go to that club on Bond Street now. To Miss Devereaux, no doubt. He would carry on and forget Cassie, and she would have to find a way to live with it.

She would simply do what she had before. She'd throw herself into Hope House—the *new* Hope House, funded almost entirely by Madame Archambeau and Miss Stone. Elyse had come to Grosvenor Square for tea, as planned, and together, they'd drawn up plans to remake the safe house into a free lying-in hospital and school for women. Madame Archambeau had mentioned a building in Stepney that she owned, and with her additional funds, they could hire a team of security. Elyse had taken their plans back to the benefactress and she'd sent a note to Cassie with the good news—they were to visit the Stepney building at the first of the year.

If she moved forward with Elyse and Madame Archambeau, she would need to do so openly. Honestly. Without a doubt, she would be ostracized from society. Perhaps even from her own brother's home. It was a risk she was willing to accept.

"Toby, get your sister a sherry," Genie said as she led Cassie to a seat on the divan.

"I'm fine," Cassie tried to say, but she had to admit, she didn't sound fine. Her voice shook.

"That bloody blackguard. I knew he was no good," Michael said. "I'm sorry, Neatham, I know he's your friend, but even you must admit now that Thornton wasn't suitable for my sister."

Hugh didn't respond to the duke. He wouldn't denigrate his friend, nor could he argue against Michael's opinion.

"This isn't about Lord Thornton," Cassie said, waving aside the sherry Tobias had brought her. She jumped up from the divan. "I have something to tell you. All of you. And I'm sorry to ruin the night, I planned to wait until after dinner, but honestly, there's no good time to do it. I can't put it off any longer."

She closed her eyes. Looking at them would make it so much more difficult. All the practiced confessions and finessed words fled her mind, and she heard herself blurting: "I've been operating a home for unwed pregnant women in the East End for a year and using my pin money to fund it."

A handful of protracted beats of silence later, she peeked out at the room. Mouths gaped. Eyes blinked owlishly. Michael seemed to have turned into a statue, his loose jaw hanging open in a most unflattering expression.

"*You're* Hope House." Audrey's whisper severed the stunned quiet. "That is why you didn't need me to look into it for Isabel."

"Who is Isabel?" Genie asked.

"It doesn't matter who Isabel is," Michael said, breaking from his stony mold. "What do you mean you've been running a...a home for...My God, Cassie! The East End?"

Genie swiped the glass of sherry from Tobias's hand and brought it to her husband, who had collapsed backward into a chair. She ordered him to drink. He did, tossing it back in a single gulp.

"I think it does matter who Isabel is," Hugh said from

where he was standing behind Audrey's chair. "Unless I'm mistaken, she's the very sort of woman Cassie has been helping at this secret home."

He implored her with a wrinkled brow to speak up for herself. She nodded, the motion jerky with her muscles so tight with nerves. "Yes. Isabel found herself compromised and the man responsible was cruel. She had no one, no family to care for her, no one to turn to for help. But then she heard of a safe place."

"And you took her in?" Michael asked. "You *hid* her?"

"Her and many more like her, yes," she said, exhaling shakily. "The home is for any woman wishing to have their child in private."

"But you're no midwife," Tobias exclaimed, appearing even more boggled than Michael. "How did you even come to have this...this radical idea?"

Audrey cleared her throat. "Sir, would you please take Catherine to the kitchens? I'm sure Mrs. Comstock wouldn't mind."

The young man scowled at the dismissal. "Things were just getting interesting," he grumbled, but took Catherine's hand and did as he was asked. Genie dismissed the footman and maid from the room, too. As soon as they had gone, Cassie turned to her younger brother.

"Toby, there are things you don't know—"

She was cut off by the butler knocking on the closed drawing room door.

"What is it, Barton?" Michael snapped. The butler entered and bowed at the neck.

"Your Grace, a visitor. Lord Thornton. Are you in?"

Numbness stole over Cassie from crown to foot as Michael bellowed, "No, we are not in!"

But as Barton turned to deliver the response, Grant shoved past him, into the room.

"You're rather loud for not being in, Fournier." Grant's eyes immediately found and hinged onto Cassie. Her lungs drained of oxygen as she stared at him, her eyes drinking him in. What was he doing here?

"What the devil, Thornton?" Michael lunged to his feet. "How dare you intrude into our home uninvited, and after what you've done?"

"My goodness," Genie said with a gasp as she no doubt saw the faded bruising on his chin and the healing gash near his eye. "Lord Thornton, you've been hurt."

Torn between holding Cassie's gaze and responding to the duchess, he quickly looked away. "It was days ago, Your Grace, I am fine."

"You won't be if you don't get out of my house," Michael retorted.

"Michael, stop," Cassie said, her voice barely audible.

"Actually, I think Thornton's timing is perfect." Hugh sounded far too cheery for the tense moment. "I was just about to share some news about Mr. Youngdale."

"Who?" Michael, Genie, and Tobias exclaimed, all in unison.

"The man who compromised Isabel," Cassie said.

Tobias groaned. "The woman you took into this scandalous Hope House place?"

The corner of Grant's lips twitched, and that adorable dimple dug into his cheek. Oh, good heavens, why did she have the urge to run to him and kiss it?

"I see you told them," he said. She nodded, and he beamed at her with unabashed pride. She dragged in a breath, her head spinning from the rush of it.

"Why should we care about this Youngdale fellow?" Tobias asked.

"Because," Hugh began, "Cassie and Thornton defended a young woman's life against him, even though they risked their own necks to do so."

Cassie shot Hugh a pleading look. "I'm sure we don't need to discuss that right now." Michael was already at the end of his rope. Hearing about the attack in the alley and then the one at the rectory would push him right off.

"Perhaps not, but I think you'd like to know that Youngdale has been arrested—again. This time for the murder of his first wife." Cassie's skin prickled as Hugh continued. "I had some officers look further into her death, and the coroner confessed that Youngdale paid him an unfriendly visit, encouraging him rather forcefully to gloss over some other markings on the woman's body that indicated previous abuse. But it was one of Youngdale's housemaids who clinched it. She was threatened to keep silent about witnessing a dispute near the top of the stairs that resulted in her mistress being shoved to her death."

What Isabel had said was true then. He'd killed his first wife, and he would have had no qualms about doing the same to her after their child had been born. He'd wanted the child. Not her.

"That is awful," Genie said softly.

"He will be going away for quite some time," Hugh said confidently. Cassie nearly swayed with relief.

"Do you mean to say that my sister was in the presence of

a vile murderer?" Michael asked, the skin above his cravat turning florid.

"I am perfectly fine, Michael," she said with an exasperated sigh. "The important thing is that a woman is safe, and a murderer is going to prison."

"Yes, a woman who compromised herself, and with a man of immoral character," Tobias said, his cheeks becoming just as red as Michael's. "Not just her but all those women. How could you align yourself with such people? Really, Cassie, a home for unwed mothers? It is shameful."

Cassie reeled from the sharp scolding. Grant took a step toward her, as though he had seen it. But he stopped short of reaching for her. Instead, he turned to Tobias.

"There is nothing shameful about showing compassion. There are too many men who sow their wild oats and never look back to see what comes of them. Your sister is protecting and caring for women who have nowhere else to turn. You should be proud of her; you should support her."

Cassie stared at him in wonder, but Tobias only grated out a laugh. "Support her as she ruins herself by associating with other ruined women?"

"Choose your next words carefully, Tobias." The lowering timbre of Grant's voice lifted the small hairs on her arms.

She went to Grant and laid a hand on his shoulder. "It's all right. He doesn't know."

Tobias was the only person in the room who didn't. At the time, he'd been away at university, and it had been easy to leave him in the dark. The fewer people who knew, the better. But now, she knew she would have to tell him.

"That doesn't make it all right," Grant argued. He took

her hand from his shoulder and held it between his palms. "I won't hear a single word spoken against you; I don't care who it comes from."

"Grant," she whispered, keenly aware of all the eyes on them. "Why are you here? The charade is over. I've asked you to stay away."

Looking at him, just hearing his voice, hurt as much as it soothed.

He lifted her hand, still clasped between his, to his lips and held her in a stare so tender and vulnerable, it made her heart ache. "The charade is over, yes. It was over long before I even realized it."

She shook her head. "What do you mean by that?"

"I don't know when it happened. It might have been when you helped me with Amir at the clinic, or maybe when you confided in me about the baby. But it could have been even earlier when I saw you for that first time at Hope House. If that is the case, and I'm beginning to think it is, then the charade ended before it ever began."

She stared at him through hot welling tears as he pressed two more kisses to her fingertips.

"*What* is the blackguard saying?" Michael hissed to someone, but Cassie ignored him. She found it simple to do while locked in Grant's unyielding gaze.

"The blackguard is saying that he's been a bloody fool." Grant lowered her hand but didn't relinquish it. He only held on tighter. "When I bullied you into that courtship, I had every intention of getting what I wanted. But because of you, what I wanted changed. By the time I'd come to my senses, I'd done everything wrong."

She sipped shallow breaths, the rest of the room and

everyone within it disappearing. Only Grant mattered. Though she could barely see him through the haze of tears.

"All of London is right. I *am* a blackguard. I'm a scoundrel of the worst ilk. I've treated you wretchedly, and I will beg your forgiveness every day for the rest of my life if I must because whether you want me to be or not, I am in love with you."

A sob lodged in her throat, and with a blink, the welling tears spilled over. "You can't be. I'm ruined, Grant. I'm broken."

"We've both been broken," he said. "But we don't have to stay that way."

Her heart threatened to burst as she clung to Grant's hands. They were the only things keeping her upright as he sank to one knee. "I want you as my wife, Cassie. And there is nothing false or pretend about that."

She trembled, her mind reeling, her heart thrashing. This wasn't real. It couldn't be.

"I want to believe you." Her voice shook. "I want to trust you. I've never wanted anything more."

He frowned. "But?"

"But you said you'd never marry again, and I can't ask you to. I can't ask you to stop loving her."

"I never will." It was resolute. Unemotional. Just bare fact. Surprisingly, the twist of envy she'd felt the few times he'd spoken of his lost wife did not come. Grant was not fickle. He was steady and tenacious, and she admired him for it.

"My love for Sarah is entirely different from my love for you." He got up from one knee and pulled her closer, holding her hands to his chest. "She was the woman I needed then. You are the woman I need now. Cassie, you're the woman I *want*. Say you want me too. Tell me you love me, and I'll spend the rest of my life trying like hell to make you smile, even if I have to make a bloody fool of myself to do it."

Cassie laughed through her tears. "Yes, you idiot. Yes, I love you." She sucked in a breath. "I love you, and I'll marry you. Genuinely, this time."

A boyish grin cut those dimples into his cheeks, and she could no longer resist him. She grabbed Grant by the collar and dragged his lips to hers. He held her to him, squeezing her so tightly she could scarcely draw breath. She didn't care in the least. She didn't need something as trivial as air when his lips were on hers.

"Thornton!" Michael's bellow severed their locked mouths, but Grant didn't let her go. He kept a supportive arm around her as they faced the room and everyone watching. Belatedly, her cheeks fumed at their display, but from Hugh's wide grin, the tears sparkling in the corners of Audrey's eyes, Genie's steepled hands pressed against her radiant smile, and even Tobias's slightly bashful smirk, Cassie realized they had nothing to be embarrassed about.

"Come to my study," Michael said after his own flustered moment. "It looks as though we have important matters to discuss after all."

Cassie linked her arm around Grant's, unwilling to let him go. She wasn't certain she'd ever want to be anywhere again without a part of him touching her. "I will come too," she said. "If the pair of you will be discussing my marriage, I will be there as well."

Michael only shook his head. "Of course you will. Come along then."

EPILOGUE

The pains had been coming sporadically for the last hour. The twinges had been easy to ignore at first, but while Cassie had been sitting in the library at Hope Clinic with some of the women who'd expressed an interest in learning to read and write, something had changed. One of the young women, Janice, had touched her hand when Cassie's fingers froze on the primer they were reading together.

"Is it the little one, milady?"

The tightening around Cassie's middle had lessened, and she'd laughed. "It is. Struggling for room to move, I'm sure."

Although, she knew this wasn't the familiar jabbing of elbows, knees, or feet.

"Maybe we should stop for today," Petra, another resident at the clinic suggested.

Cassie was reluctant to end so early. She enjoyed the lessons in the library whenever she and Grant were at the clinic. They made the drive from Thornton House to Stepney Fields three days a week, and each time Cassie marveled at how far the place had come. So much had changed in the two years since Hope House and Grant's free clinic had merged at Madame Archambeau's Stepney property. The former church with its courtyard and rectory had been the perfect location for a new lying-in home and free clinic. With its main gate and a team of security, it was a secure place for women looking to escape a bad situation. Being so close to Whitechapel, it was also easily reached by Grant's regular patients. He was no longer Dr. Brown, and she was no longer Miss Jane Banks. They had decided together that the time for hiding was over.

Cassie took Janice and Petra's advice and concluded the day's lesson. She hefted herself from the chair, needing to brace a palm on the table to do so. She'd grown so round and heavy during the last month she could no longer see her feet. As she slowly made her way from the residential wing to the clinic, she evened her breathing. She didn't want to appear panicked when she met with Grant in the clinic wing. It had taken a full year after their wedding to convince him to try for a baby. His initial disinterest had developed into outright refusal, but she hadn't taken it to heart. She'd trusted that in time, he would overcome his fear. And he had.

It was next to impossible to keep their hands off each other for any length of time, so she was accustomed to her husband coming up behind her, wrapping his arms around her waist, and nuzzling her neck. However, soon after holding Hugh and Audrey's second child, James, named after Audrey's late brother, Grant had taken Cassie by surprise. He'd come up behind her, his lips brushing the shell of her ear, and he'd whispered, "I want to see you holding our child. I'm ready if you are."

Not very long after that, she'd conceived. After some initial panic, Grant had calmed. For a while, he'd been the picture of composure. However, the last few weeks, he'd become less tranquil and more agitated. They'd argued about her refusal to confine herself in the final month. He wanted her in bed, resting, feet up, all the time, but she wouldn't have it. She wasn't a conventional woman or wife, as he already knew. They happily kept on the periphery of the beau monde and accepted that their eccentric choice to care for those less fortunate excluded them from most of society. Michael and Genie, Hugh and Audrey, and Tobias had all accepted them, of course, but Cassie no longer saw much of Jane Riverton, and only rarely had tea with Marianne, whenever Lady Dutton was not invited. However, Cassie found she did not miss them overly much, and that she was more herself with Elyse, who had become one of her closest friends. Next to Grant, of course. He was her best friend. Her lover. Her partner and confidant. And yet as she'd come closer to her own lying in, he had become a tyrant about rest.

Exhaustion felt bone deep most days, but she was also brimming with impatience and anticipation, and couldn't think of resting in bed. The only time she relented was when he climbed into bed with her. He'd hold her close and rub her swollen belly, a pleat of worry between his brows even though he insisted he was not worried at all.

Cassie, however, was more than ready. She longed to meet their baby. Every time she imagined it, she felt her eyes get hot with tears. Not a single day passed when she did not think of her daughter, imagining her life in Sweden, how old she would be, and what she might look like. She would never stop thinking about her, not for the rest of her days. But it was time to move on. It was time for her to know what it was to mother a child that she could watch grow.

The clinic was nearly empty when she arrived, and she found Grant and Hannah discussing something over a file. Hannah, to Cassie's relief, had not been upset at all when her brother-in-law proposed to Cassie, and ever since, she had become like a sister. Hannah and Elyse had also grown close, their shared interest in building up Hope Clinic developing into a deeper friendship. One, Cassie had come to understand, centered around the same devotion she and Grant had for each other. Madame Archambeau and Miss Stone had taken them under their wings, in a way, giving Elyse and Hannah a place in the demimonde where they were accepted. It was yet one more reason Grant and Cassie were happily distancing themselves from the ton these days.

Grant had his back to her when she entered the spacious room, filled with several beds, each enclosed with privacy curtains. Only one patient remained from the four that had been staying at the clinic with a mild fever. The young man coughed from behind his curtain.

Her husband seemed to always know when she was there, and right then, he spun on his heel and speared her with a vexed look.

"Cassie, I've told you to stay out of here." He left the file with Hannah and walked swiftly toward her. "If you were to catch a fever now, it could be dangerous."

She pressed her finger to his mouth to hush him and then chased it with her lips. He groaned in frustration, but as usual, could not resist, not even with her large belly pressing up against him. He took her face into his palms and kissed her in return, nibbling her bottom lip before releasing her.

"I'm ready to leave," she said. "If you are as well?"

"Everything is in hand here," Hannah called, grinning with mischief. "Take your wife home and make her put up her feet."

"Oh, not you too, Hannah," she sighed.

"Yes, me too. Nurse's orders."

Cassie laughed and tossed up her hands. "Very well then."

Grant scowled. "Oh, so you'll obey her, but not me?"

She tugged on the lapels of his doctor's coat. "I will never obey you, Grant Thornton. I thought you would have known that by now."

"Trust me," he muttered. "I do. And I've got my first gray hairs to prove it," he said, pointing to his head of thick black hair that had not even a single strand of gray.

He helped her into her pelisse, and as they left the clinic's entrance and entered the courtyard, he kept his arm hooked around hers. He was loath to even allow her to walk or take stairs on her own, and she couldn't entirely blame him. Her balance had become rather a thing of the past, and a slip and fall the previous month had nearly driven him to the brink. His stethoscope had been pressed up against her abdomen several times a day after that, as he listened for the baby's heart rhythm.

"I'm fine," Cassie had assured him. Grant had removed the trumpet-shaped device after hearing the strong woosh of their baby's heart and had planted his lips right onto the top her bare stomach. She'd nearly wept from his tenderness. He was trying, so valiantly, to be brave. Every time she began to get impatient with him, she remembered what he'd endured...and found a new reserve of patience.

Now, he helped her up into the carriage, Merryton at the reins. Patrick still drove for them too, however, he was in Essex right then to visit Tris and Isabel. The two had married before Isabel had given birth to her first child, a boy, and she had recently born a second son. Everything that had happened with Mr. Youngdale seemed so long ago now. He'd been sentenced to transportation, banished from England's soil for good. Isabel had once told her, even with all the pain he'd caused, something good had come out of it. She had Tris and their growing family, and Cassie could not have been happier for them.

Grant had just taken the seat next to her in the carriage when a ripping pain encircled Cassie's stomach and back.

"Oh!" she gasped, her hands going to her middle and her eyes squeezing shut as the contraction persisted. Stronger—much stronger—than the last.

"Cassie?" Grant gripped her arms as the contraction ebbed. She gulped in air, the relief blissful. But it would not last. She knew what was happening. Had felt it all before, and now, it rushed back to her, along with a tremor of dismay. But she was not afraid. Not really. She'd given birth once, and all had gone well. It would be so again. Before the day was done, she would be holding her child. A child she would never have to give up.

She opened her eyes and saw her husband's green stare blazing with alarm.

"I think you should go back into the clinic and find Elyse," she said, still trying to even her breaths. "We should bring her with us to Thornton House."

Grant's eyes drifted to her stretched abdomen, and his

hands cradled her belly gently. "It is time?" He heaved for air, as if he'd just quit sprinting in a foot race.

Cassie lifted his hand from her stomach and kissed his palm. "It's time."

"WHAT IS the point of holding that glass of whisky if you do not drink it?" Hugh asked from where he leaned against the wall of the upstairs landing.

Grant hadn't touched a drop of the liberal pour his friend had handed him as he paced between the landing of the stairs and the closed door to Cassie's bedchamber. They had adjoining rooms, but he never used his own. He couldn't imagine spending a single night away from her, and even now, felt the restless urge to be with his wife, inside that room. He couldn't eat. Couldn't drink. Not when his whole world felt as if it were imploding.

"Breathe, Thornton," Fournier said as Grant deposited the glass onto a credenza and continued to pace. The duke and duchess had arrived shortly after his brother James. Grant suspected Hannah had dashed off notes to them all after he'd gone running back into the clinic, bellowing for Elyse.

The ride from Hope Clinic to St. James's Square had taken an age, it seemed, and he was grateful the midwife had been with them. She kept Cassie's mind focused on breathing as the contractions overtook her, and off Grant, who had slowly started to unravel.

"It will be over soon," James said. "All will be well." He clapped a hand on Grant's shoulder as he passed by. He'd worn a rut into the carpet the last two hours, the sounds from the bedchamber enough to stop his heart. They stabbed at him, each one ripping him open.

He nodded, grateful his brother was there. The last two years had been tumultuous with the rest of his family. Lawrence and Harold had joined the marquess in his denunciation of the Hope Clinic, while Penelope and James had been in support. Lord Lindstrom had indeed cut Grant off, but as Cassie's dowry was a small fortune, it didn't much matter. He teased her all the time about how he'd only married her for her money, especially when she was being particularly stubborn about something. She would clap back with, "And I only married you for your prowess in bed, my lord, so we're even." They would end up laughing and making love every time. Good God, he loved her. He loved every little thing about her, even the parts that infuriated him, like her sharp tongue and heady temper, her mulish impatience and perhaps less significantly, her devilish pranks, like her penchant for moving the ribbons in the books he was reading so that he'd lose his page. He would endure all the misplaced ribbons in the world just to hear her laughter, see her smile, witness the heat in her eyes when they made love, and the determination that filled them whenever she was caring for someone at Hope Clinic.

This marriage was vastly different than his first. He worshipped Cassie just as he had Sarah, but there was something deeper to this union, something stronger. Cassie had once questioned how their love could work when they were each so very broken. But they had taken their broken pieces and forged something stronger out of them.

Another grating scream came from the bedchamber. It

was a blade to his chest. Grant raked his fingers through his hair and tugged.

"I need to be in there," he said. He turned to Hugh. "You were with Audrey."

"I was invited in," he clarified.

"What help would you be?" James countered. "Look at you. You're a mess."

His brother was right; he was a frantic, unmoored mess. Cassie would not need him in this state.

The bedchamber door opened, and Grant whirled toward it. Genie stood within the threshold, shielding the room from view.

"She is asking for you," she told Grant, and without hesitation, he stormed into the room.

Cassie was on the bed, her chemise bunched at her thighs, her hair loose, her skin glistening from sweat. She held out a hand to him, and he surged toward her. He gathered her into his arms.

"What is it?" he asked Elyse, who perched at Cassie's feet. "What is wrong?"

"She is doing just fine," she answered calmly, just as he would have, had he been attending a birth. He'd done so several times over the last two years. But here and now, that was not his role. "Almost there. Just a few more pushes," the midwife said with confidence.

Cassie gripped his arm and turned her eyes to his. "I just don't want to be alone this time," she whispered.

Instantly, the frantic rattling of his mind and pulse evened. He swept a damp lock of hair from her brow and forgot everyone and everything except for her and what she needed from him. She wasn't alone. Elyse and Audrey and

Genie, along with her maid, Ruth, were all present. But it was Grant she needed. It was Grant she *wanted*. He would not let her down.

"I am right here. I'm not leaving, my love." He kissed her brow, and another contraction commenced. Being at her side, with her hands squeezing his, her screams resonated differently than they had while he'd paced the landing. They were not just cries of pain, but of resolve, of fearlessness and the determination to bring their child into the world. He'd never seen her so bold, so brave and powerful as she was right then.

She wasn't frightened in the least, and because of that, neither was he.

After a final valiant push, Cassie fell back against the pillows. A shrill wail split the air. Grant watched in sheer fascination and disbelief as Elyse handled the infant, deftly clamping and cutting the umbilical cord before lifting and turning the babe for them to view. A little girl, flushed pink and squalling, quivered as she fussed. Grant could barely see her through a wall of tears as Audrey took her and swaddled her.

"Grant," Cassie said softly, her voice drawn by exhaustion. He cradled her face and kissed her brow, and for a heart stopping moment, peered toward Elyse. The midwife appeared to have been waiting for him to do so, because she merely nodded and grinned.

"All is well, my lord."

At last, the tension drained from him, and he released a shaky sob as he gently pulled Cassie.

"You are breathtaking," he whispered, kissing her temple, and feeling her melt against him.

"We have a daughter," she said, and when he peered down at her, tears streaked her cheeks too. He brushed them away and kissed her as joy consumed him.

A moment later, Audrey placed the swaddled little girl into Cassie's waiting arms.

"She's the most beautiful thing I've ever seen," he whispered.

Cassie nuzzled the baby's crown of fine, raven black hair, and breathed her in. "I could hold her forever," she said softly.

"You can, and you will."

As they gazed at their daughter, Grant felt the last of their broken pieces shift and fall. They slid into place, side by side, where they became whole again.

Right where they'd always been meant to be.

Thank you for reading The Lady's Last Mistake. Please consider leaving a rating and review on Amazon to help other readers discover the series.

If you haven't read the Bow Street Duchess Mystery series, the seven-book series is complete and available on Kindle Unlimited for binge-reading!

ALSO BY CARA DEVLIN

The Bow Street Duchess Mysteries

MURDER AT THE SEVEN DIALS

DEATH AT FOURNIER DOWNS

SILENCE OF DECEIT

PENANCE FOR THE DEAD

FATAL BY DESIGN

NATURE OF THE CRIME

TAKEN TO THE GRAVE

THE LADY'S LAST MISTAKE (A Bow Street Duchess Romance)

The Spencer & Reid Mysteries

SHADOW AT THE MORGUE (Jan. 25, 2025)

The Sage Canyon Series

A HEART WORTH HEALING

A CURE IN THE WILD

A LAND OF FIERCE MERCY

THE TROUBLE WE KEEP

A Second Chance Western Romance

ABOUT THE AUTHOR

Cara is the author of the bestselling Bow Street Duchess Mystery series. She loves to read and write across genres, but her heart is reserved for romantic historical fiction and mystery. She lives in rural New England with her husband and their three daughters. Cara is currently at work on her next historical mystery series releasing in 2025.

Printed in Great Britain
by Amazon

59321813R00202